To Chloe

Thanks for

Keeping

Reading

Alive

All the best

DADXx

To Chloe

Thanks for

keeping

reading

this

All the best

Laura

Hi, I'm the author, E. A. Stephenson. I've been writing now for over 25 years. I am very passionate about my work, I love the thought of creating something for people to enjoy and I am thrilled to have my work published. I am equally excited as I finish the second part of *Shadows and Light*, which will hopefully be on the shelves soon.

When I was younger, I encountered a few ladies who had gone through tough emotional times. The strength of these ladies inspired me to write this story to show that there is light beyond the shadows.

Shadows and Light
The Trial begins

E. A. Stephenson

Shadows and Light
The Trial begins

Vanguard Press

VANGUARD PAPERBACK

A CIP catalogue record for this title is
available from the British Library.

This is a work of fiction. Names, characters, businesses, places,
events and incidents are either the products of the author's imagination
or used in a fictitious manner. Any resemblance to actual persons,
living or dead, or actual events is purely coincidental.

ISBN 978 184386 721 0

*Vanguard Press is an imprint of
Pegasus Elliot MacKenzie Publishers Ltd.*

www.pegasuspublishers.com

First Published in 2013

**Vanguard Press
Sheraton House Castle Park
Cambridge England**

Printed & Bound in Great Britain

Dedication

In loving memory of

Anne Marie Anderson
Martin Gerald Dicken
Keith Anthony Sutton
Carol Sutton
Mr & Mrs Sutton
Derrick Douglas
Freddie

God bless and I love you all.

Acknowledgements

Special thanks to:

Samantha Roden
Mr & Mrs Ktori
Mr & Mrs Pritchard
Mrs Marcella Sutton
Dennis
Kaswell
Martin

God bless you all and thank you for all your support.

Very special thanks to:

Pegasus Elliot MacKenzie Publishers Ltd

Chapter 1

'Court is adjourned until Mrs Phillips is in a more stable condition to take the stand. All parties involved will return to court on June the twenty fourth at nine-thirty. Thank you,' said the judge.

'All rise,' said the usher. Everyone stood up as the judge left the court.

Richard handed Sarah a hanky to dry her eyes. 'I'm sorry,' said Sarah, blowing her nose and looking at Richard as though she had done something wrong.

'Sorry?' said her barrister. 'What on earth for?'

'For not being able to testify,' replied Sarah.

'Now don't be silly, remember I told you earlier, this is crown court and believe me things work a lot different from a simple magistrates' court. At the end of the day as I have said, if you can't take the stand then you can't take the stand, it's as simple as that. It's not going to be easy, but we'll get there in the end.'

Sarah and her barrister had not noticed the commotion that was going on behind them, between her husband and the man that the guards were taking down a flight of stairs. Sarah's father was holding David back and telling him that it's not worth going after him, when Sarah's barrister jumped into the conversation.

'Now look, I'm having enough trouble as it is trying to convince the judge and the jury that your wife was raped. May I remind you in case you've forgotten that the other man who raped your wife is still walking the streets. Now that may not bother you, but it sure as hell bothers me.'

Sarah's father let David go.

'Now you listen to me,' said Richard, picking up his briefcase and heading for the door. 'I'm going to win this case, it may take time, but I am going to win.'

'I know,' said Sarah putting on her coat and walking out with Richard, completely ignoring David.

Sarah's father had already taken the children out of the courtroom. He was waiting outside by his car when everyone came out. David was the last person out of the door walking with his head held low, as if he was about to be sick. Sarah had walked Richard to his car. She apologised for her husband's behaviour.

'Why do you keep apologising every time something goes wrong? Ok, your husband was way out of order, and if the judge was there he could have been in contempt of court, so he was fairly lucky, but you must understand his point of view. I mean his wife has been raped by two men, one of whom the police can't catch. The one suspect that we have is really not much use until we catch the other one all we can do is hope the judge is on our side for a change, if not to be honest, I don't think that we have much chance of winning. But please do not give up hope, anyway I must dash I have to get back to the office before I go home.' Sarah said goodbye and left. She waved to Richard as he drove his car off the car park.

Sarah's father had already left, he told David to tell Sarah that he would call her later on in the evening. David and Sarah never spoke all the way home, they just glanced at each other every now and then. Sarah was first in the door, she told the children to go out and play. Jason asked if he could go and play with his next-door neighbour Paul. Sarah said it was ok, and Lucy told her mum she was going upstairs to play with her toys.

David was sitting on the chair with a drink in one hand and the remote control in the other. He sat there flicking from one channel to the other, Sarah got fed up and went over and turned the television off.

'Hey, I was watching that!' said David, looking at his wife who was standing in front of the television.

'Were you really? Ok, what's on BBC one?' asked his wife.

'World in Action,' he said, looking thoughtfully at his wife.

'At four o'clock on a Wednesday afternoon, I don't think so somehow,' she stated as she sat down beside her husband.

David knew that his wife knew that he had no idea what was on BBC one or on any channel for that matter.

'Look, if you're still upset about what happened in court you have no need to be. I can understand how you feel, but beating up the man is not going to help me now is it?'

'No perhaps not,' said David, shaking his head, and now even managing a small smile.

'The only way this is going to work is if I handle it my own way,' said Sarah, kicking off her shoes and putting her feet up onto the sofa.

'I'm sorry, it's just that I feel so damn helpless, I want to help, but I can't you know.'

Sarah asked her husband if there was any chance of a hug, he obliged and put his arm around her and she rested her head on his chest. 'What would you do if you could?' she asked.

David sat and thought. 'You know to be honest, I can't think of a damn thing,' he replied.

'Darling,' said Sarah, in a soft voice. 'Richard gave me an idea.'

'What was the idea?' he asked, running his fingers through his wife's hair.

'Well, he suggested that we talk to someone,' said Sarah.

'Like who?' asked her husband, sitting up and looking at his wife.

'He thinks it would be a good idea if we both see a psychiatrist.'

Sarah sat up.

Sarah thought of two things that might happen at this moment in time. Now he could hit the roof and cause an argument over it or agree that they should both go and see someone. Sarah looked thoughtfully at her husband, as he sat back in his seat. Sarah rested her head on his chest just as she had done earlier. After a few minutes David said calmly, 'Do you think that we should see someone? I mean do you feel that we need to?'

'Well to be honest, I think we do. If this is the only way, then I don't see that we a have much of a choice do you?' replied Sarah.

'No I suppose you're right.' He was just about to continue when the phone rang.

'I'll get it,' said Sarah, getting up and picking up the phone. 'Hello?'

'Mrs Phillips, I'm calling about your win on the pools, I'm just calling to see when it is convenient for me to call round and deliver your cheque for ten million pounds.'

'Darling, I think we have a crank caller on the line, should we call the police?'

'I'll give you crank caller,' said Sarah's father on the other end of the phone.

'Oh, hi Dad, I never guessed it was you, you know it never entered my mind,' said Sarah, breaking into a small giggle which also made David laugh. 'By the way, how's Sandra?'

'Your sister's fine,' said her father. 'How are you and David, has he stopped sulking yet?'

'We're both ok, well, as well as we can be I guess, and yes he has stopped sulking.'

'I was not sulking,' said a voice from the kitchen.

Sarah replied, 'You were too, you had a face a mile long earlier.' Still on the phone to her father, she said, 'Dad, can I ask you a favour?'

'Go on, what mission do you want me to accomplish now?' he asked.

'Well you know that the children are not going back to school until this case is over. I was just wondering if you could have them for a while, because you know that they'll only be here being bored stiff. Would you mind looking after them for me, so David and I can have some time on our own?'

'Oh no, the dreaded grandchildren… no I don't mind, how long do you want them to stay?'

'Err… I don't know, how about permanently, or just until they reach their twenties.'

'No way, I had enough looking after you and your sister when you were growing up, never mind doing that all over again at my age. No I don't mind looking after them, but I have a better idea, I'll take Jason and your sister can take Lucy?'

'How do you know she wants to have Lucy?' asked Sarah.

'Your sister needs a break, she's not doing herself any good by sitting around the house moping all day, besides she could do with a change. I'll have a chat to her and see what she says, ok? I'll phone you back tomorrow morning. I must go she has just finished cooking, call you tomorrow, bye.'

Sarah sat back down in her seat. She watched David coming in with a tray. He put the tray on the coffee table and sat down next to his wife handing her a cup of coffee.

'What would you like to do tonight?' David asked his wife.

'Oh I don't know really, I know I don't fancy cooking tonight,' she replied.

'I'll tell you what we'll send out for pizza,' said David.

Later on in the evening David was on the phone ordering a large family sized pizza. The man on the phone said it would take about forty minutes to arrive.

'Thanks that's fine,' said David as he put the phone down.

Jason came in and sat down next to his mother.

'How do you fancy spending your holidays with your grandfather?' asked Sarah.

'I'd love to spend time with Granddad,' said Jason, kissing his mother and leaping off the sofa and running wildly for the stairs, nearly running into his father.

'Hey what have I told you about running about?'

'Sorry Dad,' said Jason as he ran up the stairs to tell Lucy the good news.

'What on earth did you say to him?' David asked, walking into the living room.

'I only told him that he could go and stay with his granddad for a while,' replied Sarah.

'Somehow I get the feeling by the way he took off up the stairs, he can't wait to go,' said David.

It wasn't long before the pizza came; David was just paying the young man as the children came downstairs.

'Ah yes,' said David, sniffing the aroma of the pizza as he was taking the pizza off the man. 'Keep the change.'

'Thank you,' replied the young man. He turned and walked back down the path.

David closed the front door and headed for the living room; the children couldn't wait to eat their pizza.

'Hey slow down, don't rush your food,' said David as he walked into the kitchen to fetch some pop.

They finished the pizza and about an hour later, Sarah told Jason and Lucy that it was time for bed.

'Make sure that you brush your teeth before you go to bed,' said their mother. David had put the empty box in the bin. He quickly washed the up the glasses they had been using then came back into the living room and sat down. Sarah had gone up to make sure that the children were in bed. David and Sarah watched the ten o'clock news and then went to bed.

The next morning Sarah woke up as though she was startled by something in her sleep. She let out a tiny yell loud enough to wake David but not the children. He came up from under the quilt to find his wife in a bit of a panic. He came to his senses fairly quickly and sat up.

'Hey are you alright?' asked David. His wife put her arms around him and started to cry.

'Hey come on, what's wrong my snoring isn't that bad is it?'

'Do you love me?' she asked

'What, course I do,' he replied.

'No I mean really love me?' insisted his wife.

'Look I've told you before, I love you as much as anyone could love a person and more. Before you ask no I'm never going to leave you for anybody else or go away and live on my own or win the pools and leave the country,' said David.

David looked deep into his wife's eyes. 'The only way I'm ever going to leave is when I die, but I do not plan on dying just yet, well not for the next two hundred years anyway.'

'I know,' said his wife, 'but I just like to hear you say it.'

'Now what brought all this on?' asked her husband.

'Oh nothing, it was just me being silly,' said Sarah.

She got out of bed and headed for the bathroom. David looked at the clock and it said seven forty-five.

David sighed, 'So much for a lie in.'

He got out of bed and had a shower after his wife and went downstairs.

David was pouring himself a cup of coffee when the phone rang. Sarah answered it. 'Hello? Good morning.'

'Sarah, it's me Jonathon, how are you?'

'Well, you know, as well as I can be I suppose,' replied Sarah.

'Is there anything that I can do for you?' asked Jonathon

'Not really, I'll let you talk to David.' She called her husband and handed him the phone.

'Hi Jonathon how are you?' asked David.

'Never mind how I am,' said Jonathon. 'How are you and Sarah?'

'Well,' said David, 'I think that we're ok considering what's happened.'

'Ok, it's just that Sarah sounded a little distant,' said Jonathon 'Are you sure that she's ok?'

'It's just that the police haven't caught the other suspect yet and, well, things are a little bit tender at the moment,' said David.

'Well this guy's never really out of the country for that long, so I'll know as soon as he comes back,' said Jonathan.

'Anyway how's everything at the office?' asked David.

While David was on the phone, Sarah drank her coffee and ate her toast, and went upstairs to make the bed. Jason was just coming to tell his mother that his sister didn't feel very well.

'Mum?' said Jason as he came into the bedroom.

'Good morning sweetheart,' replied his mother.

'Mum, Lucy doesn't look very well.' Sarah headed for Lucy's bedroom. 'She's been sick as well.'

'Look you, go and wash your face and brush your teeth, go and get dressed and then go and have some breakfast.'

'Ok Mum,' said Jason, walking half asleep into the bathroom.

Meanwhile, Sarah was talking to her daughter. Lucy began to cry as she was telling her mother that she had pains in her tummy.

'I'll get you some milk and after that you can a take a shower. If you don't feel any better we'll take you to the doctors,' said her mum.

Sarah went downstairs to fetch a glass of milk for Lucy. David was just finishing his breakfast when Sarah came into the kitchen.

'Lucy's been sick, I'm going to give her some milk and make her take a shower and if she still feels the same we'll take her to the doctors.'

David was going into his daughter's room, when Sarah was coming up the stairs with the milk. Lucy was still crying she had been sick three times since her mother was downstairs fetching the milk.

David took off Lucy's nightdress as she had been sick all over it. Sarah told Lucy to drink the milk. The milk seemed to ease the pain straight away but after a couple of minutes Lucy still looked and felt terrible. Her mother told her to take a shower. David meanwhile was taking the covers off the bed. He got some newspaper and cleaned off as much of the sick as he possibly could and put the rubbish in the bin and the linen in the washing machine and turned it on.

'Do you feel ill at all son?'

'No I'm fine Dad,' replied Jason.

David was thinking aloud, when Sarah and Lucy came downstairs, Lucy still didn't look too good.

'She was sick again,' said Sarah.

'I'll take her to the doctors, you phone whoever Richard told you to phone and I'll take your car,' said David. 'I don't even know where my keys are.' David picked up his wife's keys and left with Jason and Lucy.

Sarah was just about to go upstairs, when the phone rang.

'Oh, hi Dad,' said Sarah.

'Everything ok,' asked her father.

'Not really, it's been one of those mornings Dad, it really has.'

'Ok,' said her father, 'what's happened now?'

'Lucy's been throwing up all morning. I gave her a glass of milk, but after a couple of minutes she brought the whole lot back up. We all had pizza last night, the rest of us are ok.' She was about to continue when her father cut in.

'Ah, I think I know what made her sick, yesterday at the courtroom I bought her a cheese and onion roll from one of the machines, so that might have been it.'

'Well how come Jason wasn't sick? I take it they both had the same?'

'No they never actually, Jason just had crisps, so that might explain things I hope,' said her father.

'She should be alright now anyway, because David has taken her to the doctor's. Anyway, you never called me to hear about my problems.'

'Yes I did, but I also called to tell you that I'd be busy this afternoon, so Sandra will pick up Jason and Lucy. In fact she's on her way over right now, she's just left. Anyway I must go I'll call you tomorrow or during the week, ok bye.'

Sarah opened her bag and took out her diary, she found the number that Richard her barrister had given her yesterday at the court. As she dialled the number her sister knocked on the door; Sarah opened the door and let her in. She waited in anticipation as the phone rang she was hoping someone would answer fairly soon, she felt nervous enough as it was. When someone did eventually answer Sarah paused, she had to make a split second decision whether she was dragging her family down even more than they were already. In the end she convinced herself that she was doing the right thing. When Sarah spoke, the woman on the other end of the line convinced her that she would be ok, and that anything they discuss would be in the strictest confidence.

'Now, first of all,' said the woman. 'Can I have your name?'

'My name is Sarah Phillips,' said Sarah, trying to reassure herself she was doing the right thing. Sarah was on the phone, when the door knocked. She went and opened the door, whilst still talking to the woman on the phone, her husband and children came in.

Sarah looked at Lucy; she was looking a lot better now that she had seen the doctor.

'Where is that gorgeous looking sister of yours?' whispered David.

His wife pointed towards the kitchen, David headed for the kitchen. 'I bet you ten to one she's stuffing her face,' Sarah whispered back. David went into the kitchen to find Sarah's sister eating chocolate biscuits. David walked up and put his arms around her waist.

'Hello,' said David, kissing her on the cheek. 'Would you like to get married?'

'Yes I would, but I don't think that my adorable sister would ever forgive me for stealing you from her.'

'Oh I don't know she'd get over it eventually, she may even start talking to us after a few years,' laughed David.

'Believe me dear,' said Sarah, walking into the room. 'You could never cope with her on your own you'd probably end up doing life in prison.'

'Auntie Sandra!' shouted Lucy as she ran over to her wrapping her arms around Sandra's waist. Sandra cuddled Lucy tightly.

'Ooo, I've missed you,' said Sandra still cuddling Lucy.

'I've missed you as well Auntie,' replied Lucy.

'Are you alright? You look a little peaky.' Sarah felt slightly chuffed with herself, for a few moments everything seemed normal, it seemed like nothing in the world was wrong. She was also chuffed at the way Lucy greeted her auntie every time they met.

Sarah glanced at Jason who was strolling into the kitchen looking as though he had done something wrong. He hadn't, he just looked that way. He looked up to see his Auntie Sandra standing in front of him.

'Hi,' said Jason, looking thoughtfully at Sandra.

'Hi, is that all I get?' said Sandra, waiting for a cuddle off him. 'At least give me a cuddle and a kiss.'

'Dad, do I have to?' asked Jason, looking helplessly at his father.

'Err… don't ask me. I don't live here. I've never seen this woman before in my life, why she could be a vampire for all we know.' Jason looked at his Auntie, looked at everyone in the kitchen then gave his auntie a hug and a kiss. He then headed for the biscuits that Auntie Sandra was eating earlier.

'Did I hear someone mention a doctor?' asked Sandra.

'Ah, that reminds me,' said David, taking the linen out of the washing machine he had put in before he went out. He took them out and put them in the dryer. Sarah, her sister and the children went upstairs; Sarah was telling her sister what had happened.

Whilst upstairs, Sarah cleaned up Lucy's bedroom and Sandra helped Jason and Lucy pack a suitcase each. Sandra finished helping the children just as her sister put the last sheet on the bed, then the quilt back on Lucy's bed.

'Gosh, I never knew these pair had so many clothes,' said Sandra. 'I agree' said Sarah, going down the stairs. 'But David thinks that they don't have enough clothes.'

'Hey listen, I know damn well that we never had that many clothes when we were younger,' said Sandra, as she follows her sister into the kitchen.

'Yes I know, why on earth do you think I buy so many clothes now? Mind you David's the one you know. He'll say things like, god I wish I could find something to wear, or my favourite is when he says, darling I can't find a suit to wear. Can't find a suit to wear, my husband owns nineteen different suits in his wardrobe.' Sarah was about to continue when her sister jumped into the conversation. Sandra looked deep into Sarah's eyes.

'Now look, the kids are outside, David is outside and David only has fourteen suits in his wardrobe, plus there's something on your mind because you're rambling.'

Sarah was leaning on a cupboard looking out of the kitchen window at David, who was being silly with the children in the back garden. She began to cry.

'Hey come on,' said her sister. 'What's wrong?'

'What's wrong? You and everybody else must think that you're in fucking cuckoo land. Two men raped me I was the last person in the world who expected to be raped. Nobody gives a damn about me,' said Sarah raising her voice as the tears streamed down her face.

'Do you know that David and I haven't had sex since I was raped? You know how much I want him to hold me in his arms and tell me that he loves me, or just throw me on the bed and make mad passionate love to me, but nobody cares do they?'

Sarah was still crying, when Sandra began to laugh.

'What the hell do you find so fucking funny?' shouted Sarah. This made David look towards the kitchen window. He headed for the back door and he stood outside, listening to Sarah and her sister arguing. The children were still at the bottom of the garden playing together, they hadn't really noticed that their father had gone.

'What do I find so funny?' said Sandra, pacing up and down the kitchen. 'Well, ok I'll tell you. You are without doubt, the most selfish self-centred cold-hearted bitch that I have ever met. God you're incredible. In case you hadn't noticed, this is the fucking nineties and with all the things going on in the world today, you must be fucking naive to think that being raped could never happen to you. As for being in cuckoo land, well the only person there must be you. How can you stand there and say that you were the last person in the world, who expected to be raped? No woman in the world expects to be raped, you as a woman yourself should understand that. My God you can really get my temper going sometimes sis you really can. As if that wasn't bad enough as it is, you have the audacity to stand there and say that nobody gives a fuck about poor old Sarah. Well fuck you Sis, because you know damn well that everybody cares.'

By now David had heard all he wanted to and came into the kitchen.

'Well we have had a nice conversation, haven't we?' David looked at both his wife, who was just standing with a blank expression on her face, and at her sister who was foaming at the mouth with steam coming out of her ears. Well, she never really had steam coming out of her ears or foam coming out of her mouth, but you can imagine how she looked. Sarah was just about to speak, when David put his finger to his lips and gestured her to be quiet. 'Now, before we all say something that we might regret, I think that Sandra should take the children and go, and darling maybe you should go upstairs and cool down.'

'Fine by me,' said Sandra, 'that sad bitch can go and fuck herself.'

'Fuck you too!' shouted her sister.

You could cut the atmosphere in the kitchen with a knife, it was that dense. David called the children in from outside. Sarah kissed them goodbye and went upstairs, she never said anything to her sister as she left. Sarah watched her from the bedroom window. Sandra knew that her sister was in the window, but she never looked up to see. She put the cases in the boot as the children got into the car and said goodbye to their dad, she kissed David goodbye and drove off.

'Well, well, well,' said David, coming back into the house. 'What a day this has turned out to be.'

He walked into the living room, sat down and switched on the television.

Later on in the evening his wife came downstairs, she looked as though she'd been crying all evening. David looked at her, and then told her to come and sit beside him. He didn't say anything as she sat down next to him; he just kissed her on the cheek and put her head on his chest as he held her tightly in his arms. After sometime David asked her if she wanted a drink. She said 'yes,' so her husband poured her a brandy, a double brandy because she looked as though she needed it. He gave his wife her drink and he sat back down. After about ten minutes Sarah spoke.

'I made an appointment for us to see a psychiatrist. We have to see her at nine thirty on Monday morning.'

David kissed his wife, he turned off the television and they both sat quietly in the dark.

Sarah realised after sometime that they were both falling asleep, so they went upstairs and got ready for bed. David decided to take a quick shower before going to bed. Sarah washed her face and stared deeply into the bathroom mirror, which was beginning to get steamed up from the shower. Sarah finished what she was doing and got into bed. By the time David came into the bedroom, Sarah had fallen asleep. He put on his pyjama bottoms and got into bed. He hardly ever wore a top in bed, most of the time it was either too warm, or too stuffy to wear anything in bed. He leaned over and kissed his wife on the cheek; he stared lovingly at her for a while before he turned off the lamp and went to sleep.

The next three days went by fairly quickly; although Sarah and David spoke, it wasn't how they usually talked. Most of the time, the two of them were laughing and joking and poking fun at each other, but not this particular weekend.

Sarah was the first awake and out of bed on Monday, she had a shower and she even had a small breakfast. She was about to go back upstairs and wake her husband up, when he came strolling down the stairs, still half asleep. 'Morning,' smiled his wife cheerfully. David yawned and said good morning at the same time.

'Care for some breakfast, or by the look of you do you just want a cup of black coffee?'

'Err... I think I'll be brave this morning and have both,' her husband replied, yawning again and scratching his head. David went back upstairs and got dressed, he came back down looking a lot more refreshed and a lot livelier. David ate his breakfast then told his wife that it was time to go. They reassured each other that they were doing the right thing and off they went.

While they were driving along the road, Sarah imagined the place they were going to was quiet, you know like the people you meet are morbid if you like. She giggled to herself; she was thinking that the first words out of the person's mouth would be, 'Oh I'm so sorry Mrs Phillips.' David stopped the car outside a large building, Sarah looked surprised, the place was not at all like she had just imagined it to be, and there were people everywhere. The place was that hectic the automatic doors were continuously open.

David reassured his wife that everything was going to be ok, and that she shouldn't worry. David thought, that the sooner they got in there, the sooner they could get it over and done with, and the better him and his wife were going to feel. So they got out of the car, locked the doors and took a deep breath and went inside. They headed for the reception desk where a man looking as though he had just won two million on the pools, and then forgot to post the coupon, was sitting down staring at a computer. David and Sarah told him their names, and the man looked them up on the register. He told them to take the lift to the top floor and then see the receptionist up there.

Sarah apologised to herself for looking at the man at the reception desk and automatically thinking that he was a horrible nasty person, but it turned out he was very nice. When they got to the top floor, Sarah breathed a small sigh of relief, because the top floor was nowhere near as hectic as the ground floor. They made their way to the reception desk. The lady behind the desk greeted them with a cheerful good morning and a warm smile. They told the receptionist their names and she walked them to the office they had to go into. The secretary knocked on the door and then she went in.

'Miss Cartwright, Mr and Mrs Phillips are here to see you.'

'Ah yes, send them in Susan,' said Miss Cartwright.

David and Sarah entered the office, well I say office it was more like a living room than an office.

David and Sarah were a little surprised, but not in the way that you think, you see being an architectural consultant, David was used to seeing big offices even bigger, and better than the one he was in now. Of course his wife being an estate agent saw lots of big lovely offices, but I don't think that at that particular time that offices or the way they looked were on Sarah's or her husband's mind.

Miss Cartwright greeted them cheerfully and gestured them to sit down. She didn't really have what you would call office chairs, she had like two different, but matching settees and chairs. David and Sarah sat down. Miss Cartwright told David and Sarah, that because they were to see a lot of her they should call her Helen.

Helen explained that the sessions were all about opening up and the idea was to say whatever the hell you wanted, even if it had nothing at all to do with the problem in particular.

'So for instance, if you want to talk about football and how it upset you that Liverpool lost on Saturday, then you can tell me or shout at me. The whole idea is so that you feel comfortable with yourself being here and then you can tell me your problem. Everything is said under the strictest confidence, so apart from my secretary nobody will know anything unless you want them to. Let's say for instance you want to call me a fat ugly bitch, and then do so, that is what I'm here for,' Sarah smiled, but Helen still got the impression that neither Sarah nor David was ready to speak.

'Right, I'll speak until one of you thinks of something to say,' said Helen.

Helen rambled on about nothing in particular waiting for Sarah or David to butt into the conversation. After about five minutes, Helen said, 'Right, we'll start this again.'

She was about to continue when Sarah in a soft voice said, 'I was raped.' There was a silence for a couple of seconds.

Then Helen said, 'Were you really, forgive me for saying this, but you do not sound very sure.' There was another few seconds of silence.

'My sister and I were raped once,' said Helen, looking thoughtfully at David and Sarah, who in turn looked completely stunned.

Here they were with a woman they had just met, and here she was giving them her life story.

Helen continued, 'It was a very long time ago; I was nine at the time, well nearly nine anyway, my real father had died when I was about a year old, so it was no shock that later on in life my mother would remarry and she did. I was about five years old when they got married,' she smiled.

David and Sarah were getting more and more interested and more and more bewildered.

'Don't get me wrong, he was nice to my mother and he gave her money. He took us to nice places, took us on holiday and took us everywhere. Believe me, my mother never ever wanted for anything. So what made me hate him so much that I wanted to kill him? Well about a week before my ninth birthday, he came into my room while my mother was at work and my sister was in her bedroom. He asked me what I wanted for my birthday. I said I don't know, I told him that I never really gave it much thought. He then told me what he was going to give me for my birthday. I'll give you a clue, it was about eight inches long and it produces babies. I told him that I had no idea what he was on about, and told him to get out of my room, because I wanted to get into bed. He then said I'll help you get into bed; he got up and came towards me. He grabbed me and I shouted for my sister, she came in and as he turned round, she gave him a good kick in between the legs. I'll be a big head and say it was that powerful, it would have brought iron Mike Tyson to his knees. He groaned; so I saw my chance and tried to run, he grabbed my foot and I fell over. I cut my head open, because I could feel the blood running down the side of my face. He was still in agony as he slapped my sister and then he slapped me. He gave me a few more slaps perhaps just to make sure that I wasn't knocked out from banging my head, and to make sure that I was awake. Then of course he locked my sister in the cupboard and raped me. He then locked me in the cupboard and raped my sister. I remember hearing him hitting her and calling her names. He called my sister a slut, a slag and various other names, he then left whistling as he went out of my room and down the stairs.'

David and Sarah just sat there looking at each other in amazement. Here was a woman whom they had just met half an hour ago, and there she was as proud as you like telling David and his wife her life story.

'How can you sit there and talk about this thing, like you don't care less any more?' asked David.

'Now you listen to me, Mr Phillips. I have to talk about things in my past to people like you two, because most of the time people don't understand about things like this. For instance, you and your wife are supposed to be telling me your life story not the other way round. I'll be honest; I hate people who get raped, because they have no idea of what to say to anyone. Like your wife just said, I was raped. I mean let's be honest, how do you know that she isn't lying about it? How do you know that she isn't making things up as she goes along?'

'Now wait a minute,' began David, when Helen started up again.

'I think like you do. I think that all sex offenders whether male or female should be put to death, personally I think that they should hang the lot.'

She was about to continue, when Sarah shouted, 'Look, this thing happened to me not anybody else, me. My dignity was taken away from me; those bastards had no right to take my life away. It's alright everybody saying what I should be doing, but what about what's best for me?' She began to cry.

'Are you happy now?' asked David, giving Helen an evil look. 'Is this what you wanted to hear?'

'No, but it is a start.'

Sarah got fed up of all the bickering and began to shout loudly, 'I was raped!' She even screamed her lungs out saying it. She stopped; she looked at both her husband and Helen and said quietly, 'I was raped.'

She had stopped crying by this time, she got up and stared thoughtlessly out of the office window. 'You know this is almost funny to an extent.' David was about to speak, when Helen gestured him to keep quiet. 'I mean you think about it, the sexy estate agent, the drug addict and the millionaire, wonder if you could make a film out of it,' she chuckled slightly. 'God, what a life.' She sat in a chair behind Helen's desk. 'You know you go away on holiday, you spend three wonderful weeks in America and then you come back to this.' She sighed, she was thinking about the argument she had with her sister. 'We came back off holiday, and the last thing we expected to see was police in and out of our house. I think that the whole of the British police force were there. There were police with guns, police with dogs; they were in and out of my back garden. Police were talking to the neighbours, huh, police talking to each other. I mean think about it, how do you think it feels to come back off holiday, pull up in a taxi to see policemen and woman walking all over your house. It's almost as bad as being burgled by the men in blue. Some of the mess they made was unbelievable.' Helen kept Sarah talking, by asking her what had happened at the house. She also made the coffee; David gave signals with his hands as to how he and his wife liked their drinks.

Meanwhile, his wife continued.

'Well we gave the keys to my sister Sandra who I recently had an argument with so she could get a break. You know, because she was divorcing her husband and she felt really down in the dumps. So my loveable hubby and I thought we'll give her the keys so she and her new boyfriend could have some peace and quiet. At the end of the day he wanted money she wouldn't give him any and so he battered her. He put her in hospital for six weeks, he also made her lose her baby and she was three months pregnant at the time. I mean listen to this,' said Sarah, drinking some of her coffee, which by now was getting cold, because she never really realised how much or how long she had been rambling. 'We came out of the taxi, we had to practically explain every detail about our house, and some of the things that we had in there before the policemen would let us in. I can understand why the children had to stay outside. I can honestly say if we had been burgled I guarantee the mess would be just as good as the police made, and the man who had attacked my sister made there. We were trying to ask all these different policemen questions to try and find out what happened, neither one of them would give us an answer so in the end David got pissed off and shouted at one of the policemen to talk to him. It worked, a smartly dressed CID man came strolling over to us. As a matter of fact he turned out to be extremely nice and helpful. He even asked us to show him the policemen who did not give us any help, so one by one David and I pointed them out.

'Ok, I admit there were only about four to blame, but still they were not very helpful when they should have been. He got all four together and in front of David and me, he gave them a right telling off. He even made them apologise to us, then he made them go away and check some more statements. He then apologised to David and I, and then he told us what had happened. He even told us that if it wasn't for the next-door neighbour, Paul, and his quick thinking things might have been a lot worse.

'I asked if anybody had bothered to notice that my sister was three months pregnant. He said that he had received no such information. He questioned two policemen who were walking past; both of them had the information written down in their notebooks. The Inspector took their badge numbers and told them, he would have a word with them later on back at the station and he apologised once again. He was about to speak, when a young policewoman came up and spoke to him. She had to go to the hospital to get a statement off my sister and she wondered if we would like to come and find out how my sister was. He said that was the best idea that anybody had come up with so far today, so off we went.'

'How was your sister?' asked Helen.

She was pleased that Sarah started talking freely, and it seemed that Sarah had got over her shock of being with a shrink.

'Well from what the policewoman was telling us on the way to the hospital, it seemed that my sister was in a terrible state. You know the feeling when you go in and ask what ward she's in; your mind is going wild. Your thinking I wonder if she wants anything, or how badly hurt is she and so on. Anyway we found the ward eventually after asking about seven different doctors and nurses. The policewoman said that it would be better if she took a statement from my sister first, before we all went in to see her. It seemed like the policewoman was in there for ages, it might only have been about ten minutes, but it seemed like forever.' Sarah paused. 'You know I never prepared myself to see my sister. As soon as the policewoman came out I was in the room, it was that quick, I never even waited for the door to shut after the policewoman came out. When I went in and saw my sister, I was in shock and went numb all over. I tried to move but I had a few seconds of shock. The policewoman told us that my father had gone out looking for the man.' Sarah sighed deeply. She was thinking about the argument she had with her sister and why at such a testing time in their lives. When they really and truly needed each other, they had to have a silly argument.

'Meanwhile,' she said continuing. 'The thought of my sister hooked up to all those machines, she might as well have been in intensive care, she looked that bad. It may sound a bit silly, but even though it hurt me seeing my sister like that, I knew I had to get a grip of myself. She was fast asleep all of the time that I was in the room, but as soon as my daughter Lucy came in, it was like she was never asleep. She couldn't have heard them come in, but you know hospitals, the doors are that quiet you have to look at them to know that they are closed. Personally I think that the look on Lucy's face said it all. She was the last one in the room; she looked at the machines hooked up to my sister. David and I knew that she was going to cry, it was just a matter of time.'

'Did she cry?' asked Helen, looking thoughtfully at Sarah.

'I wouldn't actually say she was crying, she was more like hysterical. You know I never asked my sister this, and I don't think that I ever will ask her. But I think that even though she was in that position, I think it kind of took her by surprise. I know damn well that it took me by surprise. The last thing we expected to see was our nine-year-old daughter having hysterics.'

David was feeling a little bit left out, it was his own fault anyway he had the chance to speak but he didn't. Maybe he was a little shy, even though being a man he would never admit to it. He began telling Helen, how Sarah was holding both her sister, and daughter telling them that everything was going to be ok, but she knew that it would take a hell of a long time, before her sister ever got over what that man did to her.

'It's going to be a hell of a long time for me to get over what those men did to me,' said Sarah, looking at both her husband and Helen.

Helen looked at the clock on the wall.

'Oh well I'm afraid to tell you that your time is almost up. Now be honest, don't you feel slightly better by opening your heart? I do have one query though,' said Helen, looking slightly puzzled.

'Neither of you have mentioned, how your son felt, that's if he felt anything at all. You know because some people just don't feel anything at all, it's not their fault it's just that there aren't any feelings there at all.'

'Oh Jason, yes he felt it alright. For weeks he just moped around the house, he wouldn't do as he was told,' said David.

'The one night when I was going to bed,' said Sarah. 'I walked past his bedroom and I looked in to see if he was alright. He was fast asleep, but you could tell that he had been crying, you could see the tears had dried up on his face and left lines. I gave him kiss on the forehead and then went to bed.'

Helen got up and headed towards her desk.

'I'll make you another appointment for next Monday. I don't think I have anything on, so you and your husband will have a lot more time with me, ok,' said Helen, writing on a card and handing it to Sarah.

David had stood up, he handed Sarah her coat and he put on his own. Helen walked across the office, and opened the door to let David and Sarah out. She told her secretary to put the appointment that she had given Sarah and her husband in her diary and she did.

David asked if they would send him the bill in the post, or would he have to pay it now. Both Helen and her secretary began to laugh; even Sarah had a slight giggle to herself, even though she never knew what was so funny. Helen's secretary stopped laughing and told David and Sarah that the service was free, and that every time that someone new came in they asked them the same question.

'We even had a bloke once, who left a hundred pounds on my desk and walked off. We tried to find him of course, but we never did. So in the end, because we never saw him again we gave the money to charity,' said Helen.

David laughed and replied, 'Well, I've made a fool of myself once again.'

He pressed the button for the lift to come; it only took a couple of seconds for it to come. David and Sarah said their goodbyes and got in.

Helen held the lift so she could talk to Sarah. 'Being raped doesn't affect your body, it affects your mind.'

Sarah looked thoughtfully at Helen; she had some idea of what she was talking about. 'As for getting over it, I was raped over thirty years ago and I haven't got over it.' They said their goodbyes, as the lift closed.

On the way home Sarah asked David what he thought of Helen. 'I don't know really, she seems a hard person. I don't mean that in a nasty way. I mean, she is a terribly nice person, but she looks like she can handle herself in any argument.' His wife smiled. 'Well I think she's a nice person anyway.'

It was almost lunchtime when they got back. David noticed the light flashing on the answering machine, so he pressed the button to rewind it and waited for it to come on, it was their barrister Richard.

'Sarah, can you and your husband come down the police station, I think they've got Mr Forbes. I'll meet you there, they need you to come down and identify him. Please be as quick as possible, bye,' said Richard.

David heard a smash in the kitchen. He ran in to see his wife lying in a heap on the floor. He checked her pulse and because he knew first aid he knew that she had only fainted. After a few seconds she began to come round. David got her a brandy and told her to drink it right down and she did. After a couple of minutes she was back to her normal self. She was still a little bit shaken, but apart from that she seemed to be alright. David reassured her that everything was going to be alright. He helped her into the car and headed for the police station, which was about a mile and a half down the road.

When they got to the police station, they saw Richard and the Chief Inspector standing outside waiting for them along with a few other people. Richard asked Sarah, if she was alright. She said she was as nervous as hell, but she would be alright if everybody didn't fuss over her. After a few minutes they all went inside the station following the Chief Inspector. David was telling them, how Sarah had passed out in the kitchen when she heard the news. Richard told her, if she didn't feel up to it, she didn't have to go through with it and that everybody would understand. She told him that she was still nervous and scared, but she was still going to do it. As she said, she didn't want to disappoint anybody.

They all entered a small room. There was Richard, the Chief Inspector and one of his sergeants and Sarah and David. The Chief Inspector told Sarah that she had nothing to worry about, and that the men who would be on the line up would not be able to hear, or see her so she had nothing to fear.

Sarah took a deep breath, kissed her husband and said loudly, *'Fuck it!'*

The sergeant said, 'It's ok Mrs Phillips we understand if you can't do it, we'll just have to wait until you feel that you are ready.'

The Chief Inspector had the kind of look on his face that said, 'Oh well that's another one that gets away.'

But Sarah had other ideas, she had decided there and then to make a stand. She decided that they were not going to get away with what they did to her and her family.

She took everyone by surprise and said, 'Is it possible to see him face to face?' asked Sarah. 'If it's the right one, I'll have to see him in court anyway, so what's the difference between now and then?'

''Err… nothing,' said the Chief Inspector.

It took a lot of courage for Sarah to do that, nobody realised just how much courage though.

The Chief Inspector, led then into the room where the men would be lining up. Sarah waited patiently as the men came in one by one. Sarah only saw the first three, before she spotted her attacker. Then within seconds, Sarah was on top of the man who had raped her. She was pulling his hair, scratching his face, kicking him, you name it she did it and who can blame her. David grabbed his wife off the man and the sergeant grabbed the accused man and held him.

'Mr Michael Forbes, I am charging you with the raping of Mrs Sarah Phillips. You have the right to remain silent. You do not have to say anything, but anything you do say can and will be used against you in a court of law. If you cannot afford a lawyer, one will be appointed for you by the state. Do you understand the charge and your rights as I have read them to you?' said the Chief Inspector.

Sarah was still trying to get at Mr Forbes. She was spitting at him and calling him every name that she could think of, but her husband was holding her back.

'Yes I do,' said the man, as polite as possible. 'But I know that you have made a mistake in accusing me. That woman's mad and she needs help.'

Just then Sarah got close enough to kick him and she did, she kicked him square in between the legs. 'Maybe that will remind you of what you and your friend did to me, you bastard.'

The man dropped to his knees.

'All your money can't help you now Mr Forbes,' said the Chief Inspector. 'We've got you by the short and curlies you little shit, get him out of here,' the Chief Inspector shouted to the sergeant.

The sergeant helped Mr Forbes off the floor, the rest of the line up had been told to leave by another policeman. Richard told Sarah that he was going to win the case, and that both of the men would be going to prison for a hell of a long time. David let go of his wife, seen as though the man had gone.

'Well I must congratulate you, Mrs Phillips. I'll let you and your husband in on a little secret; we've known that Mr Forbes was a very dodgy character for some years. We were hoping to catch him on a drugs charge,' said the Chief Inspector. 'But this charge is just the beginning.'

'Yes, but if you knew all that why didn't you bring him in before now?' David asked, holding Sarah's hand.

'Mr Phillips, I don't want to sound unsympathetic, but I can say that we've been very lucky.'

David cut into the conversation. 'You mean my wife gets robbed, beaten up and then raped and you say that you were lucky, God what a joke.'

'Now you listen to me, Mr Phillips. I deal with hundreds of rape cases, each one different from the last. Let's say you have ten cases, rape cases that is, you have at least four who turn out to be complete and utter liars. You have three who are too scared to bring the charges up. You have one that will take it all the way to court and then bottle out at the last minute. Then one that will go every inch of the way and see justice done.' The Inspector began to walk towards the door.

'You left one out,' said Sarah as he walked away.

'Yes, I know,' said the Inspector. 'That's the one that commits suicide.' He held the door open to let David and Sarah out.

'As I told you, I deal with literally hundreds of these cases. I have files on my desk right now going back years. So as I said, don't ever think that you are alone. Anyway I must go I have criminals to catch,' and he walked away.

'Thank you, Chief Inspector!' shouted Sarah.

'Any time, see you in court Mr and Mrs Phillips.'

When Sarah and David got home, as soon as they got in the front door, David grabbed his wife and gave her a big kiss and held her tightly and told her how much he loved her.

'I know you do darling,' replied his wife.

'It took a hell of a lot of courage, to do what you did today,' said David, and he hugged her again.

'Anyway what are we going to do tonight?' asked David. 'Oh and you better phone your dad and tell him what's happened.'

'It would be better if you phoned him, I'm not phoning in case that fucking bitch of a sister of mine answers the phone,' said Sarah.

'Yeah, but you'll have to talk to her sooner or later,' replied David, picking up the phone and dialling.

'Will I, huh the fucking bitch will have to speak to me first, she started the bloody argument not me,' insisted Sarah.

'Alright, you don't have to talk to her if you don't want to,' said David. 'God women.'

'Hello Bob it's me David. Oh me, I'm fine. Hey look if she and her sister want to argue that's their problem not mine. Anyway forget them I have some good news, the police have caught the other man. Yes I agree it's about time; anyway your wonderful lovely daughter had to pick him out of a line up. Gosh, she only saw the first three and that was it. She just took me and everybody else by surprise, and dived on him. Let's put it this way; I'm proud of the way she handled herself today, she was absolutely brilliant. Anyway, how's that little pain in the neck of ours?'

'Oh he's playing in the pool,' replied Bob.

'Posh git,' said David chuckling slightly. 'Anyway give Jason a kiss from Sarah and me, bye.'

'Hey where's mine,' asked David, looking at his wife eating a piece of chocolate cake.

'Get your own,' said Sarah, eating the last part of her cake.

'Well,' said David, sneaking around the chair without Sarah noticing and grabbing a packet of chocolate biscuits off the tray that his wife's holding.

'Seeing as though you christened the cake, I might as well christen the biscuits,' he said smiling and sitting on the settee.

He looked across at his wife, who had put the tray down and was heading for the biscuits that he had taken from the tray. She took one step, and then she just lunged for the packet. In the end after sometime they decided to save injury and share the biscuits.

'You're very lucky, that I'm generous enough to let you have any of these biscuits,' said David.

'It's only because you love me,' replied Sarah, putting her head on his shoulder.

David picked up the remote control and started flicking from one channel to another, after getting into a programme that turned out to be pretty boring he turned it off.

'Television is getting really boring; we should get satellite television you know.'

David hadn't realised that his wife was fast asleep, until he got up to fetch a drink from the cabinet. He turned round to ask her if she wanted another drink, that's when he realised that she was fast asleep.

'Ah well, I wanted an early night anyway.'

David thought it best not to disturb his wife; he knew she'd had a hard day. He knew that there would be even harder days yet to come. He went upstairs and fetched a blanket out of Jason's room and a pillow. He came back downstairs; he placed the pillow carefully under his wife's head, as not to wake her. He then laid the blanket over her; he also took the empty glass out of her hand and put it in the sink along with the one that he had been using. He then switched everything off and went to bed.

The next morning, it was fairly late when he got up and came downstairs. The blanket and the pillow were there, but his wife wasn't. It wasn't late in the morning, but eight o'clock is late where David is concerned, he had usually done a few hours' work by then. David shouted all round the house, he even looked around the house but his wife was nowhere in sight. He was feeling slightly worried, he then noticed that his wife had taken his car keys which were usually next to the phone.

Whilst putting the blanket back on Jason's bed he thought that she might have gone to the shops, but as time went on he knew that she couldn't have. He packed the last of the things he had washed up away and he sat watching the television.

He was deep into a programme, when he realised that time was getting on. He began to get more and more worried as time went on. At about eleven o'clock, while he sat there with the television on, he heard the front door open and he jumped up off the chair.

'Where have you been, I've been worried sick about you. I was thinking all kinds of silly things,' said David, looking very relieved that his wife had finally came back home.

'I went for a drive this morning. I was going to leave you a note but changed my mind.' Sarah leaned against the doorframe of the living room door.

'I went back,' she said, cautiously looking at her husband. 'To where it all happened.'

'Why on earth did you do that?' asked David, raising his voice.

He then realised that his wife needed a sympathetic ear and not a person who was going to bite her head off. He told her to come and sit down next to him and she did. David wanted to shout and bawl at his wife, but he managed to control himself. 'Right,' he said, putting his arms around her.

There was a brief pause before his wife began to speak.

'I went back to the town centre, I was driving around this morning, and I even drove to Flansly.'

'Flansly, but that's nearly eighty miles away,' said David.

'I went back to where it all happened. At first I thought I'd have a short drive come back and go to bed, but I didn't I just kept on driving. I came back from Flansly and just headed straight for the town centre, sat right there where I was raped, and I lived every horrible nasty thing that those two bastards did to me. I sat there and I screamed as loud as I could, for as long as I could, then I just sat there and had a damn good cry. Then after a while I came home, I just floored the car all the way home.'

'Did you come to any decisions?' said her husband.

'Only one.' She got up and stared out of the living room window. She eventually sat down on one of the single chairs.

'What was that?' asked David, leaning back against the sofa.

'I finally realised how much I love you. Don't get me wrong I loved you anyway, but it seems to have grown a lot stronger than it was.' Sarah smiled, which made her husband smile.

She got up and went over to him and kissed him. 'Yes, I am definitely in love with you,' said Sarah, going into the kitchen. 'Fancy a coffee?'

'No thanks, I've just had one,' replied David.

The rest of the week seemed to go by fairly smoothly. It seemed that Monday morning just wanted to come quickly, or should I say that Sarah wanted it to come quickly. I don't suppose that David cared less, he just sat there watching the Gulf news. In a way I think that David had forgotten that it was Monday. Sarah told him to get a move on or they would be late. David turned off the television and grabbed his coat whilst going out of the front door. When they got to Clarence House, Sarah and David didn't feel nervous. They didn't even speak to the man at the desk, and they just caught the lift and went straight to the top floor to Helen's office and got out. They headed for the reception desk.

Susan the woman at the desk was speaking very quietly, she had a sore throat and she was losing her voice. She led them to Helen's office.

As they walked through the door they saw Helen on her hands and knees on the floor.

'I know I'm a bit behind with the times, but I don't think that people dance like that nowadays,' said David.

Helen began to laugh. 'You'd be very surprised to see how some of these youngsters dance nowadays, I can tell you.'

Meanwhile Sarah had found a little bear and was playing with it when Helen got up.

'Oh I give up,' said Helen, taking a huge sigh. 'I'll just have to get another one.'

'Another what?' said David, looking at his wife, while Helen was looking in her desk drawers.

'Another Garfield, I had some kids up here earlier and now, I can't find it.'

Sarah hadn't noticed that her husband was looking at her, and that he realised that she was in a world of her own.

David whispered to Helen, 'Err... does your bear look anything like this one?' and pointed to Sarah, who was still playing with the bear and still in a world of her own.

David sneaked behind the chair that Sarah was sitting on. He was talking as though the sound was coming from the bear. Sarah was startled by the noise. She looked curiously at the bear for a few seconds, before she realised that bears could not talk. She then looked up to see Helen gazing at her. Just then David came up from behind the chair. He was still talking as though the bear was talking, but by this time Sarah came to her senses. She had already noticed that Helen was looking for it and she gave it back to her.

Helen asked David, what he was doing on the floor.

'I'm trying out a new dance,' said David, feeling pretty stupid. After all he was on his hands and knees in an office.

Everybody sat down, whilst Helen made a drink. She asked them how they both were. They were as well as could be expected. Helen told Sarah that she wanted to be there with her the next time that she went to court. Sarah told her that the next court hearing would be on the twenty second of July, and that she would love to see her there. Helen also asked if everything family wise was ok. Sarah told her that the kids had gone away to stay with their auntie and granddad for a while.

'Well,' said Helen, raising her eyebrows. 'You have the whole house to yourself, two hot blooded people in the same house, God the passion in your house must be great.'

Sarah started to laugh. 'Passion David, you must be joking.'

Sarah's giggling made her husband slightly cross.

'Let me tell you a little story,' said Sarah, taking off her coat. 'Me, my darling husband and my two darling children wanted to go away on holiday. Let me rephrase that, we had to go on holiday. I mean one holiday in nine years is not good enough. Ok fair enough we were both working; we never thought of taking a break, all David and I wanted to do was work. You know, get the best for your children and so on. After a lot of thought and a few debates, we decided that because we may not be going on holiday for another nine years, we would have a holiday to remember. You know the kind of holiday that you can look back on later on in life.

'So in the end we all went to America. It cost us nearly three thousand pounds mind you, but as I said after all the debating we went.' Sarah got up and looked out of the window.

'I can honestly say that was probably the best three weeks of my entire life. Don't get me wrong mind you, I love being married to my husband, even if he is a pain in the neck sometimes, but I love him anyway. Maybe it was the change of country I don't know, or maybe it was having sex every night. I can't really say what it was, but I know we all enjoyed ourselves.' Sarah gazed idly out of the window behind Helen's desk.

'So what went wrong?' asked Helen, looking at David who was looking at his wife, who was staring out of the window.

'I don't know; I'm not blaming the loss of sex on being raped.' She paused. 'But we started to have problems way before that happened.'

36

'What kind of problems did we have?' asked David, sounding slightly surprised at some of the things that his wife was saying.

'What problems?' She was also surprised, but in a different way.

'Ok for instance one night we were watching a movie on the television, it wasn't exactly a red hot movie; it didn't have a lot of sex in it, but believe me what there was, was worth watching. Now the children were in bed and it was late at night, so no one could really disturb us. So during the film, we started to play with each other.' Sarah looked at Helen. 'Do you mind if I'm blunt?'

'No, not at all,' replied Helen. 'Be as blunt as you want, don't mind me.'

'As I said, we sat there playing around with each other. I was playing with his cock, and he was pushing his fingers in and out of me. We were really and truly enjoying ourselves. I asked him if he fancied going to bed, he said yes, so off to bed we went we got undressed, then got into bed. He then decided that because his cock had gone down, he didn't want to know any more, so he rolled over and went to sleep. He thought nothing about getting me worked up then letting me down. He just said, "Oh I would oblige you, but I am too tired." He seems to forget I've had two children, I don't care less if I never have sex again, well almost never.'

Sarah sat in the chair behind Helen's desk. 'You know, it's ironic when he wants sex it's a totally different story, he'll try every trick in the book to get me to have sex with him. The amount of times, that I've had sex when I didn't feel like it is unbelievable, but I never complained, I just got on with the job. I mean you tell him about it, but being a man he just doesn't understand. I don't suppose that it's his entire fault really, I suppose I have to take some of the blame somewhere along the line.'

'Oh, why?' asked Helen.

'Well I'm afraid to say no. Don't get me wrong, I know that he'll never hit me and even though he might not show it, but he'd be in a bad mood probably for days. It's only because I love him why I put up with it.'

Helen looked at David, who was sitting there with his mouth slightly open.

'Is there something that you want to say David?' asked Helen.

'Yes there is as a matter of fact, I had no idea you felt so strongly about these things. I wish you had talked to me about these things before. The other night when that film was on, when I was downstairs on the sofa, I wanted you so badly it was incredible. I can't help it if I got tired at that particular moment, ok it was a shitty thing to do, but you know what I'm like, as soon as my head hits that pillow I'm fast asleep.'

'But that's not the point, I was just as tired as you were if not more, because I got up before you did. I was up at least an hour and a half, before you got out of bed and even then you said you were still tired. I even told him to go back to bed, but he said it was a waste of time seen as though he was up already,' said Sarah.

David looked at his wife. 'Why didn't you bring any of these things up before? I've always said, we should talk to each other about everything.'

'Look,' said Helen. 'I gather that neither one of you realise how bad your problem is?'

'What bloody problem?' asked David, raising his voice.

'So you don't think that you and your wife have a problem?' replied Helen, looking at David. Whose cheeks were going slightly red.

'No, I don't think that we do have a problem,' replied David, 'well not a major one anyway.'

Helen asked Sarah the same question. She also said, that she didn't think that the problem was that bad, it was probably all in her head.

'So you do realise that you have a problem then?' said Helen

'Yes,' replied Sarah, 'I suppose we do.'

'Well I don't,' said David, getting slightly angry. 'I don't think that we have a problem at all and I don't think, that my wife and I should be telling a complete stranger our problems.'

'Oh so now you also admit that you have problems?' said Helen, looking at him in such a way that it made David look down to the floor. David never said anything; he just sat there looking as though he was in deep thought.

'There are things that people can't talk about to their families, but they can tell a friend or for that matter a complete stranger. You see you two think that you are the only couple in the world with problems, but you're not. Your problems don't even come close to some of the ones that I have to face every week.'

'Yeah, right,' said David, in a sarcastic voice.

'We know that there are people out there with bigger problems than us, and no we're not looking for sympathy,' said Sarah.

'Then what are you looking for?' asked Helen, raising her voice slightly.

David and Sarah never answered. After a few minutes, Helen got up and went over to her desk where Sarah was sitting. She buzzed for her secretary, after a few seconds; there was a knock on the office door. Helen told her secretary to come in and sit down. Sarah and David were puzzled. They had no idea, what Helen was up to.

Sue, Helen's secretary, was a bit reluctant to sit down; she was also puzzled as to why she was called in to the office. Helen asked her to tell David and Sarah what happened one day when a young friend of hers came into the office. Sue was a bit reluctant, she didn't want to bring all that back up again, but she knew that she had no choice. Of course she could insist that it would bring back too many bad memories and basically, beg not to bring it back up, but in the end she thought I might as well get on with it, even though it hurt her to do so.

There was a brief silence, and then slowly Helen's secretary began.

'Well, the girl that came into my office, I used to go to school with her mother, I could say that her mother and I were the best of friends, but it wouldn't be true we were just good friends. We had fights and we argued, but we always got back together in the end.' She smiled. 'I even slept with her boyfriend and she slept with mine. Neither one of us knew about it until we left school. Anyway the girl that came into the reception area was my friend's daughter, so I asked if there was anything that I could do for her, she said no, and that her mother was meeting her there, and would it be ok if she waited. I said yes and she sat down.

'Well as the day went on and the hours went by, I began to get the feeling that there was something wrong, but I didn't think to just sit there and ask her. I made her a coffee and had a ten minute chat, and then I got back to work. It was nearly lunchtime when she told me she had better be going, because it didn't look like her mother was coming. I said ok; I told her I was going to give her mother a good roasting when I saw her. I then told her to watch how she went and to be careful. She said as she went into the lift that she had realised what she had to do.

'Now usually when she was leaving, or I was leaving her she'd say goodbye and see you soon. She always said it without fail, but on that particular day she just said goodbye. Now it never dawned on me that she might have been in trouble and as I said, it was stupid of me not to ask. I mean she often came and waited there for her mother to come.' Sue sighed, she wanted to cry.

'Anyway I got up and as she went down in the lift, I noticed an envelope had been left on the chair; all it had written on it was to a very special friend. Now if I had used my brains and ran down the stairs, I probably could have caught her, but I never. As I opened the letter everything she had said suddenly started to dawn on me.' She sighed again. 'In the letter she told of how for years her stepfather was abusing her and her sister. The girl that left me the letter, she was only fifteen and her sister was about eleven or twelve, something like that. She also told how she would sit down and try and tell her mother, who would turn round and say that she was making things up. And that she just hated her stepfather, because he was a nice person. She said it went on for years and that some nights, when their mother went out; he would lock one of them in a cupboard. She said she used to scream if it was her, because she knew what he was doing to her sister. She would shout and yell, but try as she might nobody could hear her. She didn't have a father because he died in the army; apparently he got shot whilst he was in Northern Ireland. So apart from her mother, she basically had no one to talk to, ok she had relatives, but even they were not interested in hearing her cry for help.

'Why she never came to me for help, I'll never know. What was even worse was I thought if I catch the lift I might be lucky and just catch her leaving the building. I came rushing out of the lift to find police everywhere. I asked a young man what was going on. He said that a lorry had hit a young girl and that she was dead, the young man then walked off into the lift. I ran outside to see if what I thought had happened, had happened. It had, the girl had committed suicide. What had happened was that she just ran straight down the middle of the duel carriageway straight into a lorry, and as you would naturally expect the girl never stood a chance. I told a police officer about the letter and who the young girl was. I then told him that I had to go back upstairs and tell my boss. He sent two policemen with me. I told them the name and address of my friend, sorry ex friend and the name of her husband and where he worked.'

She was just about to continue when Sarah cut into the conversation.

'How did you cope?' she asked.

'Well, I don't really know, I think I just swept it to the back of my mind. I can't say that I've got over it completely, but I can say I learned to live with it. That's all you can do really. I sit behind my desk sometimes, and think that any minute she's going to walk out the lift. I know that isn't going to happen, but that's what I think all the same.'

'Do you think; I mean really and truly think that when she went down in the lift you could have run down the stairs and caught her?' asked Sarah.

'No I don't, but that's what I keep thinking. Look if a person is locked on to committing suicide, then there is no way that anybody can stop them. All the love in the world wouldn't stop them from killing themselves.'

Susan asked if it was ok if she went back to work.

Helen said, 'Yes.'

On her way out David asked Susan, 'What happened to the girl's younger sister.'

'She was taken into care and then fostered out to someone,' said Susan.

'Do you still see her?' asked Sarah.

'Well it was a very long time ago, but yes I see her everyday,' replied Susan, as she opened the door to go out.

'Does she live with you?' asked Sarah, thinking that the young girl may be living with her.

'No she's all grown up now with her own life,' said Susan.

'How do you know that?' asked Sarah with tears in her eyes.

'She happens to be my boss, and you've been talking to her for the past hour.'

She smiled, then shut the office door and went back to work.

'It, err… looks like I owe you an apology,' said David, looking and feeling slightly guilty.

'No there's no need to, as I've told you, this is the place that you can come and say and do as you want.'

'Well, I'm still sorry anyway.'

Helen was just about to speak when Sarah started to speak.

'I think I owe you an apology too.'

Helen was just about to speak, when Sarah started up again.

'God, I've been so fucking stupid!' she shouted 'I mean; there's me thinking, God of all the women in the world, those bastards had to pick on me. When in a perfect world, they would not do that. I thought that people in this place were nice kind helpful people. What a load of rubbish that turned out to be.'

Just before Sarah spoke, Helen saw her chance and jumped into the conversation.

'Look. Why don't you cut the crap, and tell me what's really on your mind. I know you want to talk about being raped, so why don't you? You have to come to terms with it sooner or later, so it might as well be sooner than later.'

There was a couple of seconds of silence, then Sarah spoke breaking the atmosphere and kind of taking David and Helen by surprise.

'Well, where should I begin?' said Sarah, with an almost solemn look on her face. 'Well I got up as usual to go to work, I had a reasonable day, and I finished work early so that I could pop into town on the way back from the office. I went into town, did some shopping, went back to the car and it wouldn't start. I sat there for a few minutes thinking shit what am I going to do now. In the end I thought, oh well sod it. I thought I'll get a taxi home. Then I decided not to, as my house wasn't that far from where I was. It was only about ten minutes away if that, I hadn't got that much shopping and the bags that I had got, weren't really that heavy, and it was a nice day so why not walk home, so I did.

I thought to myself if I cut down the alleyway beside the doctor's I should be home in no time.' Sarah smiled, just a small one.

'I remember thinking God this alleyway's long. Don't get me wrong, I wasn't walking down this alleyway alone. There were loads of people walking down going in and out of doors, people standing there talking, just people going about their business. I got near the end of the alleyway and I bumped into someone I knew. I never really liked this particular person, the only reason I knew him is because I had done some business with him,' she sighed.

'You see about a year ago this millionaire businessman came into my office and said he wanted to sell a house. I told him that I was not interested in buying the type of property that he was selling. Anyway he wanted me to buy it and I said no. So for a few weeks he kept coming into the office, and I kept on saying I wasn't interested.

'Then one day I thought, well it's not going to hurt you to go and have a look at it now is it. So the next time he came in, I went with him to view the house and it turned out to be very nice. To cut a long story short, I bought it at a cheap price and sold it for twice as much as I paid for it, which of course is what I do. Of course he heard about this and came into the office; he said that he wanted half of the money. He tried to claim that I had conned him out of money, but I didn't. I gave him the selling price he asked for and he took it and that was that. He came into the office shouting and bawling how he was going to close my partner and me down, and how we would never work in this town again. That was about a year ago and as time went on we just forgot about Mr Forbes,' she sighed deeply.

'I mean the only reason I talked to him was to be polite. You know my dad always told my sister and me to always be polite under any situation. I was, although he was being a little bit sarcastic, I was very calm and very polite. In a sense I wish I had told him there and then what I really thought of him. Anyway I told him that I had better be going, and that it was nice seeing him again and all that. Just then this scruffy looking man came running round the corner. You know ripped jeans, trainers so big that you could get two feet in one trainer, bright orange shirt with something stupid written on it like: tight buts drive me nuts, something stupid like that. Anyway he said to me "fancy going halves on a bastard". I just replied, not with a pratt like you as I was walking off.

'Before I knew it, he grabbed me and called me a fucking bitch, so I wasn't going to stand for that. So I kicked him in the balls, he dropped to his knees like someone dropping a sack of potatoes on the floor. Anyway I began to walk off when a slap came from Mr Forbes, which put me on my arse. I was dazed; I tried to get to my feet but I couldn't. I began to scream and shout, but no one seemed to care.'

Tears were rolling slowly down the side of her cheeks as she spoke. David was trying desperately to stop himself from crying too.

'They dragged me by my hair into a corner beside a car. By this time I was shouting and screaming my lungs out, but no one came. They kicked me, slapped me, punched me, you name it they did it.

'The scruffy looking one said, "Give me your purse". He then took out a knife. I told him to take the purse and go. He took the purse and said that the best was yet to come. Forbes said that he was going to go first, he said that he never believed in having seconds.'

Sarah was crying while she was talking, she kept picking the tissues out of the box on Helen's desk and drying her eyes. The more she dried them, the more she cried and the more she cried the more tissues she used.

'At a guess I'd say that I had blood coming from everywhere. The scruffy looking one was holding me down while the other one ripped off my skirt and my knickers. He took out his cock, showed it to me and then said that he was going to put it inside me. He put his hand over my mouth while the other one held me down, so that I couldn't move. Forbes kept saying, "Nice isn't it?" I wanted to scream and scream as loud as I could, but I couldn't and nobody would have heard me anyway.

I wriggled about as much as possible. But all he said was, "Yes I know your enjoying it." He got off me, and he let his sperm drip all over me and then the other one had me as well. He said that my pussy was nice, and that he could do this all day. He also said that I was enjoying it. He finished; he also let his sperm drip all over me. They gave each other a high five; you know where they slap their hands together in the air. Then Forbes said that I was a good fuck. The other one gave me a kick in the ribs. I must have passed out after I heard them drive away; I could hear their laughter as they went.

'You know I think my sister was right,' said Sarah, still crying. 'I am a cold hearted bitch. I know that it happens all the time and some of the bastards never get caught. So you could say that I was lucky in getting those two caught.' She was still crying, when she sighed. 'At first I thought, well just try to get over it as best as possible. I thought of committing suicide. I thought of just packing my things and leaving my home and this place for good, and just starting a fresh life somewhere else. But when we went to the police station, when the policeman said, I had to pick them out of a line up. I thought well why the fuck should I leave? Why the hell should I leave my family? Why the hell should I give up a business that I and my partner Susan have worked damn hard to get it where it is today? As for committing suicide that idea went straight out of the window.

'As I stood there listening to what everybody was saying. I thought why should I give up all that I have worked for, all that I have? It may not be much, but at least I have something which I can call my own. There and then at the police station, I decided that those two bastards were not going to get away with what they did to me.

'Bastards, they took my life away from me! They had no fucking right to take my life away from me! You know the worst thing is, ok they caught the scruffy looking one within a week, but Mr Forbes, because he was a millionaire, got people to cover for him. Even people in the police force covered for him. It took three and a half months for them to catch him. So I decided there and then that they were not going to get away with it. They were not going to get the chance to rape anybody else.

'The part that got to me most was when the neighbours and everybody started to gossip. The only neighbour that never said a word was Paul who lives right next door. Even the other neighbours that live a little further away from my house had a dig at my family and me. I've lost count the amount of times that David has beaten someone up in our area. You know you get the snide remarks from people: "Oh I wonder if she's telling the truth, after all he is a millionaire, why would he want to rape her?" One woman even said that I deserved it for leading them on. Leading them on, I don't think that carrying a load of shopping looks very sexy, although, some members of public may disagree with that.

'I hated the fact that ever since the trouble I had with my sister and her ex boyfriend, people have looked at my family and me like we were animals or something. But not one of them has had the guts to come up to us and say anything. They just waited until our backs were turned, they make me sick. I know that this kind of thing happens all the time, at different places, different times and the people there probably say the same things as the people here, but it still makes me sick.'

'It's true' said Helen, 'People are always the same. It doesn't matter where you go or who you are, when there are scandals they all want to poke their noses in. But when the scandal happens to them they try their best to keep it quiet. Take me for instance I've been doing this job now for nearly eleven years and I'm still shocked by some of the things I hear. Ok, take what happened to me for instance, when I was younger I wanted my relatives to help my sister and I, but not one of them came forward to try and help us. I can still remember some of the things that people used to say. You know things like: "now come on your stepfather's a wonderful person you're just being silly, because you don't like him", or the classic one was: "I think that you have been watching too much television young lady". The amount of arguments that my mother and sister had was unbelievable.

'Not long after my sister killed herself, my mum died of a heart attack. So I'll never know if she ever really believed my sister or me. Even though I was so young, I went to live with a foster family. Then I went to live with a friend, now my secretary. There was a brief silence. Oh and before you ask. No I don't feel bitter against any member of my family, or my relatives. I just feel sorry for them.

'Anyway the point is that you have more guts than you give yourself credit for. Now most of the time when people come to see me for the first time, I have to beg and beg for them to say something. Even when I shout and bawl at them, even then they are still in two minds about talking to me,' she giggled. 'Once I sat here for more than two hours with this woman who had been beaten up by her husband. For one and a half hours she never said a single word apart from hello and goodbye. I tried various ways to try and talk to her, but she never said a word.'

'But didn't she ever speak to you at all?' asked Sarah.

'Yes she did the same day, when I told her that her session was over and would she pay the five hundred pound fee when she went to reception. She went mad, telling me that she's not paying that much money and that I hardly said a word to her for hours.

'As soon as she said that she realised that she was suppose to speak, and I was suppose to listen. I let her sweat until she got to reception, before I told her that she did not have to pay a fee of five hundred pounds. She did however apologise to me, and said that she would do better the next time she came.'

Helen asked if anybody wanted a drink. David and his wife both said yes.

'What was she like the next time she came?' asked Sarah, as she took a cup from Helen.

'I don't know? She never came again. All this happened months ago, so I expect that she went back to her husband that's what they do most of the time. Anyway the point is you have a lot more guts than you think. Now I don't usually say things like this to people, but I think that you may surprise yourself in the weeks to come.'

Meanwhile, David had just sat there; he hadn't said a word for a while. He looked like he was staring at a picture on the wall. He wasn't he was just staring into space. He eventually came back to earth. Helen and Sarah never realised that David had not been listening to a word they had been saying for the past forty-five minutes. They just took it for granted that he was listening, and he never let on that he hadn't been. He drank his coffee which by now was stone cold. Helen told them that their time was nearly up.

'Well I'm glad that we got over our teething troubles. But as I said, you have to put everything into prospective. Some of these rich people have it in their heads that, because they have a lot of money, when they get into trouble their money is going to save them. Most of the time they get lucky, and they get away with whatever they've done. But occasionally, just occasionally at least two out of three get prosecuted good and proper. They don't get sent to holiday homes, they get sent to a real prison. Trust me; I used to be a lawyer, I know how the system works.'

David and Sarah got up, because their time with Helen had come to an end. Helen told them she was looking forward to their next visit, and asked Sarah when her next court date was, and that she would make some enquires for her as it's always a good idea to know what your opposition is up to.

'One more thing before you go, what is the name of your barrister?' asked Helen.

Sarah told her the barrister's name.

'Oh my life,' said Helen, taking a deep breath and letting it out rather quickly, she smiled. She had a radiant look about her all of a sudden.

'It's alright,' said Sue Helen's secretary. 'Richard Thorn and Helen used to date each other.'

'We did not,' said Helen, going slightly red in the face. 'We had a business relationship that's all.' Helen was looking very happy all of a sudden.

'Well flip me, if my marriage was as good as your business relationship, I would never have got divorced,' replied Sue.

'Ok we used to date, but it was a very long time ago. I don't even think that he'd remember me anyway.' Helen was getting slightly embarrassed, because everybody was looking at her. 'Anyway enough about me, I'll try and find out as much as I can for you ok.'

David apologised once again for the way that he acted earlier. Helen told him, that it wasn't any need for him to apologise. They said their goodbyes and then David and his wife left.

David chuckled.

'What's up?' giggled his wife. Even though she had no idea of what he was laughing about.

'I was just thinking how red Helen went just when you mentioned Richard's name to her. It's a good job she was sitting on the desk, or she would have passed out if she were standing up,' he said still smiling when he came out of the lift.

They never really said much on the way home. David asked his wife what she wanted to do that night and she said that she didn't know. For that matter, I don't suppose that she really cared.

Later on in the afternoon David suggested that he and his wife go out to dinner. She said that she didn't mind, but in the back of her mind all she wanted to do was curl up on the sofa with her husband watching television. But David was looking forward to going out, so not to spoil his evening she went out with him to dinner. I suppose there were occasions when she wanted to go out and he wanted to stop in. But I suppose he went out to make her happy.

They had a reasonable night out. David wanted to go out for a drink afterwards, but his wife just wanted to go home and go to bed. So that's what they did. He was a little bit disappointed, but he understood how she felt. Even though he knew that what he was thinking was complete rubbish.

David was first through the front door. His wife asked him if he had checked the answering machine for messages. He replied that he was about to. Sarah then took off her coat and then went upstairs. David meanwhile was checking the

46

machine, lucky enough there weren't any messages. So he put the lock on the front door turned off all the lights and went upstairs.

His wife had not even got undressed; she was fast asleep on top of the quilt. He took her clothes off, took off her shoes and put a pillow under her head. He then put as much of the quilt over his wife as he could. He then got undressed and went into Jason's room to sleep.

In the morning David was startled out of his sleep by his wife shouting and screaming his name. He jumped out of Jason's bed flung open the bedroom door, and ran to the bedroom to see what was wrong with his wife. He ran in and stopped suddenly, his wife was sitting up in bed crying furiously and shouting his name. He quickly went over to her and put his arms around her.

'Hey come on what's wrong?' he asked.

His wife put her arm's tightly around his waist, and put her head on his chest and cried.

'David don't leave me, don't ever leave me,' said his wife, who was still crying franticly. 'I don't ever want you to leave me ever.'

'Hey now calm down, alright,' comforted David. 'I'm not going anywhere with anybody apart from you. I love you more than you'll ever know. I love you more than life itself. I'd never leave you for anything, even if the Sultan of Brunei said he would give me everything that he has if I let you go. I'd still say no because I love you too much.'

They sat there for what must have seemed like eternity, but it wasn't all that long.

After about twenty minutes, David convinced his wife that it would be a good idea to get out of bed.

'Why don't you take a shower and I'll make you a nice breakfast,' suggested David.

Sarah nodded and got out of bed as her husband went downstairs. Once she had finished showering and got dressed Sarah went downstairs. David made her a cup of black coffee. He told his wife that breakfast was almost done.

'You know to be honest, I don't really fancy any breakfast,' said Sarah, sipping her coffee.

'That may well be the way you feel, but you have to eat; I noticed last night that you left most of your food when we were in the restaurant. So even if I have to force feed you; I'll make sure that you eat properly.'

Sarah had stopped crying now, she wasn't feeling any better, but at least she had stopped crying.

'What do you want to do today?' asked her husband.

'Oh, I don't know,' she replied, picking at her breakfast.

David knew that he could not force his wife to eat, he could shout and bawl at her but at the end of the day if she wasn't hungry she wouldn't eat. Sarah told David that she would wash up.

'You will not, why do you think that I spent over four hundred pounds on a dishwasher, so we wouldn't have to do things like that? Anyway if you want something to do, I'll be generous and let you make the beds.'

'Oh thanks,' said his wife, managing a small smile. She kissed her husband and said, 'I love you.'

She ran up the stairs before he could reply.

David had an idea; he was thinking how he could cheer his wife up. He thought of a big bunch of roses. He also had another idea, he phoned Sarah's office.

'Hello, can I speak to Miss Susan Hardy please?'

'Whom shall I say is calling?' said a sweet petite voice on the other end of the phone.

'It's err… Mr Phillips,' said David.

'Ok, thank you, I'll just see if she's free hold on one moment please.'

'Ok,' said David, waiting patiently.

After a few seconds the secretary came back onto the phone.

'Hello, Miss Hardy is free; I'm just putting your call through now, Mr Phillips.' After a few seconds Susan answered the phone. The secretary put her phone down.

'David, hello how are you? I couldn't tell the last time that you called me,' said Susan. David giggled.

'Liar, I called you on your birthday a couple of weeks ago.'

'Oh by the way thank you for the present,' said Susan.

'Never mind that now,' said David. 'Look can you do me a favour?' David told Susan what he wanted her to do. 'Now don't forget it has to be a big bunch of roses. I'll give you the money when you come down,' said David.

'You will not,' said Susan.

'OK, look I'm going, I can hear her coming down the stairs, see you later.' He put the phone down just as Sarah came down the stairs.

'Who was that on the phone?'

'Oh, err… wrong number,' said David quickly and then going into the kitchen. Sarah just said ok and went into the living room. She put the television on and sat down. David put all of the dirty things they had been using in the dishwasher. Then went into the living room and sat down with his wife.

'You were on the phone a long time, considering that it was a wrong number?'

'Err… they wanted to know where Micro engineering was?' David breathed a sigh of relief so slowly that you could hardly hear it.

'Micro engineering, never heard of the place,' said his wife.

Later on in the evening, Sarah noticed that her husband, every so often was looking at the clock.

'What's wrong?' asked his wife.

'Err… wrong, what makes you think that there is anything wrong?' replied David, who had not noticed himself looking at the clock.

'Well, it's nothing really it's just the way that you've been behaving since that call earlier,' said Sarah, looking at David who was looking at the clock. 'You see you're doing it now.' Just then the doorbell rang. Sarah quickly jumped up and said she would get it before her husband had a chance to move. Sarah opened the door; all she saw at first was a very big bunch of flowers and a bag.

'Now you might as well come in Susan,' said Sarah, giggling.

'How do you know that it's Susan?' said a rather muffled voice from behind the flowers.

'Well, the only person I've seen with a ring that big was Elizabeth Taylor, oh, and Joan Collins.' Susan parted the flowers, said hello and then went in. She went in to the living room where David was sitting down. He turned round to look at Susan but all he saw was her ring.

'Gordon Bennett,' said David, standing up.

He walked round the chair and took hold of Susan's hand. 'My God, I've seen a lot of things in my time but that's huge.' Susan started to laugh.

'Michael at work said the only rock he's seen that big was Mount Everest,' said Susan smiling warmly. Sarah was glued to the ring as well.

'Susan is there something that you want to tell us?' asked Sarah, who had noticed the overwhelming look of delight on her face.

'Ok, I can't keep it to myself any longer, I'm getting married.'

'Oh well done,' said David, kissing her on the cheek.

'Well, it's about flipping time,' said Sarah, who kind of expected this to happen years ago, but it didn't.

'I've been trying to keep it a secret for as long as I could,' said Susan.

'I have to ask a silly question, but are we invited to the wedding?' said Sarah. Susan looked at David and Sarah. 'Well, I have to tell you that you're not allowed at my wedding, although, it may seem strange getting married in a church without David as my pageboy, and you as my Matron of Honour. That's of course if you do not have anything planned for the twenty sixth of October. Of course that's if David doesn't mind being my pageboy and you Sarah don't mind being my Matron of Honour.'

'I think that my hubby is a bit too mature to be a pageboy.'

'Oh I don't know, get rid of his grey hair; stick him in some short trousers.' David was about to speak when his wife spoke.

'We'd love to,' said Sarah, getting slightly excited. 'Anyway who sent you the flowers?'

'Oh the flowers. They're not for me, they're for you. The one bunch of flowers are from me,' said Susan.

'Who's the other one from?' asked Sarah, quickly and getting slightly excited once again. 'Well I don't know; it has a note in with it,' said Susan.

Sarah took a card from the bunch of roses that Susan had pointed to.

While Sarah was reading the card, David and Susan were in the kitchen.

'How is she?' asked Susan, quietly.

'She's in a pretty bad way; she woke up this morning screaming my name. She thought that I had packed all my things and left in the middle of the night. When I woke up, all I could hear was Sarah screaming. I ran out of Jason's room and went to see what was wrong,' said David.

'Why were you in Jason's room?' she asked taking the Chinese meal she had bought out of the bag.

'Oh don't get me wrong, we never had an argument, she went to bed before me and fell asleep in an awkward position.'

He was just about to continue when his wife ran over to him and kissed him. David gasped for breath when his wife stopped kissing him.

'What was that for?' asked David.

'For the flowers silly,' said his wife.

'Oh that, it was nothing.' She kissed him again, but not so vigorously this time.

'Do you want to hear what the card says,' said his wife smiling.

'Yes certainly,' said Susan.

'Ok, the card says,' began Sarah:

'With all my heart I love you dear
Even through all the heartache
And through all the tears
I hope that we're still together
In the years to come
I love you more than anything
You're my number one
Love always
David.'

'Now that is nice, you know if my marriage is a good as yours when I get married, I'll be one of the happiest women alive. Look anyway enough romance is it possible that I could have some plates for this meal or it is going to get cold.'

'Oh sorry,' said David. David took out some plates and Sarah went to find some vases to put the roses in. She came back about five minutes after and sat down.

'God, what is that?' asked Sarah looking at the food on the table.

'Now, now woman,' said Susan. 'This is nice, it's chicken chow mien with rice and vegetables.'

'This is the horrible mess that you have isn't it?' asked Sarah, looking at David.

'I'll have you know woman that this horrible mess is quite nice.' Sarah cautiously started to eat the chow mien.

Hey, this isn't bad, thought Sarah.

'Hey, this is quite nice.' Sarah had taken everyone by surprise. She had almost finished her chow mien, when Susan and David were only halfway through theirs.

'God, you must have been hungry,' said Susan.

They finished their meal and just sat there for a while talking. They were not taking about anything in particular. They were just talking about things in general.

After a few minutes of silence, Susan plucked up the courage and asked Sarah if she was alright. Sarah smiled; she picked up the plates and walked across to the dishwasher.

'Of course I'm alright, why shouldn't I be?' Just then Sarah dropped the plates and started to cry. 'No I'm not alright, my life is ruined and my family's drifting apart. I'm scared stiff to open my front door. I never used to be like this. I used to love going to work. Now I'm too scared to leave my own house. Why me? Now that's a question. I ask myself a thousand times why me!' she shouted. She was crying even more. Susan got up to put her arms around Sarah.

'Get away from me, just get away from me. Leave me alone!' she shouted again. Susan grabbed Sarah and cuddled her tightly. Susan had tears in her eyes. It hurt her immensely to see her best friend in such pain, and to know that there wasn't a damn thing that she could do to help. David just sat there with his head in his hands, he was in a dilemma.

David just sat there even after his wife and Susan had gone into the living room. After a while Sarah stopped crying, she just sat there in Susan's arms. David meanwhile had took a deep breath got up and cleared the broken plates off the floor. He swept up and put all the broken things in the bin. He then put the brush back into the cupboard and went upstairs. He had the idea that Susan would be stopping the night, so he went into Jason's room and went to sleep. He woke up once again by the sound of screaming. His wife had had another nightmare. He could hear Susan telling her that she was going to be alright. He could hear his wife crying in the bedroom. Part of him wanted to go in and put his arms around his wife. The other half was saying don't bother, you've tried your best; now leave her for a while.

After a while he drifted back off to sleep. By the time he woke up, Susan had gone. Sarah was in the back garden. It was fairly late in the morning. David yawned as he went outside.

'Morning,' said his wife, who was weeding the garden. 'Did you have a nice sleep?' Sarah came over to him and kissed him, and then went back and to do some more weeding.

'I still feel tired believe it or not,' said David, yawning again.

'You can go back to bed, if you want, I don't mind.' Sarah was struggling to pull a weed out of the garden.

'Having trouble with that one?' smiled David.

'No, I can do it,' she replied, as she was going red with the strain. As she was pulling hard at the weed, David came over.

'Now stop take a breather. God, you look like you're going to pass out,' said her husband. 'Now, I'm not an expert gardener, but I do know that the best way to get rid of a weed is to find the root.' David got a shovel and started digging a little bit away from the weed. He dug a big hole, not too big and not too small just big enough to get your hand in. He got his hand in and pulled at the root, but it still wouldn't come out. Sarah then suggested that they put some water down the hole, to kind of loosen the root.

David said the main problem was that the root could be right under the ground and probably half way down the garden. Sarah started pouring the water down the hole. Then they both started pulling at the root and then finally after a few minutes the root came out.

David cleared away the mess and put all the rubbish from the garden in a bag. Then he put the bag in the bin. Sarah meanwhile had gone back into the house. She was in the downstairs toilet, when the phone rang. David was just drying his hands as he picked up the phone.

'Hello.' There was a slight pause before the person answered.

'Hi, David it's me, Sandra.'

'Hi,' said David, in a soft voice. 'Why on earth are you whispering?'

'I thought that bitch of a sister of mine might have answered the phone. She usually does,' replied Sandra, in her normal voice.

'Look, you'll have to talk to each other sooner or later,' said David.

'I wouldn't care if my sister never spoke to me again. God, it makes my blood boil thinking of some of the things she said. My sister has always been an arrogant argumentative cow. If she hasn't changed by now, then I'm afraid she never will.'

David was just about to speak when Sandra cut in again. 'Anyway, you don't want to hear me gripe on about my sister. I just phoned up to see if you are alright.'

'Liar, you phoned up to see if Sarah's alright you mean. Now come on admit it, that's the reason why you phoned isn't it?' said David.

There was a pause, after a while Sandra responded.

'Yes ok, that's why I phoned, but I'm not going to speak to her, so you can get that idea out of your head.'

'What idea? Ok, it bothers me that you two aren't talking, but there isn't a fat lot that I can do about it,' said David.

'Anyway, is she alright?'

'Well, it's hard to say, I mean some days she looks and sounds perfectly fine, other days she's ready to bite your head clean off. Plus she's been having nightmares. She said that they're not nightmares but she's had three so far, each time it seems to get worse. The other night we went out for a meal. Now despite the fact that she left nearly all of her meal and drank more wine than anything else. She seemed distant, you know as if she was only with me in spirit. Anyway we got home; she went to bed before me. I went up about ten minutes after and she was fast asleep on the bed.

'Now she was in such an awkward position that I thought it best not to move her. So I took off as much of her clothing as I could and put as much duvet as I could on her, then I went and slept in Jason's room. Early in the morning I heard screams coming from the bedroom. So like Ben Johnson, I ran in as fast as I could and there she was sitting up in bed shouting my name. To cut a long story short, she thought that I had gone or was going to leave her. Susan was with her when she screamed out last night.'

'Have you both been to see someone about all this?'

'Well, we are seeing someone at the moment. She seems a nice person even though we have only seen her twice. I haven't told her yet, so I'll talk to her about it when we go and see her next,' said David.

'Anyway, I'm going, I'm taking your daughter shopping,' said Sandra.

'Now Sandra, please don't spoil her,' replied David.

'You know me,' Sandra said giggling. 'Would I do a thing like that?'

'Anyway give Lucy a big kiss from Sarah and me. I'll talk to you soon.'

They both said goodbye and put the phone down.

David went and sat down beside his wife, who was eating some biscuits.

'No need to ask who that was on the phone?' said his wife, in a harsh voice.

'She only called to see how you were. She still cares about you,' said David, reaching for a biscuit. When his wife snatched the packet and moved away from her husband. Sarah had a serious look on her face.

'Do I get a biscuit or not?' said David.

'No you don't!' replied his wife, loudly. 'They're mine and you're not getting one, so don't even bother asking.'

David laughed.

'You childish bitch, in all my years I've never known anybody as childish as you. All I wanted was a biscuit for God's sake, not the bloody packet.'

'God, you've gone nasty all of a sudden,' said Sarah, interrupting her husband. 'Here have a biscuit if you want one, take the fucking packet if it means that much to you. God, you can't even have a laugh and a joke with anyone these days. People get nasty over the slightest thing.' Sarah offered her husband the packet. He grabbed the packet, threw them against the wall making the biscuits go all over the place.

'I told you I don't want the bloody biscuits,' David said. 'I know what's eating you. You hate the fact that I'm still talking to your sister.'

'I knew it, every time that you start arguing, you always bring my bitch of a sister into it. I'm beginning to think that you and she might have something going on. You know like Sarah I'm just popping out for an hour, or so won't be long.'

'Oh come on, be real,' said David, who was standing there looking unbelievably stunned. 'I can't believe that you're even thinking about things like that, never mind saying them.'

'Oh don't come the innocent, loving, loyal husband routine. God you hear about this kind of thing all the time. Husband sleeps with wife's sister in torrid love affair,' Sarah sighed. 'I suppose it makes a change from humping the secretary.'

David just stood there speechless.

Sarah smiled. 'Oh what's the matter cat got your tongue hey?' said Sarah, giggling.

'Maybe your sister was right; you are a cold hearted bitch,' said David.

'Am I now? Shall I tell you what really gets on your nerves? It's not me, but them.'

'What do you mean them?' asked David. Who was well and truly pissed off by now.

Sarah stood up and walked around the room.

'Now, imagine holding a woman down and having violent sex with her. I mean, as I've said before, that's all rape is "SEX". It's hurtful, it's painful or is it?' Sarah said, walking around the room.

'Let's take that point for a moment. Now some men do say that raping a woman would be ideal just the thought of it turns some people on.'

David interrupted the conversation.

'Ok, look it's late in the afternoon, I'm hungry.'

'You want to hump my sister, but we can't have everything now, can we? You hate the fact; that because I was raped, the men who had sex with me were probably better at it than you were.'

Sarah walked round in front of her husband.

'Imagine this; one of the men that raped me, he must have at least twelve inches between his legs. Imagine twelve inches going in and out in and out.'

Just then out of the blue David slapped his wife. Sarah fell backwards onto the floor. Within seconds she could feel her face swelling up. She could feel her face throbbing, but she didn't cry. David within seconds was apologising for what he had done. But as you might expect it was too late the damage had already been done.

Sarah's face was in tremendous pain, but she never gave her husband the satisfaction of seeing her cry. She took a deep breath and then she walked slowly past her husband. David reached out to put his arms around his wife. She flinched thinking that her husband was going to hit her again. She ran for the door and then she ran upstairs. David heard their bedroom door slam shut.

David just sat outside in the back garden thinking about what he had just done to his wife. He knew that his wife was sobbing in the bedroom. David looked up at the sky. He could see the previous event flashing before his eyes. Each time he thought about it, it made him feel worse, but he couldn't do anything but think about it.

He thought to himself, 'Why did you have to be so fucking stupid?' The other half was saying that the bitch deserved everything she got, she was basically asking for it.

It was now evening time and David still hadn't had anything to eat. Sarah had not come down since the incident. He knew that it was pointless asking her if she was alright, because he already knew the answer. Finally he went to sleep in Jason's room. He went to sleep feeling rather sorry for himself. He woke up at different times during the night; each time it was because he had been thinking about what he had done earlier on.

David woke up early the next morning. He kept thinking of what he had done the previous day. He knew that his wife would not forgive him that easily, if she forgave him at all. He got up, he made Jason's bed and then he went and took a shower. He crept into his own bedroom to see if his wife was alright. He couldn't see her properly, because as usual she had her head under the quilt. He very slowly took some of his clothes out of the cupboard and went downstairs. He picked up some letters which were by the front door. He also picked up the paper and then he went into the kitchen. He put the letters and the paper on the table and made himself some breakfast. He thought that he might as well have a big breakfast, because he never ate anything the day before. For some reason he went right off food. He was deep into the paper when his wife came into the kitchen.

'Good morning,' said Sarah, cheerfully. She smiled at her husband. 'Any chance of breakfast?'

David was slightly stunned; the last thing that he expected was his wife to come downstairs in a good mood.

'Err… yes certainly,' said her husband, getting up. 'What would you like?'

'Eggs, bacon, sausages, beans, fried bread, coffee. Oh and a glass of orange juice please.' David was still stunned as he prepared his wife's huge breakfast. Which really and truly surprised him, because his wife hadn't had a breakfast this big for years? The only time she ate like this is when she was pregnant. But he knew that she wasn't pregnant, because she had had a few periods since she was raped. He made his wife's breakfast, Coffee and the orange juice. When David sat back down he had a chance to look at his wife's face.

He couldn't see much when she came in, because he could only see the one side of her face, the good side.

Sarah looked up to see her husband staring at her.

'Beauty isn't it? Notice how it covers most of my face. You'll notice as well that my one eye is nearly closed. The part that you can see is as red as a strawberry. My eye is so black that it shines. Before you ask, I cannot cover it up with make-up. I can't even blink it's that painful. Anyway this is a lovely breakfast; I should eat like this more often.'

Sarah ate another mouthful of food.

David just sat there bewildered. Why was his wife behaving like this? To say that her husband was under stress was an understatement. Sarah put all the things in the dishwasher and then went to get changed. She came back down about ten minutes after.

'Right, come on then,' said Sarah. 'What shall we do today?'

'Err… whatever you fancy.' He felt guilty every time he looked at Sarah.

He was still bewildered by the calmness of his wife.

'How about we just curl up on the settee together,' said Sarah.

David was thinking that he should apologise to his wife for hitting her. But that might just upset her. Besides the guilt that he was feeling was far worse than anything his wife could say to him. David and Sarah just sat there watching the television. They never said much to each other. They just sat there for most of the day watching television, occasionally getting up and getting a drink of coffee or something to eat, but they really never did anything else. The rest of the week went by fairly quickly, and before they knew it Monday morning had come again.

They both got up. There was still a bit of tension between them. David was the first to get dressed and go downstairs. His wife came down about ten minutes after him. Her husband was watching television and drinking a cup of coffee. He knew that there was something that he had to do today, but he could not remember what it was.

'Right,' said his wife, getting on her coat.

'Where are you going?' he said looking at her.

'What do you mean, where am I going? In case you've forgotten today's Monday.'

David just looked puzzled.

'Yes, I know that today is Monday. So what's so special about this particular Monday?'

'You're joking right' she said, looking strangely at him. She could tell by the odd look on his face that he didn't have a clue what she was talking about. 'Well blow me; I do believe that the man's forgotten. Look I'll give you clue. What have we been doing every Monday morning at nine thirty for the last two weeks?'

David just looked at her, shrugged his shoulders and said that he didn't know. 'I can't remember.'

Sarah just thought that he was taking the piss out of her.

'Well seeing as though you've had a sudden lapse of memory, you might as well stay here. Let's just hope that this sudden memory loss isn't permanent, or else you're in big trouble. Right seeing as though you don't want to come, I might as well go on my own, see you later.' She grabbed his car keys off the shelf by the phone and left.

David heard his wife slam his car door, when he remembered that they had an appointment with Helen. He rushed outside just as his wife drove off the drive.

'Shit, I knew there was something I had to do.' He went back into the house and closed the door. He could have jumped into his wife's car and gone after her. As he saw it there was no point. If she really wanted him to come, she would usually have told him. She would never get upset about it.

David was sitting there, thinking allowed and feeling sorry for himself, when the phone rang. You could call it delayed reaction, because it didn't register in his brain for a few seconds that the phone was ringing. After some time, he jumped up as if he was startled by something. It was then that he realised that the phone was ringing.

'Hello,' said David, quite quickly. He was thinking that the other person on the end of the line might have put the phone down, but the person answered just as quickly as David said hello.

'Hi David, it's me, Jonathon.'

'Oh, Jonathon, hi, sorry mate I was miles away.'

'I gathered that,' said Jonathon, in a soft, but firm voice. 'You're lucky just as you picked up the phone I was ready to put it down.'

'You'll have to excuse me if I don't sound myself, I've had a lot on my mind recently so you'll have to bear with me.' David by this time was sitting down on the settee with his feet up.

'By the way, how's Sarah?' David had already told Jonathon about Sarah and what had happened to her. He had no worries about Jonathon asking about his wife's welfare, because Jonathon and Sarah were quiet close and of course Jonathon was gay.

'Sarah's fine, well as she can be under the circumstances. Err... when did you come back off holiday?' said David quickly, hoping to change the subject.

'We'll discuss me later. Never mind trying to change the subject. Look, I'll get straight to the point. I went into the office the other day and I knew something was up, but nobody would say anything. All Misha said was, "I would love to tell you what's going on, but I don't like people talking about me behind my back, so I'm not going to do it to anybody else." She just said, if you want to know ask David about his wife. So here I am asking.' Jonathon had been part owner in the company that David had worked for some time now. David told Jonathon that he had already told him about Sarah being attacked.

'Yes, but you only gave me half of the story,' replied Jonathon. David began to tell Jonathon all that had happened. To say Jonathon was gutted was an understatement.

'What was that name again?' Jonathon asked David.

'Ronald Walker.'

'No, not that one, the second one that you mentioned,' insisted Jonathon.

'Oh you mean Michael Forbes,' said David. 'Do you know how much I wanted to beat him up? I wanted to beat Forbes that bad, I could taste it.'

Jonathon was thinking aloud. 'Forbes, Forbes, Forbes. I know, I know the name from somewhere, but where?'

'Perhaps you've done business with him?' said David.

'No I don't think so; in fact I know I haven't. I would've remembered his name. No, I know the name for a specific reason.' And he thought. He was thinking when David carried on.

'Yeah, you know I wanted to kill him that bad it was incredible.'

'That's it, Oh David you're a genius,' said Jonathon, shouting down the phone. 'No wonder you're on such a huge salary. Oh God you're brilliant.'

'Hey Jonathon calm down. Tell me what you know, if you know anything that could help us,' said David.

'If I know anything that could help! Hang on a moment let me catch my breath. God, you're a genius,' said Jonathon, again.

'Look, ok. I'll tell you. Do you remember the funeral of Mr Jeffries? Well as you know, he was a well respected man in or out of the board room. Well did you ever find out, how he died?'

'No, I was led to believe that he died from a stroke. People say that he was way overworked. I didn't believe that story myself mind you. Edward was probably one of the fittest men around this area. So how he died from a stroke, I'll never know. I miss that bloke you know,' said David.

'Yes, so do I. Anyway I heard that same story. I never believed it either, so I had some of my friend's check out what happened. Now I remember that the police had a word with Mr Forbes, but nothing ever came of it. I also know that Forbes had an argument with Edward the same day he died. Now doesn't that tell you something?' said Jonathon.

'It does sound a little suspicious, but that doesn't mean that he killed Edward though does it?' replied David.

'No I suppose not. I don't suppose that he raped your wife either.' There was a brief pause, between David and Jonathon. Then Jonathon said, 'Look, ok, maybe the man's innocent. Maybe I'm just being foolish. Maybe my friends told me a pack of lies. But some of the stories which I've heard about this guy are incredible. And if there's a slim chance that I'm right. Then that piss bag would never come out of prison, and you know that's why your brain's doing overtime.'

David asked when he came back off holiday.

'Came back just before the weekend, broke my leg as well. Well I say my leg it's more my ankle downwards,' said Jonathon.

'How on earth did you manage to do that?' enquired David.

'Well I was coming down this slope fairly quickly, and even if I say so myself I'm quite a good skier considering that I taught myself. Anyway, coming down this slope, doing at least sixty-five miles an hour, this stupid American woman came out of nowhere. By the time that I noticed her, the speed I was going I couldn't have stopped. There was no way in the world that I could have stopped.

'Anyway I tried to be clever and try and swerve round this woman. I was almost round her when she panicked and stuck one her skis out. For what bloody reason I shall never know. She stuck her ski out, tripped me up. I rolled about ten times and then I came to a stop. I'll tell you the pain was unbelievable. All the

American woman said was, "I'm so sorry I never saw you coming." Never seen me coming, she was only standing in the middle of the runway while I was coming down.

'Anyway there is a funny side to all this,' continued Jonathon. 'When I walked into the office, because I was on crutches I had to wear this iron boot. So when I walked on the tiled part of the floor in the office, the boot used to tap on the floor as I walked. So Misha started calling me tap. That's what people call me now, tap.'

David laughed slightly.

'So apart from that you enjoyed your holiday?' he said.

'Yes I did, and I'm going again as soon as my ankle's better. But I have to go to Japan for a while, and then I'm off to France after I come back from there. I'll let you know when I'm going,' said Jonathon.

'Yeah do that, I want to show Sarah your new house before you go away again. I was going to show her before you went skiing, but I never had the time,' stated David.

'Yes that's fine, just let me know when, but I'm still going to check this guy Forbes out for you. Hey look, I'll take Jason and Lucy away with me soon. Well after I've done this deal in Japan anyway,' replied Jonathon.

'Are you sure?' asked David.

'Look, we'll have to talk soon. Anyway I must dash; I have a lot to do today,' replied Jonathon.

'Ok, see you Jonathon, sorry tap,' said David. They both said goodbye and put the phone down.

David paused for a moment before getting up and putting the phone back. He then went and made himself a cup of tea.

Chapter 2

Sarah meanwhile was talking to Helen. 'Yes as I said, it's been one of those weeks,' said Sarah.

'You still haven't told me, how you got the bruise on your face? Don't tell me that you walked into a door,' said Helen.

'I wasn't going to. I was going to be perfectly honest, and tell you that David did it. I know he shouldn't have hit me. But believe me, it was my own fault and I know that I deserved it,' said Sarah.

'How can you say that? I've had my fair share of slaps from people, but I can honestly say that I didn't deserve any of them. If you don't mind me saying so that was a rather stupid thing to say,' said Helen.

'I don't mean it like that,' said Sarah. 'I mean, I said a lot of things the other night that I shouldn't have done. I basically blamed my husband for me getting raped. I even turned round and said that he may even like the thought of raping me. I even went as far as saying that he was sleeping with my sister.'

'Ouch, I gather at this point is when you received the slap?' asked Helen.

'No, I think it was when I said that the rapist was better at it than he was, and his tool was at least five inches bigger than his,' said Sarah.

'My word you did go to town on him didn't you,' said Helen, looking at her.

'It put me on my arse, I can tell you,' replied Sarah. 'As soon as he hit me, I could feel my face swelling up. I had a look at it, before I went bed the night that he did it. I sat there in front of the mirror, and I thought look at the state of that. I looked like a bag of shit. Don't get me wrong, I like to look as good as the next woman, but basically people have to take me as they find me.' Sarah got up and started pacing up and down Helen's office. 'I mean if a woman's standing there in a five hundred pound dress and mine was two hundred, and if the other person didn't like it then as I say tough. You can't please everybody. So I start by pleasing myself.'

'Tell me about you and your sister. I remember you saying the last time you came that you had an argument with her. Has that been resolved yet?' asked Helen.

'Look if you don't mind, I'd rather not talk about that bitch,' replied Sarah, in a hard voice.

'Why not?' asked Helen.

'Why not because the bitch pisses me off, that's why,' replied Sarah. 'You know she turned round after all the things that David and I have done for her, and said that I was a cold hearted bitch, me, her only sister, a cold hearted bitch.'

'What did you say to that?' asked Helen.

'Me, I told her the truth,' said Sarah.

'And what was that then?' asked Helen.

'I told her plain and simple, that she was living in cuckoo land. Her and the rest of the mongrels in my family,' replied Sarah.

'What about your father?' enquired Helen.

'My father, huh, I don't think that he understands at all. We haven't spoken about what happened. We said a few things about it but that's about it. We haven't sat down and had a good talk for ages. Before we'd sit there and talk about anything, from sex in this day and age, to why John Barnes is such a good football player. We used to talk about everything but not now, not since I was raped. That's a word in itself isn't it, rape. When I think of what those …(she took a deep breath and then let it out slowly) those animals did to me. It just makes me sick. You know to most members of my family, I was just raped and eventually I'll get over it. But to me those two men took part of my life away. I can't actually put my finger on it, but those two men took something from me. Something I don't feel I will ever get back, it feels like… I don't know they've taken my life away; I can't seem to be able to explain it. You know, I keep thinking that I must have been a horrible person when I was a child. I must have been really horrible and nasty to people.' Sarah sat down and looked at Helen. 'Well, I must have done something to deserve this.'

Helen chuckled.

'All you've done since you've been here is gripe on about how everybody treats you. You haven't mentioned once, how everybody cares about you,' said Helen. 'David must love you to stay with you and put up with all your crap. You must love him as much to put up with his crap. Being raped is a terrible crime. They should get a few of these people and make an example out of them. So the next lot of people will think twice, before they do it to some other woman. But you must realise that you're not alone. At least twenty thousand women get raped every year all over the world, and almost half of them never take it to court. Most of them bottle out. You hear literally thousands of silly stories,' continued Helen.

'Like this girl on the beach with her boyfriend having sex. Now when they eventually finish, he looks at his watch and realises that the next bus is due soon, so the boyfriend kisses her goodbye and off he goes. Why on earth he never walked to the bus stop I shall never know. I suppose he had his fun and then thought sod it I'm going home, or maybe he lived further away than she did. Anyway this girl was putting her clothes right, when this old couple who were walking their dog on the beach saw her and asked if everything was ok. Now this is the part that got me. Instead of just saying that she was fine, and she just fell asleep on the beach. She would have gone home slightly embarrassed, and that would have been it. But no, she had to lie.

'This old couple's dog had found this girl knickers, and was sitting on the floor with them in his mouth when the lady owner spotted them. She took them from the dog and asked the young girl if they belonged to her. She said yes. Then out the blue, she just said that she had been raped. She said the man that they had seen running off had done it. Why she had to lie in the first place, I'll never know. Anyway to cut a long story short, the police arrested this boyfriend of hers and charged him with raping her. The truth only came out when they went to court, and the judge was about to give her boyfriend six years in prison.

'She then told the truth and shocked everybody. The judge told her that she would be charged with wasting the court and police time. The judge should have given her six years instead.'

'Well, what happened to her boyfriend?' asked Sarah.

'Oh him, he made some money by selling his story to the newspapers. After that, nobody heard anything more about him.

'Another silly one was where this woman in America said that this bloke had raped her. This bloke got twelve years in prison, and he came out after twelve years in prison. He kept saying all the time he was in there that he was innocent, but no one believed him. The day before he came out this woman went to the police station that charged him, and told them that he had never done it. The joke is that when the man she had sent to prison came out, he asked her to marry him. He just spent twelve years in prison, because of her and the soft pillock wants to marry her,' said Helen.

'Did they ever get married?' asked Sarah.

'Of course they got married,' replied Helen. 'He got millions for wrongful imprisonment, they got married and that was that. Anyway the point is that you have a solid case. There is no way that you could lose unless you back out at the last minute. Failing that happening, I can't see you losing this case. Anyway let's get back to your sister.'

'Well, what do you want to know?' asked Sarah.

'Oh I don't know tell me how you get on in general,' replied Helen.

Sarah was a bit reluctant to talk about her sister, but she knew that she had to because Helen would not give up until she did. So reluctantly she began.

'Err... well my sister's forty something, she's about five foot seven, slim, well dressed and well mannered. Well spoken, she's fairly good looking. She hasn't got loads of money, but there again she's not short of a quid or two. That's it nothing much to tell really.'

Helen looked at Sarah as if to say, well come on I want to hear some more.

'Ok, my sister and I hardly ever argue, but when we do, boy do we argue. David and I helped her a lot when she had all that trouble while we were on holiday. You know telling my sister that she could not have any more children was one of the hardest things I have ever had to do in my life. She hasn't got a boyfriend now. But suppose she meets somebody and wants to have another child. She'll know in the back of her head that she cannot have any more kids as much as she would like to.' Sarah paused for a brief moment.

'You know I've never heard her complain yet about being in hospital, or losing her baby. I've never really thought about it until now. Ok, she stayed with us for months after she came out of hospital. David and I never worried about it at all. We wanted her to stay; in fact the whole idea of her staying was down to David. Sandra just wanted to go back to her house on her own and stay there without seeing anybody. But David said no she had to stay with us. He even hid her house keys and her car keys, so she wouldn't run off back to her house.'

Sarah was just about to continue, when Helen cut into the conversation.

'Now, that was a good idea, the best thing she could have done was stay with people that love her and care about her. Well I say the best thing, it was the only thing that she could have done under the circumstances.'

'Anyway,' continued Sarah. 'I sat up with her in the night, when she was crying or when she was having nightmares. The nightmares God, when I think of all the nights that she used to wake up shouting and screaming was unbelievable. There were many nights when she couldn't sleep and I sat up with her all night. I sat up until eight o'clock in the morning with her. It never bothered me at the time. It bothers me now slightly, but that's probably because we're not speaking. Now I know she's a big girl and she can take care of herself, but I have to admit even now I worry about her.

'Ok, let me ask you a question,' said Sarah, to Helen. 'If you wanted to go somewhere, how would you go about it?'

'Err... well,' said Helen. 'First of all, I'd pick the place that I wanted to go, get some money out of the bank. Put some clothes in a bag, tell my friends where I was going and when, then I'd be off.'

'Now you see my sister is different, she went to Italy,' said Sarah. 'She never told anybody that she was going; she basically just caught a plane and went. She phoned us about a week later from Italy. At first I thought she was playing a joke on David and me, because I asked her if she took any clothes and she said no. Even so she came back with enough clothes to fill a double wardrobe twice. But she never told anybody she was going. I mean, here's my one and only sister over a thousand miles away and nobody knew until she had been over there for nearly a week, until she phoned me and told me. As I said at first I never believed her, I thought that she was playing a practical joke on me. You know I was expecting Jeremy Beadle to walk out from somewhere, but after sometime, I realised that my sister was telling the truth.

'I eventually came to terms about her running off to Italy, even if it did upset me slightly.

'You know all things were going through my head. Suppose something happened to her over there. Suppose this happened, suppose that happened. In the end David convinced me that my sister would be ok and that I was worrying over nothing. When my sister eventually came back, she was as bright and cheerful as she usually was. She brought back presents for everybody. When she told our father, he nearly died. He couldn't believe that she just got up and went away without telling a soul. She told him that it wasn't the first time that she had gone away without telling anyone where she was going. He knew what his daughter was like.

'She's done it so many times before that the family has lost count. Now we just accept it when she goes away and comes back. We just ask her if the weather was nice or did you enjoy yourself, we don't hassle her now a days about it.

'I could never do that. I couldn't just get up one morning and decide to go away somewhere. I'd have to cancel too many things. Let's see: first there would be the paperboy, then the milkman. Then I'd have to cancel my sessions with you. Then I'd have to cancel all my meetings at the office, cancel all my viewing dates. God, I'd be in it knee deep by the time I got back from wherever it was I did decide to go. I mean it's alright for my sister, she wouldn't have to drag her family with her.'

'Does she have any children?' asked Helen, getting up and heading towards the kettle. 'Would you like a drink?'

Sarah said she'd have a coffee.

'Yes, she has a son Jamey.' Sarah smiled, she felt cheerful about her nephew, even though she hadn't seen him for weeks, sorry months.

'How often do you see him?' asked Helen, bringing the drinks she had just made over to the table.

'Not very often,' replied Sarah.

Helen looked awkwardly at Sarah.

'Oh no, it's not what you think. The argument between my sister and I is a recent one. Before that we never really argued at all. The reason we don't see him is because he is away at school.'

Helen had a kind of relieved look on her face, as if to say thank God for that.

'Look I hate to sound like I'm bowstring, but my nephew has a talent. At the age of nine he could draw as good as a person who was twenty and had been drawing for years. So the family decided that such artistic talent should not go to waste. So we sent him to St James's School of Art.' Sarah was about to continue when Helen spoke.

'Isn't that a boarding school as well? I know that they have a yearly competition and the winner gets a chance to show off their work in public.'

'I never knew that,' said Sarah. 'I thought that after a certain time after they learned how to draw properly they just took an exam. Then if they pass, they would go on and do their own exhibitions, or do commercial work.'

'I suppose that they do go on to other things,' said Helen. 'But you must remember that they don't just draw, they do other things as well. They would still have to do English literature. They would still have to do history, geography, and maths. So they would still have a lot of things to do apart from drawing. Personally I think that drawing would be the last thing that they would do.

'Oh that reminds me. You do know that you're in court on Monday, don't you?'

'I am?' said Sarah, sounding and looking stunned. 'I'm sure you're wrong. My court date is not until the twenty fourth of June.'

'Sarah, I hate to say this, but I think that you're a few weeks behind yourself,' said Helen, giving Sarah a small calendar off her desk. Helen always marked off the days that had past.

'It can't be the seventeenth of June already,' said Sarah, sitting there with her eyes wide open.

Sarah asked if Helen was playing tricks on her. Helen went to her intercom and buzzed her secretary. Sue answered, 'Yes Sue, could you please tell me what today's date is please?'

'Err... yes, it's Monday the seventeenth of June, why?' said Sue, sounding slightly curious.

'Oh I just wanted to see if I had marked my calendar off today, thanks Sue.' Helen let go of the button and sat down. 'Told you,' said Helen, looking at Sarah. Sarah was stunned, she never realised that the time had gone so quickly.

She was still holding the calendar as she walked up and down the office floor. Helen was puzzled. She knew that most people forgot certain days, or even have mistaken another day for the previous day. Like some people think that Monday feels like a Tuesday, or vice versa. Helen asked what month Sarah thought it was, or what date she thought it was. There was a pause as Sarah sat down.

'Well,' said Helen, pressing Sarah for some kind of answer.

Sarah took a deep breath and replied, 'I thought that it was the end of May not halfway through June. God, I feel so stupid.'

'Why people make mistakes like that all the time, so why should you or I be any different? We humans are allowed to make mistakes you know.' Helen was doing her best to take Sarah's mind off the subject in hand. She began slowly to turn the subject into something else. Eventually Sarah began talking about something else. Thank God for that, thought Helen. We would have been on this subject for hours otherwise.

Sarah started talking about her husband and how they seem to be drifting apart.

'Oh come on you and David love each other, it would take much more than this to tear you and David apart. Personally, I think that you're just being silly.' Helen was just about to continue, when Sarah butted in.

'How long did you go out with Richard for?'

Helen went slightly red.

'Err... I, err... can't remember,' said Helen, looking down towards the floor.

'Now come on, I need a better answer than that,' smiled Sarah.

Helen thought for a moment. Should I tell her or not, I don't suppose that it's going to hurt. Besides if I can't open my heart to them, how can they open their heart to me? Helen began.

'Well it all started eleven years ago, I had just finished my job as a solicitor, it was my last week at the office when Richard was on his first. I think that he was taking my place, I'm not sure.'

'Why did you leave?' asked Sarah, looking thoughtfully at Helen.

'I left to start this place,' replied Helen.

'Can I ask you why you chose the name Judy's?'

'It's named after my sister. Anyway to cut a long story short, Richard and I kept bumping into each other during that week. Look, I'll tell you the embarrassing story, I might as well get it over and done with,' said Helen.

'Now although I never noticed at the time, Richard was talking to one of the barristers that had paid a visit to our office. Anyway the barrister went one way and Richard came towards me. Just as he said, goodbye and turned round, I pushed the door open. Now I should have been looking where I was going, so it was basically all my fault. Anyway as he turned round I pushed the door. Because he was leaning forward, I banged the door off his nose. As you can guess there was a lot of blood. I did think at the time that I had broken his nose. That's the first time that we really met. There I was apologising to him as much as possible, while he was lying on the floor in tremendous pain. After that we really got to know each other. I took him out to dinner to make him realise that I was really and truly sorry. Anyway we got to know each other. As far as I know we never really split up, we just didn't see each other, as often as we would have liked to. I think we just eventually drifted apart. Anyway enough about me, how is David?'

'I thought we'd finished talking about him,' said Sarah.

'How can you say that? He's your husband and I'm sure that he loves you a lot. I bet he loves you more than you realise,' commented Helen.

'That may well be, but at the moment he's pissing me off,' said Sarah. 'You know we sit there together and half the time, we never say a word and when we do, all he did was argue.'

'So you can honestly say that you never ever cause an argument between you and David?' asks Helen.

'No, I try my best not to argue with him, but when he starts, that's it. And you can never get a word in edgeways,' replied Sarah, staring awkwardly around the office.

'Look Sarah,' said Helen, getting slightly cross, even though Sarah never noticed. 'You know and I know that David can be slightly arrogant when he wants to be. But as far as what I have seen of him, I don't think that he is the argumentative type. I have hundreds of different women come in here for one reason or another, and of course most of them are like you – self centred.'

'How can you say that me of all people is self centred?' said Sarah butting into the conversation and noticing that Helen was a little bit pissed off by Sarah's attitude.

'Look, you've sat there for nearly an hour and a half whinging on about how bad your family treats you. I wouldn't like to know what you think about your mother and father. Do you hate them as much as you hate David, or your sister or yourself?' asked Helen.

'Number one: my mother died of cancer when I was a little girl. I don't remember much about her. But the memories I do have are good ones. My father's a really great person; he'll do anything for anybody as long as it's appreciated. He must have been a hell of a person to bring up two kids on his own. Go to work as often as possible, come home and still look after us.

'Ok, I must admit when I got to the age of about eleven, my sister was in her twenties. We had to look after ourselves, while dad was at work. Number two: David and my sister can't disagree on anything. Number three: I hate myself. I hate myself for being born even though I had no choice in the matter. I hate myself for the way I've behaved these past few months. To put it in a nutshell, I've basically been a real bitch to the people I love most. I've been a terrible mother for the past few months and, most of all, I hate the fact that I was raped. (Sarah sighed deeply.) None of this would have happened, if I hadn't been raped.'

'You can't say that. Personally speaking, I think that your marriage was going downhill before you got raped,' Helen suggested.

'Listen,' said Sarah, quickly. 'My marriage was fine until I got myself into this mess.'

'Was it really?' asked Helen, in a very sarcastic voice. 'Well let's see then shall we. Starting on Monday morning, what happens on that day? Starting when you get out of bed in the morning, what do you do first?'

'Well nearly all the time, it's David who gets out of bed first. He gets up about five in the morning; he's out of the house by six at the latest. I get up about six thirty, I get myself ready for work, I have breakfast, then about seven o'clock I get the children out of bed. They get ready for school, have their breakfast and then I take them to school before I go to work.

'I usually pick them up from school or if David finishes work early he will call me to say he's picking them up, which gives me a chance to work over at the office. Anyway I finish work about four o'clock, so I go straight from work and go and pick the children up. David usually finishes work about six to half past, sometimes seven o'clock, if he works over. We watch television from seven till about nine; sometimes we watch the television in the bedroom just to catch up with the news.

'By half past ten at the latest, you can guarantee that if we don't make love, David and I are fast asleep. That goes on every day until the weekend when we stay in bed until fairly late in the morning. Well I say late, we get up about eight or nine in the morning. The only time David stayed in bed for longer is when he had Chinese flu, then I had the same thing a couple of weeks later. The amazing thing is that not one of the children caught it.'

'So basically all you do,' said Helen. 'Is go to work, pick the children up from school and watch a little television, then go to bed. Perhaps make love that's if you're not too tired and you feel in a randy mood. So you have no recreational activities. No outside life, just the same routine day in day out. What about things like, golf, swimming, keep fit, jogging, playing snooker, fishing or just going to an art gallery, or taking a stroll in the park. Not even a day out to a theme park every now and then. I mean most of the people I know have some kind of hobby. Even I have a hobby.'

Sarah smiled, she never imagined Helen as a hobbyist, even though she does know some people with strange hobbies.

'What is your hobby?' asked Sarah, waiting in anticipation to hear what Helen was about to say.

'My hobby, my hobby is collecting racing car sets and building tracks in my loft at home, I have a hundred and fifty-five foot track. I have thirty-five different cars and trucks; I even have motorbikes for it. Before you ask, I've been doing it for about three years. I could have done it sooner, but I just couldn't be bothered. I have at least three hundred different figures, men, women, children, animals and so on. I also have all the bridges, the lane changeovers. I have everything in fact, I was thinking that you and David should come over for dinner one night and I could show it to you,' said Helen.

'I don't mind coming over, as long as it is not on a court date. Well I am surprised, I never imagined you as a hobbyist, not one that collects racetracks anyway,' giggled Sarah.

'Well you never know what people do behind closed doors,' stated Helen.

'I'll tell you a story, I'm not supposed to but I don't suppose that it's going to hurt just this once. I have a man who comes to see me on a Thursday morning, who collects toys. At first I thought he meant kids' toys. But as I got to know him, I found out he meant adult toys. You know like vibrators, chains, whips, leather boots, handcuffs and feathers. He collected all kinds of things like that; he said that he had thousands of condoms, he never used any of them, just collected them. Well not that often anyway.' Helen started to giggle. 'He even asked me if I would like to sample some of the toys he had. He said that he would be gentle with me even though he said that I looked like an experienced woman. I thanked him for his kind offer and then politely told him that he should play with his own toys and I shall play with mine. He never really asked me after that.

'The one time, he said that he tied this woman up. After he had done whatever he was doing with her, he fell asleep and left her tied up. The only time he remembered is when he woke up in the morning, he said that even though she had been in that same position all night, he took advantage of her while she was asleep. She woke up during the process and began to enjoy what he was doing until he had finished. Then she felt the pain of being chained up and left in the same position all night.

'But as I said, he said that he collected them for fun. God, can you imagine being chained up all night. Staying in the same position and not being able to move. I couldn't even begin to imagine how she felt in the morning,' said Helen. 'The whole of her body must have hurt.'

'Yeah, I think I might do that,' said Sarah, with a bewildered expression on her face. 'It may put the spice back into my sex life. Maybe if I sat there playing with myself, he might want to take me to bed. That's if we're not in bed already.'

'Well that may not be as daft as it seems,' said Helen, looking thoughtfully at Sarah. Who in turn had a surprised look on her face.

'Could you imagine what David would think, if I suggested something like that? I know what I'd say if he mentioned it to me. I'd automatically think that he was getting kinky in his old age,' laughed Sarah.

'So what we're talking about, what makes you and your husband happy?' asked Helen.

'Ok,' said Sarah, who now realised that Helen wasn't joking. 'Do you use toys in bed?'

'Yes, I do actually; sometimes I use a vibrator if I'm on my own. When I used to be with Richard, we did all kind of things with all kinds of toys. I would never like to be chained up. Just the thought of being tied or chained up makes me cringe.'

'Now come on,' said Sarah, looking at Helen with kind of a half smile on her face. 'Are you telling me that I should use toys in bed with my husband? Don't get me wrong, I've often sat there and wondered what it would be like using a vibrator. I've even sat there and thought what it would be like, if I dressed up in a long blonde wig and wore a leather suit and thigh long leather boots. But as I said, it was just a thought; I've never really taken it seriously.'

'Well perhaps you should take it seriously,' replied Helen. 'I mean as you said your sex life is down the drain, so why not live a little for once in your life. If your sex life is as bad as you say it is, then I'm afraid if you're sitting there waiting for something to happen, then you might be sitting there for a hell of a long time.'

'But I was raped for God's sake,' said Sarah loudly. 'That nightmare won't go away on its own you know.'

'Listen, you should stop thinking about yourself for once and think about the people that care for you the most. Plus I think that you should call your sister and make it up with her. You come in here pleading for help. But all you've basically done so far is whinge about how bad your family are to you, when realistically they're probably not that bad. But I will agree with you on one thing though, the thought will never ever go away, so you just have to put it at the back of your mind and try and get on with your life, the same as thousands of other women.'

'Yes, but,' began Sarah, when Helen cut into her conversation.

'You could think of this in another way,' said Helen, looking at Sarah who was fidgeting with her fingers.

'What way is that?' asked Sarah, stopping suddenly and noticing that Helen was looking at her. Which kind of made Sarah feel a little bit foolish.

'Well for instance, I mean you were only raped,' said Helen, who was about to continue, when Sarah jumped into the conversation quite quickly.

'What the hell do you mean, I was only raped? Two vicious animals raped me and you sit there and say, but you were only raped.'

'Well you were,' continued Helen. 'Ok, I'll ask you a question. Now, I touch wood that this never ever happens. But let's say that a mad man kills your daughter or any family member, either with a knife, a gun or their bare hands, or let's say that you lose the whole of your family and the only person left is you.

Now how would you feel if that happened? But as I said, touch wood that it never does.'

Sarah sat there, thoughts going through here mind.

'Err… well I'd probably go mad after a while.'

'No you wouldn't,' said Helen. 'If you had no mother, no father, no sister or no children, all you would want to do is commit suicide, which would be the only thing that you could consider doing. I know what you're thinking, but believe me that would not work.'

'I know, I just realised what I had thought,' said Sarah. 'Don't tell me, I know wherever I go and whatever I do, all I would think about was my family. I do suppose that in the end it would drive me to that extent and I suppose I would take my own life.'

'Let's take the principle of that question. Let's talk about how you would feel now depending on the way they died, let's say for argument's sake that they were murdered. Now apart from feeling remorse, there would be the guilt, you'd feel guilty for a lot of reasons,' said Helen.

'I know,' said Sarah. 'I feel guilty now.'

'Why?' asked Helen.

Sarah took a deep breath and sighed.

'Well I've been so preoccupied with myself, I haven't given you or anybody else much thought. I suppose you could say that all I wanted was sympathy, and as I said, I haven't given anything or anybody much thought.

'You know, I sit there sometimes and think why me? Of all the women in the world, why on earth did they pick me? Even though I say this now, but I never said at the time when I was arguing with my sister. She was right in everything she said; I am a cold hearted bitch, I don't care about anybody but myself. You know as I said, I sit there and think why me? When what I really should be thinking is why anybody? I have this terrible feeling, I've got it now, it's like I'm somewhere else watching everything that's going on. You know, like I'm watching myself on TV and even when you turn off the TV the picture is still there. I don't know what it is or what they call it, but it's a horrible feeling.

'Plus, I get touchy about the slightest thing, for instance, the other day David was on the phone talking to my sister. Now I came out of the kitchen, at least I think it was the kitchen, anyway I came into the living room, and all David said was your sister just called to see how you were. Then he asked me politely for a one of the biscuits, and that was that, without thinking I started an argument with him and of course the rest you know. I accused him of humping my sister, I said he was jealous of me being raped, because the bloke was better at it than he was,' said Sarah, sighing.

'You know you're lucky, I have people come in here that would beat the hell out of you for less than that. There was a bloke who confessed to beating up his wife because she didn't post his football coupon. You call your husband virtually everything and all you get is a slap. Do you realise how fortunate you are to have someone like that?' said Helen, with a half smile on her face and her eyebrows raised.

'How long have you and David been married?'

'Nearly ten years,' smiled Sarah, reminiscing on the time that they first met.

'In ten years how many times has your husband hit you?' asked Helen.

Sarah looked thoughtfully at Helen.

'The other day was the first time, before all he used to do was sulk. You know when David's at work, he'll argue until he's blue in the face. That's why at work they call him the bull, well the pit bull actually.'

Sarah was about to continue, when Helen started to giggle.

'Why on earth do they call him the pit bull?'

'Well a pit bull, when it's fighting never gives up until it's dead or the opponent's dead and a pit bull isn't scared to fight; it's always prepared for any situation. As I said, it just keeps going until the opponent has given up. Now they do say, that when David argues at work, he could and has argued for hours. But when we have some of his friends round for dinner, or they just come to pay him a visit, I tell them he never argues with me, they find it hard to believe. Not because I'm his wife and he's too scared to argue, but because of his reputation at work. Anyway that's why they call him the bull or the pit bull, whichever you prefer.

'You know you're right,' said Sarah, looking at Helen as though she was going to give her a medal or something.

'Oh really, why?' asked Helen, feeling a little surprised.

'Well to begin with I pay too much attention to the way I feel, and I don't really think about anybody else's feelings, I blame everybody else for the way that I am.'

'Yes that may well be the case, but you have to deal with the fact that it was you who was raped, and that you have worse days than the previous ones yet to come. Look I'm not saying that it was your fault or anything like that, but you must give some leeway to the people that love and care about you, they are trying to deal with what's happened to you too. You can't ever think that because of this you can have everything your own way and that everyone should be pampering to your needs, even though your family are trying to support you by walking on egg shells when they're next to you. You have to carry on as best as possible, but it would be a good idea to express the way you're feeling at the time calmly and openly to them, it helps all of you in the long run,' suggested Helen.

'We need to discuss your case and prepare for the next court date. Now can you tell me the date that the attack happened?' Helen asked, picking up a note pad and a pen.

'Yes, it was the twentieth of February.' Helen wrote the date down on her pad.

'That's one date, I shall never forget,' sighed Sarah deeply.

Helen asked Sarah some more questions about her last court date. As Sarah spoke, Helen wrote what Sarah was saying down on her pad.

'Oh, have I told you anything about your judge?' asked Helen, who was still writing things down on her pad.

'I think so, but to be honest I can't really remember,' Sarah replied.

'Well, I'll tell you again just to refresh your memory. The judge's name is, Thorp, Judge William Anthony Thorp QC, as he should really be known as. He's sixty years old and as I remember, he doesn't like anybody, don't get me wrong, if he knows that you're lying you're in trouble, deep trouble. He has the same motto as the US Marines,' stated Helen.

'What's that?' asked Sarah. 'Don't take any shit.'

'That's right, how on earth did you know that?' asked Helen.

'I didn't,' Sarah giggled, furiously. 'It's just that we say that in the estate agency business. We mean it as: don't take any crap houses from anybody, not in the way that you mean it.'

'Well Judge Thorp means it; if you pratt about with him that's it, do not expect any sympathy. But if he feels that you're telling the truth, he'll back you all the way home,' said Helen.

'Yeah, well he hasn't been on my side yet,' commented Sarah.

'Remember the first time that you and your husband came to see me,' Helen smiled 'For about fifteen minutes nobody apart from me said a single word.'

'Yes, I remember. God, I must have seemed awful,' said Sarah.

'No not really,' said Helen. 'You see most people who come to see me are kind of forced by someone to come. You and your husband came on your own accord.'

Sarah never let Helen know that it was Richard who gave her the address, and the phone number.

'What are you thinking about?' asked Helen, looking thoughtfully at Sarah.

'Alright I'll confess, I'm still wondering what it would be like to use a vibrator. I'm not prudish or anything like that, I'm not saying that it's disgusting to use one, but it just seems weird the thought of it, even though the fun that you could have would be unbelievable,' replied Sarah.

'Well I have to tell you that your time is almost up. Now one thing that I think that you should do is go home and have a long talk with your husband. I also think that you should call your sister and settle your differences with her. I believe you need her as much as she needs you, so when you go home make it up with her please, family is important. Don't be ashamed or too pig headed to say that you're sorry, you might find that if you talk and confide in your sister, she may do the same with her experiences with you,' suggested Helen, opening the door and letting Sarah out. She handed her secretary, the pad that she had been writing on and asked her to type it up for her. Both the secretary and Helen said goodbye to Sarah as the lift opened, and Sarah got in. They all said goodbye as the lift closed.

Chapter 3

Sarah came out the building got into David's car and went home.

Sarah pulled up on to the drive to see her husband washing her car. David waited in anticipation to see what kind of mood Sarah was in. As she came out of his car, he spoke hoping for the best.

'Hi, how did it go? Was it alright?'

'Alright, it was brilliant,' said Sarah as she kissed her husband.

'What's that for?' asked David.

'That's just because I love you, and I think that you're the most wonderful person in the world.' Sarah smiled and went into the house.

'Hey if that's what these sessions do for you when you go on your own, perhaps you should go on your own more often,' laughed David, as he rubbed the soapy sponge over her car.

Sarah went upstairs and got changed; she looked at the phone in the bedroom, she paused for a few minutes and sat there just staring at the phone. After a while she thought, ah forget it she's bound to phone sooner or later, I'll talk to her then. She finished getting dressed and went down the stairs; she stopped suddenly when she was halfway down. All she could hear was the argument she had with her sister a few weeks before, it seemed the more she tried to stop it, the stronger it became. Then she heard David's voice, who at the time, had come into the kitchen when they were arguing. She remembered David telling them both to calm down, then him telling Sandra that it would be better if she took the children with her and leave. Then she heard the voice of Helen, and the voice of her father telling her that she must speak to her sister, or she may regret it for the rest of her life.

Sarah sat down on the step where she stood. She had all the things that people had said running around in her mind, now the question is will she have the courage to pick up the phone and call her sister or not?

In the end Sarah went downstairs and picked up the phone, she dialled Sandra's number; Sarah was just about to put the phone down when Sandra answered. 'Hello, now don't put the phone down just listen, get yourself over here as soon as possible.'

'Ok,' said Sandra and they both put the phone down.

Sarah watched David cleaning his car from the living room window.

After about twenty minutes Sandra pulled up in her car. David looked surprised; the last person that he expected to see was Sandra, not with the way things were between Sandra and her sister.

Sandra got out of her car and headed for the house.

'Hi, anything wrong?' asked David, still looking a bit surprised.

'Hi, I'm fine and there's nothing wrong. Oh if you're wondering where your daughter is, she's gone fishing for a few hours while I'm down here. Hey, this wasn't your idea, was it?' asked Sandra, looking thoughtfully at David.

'No, it wasn't,' said Sarah, standing by the front door. 'It was mine, are you coming in or not?'

'You can stop outside and finish cleaning my car; you might as well do yours as well,' suggested Sarah, throwing David his keys. 'You might as well do Sandra's as well, seeing as though she won't be leaving for a while,' and went back into the living room.

'Ah well,' whispered Sandra, giving David her car keys. 'I wonder what the bitch has got up her sleeve now.'

'God knows, just close the front door on your way in, I don't want the neighbours to hear you pair arguing,' smiled David.

Sandra went into the house and shut the door behind her. She took a deep breath, sighed and then went into the living room where her sister was waiting to talk to her.

'You can sit down you know, I haven't started charging people yet,' said Sarah. Sandra walked around the sofa and sat down.

'I'll get straight to the point,' said Sarah, looking thoughtfully at her sister.

'Please don't interrupt me until I've finished, just hear me out first.' Sandra nodded to her sister.

'Well, where shall I begin? First of all I'd like to apologise for the things that I said to you in the kitchen the other week. The thing is nobody really understands how I feel; I don't even understand it myself, so I can't expect anybody else to understand it. Now this may sound silly, but I've been acting strange these past couple of months and I can't seem to help it, I'll give you an instance. The other day when you phoned here, David had only just put the phone down, I started an argument with him, it started over a stupid biscuit and it just went on from there.

'I accused him of all sorts of things, and I knew damn well that he hadn't done any of them, at the end of the day I said certain things that I had no right to say to him, and that's why he gave me black eye.'

Sandra stood up with a serious look on her face and had a good look at Sarah's eye.

'Well I say black eye, it is still bruised, but it's a lot better than it was the other day,' suggested Sarah.

Sandra had never noticed it when Sarah was standing by the front door that she had a black eye, and it still never dawned on her, when they were both sitting down, why Sarah was sitting at an angle and hiding the right side of her face.

Sarah could see the temper boiling in her sister as she looked at Sarah's eye. Sandra was just about to speak when Sarah spoke before her.

'Don't be angry with him, It wasn't really his fault and he didn't mean to hit me. I suppose what I said was just too much for him to take,' explained Sarah.

'You can never say that. Look Sis, I must apologise as well for some of the things I said, don't get me wrong, I'm not apologising for all of them. When I said that you were a cold hearted bitch, I meant it.'

Sarah looked furiously at her sister as she continued to speak. 'I meant it because it's true,' said Sandra, getting up and looking out of the window. 'I mean it because you just don't understand.'

'Oh, I understand alright,' said Sarah, getting cross with her sister. 'There's me trying to make up and all you can do is take the piss out of me.'

'You see what I mean, you don't even understand.' Sarah was just about to speak when Sandra carried on.

'Ok, let's really get things out into the open, when I called you a cold hearted bitch, I meant it. When I said that you are naive I meant it, and by God you are. The thing that you don't grasp is that when I was in hospital all that time apart from being in tremendous pain, I had time to think. I thought about all the things that I had done over the past ten years, and all I can remember is being separated from my husband. People taking advantage of my good nature, being slapped about by someone whom I thought cared about me, and then finally have the same bastard make me lose my baby.

'Now despite the fact that I have my own life and my own problems to deal with, I find out that two people raped my sister. How do you think that made me feel? I felt like I'd been kicked in the stomach so many times and I worry sick about you all the time, after all you're my baby sister. Then there's dad who's always on my mind. I know he seems and acts fine, but I do worry about him as he's getting on a bit these days. Look,' continued Sandra, sitting down next to Sarah and holding her hand.

'I don't mean these things I said about you in a nasty way, I just mean that in this day and age you can't say that this shouldn't happen to me, or they shouldn't do that to so and so, or why did they kill that little boy, or if only I never drank so many pints then it would not have happened. The point is you can't sit there and think that it won't happen to you, because in this day and age you have to believe that all things are possible.'

Sarah looked deep into her sister's eyes.

'I know what I said and I didn't mean any of it, it was just what I said in the heat of the moment, of course I know that all things are possible. I know people don't expect to be raped, but they always know that the possibility is always there.

78

'They don't expect to go out for the evening and come back to find that their house has been broken into, but they do. I know all the things that happen in the world shouldn't happen, but they do.'

'I think it's time we forgot about all this and start all over again, or we'll be here all night,' suggested Sandra.

'Ok, on one condition,' said Sarah.

'What's that then?' asked Sandra, getting up and looking out of the window again.

'Don't say anything to David or anybody else about my eye please, just leave things as they are, and we'll sort them out ourselves,' pleaded Sarah.

Sandra agreed and then headed for the kitchen. 'Come on, I know that you've got milk and chocolate biscuits in here somewhere.'

Whilst Sarah and her sister were in the kitchen, David had just finished washing all the cars; he was outside pondering whether or not he should go into the house. In the end he decided to go in, he thought to himself if they tell him to get out he'll go upstairs, and watch TV in the bedroom or take a shower. He went into the house and heard laughter coming from the kitchen. He knew from the noise they were making, that they must have settled their differences. He went towards the kitchen and noticed that Sarah and her sister were munching away at his chocolate biscuits. He also noticed that they had not heard him come in, so he crept as close to the kitchen as he could, he waited until both his wife and her sister were about to drink their tea. He leapt into the kitchen and shouted at the top of his voice.

'Who said that you could steal my biscuits, huh?'

Sandra and her sister spilled their tea everywhere, there was tea on the floor on the table; luckily they never spilled any on their clothes.

'Ooh, you idiot,' said Sandra, jumping out of her seat. 'You frightened the living daylights out of me.'

'Oh my God!' shouted Sarah, who had her hand on her chest and was breathing heavily, so, too was Sandra.

David put his arms around Sandra and apologised for scaring the life out of her.

He thought that she looked at lot more distressed than his wife did.

'Ooow, I could strangle you,' said Sandra.

Sarah began to laugh, contagiously as they all started to laugh in the end, because the face that Sandra had pulled was so funny. They were laughing and giggling for a good five minutes, when David realised that the front door was knocking and went and opened the door.

'Jamey,' said David surprisingly. 'Well, I err... how are you? Oh my God it's good to see you, well come in.'

'Hi uncle, I called round to moms but there was nobody there. Granddad's gone out as well, so you were my last hope,' said Jamey.

'By God, it's good to see you.'

'David, who's at the door?' shouted his wife, from the kitchen.

'Err… nobody just stay where you are. Come on your mother's in the kitchen,' said David.

'I thought so; I could hear her laughing as I came down the driveway,' laughed Jamey.

David gestured Jamey to stay where he was while he went into the kitchen.

'Who was at the door?' asked Sarah again.

'Oh, nobody special, do me a favour and stand just there, both of you and close your eyes. Now first of all promise me that you won't rush,' David demanded.

'What are you up to?' asked Sandra, looking curiously at David.

'Just promise me that you'll keep your eyes shut until I tell you to open them, ok,' insisted David.

Sandra and Sarah both agreed to do as David said.

'Now remember,' David repeated, 'I said, don't rush and keep those eyes closed.'

'Ok just hurry up and get on with it; anybody would think that you've got something special to show us,' said Sarah.

'I think that he's just messing us about,' said Sandra. 'He might be trying to frighten us again.'

David brought Jamey into the kitchen and whispered to him to stand in front of the two women.

'Come on David, my legs are getting tired,' said Sandra.

'Alright,' said David, 'now remember what you promised not to rush.'

'Yes, alright if we must, can we open our eyes now?' asked Sandra.

'Yes, alright if you must,' said David.

As they opened their eyes, they both shouted 'Jamey!' and at the same time rushed towards him.

'Ooh, it's so good to see you,' said his mother, wrapping her arms around him.

'Hey, leave some for me,' said Sarah, cuddling Jamey at the same time.

'My God, you look good,' said Sarah.

'Thanks Auntie. Hey! Enough of trying to squeeze the life out of me you two. Doesn't anybody care, that I've had to suffer a three and a half hour train ride and having to suffer British rail's food. I couldn't wait to come home and get something decent to eat, I'm starving,' laughed Jamey.

'Hey come on, give the guy some room,' suggested David, trying to prise Sarah and Sandra off Jamey, they eventually let go of him and sat down.

'What would you like to eat?' asked David.

'Err… how about, replied Jamey.

'Yes sir,' said David. 'That's what I like to see, a man who isn't afraid of food.'

'God, it's good to see you,' said Sandra.

'Calm down Mum before you pull something and end up in tremendous pain,' said Jamie.

They all started to laugh.

'I'm sorry; it's just that I'm so glad to see you,' smiled Sandra.

'So much for promises,' said Jamey, looking at David, who had just taken some frozen chips out of the freezer.

'Hey, now come on you should know by now that women never keep their promises,' laughed David.

'What happened to your eye Auntie?' asked Jamey.

'Err… I walked into a cupboard door, would you believe. Anyway, we weren't expecting you home from school so soon,' said Sarah, changing the subject rather quickly.

'Well, in a sense,' smiled Jamie. 'I'm not supposed to be here.' He was about to continue, when his mother jumped into his conversation.

'I hope that you're not skiving school, I hope that you haven't given all that education up.' His mother was about to continue, when Jamey jumped into her conversation.

'Mum, I haven't quit school, I haven't got anybody pregnant, I'm not on the run from the police so stop worrying and let me finish.'

His mother apologised to him for jumping to the wrong conclusion.

'The reason why I'm here is that I won't be coming home for the holidays,' said Jamie.

'Why not asked his mother with a sad expression on her face?'

'Well, I have to draw three pictures for an exhibition, so they've sent the bulk of us home to find out what we're going to draw. Before you ask, the six best pictures will be shown in art galleries in and around our hometown,' replied Jamie.

'That's great,' said David, handing him a mug of tea. 'Hey, if you need any ideas don't be afraid to ask.'

'Oh, I'm so proud of you JJ. It's unbelievable,' said Sandra hugging him again.

'Yes, so am I,' said Sarah as she came over and hugged him.

'Hey, we all are,' said David. 'We hope that you win the lot of them.'

'I hope so too, but believe me there are really talented people in my school. The kid in my class won it last year,' replied Jamie.

'Anyway here's your food,' David said, handing Jamey the piled up plate of food. 'Eat up, and you can tell us all about it later.'

Later on in the evening, David decided that he fancied Chinese.

'I wouldn't mind one either,' said Sandra.

'I'll tell you what, let's get the one we had the other day, remember when Susan was here,' suggested Sarah.

'Oh, you mean the chow mien,' laughed David. 'You know for months she was saying that the chow mien I ate looked horrible. The other day she decided to try some, she ended up eating a plate and a half of the stuff.'

'Hey come on Sis, you and me will go, we'll leave those two here on their own,' suggested Sandra.

'Those two on their own who knows what they might get up to? Why they could get up to all sorts of things,' said Sarah.

'Come on,' said Sandra, pulling Sarah towards the door.

'Back in a bit you two,' said Sarah, picking up her husband's car keys and putting on her coat.

'Don't be too long I'm feeling hungry now,' said David.

'Ok,' said Sarah as she closed the door on her way out.

There was a couple of seconds of silence and then Jamey spoke.

'What happened to Auntie Sarah's eye?' asked Jamey.

'She told you, she walked into a cupboard,' said David, looking at Jamey and hoping to change the subject but not getting anywhere.

'I'm not an idiot, I know when someone's slapped someone else, the only thing I want to know is why you hit her?' asked Jamie.

'Who said that it was me? Look, there's a lot that you don't understand, things have happened since you came and visited your mother, when she came out of hospital,' replied David.

'A man isn't a man if he hits a woman,' said Jamie.

'It just happened; I never meant it to happen,' said David, looking directly at Jamey who was looking directly at David. 'Sarah said something's that was way out of line, things that weren't true and she should never have said them to me.'

'Ok, so she said something's that you didn't like but that's no need to go and beat her up now is it?' insisted Jamie.

'Wait a minute; now let's get one thing straight, I only slapped her, if I gave her a beating, she would look a hell of a lot worse than that believe me,' said David, turning off the TV. 'Look JJ, as I said there's a hell of a lot that you don't know.'

'Look all I'm saying is that you shouldn't hit a woman under any circumstances,' insisted Jamie. 'Even if she's trashed your best stereo that's still no reason to hit her.' Jamey looked at David. 'You're nothing but a bastard to her.'

'Now that is enough,' said David, standing up and pacing the room. 'Look, I'm not going to stand here and dictate my life to you, and I don't want to hear you swear in my house ever again.'

'Don't stand there and shout at me like that, you're the one in the wrong, you're well out of order putting a hand on a women,' stated Jamie.

David took a deep breath and sat down next to Jamey. Jamey moved along to the end of the settee.

'What are you going to try and pan me out now, are you?'

David had no idea what the word pan meant, but he just had to have a guess.

'No, I'm not going to hit you.' David decided to tell Jamey what had happened to his wife. 'Jamey, look I don't want to argue with you, especially when your visits are not that long.'

'The last thing I wanted to do was argue with my uncle, I only said that you should not have hit her,' said Jamey.

'Yes I know your right, but there were unmitigating circumstances. I can't say that I had to hit her; it's something I felt that I had to do at the time. I regret doing it in one sense, but I should have done it a long time ago in another sense,' said David.

Jamey was just about to speak when David continued, 'Look Jamey, Sarah was raped a couple of months ago.'

Jamey sat there for a while in disbelief before he spoke.

'Sorry, I don't believe you. You're just trying to make excuses.'

'She was driving home from the office; she said she decided to do some shopping in the town. She was going to find a car park, but her car broke down just outside the high street. She did the shopping, as far as I know it wasn't much. She took a short cut down Deer Walk; you know the alley that leads you into town. Then just as she was coming down the alley two men jumped her.'

Jamey cut into the conversation.

'They shouldn't have late night shopping, it's dangerous.'

'This was broad daylight. The alley was fairly busy what with people driving and walking up and down it. Look, I know that I shouldn't have hit Sarah and I can't say that she deserved it, but she was way out of order.' David could see the tears in Jamey's eyes.

'How the hell can somebody get raped in broad daylight, and not get noticed by people walking up and down?' asked Jamey.

'Jamey if you're going to cry can you please go upstairs. I don't mean to be rude, but I don't want Sarah upset any more than she already is.' Jamey got up and headed for the door.

'You know,' said Jamey. 'When it's light in the morning you should go outside and see if there's a black cloud over the house.'

'What on earth for?' asked David.

'Well since you've come back off holiday you've had somebody write off your car. A mad man tried to kill my mother and two men in broad fucking daylight raped my auntie,' blurted Jamey.

David was just about to speak, when Jamey apologised for swearing. David told him that it was alright under the circumstances. Jamey asked for a towel so he could wash his face. David told him where the guest towels were.

Jamey was just coming back downstairs, when Sarah and his mother came through the front door. Jamey was tempted to ask if Sarah was alright, but he decided that at this present time it would not be the right thing to do seeing as though his auntie was in such high spirits. Jamey came downstairs and went back into the living room.

'Are you alright now?' asked David.

'Yes, I'm fine,' replied Jamey.

'Were you ill?' asked his mother.

'No, I just felt a little peaky that's all, but I'm alright now,' said Jamey.

'Are you sure that you can manage to eat this Chinese?' asked his mother.

'You bet, just try and keep it from me,' replied Jamey.

The rest of the evening went fairly quickly. Just as the news started Sandra decided that it was getting late, and that she and Jamey were going home. They all said their goodbyes and left.

Sarah closed and locked the door, and then she went upstairs. David was already in bed.

'God, you're keen,' said his wife, coming into the bedroom. 'Did you hurry to get into bed so that you could have your wicked way with me?'

'No, I got into bed so that I could get some sleep actually,' replied David. He never meant that in a nasty way, he just meant it as he was tired and wanted to go to sleep. But Sarah didn't think that he meant it that way. She thought that he was just being spiteful. She never made an issue out of it. She just kind of sulked around the bedroom. She was even sulking as she got into bed. She looked over at her husband who was fast asleep, and sighed.

Ah well, she thought. Maybe I'll get a bit tomorrow or maybe I won't. Then she had an idea, she thought why not give myself an orgasm seeing as though she hadn't given herself one for a while. David usually makes her orgasm, but seen as though he wasn't having sex with her for now. Not until she got the all clear from the hospital anyway. She thought, well, I might as well start giving them to myself seeing as David isn't going to.

She put her hand in between her legs and started moving her fingers up and down, and her fingers in and out of her vagina. She started moaning with excitement. The faster she moved her fingers, the faster she began to pant. She wriggled on the bed in excitement and after a short time, she orgasmed; she was breathing heavily and then as she relaxed she began to calm down, she smiled, she felt as though she was on top of the world.

As she thought to herself how good she felt, she went to sleep smiling to herself. She didn't care that David might not want to have sex with her, for now. She thought more and more about getting a vibrator, she even dreamed about it in her sleep. She woke up in the morning to find David looking at her. That's probably why she woke up; because she got the feeling someone was watching her.

'What's wrong?' asked Sarah, sitting up in bed.

'Nothing it's just that you look so peaceful, when you were asleep. Plus, you had a smile on your face. Were you dreaming about something nice?'

'To be honest, I can't remember,' replied Sarah.

They got out of bed and got dressed, they then went downstairs. The rest of the day went fairly quickly, so for that matter did the rest of the week. It seemed that in no time at all the twenty fourth of June had come round. It seemed for Sarah that the whole world was waiting for that date.

They got to the courtroom about an hour earlier than they should have. They went inside the court, but there was nobody there apart from the cleaner, but after a few minutes the cleaner left.

'God isn't it quiet?' said Sarah.

'Yes, I know,' said David. 'The quicker we get all this out of the way, the better off you'll be.'

Sarah agreed with her husband even though she knew that her life could never be the same. David explained to Sarah how he told Jamey about her being raped.

'Well, I can't say I didn't want to tell him myself, but on the other hand I don't suppose that you had much choice,' said Sarah. She was just about to ask how Jamey took the news, when Richard came in.

'Ah Sarah, David, good I'm glad that your here early,' said Richard. 'I phoned you this morning but you must have already left.'

'There's no problems are there?' asked |David.

'No, no problems for us but plenty for the opposition,' replied Richard.

'What do you mean?' asked Sarah.

'I'm going to ask the judge for another adjournment.' Richard was about to continue, when David jumped into the conversation.

'What do you mean you're going to ask for another adjournment? That's the second time we've had this trial adjourned. God, when are we ever going to get these people sentenced?' asked David sternly.

'If you can manage Mr Phillips to keep your mouth shut for ten minutes, then I'll tell you why I have to have this adjournment. There are a few things which I need to check out. Is he always like this?' asked Richard to Sarah.

'He's just worried about my welfare,' replied Sarah.

'Well from now on whilst you are in court Mr Phillips, you can calm down on your worrying. The police think that they may be able to stick a conspiracy to commit murder charge on him,' stated Richard. 'So when we are in court and I bring all that out, the better your chances are. The more the judge and the jury know about him and Walker the better for us.'

'Is it the murder of Edward Jeffrey's?' asked David.

'Err… yes,' replied Richard. 'But how did you know about it?'

'Well it's a long story really, but me and a couple of friends knew that Edward did not die of a heart attack,' stated David. 'That's just what the police report put it down to. But Edward was one of the fittest people we knew. I'm damn sure; he never died of a heart attack. I used to work with him a lot, he was a work alcoholic but he was a damn nice person.'

'Mr Phillips, would you be willing to go on the stand and say that?' asked Richard.

'Err… yes of course, why not,' replied David.

'I'm only going to bring it up for our benefit just so people can see a different side to these people. Don't forget, this is a rape case not a murder case,' said Richard.

They noticed that people were coming into the courtroom.

'Come on, we'd better sit down,' suggested Richard.

After about ten minutes the judge came in. The usher told everyone in the court to stand up. They all sat back down when the judge sat down.

'Your Honour, I'd like to ask for an adjournment, if I may,' stated Richard.

'Any particular reason for this Mr Thorn?' asked the judge.

'Yes, Your Honour, I have some further information that I need to check out in more detail, I have only recently received this information and I feel it is vital to the case Your Honour,' explained Richard.

'Do you have any objections Mr Chevron?' asked the judge.

'No, Your Honour,' said a rather stony-faced Mr Chevron.

'Very well, this court will adjourn until nine thirty tomorrow morning,' instructed the judge.

Everyone in the court stood up as the judge left his chair.

'You've got fuck all on me bitch,' said one of the men, being led down a flight of stairs by one of the guards. It was lucky for him that the judge had already left the courtroom. Forbes was slowly walking down the stairs. He stopped halfway down and looked at Sarah. He then blew her a kiss, and then one of the guards hurried him down the stairs.

'I hope that those two get such a long sentence that they die in prison, the bastards,' said Sarah.

The usher shouted, 'All parties will return to court on the twenty fifth of June, thank you!'

Richard was packing some papers away in his briefcase, when Sarah asked him who Helen Cartwright was. Now Richard did the same as Helen did, went as red a beetroot.

'She's just an old friend,' said Richard, locking his briefcase.

'That's exactly what she said,' said Sarah, putting on her coat and walking towards the courtroom door.

'We went out to dinner a couple of times that's all,' insisted Richard, coming out of the door behind Sarah.

'I know, she told me,' exclaimed Sarah.

'What else did she tell you?' said Richard, smiling at Sarah.

'Nothing, it's just the fact that every time I mention your name to her she goes weak at the knees, and you nearly passed out when I mentioned her name to you,' smirked Sarah.

'Well, I can't help it if she's a nice person,' replied Richard.

Just then Helen came through one of the doors. As soon as she saw Richard she went as red as a beetroot.

'I'll leave you two to talk. Oh hi Helen,' smiled Sarah as she walked past.

David had been talking to Helen while Sarah was talking to Richard. As his wife walked past Helen, David said, 'Watch out Helen, my wife is playing cupid.'

'I know,' said Helen. 'But I don't need any help with this one.' David laughed and said that he would see her tomorrow.

'So what happened?' asked Helen, as Sarah walked past.

'I think I'll let Richard tell you, see you tomorrow,' smiled Sarah with her eyebrows raised.

'Ok, cupid,' replied Helen, shaking her head side to side and smiling.

'Bye, see you in the morning Richard,' said Sarah and David.

'Yes, bye,' replied Richard, who was still blushing a little.

Then Sarah and her husband walked towards the exit. Sarah kept looking back to see if she could see what they were up to, but she couldn't see them.

Chapter 4

Sarah and David never got much sleep that night. David kept tossing and turning, he must have woken up three or four times. Each time he woke up Sarah wasn't there, but he could hear his wife moving about downstairs. He stayed awake for a few minutes, and then he would slowly drift off back to sleep. Meanwhile Sarah was watching a video. She was doing herself something to eat; she went into the living room and sat down and pressed play on the remote control for the video and waited for the film to start. She sat there eating her sandwiches and drinking her tea, she began to think about her life in general. As she finished her sandwiches and her tea, she slowly went deeper into thought, talking to herself in her mind.

'God Mum, why couldn't you have lived a little longer? Why did you have to die when I was so young? If only you knew how much I need you and how much I love you.' She remembered some of the arguments she'd had with her sister.

'God, you've had some right stinkers in your time Sarah, you really have.' Then she remembered things like, her dad telling her to go and wash her face when she was a little girl and to tidy her room. Then she remembered her first boyfriend, she smiled.

'Just think how everybody in the school hated him, because of the way he used to dress. Then you turned him into a super stud. God those were the days.'

Then she remembered him running around with different girls behind her back.

She also remembered the first time she saw David and thought what a smartly dressed young man he was and how he was definitely going up in the world.

Then she saw herself being raped by those two vicious animals, it was like being on the outside of a window and looking in, watching yourself being raped.

She woke up quickly and in a bit of a panic.

David came in from out of the kitchen.

'Are you alright?' he asked, coming over and sitting beside his wife, wrapping his arms around her. 'Hey come on, you were dreaming.'

Sarah felt as though she wanted to cry, but as much as she tried it would not come out.

'What are you doing up so early?' asked Sarah, a few minutes later.

'Early, what do you mean early it's quarter past eight?' replied David.

'Oh shit, we're in court at nine thirty,' said Sarah jumping off the chair.

'Don't panic you have plenty of time,' suggested David.

'I know it's early, but I told Richard that we would be there early,' said Sarah running up the stairs.

David picked up the tray Sarah had used and carried it into the kitchen and washed up; he then went upstairs to get dressed.

'Oh, by the way,' said David, walking into the bedroom. 'Your darling sister called this morning.'

'This morning? But it is morning,' said his wife, bewildered.

'Well I mean about six o'clock this morning,' replied David.

'What did she want?' asked Sarah, putting on a pair of black see through knickers. David paused for a few moments watching his wife, Sarah puts her long baggy skirt on and a camel coloured check top and a pair black shoes.

'Oh, she just wanted to know why we weren't at the court yesterday, when she, Jamey and your dad turned up, oh and the children. I told her what had happened and that we would see them in the court today,' said David, walking towards his wife, who was standing up and brushing her hair in the mirror.

'Did I tell you how gorgeous you look this particular morning?'

Sarah was just about to speak.

'Did I also tell you how much I love you?'

'Well not for a while,' said Sarah, turning round and putting her arms around him.

'Well you do look gorgeous and I do love you, now shall we go?' asked David.

David and his wife went down the stairs. Sarah put her coat on; David just put his baggy leather jacket on, picked up his car keys, switched the answering machine on and then left for the court.

Richard had just arrived, when Sarah and David drove onto the car park and pulled up beside him. 'Morning,' said Sarah, jumping out of the car. 'How did you and Helen get on last night?'

'You know, it's great isn't it?' said David, locking the car door. 'She doesn't want to know how you are, she just wants the gossip.'

'Well, that's women all over for you,' said Richard, walking towards the court followed by David and Sarah. 'Well, there's not much to tell, we just went out to dinner... then back to her place for a coffee.'

'Then what did you do when you got to her place?' Sarah asked eagerly.

'Sarah,' said David, in a calm but forceful voice. 'Use your imagination.'

'We just went back for coffee, not that we got the chance to drink it mind,' smiled Richard, opening the courtroom door.

'Does that satisfy your wicked sense of curiosity?' asked Richard, as he held the door for David and Sarah to go through.

They all sat down, Richard and Sarah sat together while David sat behind them. After a few minutes Helen came in followed by Sarah's father, sister, Jamey and the two children. Everybody said good morning to each other. Jason and Lucy gave their mother and father a big kiss then sat back down with their auntie and Jamey. They were talking about things in general, when two guards and Mr Chevron came up a flight of stairs with the two prisoners. The one man looked at Sarah, and then when he sat down, he stared long and hard at David. David just sat there and stared right back at him.

After a while the prisoner started to get mouthy. He said things loud enough for David and everybody else to hear. Then he shouted over to David.

'What the fuck are you looking at dickhead?'

The guard told him to be quiet but the man was persistent. He looked at David again and asked him, 'Have you been giving your wife enough, no, why not?'

David jumped up; he was halfway across the floor when he was stopped by Sarah's father. He was also stopped by one of the guards.

'Come on; let's see if you've had your Weetabix,' said the prisoner, being held back by one of the guards.

'Now, I know it's not your fault but you must try and control yourself sir,' said the guard to David.

'You expect me to sit here, while he takes the piss out of my wife, just let me bang him out and be done with it,' suggested David.

'Yes I do, as I said you have to control yourself sir or I will escort you out of the room,' said the guard.

Just then the judge came in as David was going back to his seat.

'What the hell's going on in here?' asked the judge, who looked at Sarah and at the other people in the court. It looked like the judge was about to breathe fire. He didn't of course but that's the way he looked.

'Err... it's all under control Your Honour,' said Mr Chevron. The judge sat down. There were now three guards standing beside and behind the two prisoners.

'Before we start these proceedings, let me make one thing quiet clear,' explained the judge. 'I will not tolerate any outburst from anybody in this courtroom. Mr Thorn, do you think that you could calm down the gentleman on your side that has the short temper?'

'Watch this,' whispered Richard to Sarah, as he stood up.

'Yes certainly Your Honour,' said Richard. 'But I must insist that my learned colleague Mr Chevron, keep those two prisoners under strict control. Mr Chevron's two clients were provoking Mr Phillips.'

Richard sat back down. 'Watch this,' whispered Richard to Sarah.

'Mr Chevron, if you cannot control your two defendants then I'll have no choice but to have them sent back to their cells.' Mr Chevron was just about to speak, when the judge carried on.

'If the guards cannot handle the prisoners, then maybe they should find another line of work. I will not have any of the outbursts which I've witnessed in pervious court appearances in my courtroom. Do I make myself clear?

'Right, the court is now in session,' stated the judge as he banged his gavel hard.

'Mr Thorn, would you like to begin the session by making your statement to the court.'

'Yes, Your Honour, thank you,' said Richard. Richard stood up. 'I am about to prove that Mr Ronald Walker and Mr Michael Forbes are guilty of viciously attacking and raping Mrs Sarah Phillips. I hope the judge and the jury and indeed the rest of the court keeps an open mind on this case. See the facts as they are and give a fair and truthful verdict. Once all the witnesses have been called and all the evidence has been heard. Thank you,' said Richard, walking back to his seat.

Then Mr Chevron stood up.

'I hope to clear the names of Mr Forbes and Mr Walker,' stated Mr Chevron. 'I shall prove beyond a shadow of a doubt that they did not rape anybody. I also hope that you listen to the evidence and give a fair judgement of the case. As I know at the end of this trial, a not guilty verdict will be reached. Thank you,' said Mr Chevron, going back to his seat.

'Call your first witness to the stand please,' said the judge.

Richard stood up.

'I call Mr Josh Mackoshie to the stand.'

The usher shouted for Mr Mackoshie.

Then a rather neatly dressed Japanese man came strolling down the aisle. Sarah looked thoughtfully at him as he walked past. He looks fairly young, she thought to herself. Mr Mackoshie took the oath and sat down in the witness box. Richard bid good morning to Mr Mackoshie.

'Could you tell the court your name and your job title please sir,' asked Richard.

'Yes certainly, my name is Josh Mackoshie and I am a businessman.'

'What kind of business do you do?' asked Richard.

'I deal in jewellery and computer games,' replied Josh.

'What kind of jewellery do you deal in Mr Mackoshie?' asked Richard.

'I supply oriental jewellery to shops in England and America, and some European countries,' replied Josh.

'It seems very lucrative Mr Mackoshie. I bet that your computer business is very lucrative as well Mr Mackoshie,' suggested Richard, walking up and down in front of the witness box.

'Yes, I can say that I do alright,' stated Josh.

'How old are you, if you don't mind me asking?' enquired Richard.

'No, not at all,' said Josh. 'I'm forty-four.'

Sarah looked at him in disbelief. Well I never, thought Sarah, who would have guessed that he was forty-four, he looks more like thirty-four. I hope I still look that young when I'm that age.'

'Forty-four, I'd have said that you were thirty at the most. I must admit that you look after yourself fairly well Mr Mackoshie. Can you tell the court, what you were doing on Wednesday the twentieth of February please?' asked Richard, who was now leaning against his table.

'Yes certainly, I was working in my office on my computer,' replied Josh.

'What time did you start work, Mr Mackoshie?' asked Richard, who was walking up and down once again.

'Yes, I started work at nine thirty,' reported Josh.

'What time did you finish?' asked Richard.

'I finished about one o'clock, then I went for something to eat,' responded Josh.

'And what time did you get back?' asked Richard.

'I got back about two thirty,' replied Josh.

'So when you got back the police were still there then,' asked Richard.

'Yes, there were a lot of policemen about but I never paid it any attention,' replied Josh.

'So you didn't ask anyone what was going on?' asked Richard.

'No, I did not,' replied Josh.

'Why not?' asked Richard.

'Well, it was not my concern at the time. It had nothing to do with me, so I didn't involve myself with it,' replied Josh.

'When did you involve yourself with it?' asked Richard.

'When I read the paper five days later,' reported Josh.

'So it took you five days to get in touch with the police. Was there any particular reason for this late involvement?' asked Richard.

'Yes, I was away in London,' Josh replied.

'You never got back until the Monday, is that right Mr Mackoshie?' asked Richard.

'Yes, that is correct,' said Mr Mackoshie, nodding his head at Richard.

'Could you tell us about the screams that you heard?' asked Richard.

'Well,' said Mr Mackoshie. 'People are always screaming and making silly noises in that part of town, so you get used to it after a while,' stated Josh.

'What did you see on that Wednesday?' asked Richard.

'I saw two men run from out of the alley,' Josh explained.

'Are those same men that you saw running out of the alleyway, here in this courtroom?' asked Richard.

'Yes they are,' replied Josh.

'Could you point to them, please?' asked Richard.

'Yes certainly it was those two men there,' Josh pointed to Mr Forbes and Mr Walker. There was a lot of murmuring and whispering around the courtroom. The judge called for order and then it all went quiet again.

'What were they doing by the car?' asked Richard.

'Well, after they gave each other a high five, at least I think that's what they call it. The one man in the suit got into the car first. The second one was tidying himself up and tucking his clothes in, he then got into the car as well,' explained Josh.

'Have you seen the two accused men before?' asked Richard.

'Well, I've seen Mr Forbes in the local paper but both men are at the surgery on a regular basis,' answered Josh.

'Are they really?' said Richard, looking at the two accused men sitting in the dock. 'No further questions Your Honour.'

'Mr Chevron would you like to cross examine the witness?' asked the judge.

'Yes, I would Your Honour,' said Mr Chevron, as he stood up.

'Mr Mackoshie when you heard the first scream, why didn't you get up and go to the window?'

'As I said before, lots of people scream and make loud noises around that part of town,' replied Josh.

'So what made you get up and look out of the window?' asked Mr Chevron.

'Well, it was when I heard the second scream,' explained Josh.

'Yes, so you said in your statement. But wouldn't you agree and say that it was possible that when you heard the first scream, the men that raped Mrs Phillips could have run away?' suggested Mr Chevron.

'Yes, I suppose they could have,' replied Josh.

'So you can't be sure that my two clients raped Mrs Phillips, can you?' inquired Mr Chevron.

'No, I cannot say whether they did or not,' replied Josh.

'Thank you, no further questions Your Honour,' Mr Chevron sat back down.

'Mr Thorn, have you any more questions for this witness?' asked the judge.

Richard stood up.

'I have no more questions at this present time Your Honour,' Richard sat back down.

'You may step down Mr Mackoshie,' insisted the judge.

'Would you like to call your next witness Mr Chevron?'

'Yes, Your Honour,' said Mr Chevron standing up. 'I would like to call Miss Donna Woodfield to the stand.'

The usher called the name of Miss Woodfield. Sarah waited in anticipation.

Then just as Sarah was beginning to think that Miss Woodfield was not going to turn up she did. A young woman walked slowly down towards the dock, she looked across at the two prisoners who were sitting in the dock. She walked very sleekly and sexy towards the dock.

'Miss Woodfield, may I remind you that this is a court of law and not a catwalk. You are here to impress the jury and I not those men in the dock. Do I make myself clear?' ordered the judge, noticing that she kept looking at the two prisoners.

'Yes, Your Honour,' said a soft voice. Miss Woodfield took the oath and sat down.

Mr Chevron walked over to the witness box.

Sarah meanwhile was staring at Miss Woodfield, who was staring at the men in the dock.

'Could you tell everyone your name and your occupation?' asked Mr Chevron.

'Yes, my name is Donna Woodfield and I am a doctor's secretary,' replied Donna.

'How old are you Miss Woodfield?' asked Mr Chevron.

'I am twenty-six years old,' she replied.

'I would like you to tell the court what you were doing on Wednesday the twentieth of February,' asked Mr Chevron.

Sarah was whispering to Richard.

'Have you noticed that since she has come into the room, she hasn't taken her eyes off the two bastards in the dock?'

'Calm down,' whispered Richard, 'I noticed that as soon as she walked in, anyway let's hear what she has got to say.'

'Well I came back from doing my shopping. I went into the surgery and made myself a cup of coffee after I sorted out some papers for the doctor to sign, when he came back in,' replied Donna.

'So after you sorted out the papers for the doctor, you made yourself a cup of coffee. Then what did you do?' he asked, walking up and down, in front of the witness box.

'I read the paper that I had bought while I was out shopping,' replied Donna.

'What happened after that?' asked Mr Chevron.

'Well I thought I heard a noise, but I never went outside to see what it was, I just carried on reading my paper,' replied Donna.

'What did you do after that?' he asked.

'Well then I heard a scream, then a car door slamming. Then the car drove off fairly quickly, so then I got up and went outside,' exclaimed Donna.

'Is that when you heard the victim calling for help?' asked Mr Chevron, who had one hand on the witness box.

'Yes I walked down the alley and that's when I saw the victim slumped in a corner. Then the doctor came back from his lunch break, and also called the police, she explained.

'So you never saw the two men that attacked Mrs Phillips?' asked Mr Chevron, looking at her.

'No I never,' insisted Miss Woodfield, looking once again at the two prisoners.

'Thank you, Miss Woodfield. No further questions Your Honour,' said Mr Chevron, sitting down.

'Oh how the mind wonders,' said Richard, standing up. He'd already gone before Sarah had a chance to ask him anything.

'Miss Woodfield do you ever lie?' asked Richard. 'For instance, if I was walking along the road and I dropped my wallet would you give it back to me?'

'Yes, I probably would,' replied Donna.

'Ah, probably, so it would be a fifty, fifty chance that I would get my wallet back. Let's get back to the subject of lying. Do you ever lie?' asked Richard, leaning against his table.

'No, I don't suppose I do tell lies,' stated Donna.

'Well, there's a lie for a start,' suggested Richard, walking up and down in front of the witness box.

'I object to these horrendously stupid questions Your Honour,' said Mr Chevron, standing up.

'Overruled,' stated the judge, 'I want to see where Mr Thorn's questions are leading. Continue please Mr Thorn and I hope for your sake that there is a point to all of this questioning,' insisted the judge, looking cold and hard at Richard.

'There is Your Honour,' stated Richard walking back to his desk and opening his briefcase. 'I have a copy of the statement that Miss Woodfield made to the police on the day that my client was raped.' Richard gave a copy to the judge, a copy to Miss Woodfield and then a copy to Mr Chevron.

'Would you care to read the top line of the statement that you gave on the twentieth of February, Nineteen ninety-one,' asked Richard.

'Yes, I came back from my lunch break, I opened the surgery and went inside,' replied Donna.

'So you went for your lunch?' Richard stated quickly.

'Yes, I did,' said Donna.

'Your lunch break is what being a doctor's secretary, perhaps half an hour at the most. Am I correct?' asked Richard.

'Yes, you are,' she replied.

'May I ask what you had for lunch that day?' asked Richard.

'Yes, I had chips, fish and a can of pop,' she recalled.

'Then why did you tell my learned colleague that you went shopping?' asked Richard.

'I did go shopping,' insisted Donna.

'Can I ask you, how long it took you to eat your meal?' he asked.

'About twenty minutes,' replied Donna.

'How long did it take you to do your shopping then?' asked Richard.

'Only about fifteen minutes,' replied Miss Woodfield. She looked at Richard oddly thinking that the questions he was asking her sounded pretty stupid.

'Miss Woodfield, do you really think that you are superwoman?' he enquired.

'Err… no,' replied Donna, looking oddly again at Richard.

'Miss Woodfield, I know that your lunch break starts at one o'clock. So without being a maths professor, you know that you have to be back at work by at least one thirty,' suggested Richard, leaning against his table once again. 'There is no chip shop within a ten minute walking distance from the surgery where you work. So can you explain how you managed to do all that in the time stated?' began Richard, as Mr Chevron stood up.

'I object Your Honour, all this is physically possible,' suggested Mr Chevron.

'Do you also think that you are superman?' asked the judge.

'No, Your Honour,' said Mr Chevron.

'Well, would you care to explain to me and the rest of the court, how you can eat fish and chips and go halfway across the town to go shopping. Then come back across town and then go back to the surgery all within half an hour.

'Now despite the fact as Mr Thorn had just pointed out that there wasn't a chip shop in that part of town, she would have to drive pretty quickly to do all that. Wouldn't you say so Mr Chevron?' asked the judge, in very deep voice and looking over his glasses at Mr Chevron. 'Because, there's no way that she could have walked, it would have taken her even longer than that wouldn't you say so Mr Chevron?'

'Yes, I would Your Honour,' he replied.

'Then please sit down Mr Chevron, and stop being such a nuisance,' stated the judge.

'Yes, Your Honour,' said Mr Chevron, sitting down. He looked as though he was in a bad mood, he was probably seething slightly, but I suppose that's part of the job he has to take the rough with the smooth.

'You may continue, Mr Thorn,' said the judge, looking over his glasses at Richard.

'Thank you, Your Honour. Now I'll get back to the reason why I asked you that particular question later. Now earlier, when my learned colleague was questioning you, you said that you heard the car door slam, then you got up when they drove away to see where the scream that you heard was coming from, is that right?' asked Richard.

'Yes, that's right,' she replied.

'That's why in your statement to the police, you clearly stated that you got outside just as the two men were going into the car.' Richard could see that the judge could not find the line that Richard was talking about. 'It's the ninth line down Your Honour.'

'What, oh yes, thank you Mr Thorn,' said the judge, looking slightly happier now that he had found what he was looking for.

'Now in your statement, you basically say that you had one foot out of the door. Would you say that you were almost out of the door when you heard the two men jump into the car and drive away?' asked Richard, standing right beside the witness box.

'Err… yes I suppose I would,' Donna replied.

'Then when you were outside you should have seen one of the men outside the car tidying himself up. Would you not?' he said, walking up and down the floor in front of the witness box.

'When I came outside I saw nobody, I didn't even see the car driving away,' insisted Donna.

'Then Mr Mackoshie must be lying, because he said that one of the men was standing outside the car tucking his tee shirt into his tracksuit bottoms, then zipping up his tracksuit top. That's after they gave each other a high five, then they jumped into the car and drove off. Now did you see any of that, Miss Woodfield?' asked Richard.

'No, I did not,' stated Donna.

Sarah noticed that Miss Woodfield was now looking slightly nervous and she began to fidget. Serves her right for lying in the first place, doesn't it, thought Sarah.

'Let's take this from a completely different angle; we'll forget the previous line of questioning for now I'll tell you my theory, if you think that it's wrong feel free to stop me and correct me at any time,' stated Richard.

'Firstly, I think that you did go to the chip shop to have your lunch and you did take your car, instead of walking a mile to get to the chip shop. I think that you came back the long way round, so you could finish what you were eating before you got back to the surgery. Then you went into the surgery to make a cup of coffee and that's probably when you heard the noise from outside. I think that your curiosity got the better of you, so you went outside and saw the two men running from down the entry.

'You then saw Mrs Phillips lying down on the floor next to the car. You then asked one of the men what he had been doing to the woman. He then gave you a few choice words, and told you to get into the surgery and knowing Mr Walker, he probably turned round and said something like. "If you tell anyone, I'll kill you."

'You then went into the surgery and finished drinking your cup of coffee, that's why Mr Mackoshie saw nobody apart from the two men, when he looked out of the window of his office across the road. Now Miss Woodfield is that true or not?' asked Richard, standing in the middle of the room looking at Miss Woodfield. After a few seconds Richard spoke again. 'I would like an answer from you Miss Woodfield.'

'I object Your Honour; Mr Thorn's questions are purely circumstantial. They have no solid foundation and there isn't a word of truth in any of it,' suggested Mr Chevron, standing up.

'Well, until the lady answers Mr Chevron we shall never know if Mr Thorn's comments were right or wrong, shall we,' stated the judge, peering over his glasses.

'Will you please answer the question Miss Woodfield?' asked the judge, looking down at Miss Woodfield.

'Is that what happened, because I've notice that each time that you are asked something, you look at the two defendants.' Miss Woodfield had tears running down the side of her face.

'Yes,' she replied.

'No further questions Your Honour, but I reserve the right to question the witness again,' exclaimed Richard, returning to his seat.

'I would like to ask for a fifteen-minute recess Your Honour to talk with my clients,' asked Mr Chevron.

'Do you have any objections to this Mr Thorn?' asked the judge.

'No, Your Honour,' replied Richard.

'Very well then, this court will take a fifteen-minute recess,' suggested the judge.

'All rise,' said the usher, as the judge stood up and left the courtroom.

'How did you know all that?' asked Sarah.

'I didn't, all of that was pure guesswork, if you noticed I did have my fingers crossed,' smiled Richard.

David and his father-in-law had gone out and bought drinks from the machine for everybody including Richard.

'It's only eleven thirty; they'll be another recess for an hour for lunch, then we will continue until about three o'clock. You won't be called up to the stand today, but prepare yourself for the days to come, because it is going to get very nasty inside this courtroom,' stated Richard.

The fifteen minutes went pretty quickly

'All rise,' said the usher. Everybody stood up, as the judge came back in and sat down.

'Would you like to continue your questioning of Miss Woodfield Mr Thorn?' asked the judge.

'Not at this present time Your Honour,' replied Richard.

Mr Chevron also said that he would question Miss Woodfield at another time.

'Very well, you may call your next witness Mr Thorn,' stated the judge.

'Yes, Your Honour, I would like to call Mr Jassed Agpatel to the stand.'

The usher shouted the name of Mr Agpatel. Mr Agpatel came in, took the oath and sat down in the witness box.

Richard stood up and spoke.

'Could you tell the court your name and occupation please sir?'

'Certainly, my name is Jassed Agpatel and I am a family practitioner.'

'How long have you been a doctor, Mr Agpatel?' asked Richard, just managing to get his name right.

'I have been a doctor for twelve years,' he replied.

'How long has Miss Woodfield worked for you?' asked Richard.

'Miss Woodfield is a very good secretary, she is extremely good at her job and she has worked for me for three years now,' he stated.

'When you came back from your lunch break what was Miss Woodfield doing?' asked Richard.

'She was standing by my car in the alley way,' replied Mr Agpatel.

'What did you say to her?' Richard was now standing in front of the witness box.

'Well, I asked her what she was doing in the alley. It was then that she told me about the victim in the alley,' he replied.

'Then what did you do?' Richard had now moved from the witness box and was leaning against his table.

'Well, while I tended to the victim my secretary called for an ambulance and the police,' replied Mr Agpatel.

'Mr Agpatel did your secretary phone the police straight away?' inquired Richard.

'Yes, as far I know, I can't really say, I never saw her use the phone; I was outside treating the victim,' he replied.

'That may well have been the case,' said Richard, walking up and down slowly in front of the witness box, looking at Mr Agpatel every time he asked him a question. 'But what if I told you that your secretary did not ring the police straight away? What if I told you that she rang somewhere else first? What would you say to that Mr Agpatel?'

'Well, I'd be disgusted of course, If my secretary did do that then she should be on trial here as well,' he suggested.

'Thank you, Mr Agpatel. No further questions Your Honour.' Richard sat down.

Mr Chevron stood up. He did up the button on his single-breasted jacket and then glanced quickly at Sarah and Richard, and then stood in front of the witness box.

'Mr Agpatel, how many rape cases would you says you have dealt with over the years?'

'Not as many as people might think. People think that because you're a doctor you must have dealt with thousands of rape cases. In twelve years at a guess without checking my records, I'd say about a hundred maybe slightly more but not by much.'

'Yes, but even so, a hundred is an alarming rate,' stated Mr Chevron.

'Yes, it is, well one is an alarming rate, but when you consider that over a thousand women are raped or sexually abused every day, it's basically a drop in the ocean. Sorry to put it so crudely but that's the way it is,' replied Mr Agpatel.

'In your statement to the police, you said that you were in a restaurant having your lunch when you heard a car racing its engine. Did you manage to see the car?' asked Mr Chevron.

'No, I did not; I was sitting in a far corner of the restaurant,' he replied.

'So you couldn't say whether my two clients were in the car?' asked Mr Chevron.

'No, I'm afraid that I couldn't.'

'Thank you Mr Agpatel. No further questions Your Honour.' Mr Chevron went back to his seat.

'Would you like to question the witness Mr Thorn?' asked the judge, peering over his glasses.

'No, not at this present time Your Honour, thank you,' replied Richard.

'Very well, this court will take a one-hour recess,' stated the judge, banging his gavel.

'Court will resume at one thirty!' shouted the usher. 'All rise!' They all stood up as the judge left the courtroom.

'Well, that was a turn up for the books. Fancy that bitch of a doctor's secretary doing that,' exclaimed Sarah.

'Hey now, steady on,' suggested Richard, putting some papers into his briefcase. 'There's a long road to go yet, this was just the first bump in the road and don't forget that this road has many ditches, big ones as well. I mean you're cursing and swearing now. What are you going to do when we get them on the stand and they start lying?'

'Then I'll probably have steam coming out of my ears and foam coming from my mouth. But for now, I'll try and keep my temper. How come she called somewhere else first before she called the police?' asked Sarah.

'Well, I don't know, but I'll try my best later to find out,' insisted Richard.

Sarah suggested that it would be nice if they all had lunch together. Richard was chuffed with the idea, most of the time he had lunch by himself because he just never had the time to have lunch with anybody else.

They all had lunch and then came back just as the courtroom was beginning to fill up as people came from having their lunch. David and Sarah came through the door first, followed by Sarah's father, the two children, Sandra, Jamey then Richard and Helen and some of Sarah's friends from work including her business partner Susan. They all came in and sat down. They were beginning to speak when the usher shouted:

'All rise, The R.T. Honourable Michael Thorp presiding.'

Everyone in the court stood up as the judge came in and sat down.

I wonder why they do that thought Sarah, as she sat back down; perhaps they do it as a mark of respect. Either that or they think that he's Hitler. Another thing, I wonder why they say the right honourable; he's never right in this world. If the truth was known the judge is probably just as daft and shifty as the rest of the people in this room. Now because Sarah was miles away in deep thought she hadn't noticed that another person was in the witness box.

'Now, Mrs Smith could you tell the court your job please?' asked Richard.

'Yes certainly, I'm a private consultant.'

'What does your job entail Mrs Smith?' continued Richard.

'Well, as I said I'm a consultant. You could call me a private doctor, that's all I am really is a doctor, but I do not stay in the one place unlike ordinary doctors, I have to travel to all of my patients,' she stated.

'How long have you been a consultant for, Mrs Smith?' Richard was rubbing his chin as if he was wishing for something.

'I have been a consultant for nearly twenty years.' Mrs Smith was smiling slightly as she spoke.

Sarah snapped out of her deep thoughts. As she looked up she thought to herself, when the hell did she come in? God, I must have been miles away. Flip me woman, you must control yourself. She also had that thought again like she was watching herself on the TV. And of course she could not control what was happening to her. She snapped out of it just as quickly as she went into it. She had to force herself to concentrate and in the end, she just pinched herself which seemed to do the trick.

'That's a long time to be in the same job Mrs Smith. So I can say without question that you're an expert in your field,' suggested Richard.

'Well yes, I've never thought of myself quite like that before, but yes I suppose that I am well experienced in my job,' she replied.

'Oh please you're doing yourself a grave in justice. Anybody would agree that having a job for that length of time must mean that you're very good at what you do,' insisted Richard.

'Yes I suppose so, but I do make few mistakes,' stated Mrs Smith

'That may well be Mrs Smith, we all make mistakes at some point in our lives, nobody's perfect, but I don't think that a person with a job like yours makes that many mistakes. Dispute the fact that you can't afford to, it would put a lot of lives at risk, wouldn't you agree?' asked Richard.

'Yes, I suppose you're right I've just never thought of it like that,' she replied.

'Well, let me put it another way, on the twentieth of February nineteen ninety one. Do you think that you made any mistakes at all on your examination of Mrs Phillips?'

'No, I do not think that I made any mistakes on that day. I'm sure that I did my job carefully and professionally.'

'Indeed you did, Mrs Smith. Your whole examination took over two hours to complete, did it not?' Richard was pacing slowly up and down the floor in front of the witness box.

'Yes, it did,' stated Mrs Smith.

'So it was quite a detailed analysis?' suggested Richard.

'Yes, it was, it had to be checked and double checked in cases like this,' she stated.

'Now in your report, you said that Mrs Phillips had immense bruising to her right eye. How would you say that was caused Mrs Smith?'

'Well, I'm pretty sure by the tests we ran that it was caused by a slap to the face.'

'What about the closing of her left eye and the gash to the forehead, how would you say that they were caused?' continued Richard.

'We know that the closing of the eye was caused by continuous punching of a fist to that part of the face. The gash to the upper left hand side of her forehead was caused by a fall onto a concrete step,' stated Mrs Smith.

'Are you sure about that?' asked Richard.

'Yes, we found cement dust on the forehead and on the hair. Also we found some on her clothes and some on her legs. We also examined the area where the incident took place and found traces of hair and blood there.'

'She also had a large head wound did she not?' asked Richard.

'Yes, she did.'

'Could you tell us what was that caused by?' Richard asked.

'That was caused by a fall onto a hard surface. Maybe concrete but we couldn't get an analysis of that particular wound,' stated Mrs Smith.

'Oh and why not?'

'Well for a start, there was too much blood and because, Mrs Phillips had a lot of hair we had to cut some of it out to get to the wound. But we couldn't really analyse it because of all the blood,' continued Mrs Smith.

The whole courtroom was shocked by some of the things that they were hearing. Sarah herself had started to cry, not loud just kind of whimpering. This was the first time; she had heard what those two men had actually done to her. She felt it more for her children, whom her father had taken out of the courtroom. He did not want the children to hear anything of what happened to their mother.

He was sitting outside the courtroom when one of the officers came out, and told him that he would look after the two children while he rejoined his family. Bob told the children to behave themselves for the policeman. He told them when they asked why they couldn't be with Mummy, that there were things being said that they were too young to hear.

'I hate grown ups,' said Jason, sitting on a bench. Lucy had started to cry.

'Look, we won't be very long.' Bob was trying to comfort his granddaughter.

'But, why can't I be with Mummy?' Lucy was wrapping her arms around her granddad.

'Because you can't, look, do you and Jason love your mum and dad?' The two children said yes.

'Then just this once, can you be grown up and stay with this nice policeman while we stay in there and help your mother.'

'Ok. Granddad, we'll be good.'

'I hate grown ups,' said Lucy as she sat down on the bench next to Jason and the policemen.

'So do we sweetheart, so do we,' said Bob. Bob said thank you to the policeman and went back into the courtroom.

'Now also in your report, you said that Mrs Phillips had a broken nose in two places. She had three broken ribs and she had bite marks on her shoulder. Can you explain that?' asked Richard.

David meanwhile had noticed his wife crying. He went and sat beside her and put his arms around her, he had already given her a hanky. She put her head on his shoulder and cried endlessly. David just kept whispering that everything would be alright, but that didn't stop Sarah crying though.

She stopped after about ten minutes and just sat there holding her husband's hands.

'Well, the nose was broken by a punch, which split the nose right down the middle breaking it in two places. The bite marks on her shoulder were teeth marks, human teeth marks. We checked them with dental records and found that they belonged to one of the men accused of raping her,' stated Mrs Smith.

'Could you tell us which of the accused had bitten Mrs Phillips on the shoulder?'

'The dental records and moulds taken from the victim, matched without a doubt to Mr Forbes,' stated Mrs Smith.

The court then became restless. The judge began banging his little mallet.

'Order, order, I will not have this racket in my courtroom thank you,' insisted the judge, peering over his glasses.

'Please continue will you Mr Thorn,' asked the judge, looking down from his bench at Richard.

'What about the broken ribs?' asked Richard.

'Well, they were caused by a kick, maybe two to the side of Mrs Phillips. That's why she had three broken ribs.'

'What about the bruising to her breasts and thighs?' he continued.

'Well, the bruising to the breasts were caused by a hand squeezing them tightly therefore causing the bruising to breasts. Forceful sex caused the bruising to the thighs.' Mrs Smith was just about to continue, when Richard cut into the conversation.

'What do you mean by forceful sex?' asked Richard.

'Well, I mean someone who's impatient. When most people have sex the legs are usually open far enough apart, so that the both partners are comfortable, but in this case the legs were not open as wide causing the person to lie on top of the thighs. Add that to a heavy body and that's how Mrs Phillips got the bruising to her thighs and vaginal area. That's why the vagina was very red and swollen,' added Mrs Smith.

'What about the grazing on her buttocks and the marks around her wrist?' asked Richard.

'Well someone dragging the victim across a very rough surface caused the grazing on her buttocks. Holding the wrists tightly and almost stopping the flow of blood caused the bruising around her wrists.' As Mrs Smith was about to continue, Mr Walker was starting once again to get abusive with David, even though David had not been looking at him.

Mr Chevron and one of the guards told him to be quiet, but he carried on much to the annoyance of the judge.

'Mr Walker, seeing as though you intended to keep on interrupting these proceedings you can spend the remainder of today's court session in the cells below. Guards please take him down,' ordered the judge.

Mr Walker knew that he had upset the judge, and so he decided to keep his mouth shut whilst he was being taken down the stairs to the cells.

The judge called for order as he banged his gavel a few times. He then told Richard that he was free to continue.

'Thank you Your Honour,' replied Richard, looking at the judge.

'Now, this is really what I'm interested in, what about the sperm and the blood found on Mrs Phillips?'

'Well, that was interesting. I tested both the blood samples that I found on the body and the sperm samples as well,' said Mrs Smith.

'What did you come up with?' Richard had put Mrs Smith's assessment paper of Sarah back on his table.

'Well, first of all I'm going to apologise now to Mrs Phillips and to her family. They are going to find that what I am about to say next may be very distressing.' The whole courtroom started to become restless again.

'Order, order,' insisted the judge.

There was a few seconds of silence.

'Are you sure you know what you're going to say is going to hurt Mrs Phillips and her family?' asked the judge, peering over his glasses and looking down at Mrs Smith in the witness box.

'If I have to answer the question I do, yes,' she replied.

'Is this questioning relevant Mr Thorn?' asked the judge.

'Yes, I'm afraid so Your Honour. If Mrs Smith doesn't answer my question then we shall never know if the sperm or the blood belonged to any of the accused. Thus making them walk free,' replied Richard.

'Ok, but do try and make it as brief as possible Mr Thorn. Now would you please continue Mrs Smith?' ordered the judge.

'Well, the sperm from the men accused were both different. I know that they are different anyway, because they are from two different people. But the sperm from Mr Forbes is ok but the blood is not. The sperm from Mr Walker is not ok but the blood is.' Richard looked oddly at Mrs Smith.

'What does that mean?' asked Richard

'Mr Walker has a very low sperm count, but if he finds with a very fertile woman he can have a fair few children. Mr Forbes on the other hand can have children with any woman; as long as she can have children he's fine. He can have ten children if he finds the right woman, but it was the blood that really interested me.'

Mrs Smith was about to continue, when Richard cut into the conversation.

'Why did the blood of the two men accused interest you so much?'

'Well, both of the men are drug users, but I must state that Mr Walker only uses small drugs like marijuana, speed and ecstasy, but Mr Forbes uses cocaine,' stated Mrs Smith.

'Well, if you think about it with all the money he has Mr Forbes can afford to smoke such things,' suggested Richard.

'Oh he doesn't smoke it, he injects it. We worked it out that he has been a user for about four years,' exclaimed Mrs Smith.

The whole courtroom became restless once more.

'Order, order,' insisted the judge, in a deep thrusting voice.

'Are you sure about this?' asked Richard.

'Yes, I am one hundred percent sure,' she replied.

'Thank you Mrs Smith, No further questions Your Honour,' concluded Richard.

Mr Chevron stood up, he was just about to go and question Mrs Smith. Richard was also just about to sit down.

'There's something that you should know Mr Thorn,' continued Mrs Smith

Mr Chevron was still standing up behind his table.

'Oh, and what's that Mrs Smith?' asked Richard as he turned round.

'Mr Forbes has the Aids virus, he is HIV positive.'

'Are you sure about this?' insisted Richard.

'Sorry, but yes absolutely positive,' she replied.

The whole courtroom went wild.

'Order, order, I say order. I must have order in this courtroom,' bellowed the judge.

Sarah was standing up crying and shouting loudly.

'You bastard, you've ruined my fucking life, you bastard. I hate you, I hope you fucking rot in hell!' She was crying loudly.

'Under the circumstances court will adjourn until ten o'clock tomorrow.' The judge stood up. Nearly all of the people in the courtroom were standing up.

Sarah was shouting and going wild.

'Bastard, I hate you, all of you.'

Sarah's father never hesitated; he walked up and punched his daughter on the chin. Because he was a former top amateur boxer, he knew just how hard or how soft to hit someone. Sarah went out like a light.

'I'm sorry, but it's for your sister's own good,' said Sandra's father, picking his daughter up off the floor and putting her over his shoulder.

'We are all stopping at yours tonight,' said Bob to David.

David was just stunned, he wanted to speak but he couldn't the words just wouldn't come out. They all left the courtroom and went straight to David and Sarah's house.

David opened the door and all the family went in. All of Sarah's friends had gone; they all thought it best that Sarah didn't have too many people around her at this present time. Bob carried his daughter upstairs and lay her on the bed in her room. She looked peaceful.

'I'm sorry.' He was just about to leave when Sarah began to wake up.

'Dad, what are you doing here and why does my head hurt?' Sarah was trying to sit up.

'Do you remember what was said?' asked Bob.

'Yes, I remember everything. Don't worry Dad I'm not going to get hysterical again.' She was kicking off her shoes.

'I wouldn't blame you if you do get hysterical,' replied Bob. Sarah gestured for her father to sit down on the bed and he did. Sarah had sat up; she put her arm around her father's waist and put her head on his shoulder. He put his arm around her.

'Where did I go wrong Dad? What did I do when I was younger that was so terribly wrong that I had to be punished when I was older for it?' She had begun to sob gently.

'When you were younger you played up like all children do when they're young,' said Bob.

'I know I played up when I was younger. I can tell you that I was a right little tyrant,' said Sarah.

'You can't blame yourself for what happened and God had nothing to do with it. Look, you were raped; you have to find a way to deal with that.'

'I thought of committing suicide you know. Not now but a few days after it happened,' admitted Sarah.

'Where would that have got you?' asked Bob.

'It might have solved the problem,' suggested Sarah.

'Oh, how?' replied Bob.

'Oh, I don't know, maybe if I wasn't here then people could just get on with their lives and forget about me,' she replied.

'Now, you listen to me. I've already lost the woman I love. Ok it was a long time ago, and I do still love her and think about her. But I don't want to lose another one. As for the problem being solved, well, it wouldn't be, would it? For instance, I would be grieving over the loss of a daughter. Sandra would be grieving over the loss of a sister. David would grieve over the loss of a wife. Then there are the children; to say that they would be devastated would be an understatement.

'Plus there's Jamey, wouldn't you want to see him succeed in life, the same as you and your sister have? Jamey is extremely talented, there's not that many kids get the help and support that he has. There aren't many parents who have the money to send their children to private school, like we have.' He was about to continue, when Sarah spoke.

'Yes, I understand what you're saying Dad, but if I have Aids then I'm going to die anyway, so what would be the point in living? I wouldn't want my children to see me like that; I wouldn't want anybody to see me like that. I don't want people avoiding me in the street or when I go shopping, or even if I go to work people are going to think. Oh I'm not sitting by her, she has Aids. Aids the small word that does a lot of damage,' said Sarah.

'Well we'll deal with these things as and when they arrive, but for now don't worry about it ok. Let's get those two behind bars where they belong. Then we'll worry about other things when they come up, shall we go downstairs?' suggested Bob.

'No, you can if you want. I want to have a sleep I feel tired all of a sudden.'

Sarah's father asked if there was anything that she wanted. Sarah said no she just wanted to sleep.

Sarah's father went downstairs to join the rest of the family. Richard and Helen were downstairs.

'Hi,' said Bob, walking into the living room with a smile on his face. He didn't feel like smiling, he didn't know what he wanted to do. I mean would you?

'How is she?' asked Helen.

'Well, she's calmed down; she's not as hysterical as she was even though I can't blame her. She's sleeping now, she might come down later,' replied Bob.

'Oh yes that reminds me Mrs Smith said that Sarah's tests will take about six weeks to come through. By then we should know whether Sarah is HIV positive

108

or not, we should get the results from the hospital about that time too,' said Richard.

'What about Mr Walker, surely he's HIV positive now,' suggested Bob, sitting on the arm of the chair next to David.

'He might well be as it happens, let's all keep an open mind about all of this, Sarah might not have anything.'

'I hope to God that you're right,' replied Bob.

'Anyway, I'll see you in court tomorrow. I'm going to put Sarah on the stand while the judge is on our side,' suggested Richard.

'Is that absolutely necessary?' asked Bob.

'Yes, I'm afraid so, the judge is one of these people who believes the evidence he hears and sees. I've been lucky so far that he's not been too bad with us, so let's hope that it lasts. I'll tell you something, I'm really not supposed to, but under the circumstances it can't make things any worse. I had Mr Chevron come to see me just before I left the court,' said Richard.

'What did he want?' asked Bob, in a deep thrusting voice.

'Well, he wanted to make a deal.'

'What sort of deal?' asked David, interrupting Richard.

'Well, he wanted me to drop the rape charge on both Mr Forbes and the armed robbery charges two counts against Mr Walker. I'll see myself out,' said Richard, heading for the living room door.

'What did you tell him?' asked David.

'Me, I told him that he has no chance of winning this case. I also told him that I was going to nail his arse to the wall. Anyway, I must go.' Helen and Richard said their goodbyes and then left.

'What a cheek to ask Richard to drop some of the charges,' suggested David.

'They're heavy charges as well. Armed robbery is basically in the same category as murder, which means that it can carry the same sentence as someone who has committed murder depending on the circumstances. Which for that alone can get you ten to fifteen years in prison and he has two charges against him. Rape is about seven years, maybe ten,' said Bob.

Jamey and his mother just sat there, I suppose they were both still in shock.

'What are we going to do, about Sarah?' asked Sandra.

'Well, there's not a lot that we can do,' said Bob. He was really thinking the same thing, but Sandra asked the question before he did.

'Look, we're talking Aids for God's sake. If she has got Aids, what are we going to do?' implied Sandra.

Just then, David got up and shouted for the children to come in from outside, because it was time for bed.

It was still pretty light outside even though it was getting late. They moaned for a few minutes, before their father told them to get in now.

'Kiss Auntie Sandra, your granddad and Jamey goodnight. No playing about upstairs,' said David, locking the back door, and then watching the children run upstairs.

'Goodnight,' said Jason and Lucy, going up the stairs. 'Goodnight.' David went upstairs and told Jason to get in to Lucy's bed so that their granddad could use his bed for tonight.

'Ok Dad,' said Jason, getting out of bed and walking half asleep into Lucy's room.

'Lucy, Jason is sleeping in your bed with you for tonight.'

'Ok Dad if he has to,' replied Lucy. Lucy was probably wishing that Jason would go back into his own room and sleep in his own bed, but she accepted the fact that Jason was in her bed for the night.

'Dad,' said Lucy, in a soft voice. 'Is Mummy going to be alright?'

'Yes of course she is, why?' He was trying to avoid the question.

'I was just wondering why granddad was carrying her.'

'Your mother felt unwell that's all,' said David, swallowing hard.

'As long as she gets better soon,' replied Lucy

Jason was already asleep, Lucy bid him goodnight then went to sleep.

David looked in on his wife who he thought was fast asleep. He walked over to the bed but he could not see his wife's face, because she was under the quilt. David sighed and then walked back towards the bedroom door.

'You know, I don't suppose you'll ever know how much I love you will you?' said David as he went through the door, he paused then shut the door and went back downstairs.

Sarah meanwhile was under the quilt with a little smile on her face.

If only you knew that I had been listening, thought Sarah. She whispered 'I love you to darling,' then slowly went to sleep.

David went into the living room and told them about the sleeping arrangements.

'Right, Sandra can jump into bed with Sarah, Bob, you can jump into Jason's bed, as I've put him in Lucy's room and Jamey you get the settee.'

'What about you?' asked Jamey.

'Me, oh I don't think that I'll be able to sleep much tonight.' David sat down in one of the armchairs. There was a few minutes' silence.

'I was in Lucy's room just a while ago,' he smiled as he remembers tucking her into bed. He paused for a split second.

'She asked me why her granddad was carrying her mother; I stood there for a few minutes thinking, what the hell am I going to say? How can I explain to my nine-year-old daughter that her mother might have a killer disease and that she may die in a few years' time?'

'Look,' said Sandra. 'They may be young, but they still have a right to know what's going on, they might not understand, but you should sit down and tell them all the same.'

'Yes, I know, but how do I tell them? I can't just sit them down and tell them, two people raped your mother and now she might have Aids,' said David.

'No, you sit there and explain it to them step by step. You explain every detail, every question to them so that they know what's going on,' suggested Bob.

'I will you'll just have to give me some time to work out the best way to tell them,' replied David.

'Well, it's been a very long day, goodnight all,' said Bob and Sandra, going through the living room door.

Jamey had not said a word the whole time everybody else was talking. It would have been nice if somebody spoke to him and asked him what he thought of the whole situation. But then again, he was always led to believe that you spoke when you were spoken to and not before.

'Are you, ok?' asked David, looking thoughtfully at Jamey.

'Yes, I'm fine, actually no, I'm not,' said Jamey sighing deeply. There was a few seconds of silence. 'Being raped is bad enough, no woman whatever she's done should have to go through that, but to get raped by two people is twice as bad. You have twice the pain, twice the anger, twice the hate, two of everything. But the thought of catching Aids, I don't really think that we've really thought this lot through. Aids: did you know that nearly a quarter of the population of the world has Aids, that's millions and millions of people? One person is bad enough, but to have millions with the same killer disease. If it carries on like this by the year two thousand most of the humans will be extinct.'

'Yes, I know, but until they find a cure for it people will just have to cope as best as possible. I'm hoping to God that she hasn't got it,' replied David. 'I disagree; I think that everybody in their own way has thought this lot through. I even think that the children understand what's going on. As I said we'd just have to cope with things as best as we possibly can. I know it's hard but we'll cope.'

'Maybe I should quit school,' said Jamey, looking at David and then thinking, oh, what have I said?

'That's a good idea. Well for instance, you could get a job; you could even join the army. Then when you're about twenty and you have four children, no job and no money, you'll think to yourself: God I wish I'd have stayed in school and studied harder then maybe I'd have got somewhere with my life,' said David.

'As I sit at home in my two bedroom flat with my girlfriend and the four kids,' said Jamey, jumping into the conversation.

'And the four kids,' said David, raising his eyebrows and looking at Jamey.

'Well, it was just a thought,' smiled Jamey.

'Look, there isn't anything you can do that we can't and visa versa, so you might as well stay in school and learn as much as possible however hard it is. Anyway talking about school, have you thought about what you are going to draw for your project?' asked David.

'N, replied Jamey.

'Well, I'll let you get some sleep and about five o'clock, I'll show you somewhere that you can draw your picture,' suggested David.

'In the morning?' said Jamey, slightly stunned.

'Yes that's the best time to see it as far as I know. We'll have to be there before the sun comes up,' said David.

'But, I left my pencils and stuff down Mums. I have nothing to draw with or on.'

'Jamey have you forgotten that I am an architect?' said David.

'No, I hadn't. Oh, you're an architect so you've got lots of paper, silly me,' he giggled.

'What's so funny?' asked David.

'I have an architect in the room and I'm wondering where to get pencils and paper from, God what a dope.'

David giggled for a while then told Jamey that he should get some sleep. He got Jamey a blanket and a pillow. Then Jamey went straight to sleep.

About four thirty, David woke Jamey up and told him that it was time to go. He told Jamey to wash his face just to make sure that he was awake. Jamey came back downstairs a few minutes later looking at lot more refreshed and wide awake. David got his car keys then he and Jamey left.

'What's the name of this place?' asked Jamey as they drove down the road.

'The house is called the manor. The house belongs to a friend of mine and it was built in about the late eighteenth century. He has restored it piece by piece, he even imported genuine Italian marble for certain parts of the house,' replied David as he pulled off the motorway.

The drive took about forty minutes. David drove down the drive of the house.

'God, how long is his drive?' asked Jamey, looking at the house which was getting nearer and nearer.

'Just over half a mile long,' laughed David, stopping the car about five hundred yards from the house.

'Right, how long will it take you to do this?'

Jamey was in a world of his own, he was stunned by the size and style of the house.

'Jamey,' said David, in a strong but smooth voice. 'If you don't get back into class I'll give two hours of detention.'

'Yes sir,' began Jamey as he turned and looked at David who was giggling. 'You got me there, God for a split second I thought I was back at school.'

David slowly stopped giggling. He asked Jamey once again:

'How long will it take you to complete the picture?'

'Oh, about an hour and a half, I'll do a rough sketch of it first, then later on tonight when I'm at yours or Mum's I'll draw it properly. It'll take me about four hours to do it properly.'

David gave Jamey all the things that he said that he needed. David then told him that he was going to get some sleep in the car while he got on with his picture. About an hour later Jamey woke David up and told him that he had finished. By this time the sun was shining brightly in the sky and there were not many clouds about. David got out of the car and stretched.

'Do you want to see it, as I said I've only done a rough sketch?' asked Jamey.

'Wow!' replied David, looking as though he had lost a pound and found a thousand pounds.

'That's incredible, how did you get the shadow at that angle?'

'That was the sun when the sun came up earlier; it stretched the shadow longer and longer. The higher the sun went the longer the shadow went. Anyway, as I said it's only a rough sketch.'

'That's a damn good rough sketch; you should come and work with me. If my drawing was half as good as your rough sketching, I'd probably be a lot richer and more talented artistically. Anyway, we might as well make our way back,' David suggested. They packed everything back into the boot of the car, before setting off for home.

The rest of the family had already woken up and had breakfast by the time David and Jamey got back.

'Where have you two been?' asked Sandra. 'We've been worried sick about you.'

'Show them the picture,' David suggested to Jamey as he sat down on the arm of the chair next to his father-in-law.

'It's only a rough sketch,' Jamey slowly opened the large sheet of paper and showed everybody the picture he had done.

'That's excellent,' said his mother, walking towards him and giving him a huge hug and a kiss on the cheek.

'Well, at least we know that the money your father and mother pay for your schooling is not going to waste,' said Bob.

David went upstairs to his wife and Jamey went into the kitchen to make himself a cup of tea. He asked if anybody else wanted one, but they all said no. So he just made one for himself. He found a pencil in the kitchen and he was sketching bits of the drawing, shading in bits here and bits there. He overheard his mother and granddad talking about his father.

'Dad, I just wanted to thank you,' said Sandra.

'What on earth for?' replied Bob.

'You see, well I just wanted to thank you for just being there for Sarah and me.' Sandra paused for a moment.

'Look, don't be silly, you two both mean the world to me, you know that.' Her father was looking at her and smiling.

'Anyway, I just wanted to say thank you. I called Robert the other day.' She thought that if she dropped it into the conversation quickly, her father might not get that upset.

'What on earth for?' asked her father, with a bewildered look on his face.

'Well, I wanted to talk to him. Don't look at me like that; he is still the father of my son.' Sandra felt that for now there was no point in talking to her father about Robert, not the way that he felt about him anyway.

'Well, I suppose that he should know how his son is doing,' replied Bob.

Sandra never told her father, but Robert saw his son a lot more than they knew.

Just then, David and Sarah came downstairs followed a few minutes after by the children. Sarah was in a cheerful mood, she was singing as she came into the living room.

'Right, I think that we should be going. Oh by the way have you seen Jamey's picture?' said David, leading his wife into the kitchen. Jamey jumped slightly when Sarah spoke.

'Come on; let's have a look at your picture then.'

'God, you frightened the life out of me,' said Jamey, looking up.

'It's only a rough sketch.' Jamey showed his auntie the sketch he had done.

'My God that is good' replied Sarah. They all headed for the front door.

'Personally, I think that the picture's great,' said David.

'Me, too,' said Bob.

'You're joking, if I want to win the competition this year, my picture will have to look a lot better than that,' suggested Jamey getting in his granddad's car. Jamey thought to himself as they drove down the road. 'I wonder what my teacher would say. God, he'd have kittens if he saw my picture.'

'Mr Jones how could you, one of our most talented students, present the school with such rubbish?' He smiled to himself.

I know that I'm going to win this year, he thought to himself.

They all got into the courtroom and sat down. Mr Walker and Mr Forbes had not yet arrived. Sarah said good morning to Helen and Richard, and everybody said good morning to each other and then they all sat down. About ten minutes later some guards brought the two men from the cells downstairs. Mr Forbes looked as calm as he could possibly look, whereas Mr Walker on the other hand looked slightly distressed. Although neither one of them were their usual selves.

At least they weren't staring at us, thank God. Someone must have given them a good talking to, about bloody time as well, thought Sarah, jumping slightly as the usher shouted for everyone to stand up as the judge came in.

'Mr Chevron, I hope that you can keep your clients under control today,' stated the judge, looking hard at Mr Chevron.

'Err... yes I will Your Honour,' said Mr Chevron, standing up and then sitting down just as quickly.

I wonder why they do that, thought Sarah. Why not just stand up for a few seconds and then sit back down, wouldn't that be easier, but then again I suppose they do it for a reason.

'Would you like to call your first witness please Mr Thorn?'

'Yes Your Honour, I would like to call Mr Tony Begia to the stand please.' Richard looked towards the courtroom door and waited patiently for Mr Begia to come in. Mr Begia walked down the aisle, took the oath and then sat down in the witness box.

'Can you tell the court your job please Mr Begia?' Richard was standing in the middle of the floor.

'Yes, I'm a family practitioner,' he replied.

'How long have you been a practitioner?' asked Richard.

'I have been a practitioner for about forty-five years,' replied Mr Begia.

'That's a very long time; you also delivered Mrs Phillips into the world, did you not?' asked Richard.

'Yes I did,' he replied.

'Now you work with different doctors, don't you?' asked Richard.

'Yes, I do,' stated Mr Begia.

'Why is that?' asked Richard.

'Well, I'm retiring fairly shortly, so I kind of just lend a hand here and there. I work mainly with other doctors; well I say I work with different doctors. I only work with Mr Agpatel now,' stated Mr Begia.

'He is their family doctor is he not?' asked Richard.

'Yes, he is, well, now that I am retiring,' he replied.

'So how is it that you happened to work with Mr Agpatel?' asked Richard.

'Well in the last few years, I mainly worked as a relief doctor and because I was retiring I needed to find a replacement to take over my surgery. I guess I was working with Mr Agpatel quite a lot, so I just ended up working with him permanently. It was still my surgery but he took over more and more and I began to do less and less work,' Mr Begia replied.

'So you examined Mrs Phillips the day after she was attacked, is that correct?' asked Richard.

'Yes, it is. Mr Agpatel treated her at the scene until the emergency services arrived,' replied Mr Begia.

'Can I ask why you examined her the day after?' asked Richard.

'Well, I suppose as her friend and doctor I felt that I should do my own report on her. Plus it's wise to have a second opinion,' he suggested.

'Now in your report, you said that Mrs Phillips had a cut on her head and a gash on her forehead. For the benefit of everyone in this court, could you tell everyone the difference between a gash and a cut?' Richard asked as he leaned against his table.

'Yes, certainly, a cut is usually a straight wound, it is usually deep, but it is still straight. With a gash it is more jagged. If you get a sharp knife and cut a piece of silk it just cuts straight. If you have a knife that has a few teeth missing or a piece missing and you cut the same piece of cloth, you would get a jagged cut,' stated Mr Begia.

'So did Mrs Phillips have a gash on her head or did she have a cut on her head?' asked Richard, rubbing his chin as he was walking across the floor.

'She had a cut on her head.'

'And did she have a cut or a gash on her forehead?' asked Richard.

'She had a gash,' replied Mr Begia.

'Now you also say in your report that Mrs Phillips had a closed left eye and a bruised right eye. How do you think that they were caused?'

'Well they were both caused by punches to the face. The left hand side took more than the right,' suggested Mr Begia.

'What about the bite marks to her shoulder?' asked Richard.

'Well the bite marks were human; I couldn't say which human teeth they were, but they were definitely human,' stated Mr Begia.

'Did you take any blood samples from Mrs Phillips?' asked Richard.

'Yes, I did. Well, I took samples from under her nails; even though she had a shower there was still quite a lot under her nails,' stated Mr Begia.

'And what was the result of your tests?'

'Well, I have sent them away for analysis; they should be here within the next six weeks,' stated Mr Begia.

'What was your overall analysis of Mrs Phillips?' asked Richard.

'Well, my overall analysis is that Mrs Phillips had been raped,' stated Mr Begia.

'Thank you Mr Begia. No further questions Your Honour,' said Richard, walking back to his table and sitting down. He told Sarah to prepare herself because she was going to be called up next. Richard asked Sarah if she was ok. She said no, but she wasn't prepared to give up so easily.

Meanwhile, Mr Chevron was questioning Mr Begia.

'Now Mr Begia, you said in your report that Mrs Phillips had a lot of bruising on her body. Did she ever tell you how she got them?'

'No, she was really in no fit state to tell me anything like that,' suggested Mr Begia.

'Mr Begia has Mrs Phillips ever come to you with any sexual problems?' asked Mr Chevron.

'Objection Your Honour,' stated Richard, standing up in a hurry.

'My client's sexual behaviour is not in question and I think that Mr Chevron should apologise to my client for making such derogatory remarks. My client is in enough distress at the moment without my learned colleague throwing things like that at her and her husband.'

'Sustained,' said the judge. 'Unfortunately, I am forced to agree Mr Thorn. Mr Chevron may I remind you that you are in a courtroom and not a psychiatrist's office. Kindly refrain from questioning the bedroom behaviour of Mr and Mrs Phillips. Be careful Mr Chevron, your case is as thin as toilet paper as it is. Don't make things any worse for yourself than they already are. Now, please continue,' stated the judge, in a hard voice and looking down on Mr Chevron.

Mr Chevron apologised to Sarah and her husband. He then turned back to Mr Begia.

'Mr Begia, you said that you didn't know who the teeth marks belonged to. I mean for all you know they could belong to anybody is that right.'

'Yes, they could,' suggested Mr Begia.

'So you could not say who actually caused the bruising or the cuts to her head, could you?'

'No, I could not,' stated Mr Begia.

'Thank you Mr Begia, no further questions Your Honour,' said Mr Chevron, going back to his seat.

Sarah meanwhile, under her breath was calling Mr Chevron every name under the sun as she watched him walk back to his seat.

The judge asked Richard if he had any more questions for the witness. Richard said he had only one more question for Mr Begia.

Richard stood up and walked towards the witness box.

'Mr Begia, what was overall conclusion on examining Mrs Phillips?'

'My conclusion is that Mrs Phillips had been raped,' stated Mr Begia.

'Thank you Mr Begia. No further questions Your Honour.' Richard casually walked back to his seat.

The judge asked Richard if he wanted to ask Mr Begia any more questions. Richard said not for now. The judge told Mr Begia that for now he could step down.

The judge asked Richard to call his next witness.

'Thank you Your Honour. I call Mrs Sarah Phillips to the stand.'

Sarah took a deep breath then she stood up. Richard took her hand and led her to the witness box. Sarah took the oath and sat down.

The judge looked down at Mrs Phillips.

'Mrs Phillips, if at any time you feel that you cannot continue please say so and you will be allowed to leave the box.'

'It's ok, Your Honour, if I don't get it over and done with this case might go on forever, and it won't do anybody any good. It's going to be painful, but I want this whole thing over and done with.'

'I admire your strength Mrs Phillips. You may continue Mr Thorn.'

'Thank you Your Honour,' nodded Richard.

'Mrs Phillips, could you tell me your occupation?'

'Yes,' said Sarah, in a soft, but reasonably loud voice. 'I'm an estate agent.'

'How long have you been an estate agent?' Richard walked back to his desk.

'About twelve years now.' Sarah was watching Richard as he walked towards her.

'That's a long time to run a business. Still it's good to see that businesses like yours can still survive in this day and age. Now, Mrs Phillips how long have you been married?' asked Richard.

'Over ten years,' Sarah stated.

'Do you have a good marriage?'

'Yes, we have arguments the same as most people, but yes I can say that I have a good marriage,' suggested Sarah.

'So, on the twentieth of February nineteen ninety one, your marriage was basically the same as it was any other day?' Richard was looking at Sarah as he walked up and down in front of the witness box.

'Yes, it was,' replied Sarah.

'So what happened starting from the time you got out of bed to the time your car broke down?' Richard had walked back and was leaning against his table.

'Well, it was like any other day. I got up about six o'clock; I took a shower, got dressed, got the children ready for school, had some breakfast and then went to work after dropping the children off at school. Then about lunchtime, I decided to leave work early because I wanted to do some shopping. I had just got to the outskirts of the town when my car decided to break down. I cursed and swore for a few minutes then I decided to go shopping.'

'Why didn't you call the AA, or the RAC?' asked Richard walking back towards the witness box.

'I thought that if I did my shopping first when I got home I could call them then.'

'But didn't you think that it was a bit silly leaving your car unattended, suppose your car had been stolen?' suggested Richard.

'The shopping only took about an hour if that. Anyway, because you have to be there to sign for your car when it is brought back to your home just to say that you have received your vehicle, I thought, why not leave it until I got back to the house.' Sarah was thinking, God, Richard you're supposed to be helping me not trying to see how fast you can put me away. She knew that he must have been doing this for a good reason, so she just carried on as best she could; she was still very nervous.

'Why didn't you catch a taxi back?' asked Richard.

'Because my house is what, fifteen minutes walk from the town, so why waste money like that. It must be a crime in itself, if a girl can't leave her car somewhere do a bit of shopping, then if she wants to walk home, especially when it is such a nice day like that day was, considering the month that we were in at the time,' stated Sarah,

'That may well be true Mrs Phillips, but some members of Joe public do not think so. The two men who attacked you didn't care about your car breaking down. They didn't care about how much shopping you had or how long it took you to get it. They didn't even care that you were only fifteen minutes away from your home. All they saw was you. They weren't interested in anything else, all they saw was you. So when you walked down the alley what happened? Was the alleyway packed, were there many lorries that sort of thing?' asked Richard.

'Well, to be honest there weren't that many lorries. There were a few lorries but not many. There was a reasonable amount of people and to be honest I never really took that much notice of the alley. I've walked through that alley hundreds of times and never took any notice of it,' she stated in a soft voice, 'And I never thought that day would be any different.'

'Ah, but it was different wasn't it Mrs Phillips, because two men raped you when you got to the end of the alley. Two men who had nothing better to do with their time. But please let me clarify something for the benefit of the court. Are the two men who raped you sitting in this courtroom?' asked Richard.

'Yes,' said Sarah.

'Could you point them out please?' asked Richard.

119

Sarah had tears rolling down her cheeks as she pointed out Mr Walker and Mr Forbes.

'Now, for the benefit of the court, I must state that Mr Forbes and Mr Walker may not have gone to town specifically to rape Mrs Phillips as far as we know, although they have gone to town to do some other wrong doings. But none the less they did rape Mrs Phillips.' Sarah by now was shaking; she felt that any minute now her head was going to explode.

'They might have followed you Mrs Phillips, but it is highly unlikely.' Richard was now pacing up and down in front of the witness box. 'I mean, it could have been any normal day as you well thought it was Mrs Phillips, but you just happened by chance to bump into Mr Forbes and Mr Walker.'

'Why don't you tell the truth?' shouted Mr Walker. 'Instead of trying to fit us up.'

Sarah was just about to speak, when the judge told Mr Walker to be quiet.

'You never went to town for the specific purpose of meeting Mr Forbes and Mr Walker did you Mrs Phillips?' asked Richard.

'No, certainly not,' stated Sarah.

'So it was by chance that you meet the two men accused?'

'Yes, it was by chance,' stated Sarah.

'When you got near the end of the alley, who did you see first Mrs Phillips?' asked Richard.

'I saw Mr Walker first,' replied Sarah.

'And what did he say to you?'

There was a slight pause before Sarah answered, she took a deep breath and said, 'He said, "How would you like to go halves on a bastard".' There were slight murmurs in some parts of the courtroom.

The judge was banging his gavel on his desk saying, *Order, Order!*

'Please continue Mr Thorn,' suggested the judge, looking as though he was half asleep.

'So Mr Walker, said that right out of the blue having never seen you before, or you may have seen him and not known who he was. How would you like to go halves on a bastard and what was your reply?' Richard was standing in the middle of the courtroom.

'I just said not with a pratt like you and continued walking,' stated Sarah. There were slight giggles around the courtroom even Richard chuckled to himself slightly.

They all stopped as soon as the judge looked up over his glasses. He never actually said anything, but with the way he looked at people over his glasses was enough to say anything he wanted. He was the kind of person, who could silence you without saying a single word or without making a single gesture.

'Then what happened?' asked Richard.

'Well, then I tried to walk around him, but when I went one way he went the same way and it carried on like that for a few seconds,' replied Sarah.

'So,' said Richard, cutting into the conversation. 'Mr Walker deliberately stopped you from getting past even though he never touched you; he still obstructed your path.'

'Yes, he did,' stated Sarah.

'Then what happened?'

'Well, he took out a knife and told me to hand over all of my money. That's when I kicked him in between his legs.' Sarah quickly looked at the two men in the dock.

'Then what happened?' asked Richard.

'I then tried to walk off when a slap came from Mr Forbes.'

'How many times did Mr Forbes slap you?' Richard was rubbing his chin.

'He slapped me countless times. Mr Walker also hit me a fair few times as well. I tried desperately to get up off the floor,' suggested Sarah.

'Then what happened?'

'Well, I tried to get to my feet, but I couldn't, I was in too much pain. I shouted and screamed at both of them but they would not stop. They just kept coming towards me.' Sarah looked as though the entire colour was slowly being drained out of her face and probably the rest of her body as well.

'Did any of the two accused men threaten you at all Mrs Phillips?'

'Yes, they both threatened me,' stated Sarah.

'In what way, did they threaten you Mrs Phillips?' asked Richard.

'Well, Mr Forbes only shouted at me, he never used a weapon, but Mr Walker threatened me with a knife.'

'Mr Walker threatened you with a knife,' repeated Richard.

'Yes with a knife,' repeated Sarah.

'In your statement to the police, you said that Mr Forbes said that quote, *you'd better do as he said or he might terminate you for good as he has done before, unquote,* asked Richard, walking towards the witness box with Sarah's statement paper in his hand.

'What did you think Mr Forbes meant by that remark?'

'I thought it meant that he was going to kill me,' stated Sarah.

'You also state that Mr Walker after he robbed you at knife point, and after beating you up, he said to Mr Forbes come on let's blow this place. Then Mr Forbes replied, seeing as though you've taken something from her, I'm going to take something from her as well and it isn't money. What do you think Mr Forbes meant by that?' asked Richard.

'I knew exactly what he wanted and I was determined that he wasn't going to get anything out of me.' Sarah spoke in a soft petite voice.

'I don't really want to ask you this Mrs Phillips, but can you say specifically what Mr Forbes said he wanted from you?'

Sarah paused and looked across at David. David nodded as if to say go on then tell them you might as well, so she did.

'Mrs Phillips,' said Richard, who was about to continue when Sarah cut into his conversation.

'He said he wanted to show me what real love was all about.' Sarah looked across at David again who smiled warmly at her. This in turn made Sarah feel a little bit more confident.

'So Mr Forbes basically told you that he wanted sex with you?' Richard was walking across the courtroom floor.

'Yes, he did,' stated Sarah.

'No more questions Your Honour,' stated Richard. Richard walked back to his seat.

Mr Chevron stood up and walked from behind his table to the middle of the courtroom floor.

'Mrs Phillips, isn't it true that you conned my client out of money?'

'No, I don't believe that I did,' Sarah, said firmly.

'Mrs Phillips, is it not true that my client first came to you on the third of March nineteen eighty-nine asking you to sell his house?'

'Yes, he did. I can't remember the exact date he came in, but yes I remember him coming into my shop,' stated Sarah.

'And, isn't it also true that he came in countless times after that asking you to come and view his property, and each time he came in, you said no?' asked Mr Chevron.

'Err… yes I did…' She was about to continue, when Mr Chevron cut into the conversation.

'Why was that?'

'I just wasn't interested in buying his house. I had no need for a house of that kind or of that size,' stated Sarah.

'But why didn't you take a look at the house anyway, then make a decision?' asked Mr Chevron.

'Our company wasn't interested with a house of that size. The house had eight average sized bedrooms with a bathroom and toilet in each one. Each bedroom had its own telephone; it had two big living rooms, one big dining room and a huge kitchen plus a toilet downstairs. It had three garages, a garden the size of a football pitch, which needed one of those lawnmowers that you sit on to cut the grass.

'Now, I must admit that the house was nice, but Mr Forbes must understand that not everybody can afford three hundred and eighty-five thousand pounds. Not everybody has that kind of money sitting in a bank.' She glanced quickly over at David and her family; they seemed pleased that Sarah had the courage to defend her job.

'The point is Mrs Phillips, you've never liked my client have you that's why you conned him out of that vast amount of money?' suggested Mr Chevron.

'No, it wasn't, it was just business,' said Sarah defending herself. Now, Richard would normally object to this kind of questioning, but he knew that he could just ask Sarah what happened after Mr Chevron had finished with her. So he waited for him to finish.

'I don't call conning my client out of nearly a hundred thousand pounds just business do you?' Sarah was just about to speak, but it didn't matter; Mr Chevron cut in 'No further questions, Your Honour.'

Richard stood up. He smiled at Sarah trying to reassure her that everything would be alright. He never said that but Sarah could tell just by looking at him.

'Mrs Phillips, when you bought the house from Mr Forbes who chose the asking price?'

'Err... he did,' stated Sarah.

'So even though you could have done so you never made him any kind of offer?' asked Richard.

'No, I didn't.' Sarah had calmed down a little bit by this time, perhaps she just felt comfortable talking to Richard.

'But you have expert valuation experience, so why didn't you value the house and give him a price?' suggested Richard.

'It was an awkward house to price; it had so many small things in it like the phone in every room for instance, the huge dining room which could easily seat at least twenty five people. Then there was the kitchen that had built in microwave, cooker, it even had a built in TV. It had everything so I just thought that it would be easier to ask him how much he wanted for it.'

'And, how much was it that he wanted for it again?' asked Richard, walking back to his table and picking up a piece of paper.

'He wanted three hundred and eighty-five thousand for it,' stated Sarah.

'That's what he was asking for?' asked Richard, walking back to the middle of the floor with some papers in his hand.

'Yes,' stated Sarah.

'Your Honour, I have here a copy of the actual bill of sale. Now it clearly states that the house was sold for four hundred thousand exactly.' Richard gave a copy to the judge and to Mr Chevron.

'Now on the back of this, you'll find how much Mr Forbes actually bought the house for two years before in nineteen eighty-seven. The house was valued at two hundred and fifty thousand at the most. We know that he hasn't added anything to it. In fact the house was sold in exactly the same condition that he bought it in. So it looks like Mr Forbes conned a hundred and fifty thousand pounds out of my client, and not the other way around like my learned colleague suggested.' Richard put the paper he had in his hand back on his table.

'Mrs Phillips, did you like Mr Forbes?'

'Well, until he came into my office for the first time I had never met him. I was like everybody else; I respected him for his generosity and his charity work. But I found the man himself, when I met him slightly arrogant to be perfectly honest,' stated Sarah.

'Oh, why was that?' asked Richard.

'Well, I don't know, perhaps because he was used to having his own way, and he then found someone that said no to him. I suppose for a man of his calibre it was a bit hard to take.'

'Now, you say in your statement that when you were shouting and screaming and struggling to get away, that just seemed to excite them all the more. What did you mean by that?' asked Richard.

Sarah paused.

Richard called to Sarah, once again.

'Sorry, err... what was the question again?' asked Sarah, looking thoughtfully at Richard as though he had made some kind of mistake. Richard repeated the question and waited patiently for Sarah to answer.

Sarah sighed deeply then she spoke.

'Well, when Mr Walker grabbed me by my hair and he was pulling me, Mr Forbes seemed for a short while to be very excited. He was kind of like when you take a child into a toyshop for the first time, you know you see them smiling, looking enthusiastic. Well, that's how Mr Forbes looked only on a much larger scale.' Sarah sighed deeply once again, and then looked deeply at the two men in the dock.

'No more questions, Your Honour,' stated Richard.

'Mr Chevron would you like to cross examine Mrs Phillips?' asked the judge.

'No, not at this present time Your Honour but I would like to call her at another time, if I may,' stated Mr Chevron, standing up and then sitting down a few seconds later.

'Very well,' said the judge, looking over at Mr Chevron who was watching Richard.

'You may step down for the moment Mrs Phillips.'

Sarah responded in a soft voice to the judge, 'Thank you.'

Deep down inside, Sarah wanted to cry and cry and cry. But, she wanted the whole court to know that she wasn't going to give anybody the satisfaction of seeing her cry. She walked slowly back to her seat and sat down.

The judge told the usher that they would take a ten-minute recess; everyone stood up as the judge left.

Richard was telling Sarah how well he thought that she was doing. The ten minutes went in no time at all, the judge was back in and was sitting down.

'Would you like to call your next witness please, Mr Chevron?'

'Yes, Your Honour. I would like to call, Miss Donna Woodfield to the stand.'

Miss Woodfield came walking down the aisle. She walked a lot quicker this time; she never looked at anybody. She just took the oath and sat down once again in the witness box.

'Miss Woodfield, did you notice any unusual cars parked outside the surgery?'

'What do you mean unusual cars?' she asked.

'Well, I mean cars that you don't normally see around that area. You know like flash expensive cars, the kind of cars that cost a fortune to buy and just as much to run,' asked Mr Chevron.

'Well, to be honest, I never really took much notice of the cars that were parked outside the surgery, because there's always so many nice cars parked outside there, so that day wasn't any different from the rest,' stated Miss Woodfield.

'How long is your dinner break?' asked Mr Chevron who was standing by the witness box and then walking back towards his table slowly.

'It's half an hour long,' stated Miss Woodfield as she watched Mr Chevron as he walked across the floor.

'So when you came back from having your lunch break, you saw nothing whatsoever out of the ordinary?'

'No, I did not,' she stated.

'So you never saw anybody hanging about and you never saw Mrs Phillips?'

'No, I saw nobody,' stated Miss Woodfield.

'So having not seen anybody you would not be able to point out the people that raped Mrs Phillips could you?' asked Mr Chevron.

'No, I couldn't,' she replied.

'Thank you Your Honour, no further questions.' Mr Chevron sat down.

Richard stood up as quickly as Mr Chevron sat down.

'Miss Woodfield, do you have any children?'

'No, I don't have any children,' she replied.

'Do you plan on having any children in the near future?' asked Richard.

'Yes, I will in the near future,' she replied.

'How about marriage, do you plan on getting married at any time in the not too distant future?'

'Yes, maybe I haven't really thought about getting married yet,' stated Miss Woodfield.

'Why is that Miss Woodfield?' asked Richard, who could see that Miss Woodfield was getting rather unsettled.

'Err... well, as I said I haven't really thought about it,' she stated.

'Miss Woodfield, how do you think that you would feel if Mrs Phillips was your daughter?' asked Richard.

'Well, err... I don't know really. I'd be devastated of course.'

'Yes, of course, now, you do understand that you are under oath do you know what that means?' asked Richard walking up and down in front of the witness box and looking occasionally at Miss Woodfield, who looked away every time Richard looked at her.

'Yes, I do. I promised to tell the truth, the whole truth and nothing but the truth,' she recited.

'So, if I ask you any question within reason you should answer truthfully, shouldn't you?' suggested Richard.

'Well yes, of course,' she replied.

'Good, now we know that you are a very good secretary and you like your job, but isn't there a more sinister side to you working there,' suggested Richard.

'Your Honour, I object!' shouted Mr Chevron. 'These questions have no bearing on the case whatsoever.'

'Counsel will please approach the bench,' said the judge, firmly. 'Mr Thorn, you're doing well enough so far without having to resort to asking seemingly unimportant questions like that. And you Mr Chevron, you might as well give up now because I haven't heard anything concrete from you so far. All I've heard from you so far is a load of rubbish, so you needn't chastise Mr Thorn,' suggested the judge.

'But Your Honour, we now know that she is the main witness, and I feel that there is a lot that she is holding back from us. Wouldn't it be better for us all to know what kind of person she is? It may be useful for both Mr Chevron and myself depending on the information that she gives us, it could help this case a lot,' stated Richard.

The judge pondered for a second or two while Mr Thorn and Mr Chevron argued amongst themselves.

'Your Honour, if she doesn't tell us anything useful about Mr Forbes or Mr Walker then you can rap me on the knuckles or do whatever you wish to do to me,' suggested Richard.

'I hope for your sake that she does tell you something useful, or by God, you're in deep trouble Mr Thorn, and it's no good protesting Mr Chevron, my word is final. You may continue Mr Thorn,' stated the judge.

Mr Chevron went back to his seat feeling somewhat disappointed with himself.

'Miss Woodfield, according to Mr Mackoshie the two accused men are there at the surgery on a regular basis, but yet you say that you have never seen them until you saw them in court, is that correct?' Richard like the rest of the court waited in anticipation for Miss Woodfield to answer, they waited a few seconds, it seemed like hours but it was only a few seconds.

'Miss Woodfield, you are under oath remember.'

'Miss Woodfield, would you please answer the question?' stated the judge, peering over his glasses at Miss Woodfield.

'I have seen them before,' she said finally. The whole court began to talk quite loudly just as the judge had restored order to the courtroom.

Mr Walker began shouting across the courtroom. 'You stupid bitch, how could you be so fucking stupid? They never knew anything, I should have known not to go out with a dumb bitch like you.' He was so furious at Miss Woodfield. Two guards quickly pounced on Mr Walker; they handcuffed him behind his back, they were trying to hold him still, but they couldn't because he was shouting and kicking at them and shouting at Miss Woodfield at the same time.

The judge started banging his gavel and shouting 'Order, order.' He then ordered Mr Walker be taken down to the cells and kept there until further notice.

'Mr Chevron, I am warning you for the last time, if you cannot control your clients then they will be kept in their cells all the way through this trial, do, I make myself clear?' stated the judge.

'Err... yes Your Honour.'

'Court will take a one hour recess for lunch. All rise!' shouted the usher, as the judge stood up and left rather hastily.

'Come on, let's have some lunch,' suggested Richard to Sarah.

'I'd like to sit here on my own for a while, if you don't mind?' replied Sarah.

'Would you like me to stay with you?' asked David.

'No, thank you for offering, but I just want to be by myself for a while,' insisted Sarah.

David kissed his wife on the cheek, and asked her if he could get her anything.

'Yes, a nice cup of coffee please,' she replied.

Someone had overheard Sarah saying that she wanted a cup of coffee. A few minutes later, one of Sarah's friends handed a cup to David, who in turn handed it to his wife.

'Thanks,' said Sarah, loud enough so that the person who bought the drink in could hear her.

'Are you sure that you want to be on your own?' he asked her once again.

'I have to be on my own to think things through,' she insisted.

David said 'ok' and kissed his wife once again on the cheek and then left the courtroom.

David was the last person to leave the courtroom; he was met by all of Sarah's friends and family outside, all of them wanting to know how she was feeling. David just told them that she was alright and that she just wanted time by herself, and bit by bit he changed the subject.

Sarah meanwhile was sitting drinking her coffee and looking around the courtroom, she giggled, slightly. I wonder how many criminals have been sent down in here, she thought. She must have been thinking aloud because she jumped when a voice said:

'A fair few Mrs Phillips, in fact so many I wouldn't know where to begin.' The judge had come back into the courtroom, Sarah stood up quickly. The judge giggled. 'They all do that you know,' said the judge, walking down to the courtroom floor. 'I don't know why people do it, but they do.'

Sarah sat back down on her seat; she was thinking how different the judge looked without his wig or his cloak, the judge sat down beside Sarah.

'I thought that people had to stand up when the judge came in,' inquired Sarah.

'That's what most people think, but if there's a law against not standing up when the judge comes in, I'm one of the few people who know nothing of it. Some judges are so used to people standing up for them that they wouldn't settle for anything else,' he smiled.

'I was supposed to sentence a man once, a policeman at that. He was doing indescribable things with young girls, I mean, girls of about nine or ten.' The judge was about to continue when Sarah butted into the conversation.

'Why wasn't he sentenced?'

'Oh don't get me wrong; if he had come in front of me he would have got a sentence to a mental institution, so long it would have made legal history. The fact of the matter is a group of vigilantes got to him before I did. I overheard a story about it once, someone said it's a good job the lynch mob got to him before the judge did, or it could have been worse.'

'You don't look that vicious,' suggested Sarah.

'I can be,' laughed the judge.

'Another thing is that this policeman had the most gorgeous understanding wife that I had ever met. Don't get me wrong, I've met a lot of nice men and women over the years, including yourself may I add, but if you take into account the job and life of a policeman, for instance, he can't go home without taking his job with him and he can't go to work without taking his home life with him.

'You're lucky; you're not married to a policeman, it is rather a hectic life for a woman, believe me. But with a wife like he had not many policemen have that kind of person to go home to.'

'I can guess how they must feel,' suggested Sarah, drinking some of her coffee. 'I'm married to a man who I get to spend just basically the weekends with.'

The judge looked at the clock on the wall, stood up and sighed.

'My God, it's nearly time to begin again. You know if people saw us talking together like this, they would think that we're either mad or up to no good,' he smiled.

Sarah told the judge that it would be just their secret. She thanked the judge for the polite conversation and friendly chat.

'Any time, and the honour was all mine, maybe we can talk again sometime,' he said.

'I hope so,' suggested Sarah.

'One more thing, Richard Thorn is a very dear friend of mine and a damn good barrister, so all I can say is good luck and have a bit of faith in Richard and the system. Oh, did you know that this conversation never took place,' the judge smiled at Sarah.

Sarah smiled back, the judge turned and went through his door, as the door closed behind him, the courtroom began filling back up.

Well, well, well thought Sarah, fancy the judge talking to me; then she had another thought. I can't tell anyone anyway. If this kind of thing got out what on earth would people say? Imagine the publicity; I can see it now. *Top Judge in rape trial disgraced by helping the alleged victim.* 'Gordon Bennett.'

'Who's Gordon? Bennett, when he's at home?' asked Richard, putting his briefcase on the table, then sitting down and looking at Sarah.

'Who, what?' said Sarah, jumping slightly.

'Who's Gordon? Bennett? You are alright aren't you? You didn't have any strange visitors while we were out, did you? Any ghostly figures,' giggled Richard.

'No, don't be silly. You know when you have a wild thought about something completely strange, and you think God struth, you know Gordon Bennett and all that.'

'Oh, I know what you mean,' smiled Richard.

Richard and Sarah were both so engrossed in conversation, they never noticed that the judge had come in and that Miss Woodfield was back on the stand.

'Mr Thorn, when you have finished having a private conference with your client maybe we can resume,' suggested the judge to Richard.

'Err… yes sorry Your Honour.' Richard stood up rather quickly.

Richard walked out from behind his table and took a deep breath and then spoke.

'Miss Woodfield, we know now that Mr Forbes and Mr Walker are by the surgery on a regular basis but from what you have told the court, you've never seen them before, is that true? Also, every time my learned colleague or I ask you something, you look directly at the two defendants, may I ask why that is?

'Do you have a boyfriend?' asked Richard. She looked once again at the dock. Mr Forbes just glared at her each time she looked at him.

'Let me tell you another theory if I may, Miss Woodfield. You may stop me if you feel that anything that I say happens to be untrue.'

'A few times,' replied Miss Woodfield, looking down towards the floor.

'Miss Woodfield, I'll come straight to the point. We know by Mr Walker's outburst just before lunch that you are his girlfriend, something that you neglected to mention to the court.' Richard walked back to his table and picked up some papers, he gave one to the judge, and one to Mr Chevron and he kept one himself.

'Now, in nineteen eighty-eight you met Mr Ronald Walker, and then almost eighteen months later you had an abortion. Now, I'll apologise for having to be so personal, but the court has to know all relevant facts about the defendants,' continued Richard, looking at her. You had your first abortion at the end of nineteen eighty-eight. Less than a year later, you had your second abortion. In all, you have had three abortions, haven't you Miss Woodfield?'

'Yes, but …' began Miss Woodfield, but it was too late; Richard had already carried on speaking.

'But you never went to any back street clinic, did you Miss Woodfield? You went to Fairhurst, one of the best clinics in the country, and you never paid for the abortion yourself, did you Miss Woodfield? And of course, we know that Mr Walker does not have that kind of financial stability, in fact I'd say that Mr Forbes is a rather generous man, wouldn't you say so Miss Woodfield paying for you to have all those abortions?'

'I object to this line of questioning Your Honour!' stated Mr Chevron, standing up rather hastily.

'I quite agree,' stated the judge.

'There's no crime against having an abortion!' shouted Miss Woodfield.

130

'No, there isn't, but, there is a crime against being raped and having your life destroyed. I withdraw my last line of questioning Your Honour, and I have no further questions Your Honour.' Richard sat down.

Mr Chevron glanced over quickly at Richard and then stood up. Richard was telling Sarah that Mr Chevron did not have much of a case, and that he was just fumbling along helplessly.

'Miss Woodfield, why did you have so many abortions?'

'It was a mutual agreement between my boyfriend and I.'

'Oh, what mutual agreement was that?' asked Mr Chevron.

'Well, err… we just both decided that we were not ready to have children at that particular time in our lives,' she replied.

'Do you plan on having children in the future?'

'Maybe one day, when I have enough money to support my child, but for now I'll just have to wait,' said Miss Woodfield, fluttering her eyelids a little bit at Mr Chevron, who in return smiled warmly at Miss Woodfield. He then said that he had no further questions for her at this present time and sat back down.

Richard of course had other ideas; he wanted to ask Miss Woodfield a lot more questions. He stood up and walked to the middle of the courtroom floor.

'Miss Woodfield, you said a few minutes ago that it was a mutual agreement between you and your partner, and you both agreed three times that you should have an abortion, do you love Mr Walker?'

'Err… yes I do,' she replied.

'Well forgive me for saying so, but you don't sound very sure,' suggested Richard, looking directly at Miss Woodfield, who had no choice but to look at him.

'Of course, I'm sure,' she replied.

'Just listen to what I'm about to say, if at any time you disagree with anything that I say. If anything I say hasn't an ounce of truth in it, then you stop me and put me on the right track ok?' suggested Richard.

'Yes,' replied Miss Woodfield.

Richard was walking up and down the courtroom floor. 'Now, I think that you love Mr Walker more than words can say, and I think that each time you got pregnant you wanted desperately to have his child, but he didn't want to have one. As much as you tried to have one he didn't want to know. He probably kept shouting and bawling at you, he may have even gone so far as to hit you when you suggested that you and he should have a child. I can understand the first time that you got pregnant by him; it came as a bit of a surprise to the both of you, and I also think that you thought it best to have an abortion. But I also think that each time that you got pregnant after that you wanted to have his baby. I even think

131

that you would go to extreme lengths to try and have a child, it's just that he never wanted one.'

He was about to continue, when Miss Woodfield cut his conversation short.

'You don't know what it's like wanting to have a child with someone you love, you could never imagine how I felt after having three abortions – the fights that we used to have and the arguments. God the arguments we had, some right corkers I can tell you.'

'The point I'm trying to make Miss Woodfield is that your boyfriend seems like a nasty piece of work, but I must apologise slightly for being so hard on you. I mean you are not on trial, but you must understand we need to know as much as possible about Mr Walker and Mr Forbes for that matter,' continued Richard.

Meanwhile, certain people in the courtroom were beginning to feel sorry for the life, which Miss Woodfield had with a monster like Mr Walker. If and when an argument broke out, she had no choice but to take whatever punishment he was offering at the time.

But Sarah, in the meanwhile, was boiling with fury. You think about it, Sarah has to sit there and listen to some woman babble on about how bad her boyfriend was to her. Never mind, the fact that he raped Sarah and basically ruined her life and her family's life in one way or another. After a while, Sarah got fed up with listening to people going 'oh' and 'arh' every time Miss Woodfield said something sad. Miss Woodfield was saying that as bad as he may be he would never hurt anyone intentionally.

Richard was just about to speak, but it was too late, Sarah had heard all the crap from Miss Woodfield that she cared to. She jumped up and started shouting at Miss Woodfield.

'You call yourself a human being; you're just as fucking bad as he is. I was raped for God's sake, I was raped by that no good bastard of a boyfriend of yours, and that no good pratt friend of his sitting in the dock. Here you are in court telling the whole world how bad he was to you! He ruined my fucking life, you stupid bitch. He took my fucking life away from me. My life will never be the same again thanks to your fucking friends, if I had my own way I'd have fucking killed them both already!'

Sarah was screaming abuse at Miss Woodfield. David locked his arms around his wife, holding her tightly as she was kicking and shouting at her husband to let go. Richard was there trying to calm both of the women down, but as you can guess he had no success. David was successful in the fact that he held on tightly to his wife and did not let her go. He could even suffer some of the names that she was calling him. The judge called for an immediate fifteen minute recess. He told Richard to calm his client down by the time court restarted, Richard said that he would.

Sarah in the mean time was still fuming, she watched as Miss Woodfield walked towards her.

'You bitch,' said Sarah, in a really nasty voice.

Richard took Sarah to one side away from everybody else.

'I know, I know. I shouldn't have done it but I just couldn't help myself, it was that bitch getting everybody to be so sympathetic towards her, it got to the stage where even I began to feel slightly sorry for her. Then I remembered why I was here, and then I just flipped, alright go on I know that you're going to give me a lecture.' She looked at Richard, who smiled warmly.

'Now, why should I give you a lecture? I can give you a lecture on law if you like, it only takes about seven hours if we hurry that is.'

'Err... I thought that you would be mad at me,' said Sarah looking slightly puzzled.

'I am mad at you since you mentioned it, but not for the reason that you might expect.' Richard glanced quickly at his watch.

'You've just found out that the man who raped you, his girlfriend is a material witness in the case against him,' said Richard.

'So you're not mad at me for losing my temper?' Sarah still looked baffled, by what Richard was saying.

'The reason why I'm slightly mad at you, is that you waited too long to say what you did. You let me babble on about nothing in particular. OK, I got some good information out of her and I haven't finished with her yet. I think that she has more to tell me. But you still let her babble on, you took your time in realising that she was after the sympathy of the court. When she spun the first line on how badly she had been treated, I was waiting for you to say something then. Anyway, come on it's nearly time to restart,' said Richard.

They both went back and sat down. The judge had already came back in and sat down.

'I trust that your client has calmed down, Mr Thorn,' asked the judge, peering over his glasses and looking sternly at Richard and Sarah.

'Err... yes Your Honour, she has, sorry Your Honour.'

'Good, I hope so, may I suggest you continue to question Miss Woodfield another time.'

'Yes, Your Honour,' agreed Richard.

'Then please call your next witness Mr Thorn,' suggested the judge.

Richard looked at Sarah and asked her quickly if she was alright. Sarah nodded, Richard called his next witness.

'I call Mr Ronald Walker to the stand.' Everyone in the court started mumbling amongst each other.

'Mr Walker is on his way from the cells, Your Honour,' informed one of the guardsmen. The judge was banging his gavel and telling everyone to keep quite.

Richard seized that moment to have a quick word with Sarah.

'Now, no matter what this guy says ignore him as much as you possibly can, do you understand, ignore him for as long as you can.' Richard asked David to come and sit beside his wife for a while to give her a shoulder to cry on.

Sarah was about to speak, when the guards brought Mr Walker up a flight of stairs. You could say that they heard him coming; everyone in the courtroom could hear him cursing and swearing at the guards.

'Now, remember what I said, unless you get to the point that you cannot and will not take any more, then you can start shouting. But it would be better if you could keep your cool,' suggested Richard as he shut his briefcase.

'Why?' asked Sarah holding her husband's hand.

Richard turned round and leaned against his table.

'Why? Because, I'm going to tear him apart strip by strip until all you can see is bare bones.'

The whole court watched as Mr Walker took the oath and sat down in the witness box.

'Could you state your name for the benefit of the court please sir?'

Richard leaned off his table and walked forward slightly, then stopped suddenly. There was a long pause before Mr Walker answered, and even then it was the judge who made him speak.

'Ronald Walker,' he answered in a firm voice.

'And your age?'

'I'm twenty-eight,' answered Mr Walker.

'Do you have a job?' asked Richard.

'No, I don't,' he replied.

'We'll come back to that in a moment. Could you tell the court, what you were doing on the twentieth of February nineteen ninety-one?' asked Richard as he walked up and down the courtroom floor.

'Yes, I was at the cinema with my friends.'

'You were at the local cinema with your girlfriend? Now, there's a thing wouldn't you say so Mr Walker?'

'What taking my girlfriend to the cinema?' he snorted.

'Yes, taking Miss Woodfield to the cinema and having a wonderful time and seeing a wonderful film. What was the name of the film which you and Miss Woodfield went to see?' asked Richard.

'Err… to be honest I can't remember,' he replied.

'Oh, come now you go to the movies with a pretty girl and you cannot remember what you saw?'

'No, as I said I can't remember,' repeated Mr Walker.

'Do you know a Mr Michael Forbes?' asked Richard, now standing in front of the witness box.

'Only from what I read in the papers,' he replied.

'And what's that?' asked Richard, looking directly at Mr Walker.

'Well, you know he's loaded, drives nice cars, has a huge mansion with a pool, a Jacuzzi, pulls the best birds, seems like he's doing alright for himself,' he replied.

'Do you know how he got his money?' asked Richard.

Mr Walker was about to say something when Mr Chevron stood up.

'Objection Your Honour, I cannot see the reason for asking that kind of question. Mr Forbes' wealth is not a crime.'

'Maybe not, but we must know all relevant information Mr Chevron. This line of questioning is relevant I presume Mr Thorn?' inquired the judge.

'Yes it is Your Honour,' replied Richard.

'Then please continue.'

'Thank you, Your Honour.' As my learned colleague has pointed out Mr Forbes' wealth is not an issue here, but I'm just curious about certain things.' Richard was pacing up and down in front of the witness box.

'Like what?' asked Mr Walker in a rather sharp tone.

'Well for instance, when the police raided your home, they found that you have vast amount of electrical goods in your flat, you also have a wardrobe full of designer clothes. Now as I said, wealth is not a crime, but for a wealthy man to have such luxuries it's ok, obviously he has the money, but for an unemployed man who gets just forty four pounds a week social benefit it seems rather odd that you can afford the things that you have.'

'So what,' said Mr Walker, sternly. 'It's not a crime to have a few nice things in your house is it?'

'No, you're quite right Mr Walker, but you do have rather more than a few things,' suggested Richard.

'So what, jealous are we?' he asked.

'Indeed I am,' replied Richard, walking to his briefcase and taking out a piece of paper.

'Now taking into account that you have a small one bedroom flat, you seemed to have amassed quite a few belongings. Let's see, according to the police report you have four television sets, three state of the art video recorders, two camcorders and one tripod, one home computer with all the extras, two very powerful hi-fi systems and two microwave ovens. Don't you think three would have suited you better?' Richard looked up from his paper at Mr Walker. You could see that Mr Walker was about to say something sarcastic, when Richard carried on.

'Now Mr Walker, as well as having numerous electrical goods, you also have new carpets throughout your flat, new furniture, three piece suites, bed and cooker.' Richard was about to continue, when Mr Walker spoke.

'So what I've a few nice things, what can I say, I like to feel comfortable.' Mr Walker had a big smile on his face as he was talking to Richard.

'Oh please Mr Walker, you may act like you own half of England, but your income clearly states that you cannot afford the things that you have. Now as well as having a nice home you have a nice new car,' stated Richard.

'Look like I said, I like nice things, there's nothing wrong in that,' argued Mr Walker.

'There is when you have no evidence of how you paid for them,' suggested Richard.

'I lost all of my receipts, didn't I,' said Mr Walker grinning stupidly at Richard.

Richard paused for a split second and then spoke again.

'When the police forensics were taking your clothing from the flat, they noticed that you had a lot of designer clothes; one policeman went as far as to say: "he has more clothes than my wife".' There was slight giggle around the courtroom. Mr Walker just sat there looking at his barrister.

'Now, you also use small quantities of soft drugs, have you used cocaine or heroin?' Richard was looking towards the jury.

'Tried coke once, but didn't like it so I stopped taking it. Stuck to smoking spliffs instead,' he replied.

'You mean cannabis?' asked Richard.

'Yeah course, most people do it don't they?' suggested Mr Walker.

Richard was shaking his head, and then he said:

'No, I'm afraid they do not.'

'Well, all I can say is that you lead a boring life,' suggested Mr Walker.

'Why's that?' asked Richard raising his eyebrows.

'Well, you've got to have a smoke and a laugh or you'll go mad,' he replied.

'I may well be boring Mr Walker, so may the rest of this courtroom, but most people as far as I know don't see the point of taking drugs, no matter how small the quantity. As far I see it, a drug is a drug. Ok you could argue that some drugs are stronger than others, but it's still a drug nevertheless.' Richard was now standing beside him.

Sarah meanwhile had slipped into a world of her own again, she was thinking about some of the things that Richard had asked Mr Walker.

Fancy having all that stuff in one flat she thought. You wouldn't be able to move around very well. She looked across at Mr Forbes, who looked as though he was about to be sick. Wanker, thought Sarah, I bet he bought all that stuff for him, paying him off for a job well done. Ah, never met him my arse, liar, you know Forbes probably had him as a henchman or something like that, makes you laugh it does. Why can't they let me kill them slowly and painfully? I'll even clean up the mess once I've done the job. Sarah continued thinking of all the nasty painful things that she could do to both of them.

'Yeah, well whatever you say,' said Mr Walker, arrogantly and rolling his eyes.

'I'm not saying that a young gentleman shouldn't have a nice house. I'm just saying that for an unemployed man you seem to have acquired a lot of expensive things,' argued Richard.

'I got them while I was working,' he responded.

Richard walked back to his table and fetched a piece of paper out of his briefcase.

'We'll skip that particular line of questioning for now. Instead, may I read you a copy of your statement?'

Mr Walker looked at his brief and Mr Forbes. 'If you want,' he said.

Richard said quite sternly, 'Now in your statement to the police, you said that at the time that victim was raped you were at the local cinema with your girlfriend. Is that correct?'

'Yes,' answered Mr Walker, looking at his barrister once again.

'At what time was that?' asked Richard.

'Well, I can't really remember,' said Mr Walker looking slightly agitated.

'Oh come now Mr Walker, we're talking rape; it carries a sentence from anything to five years to life in prison. Now, I must state that it is not my job to say whether you're guilty or not guilty, that's for the jury to decide. But I must give them the facts the same as Mr Chevron has to give clear and precise facts, for your own sake you must try and remember,' suggested Richard.

'Ok. Ok,' said Mr Walker, interrupting Richard.

'Look, as I said I couldn't remember the name of the film, because I never saw that much of it, but I think that it was one of those Steven Segal films.'

'And what time was that?' asked Richard.

'I dunno, about two fifteen.'

'Mr Walker, I know that you weren't at the cinema, because nobody there can remember you being there on that day. They can vouch that you go there on a regular basis, but you did not go on that particular day, did you?' Mr Walker was about to speak, when Richard carried on.

'And we would all like to know, how you came to be at the cinema with Miss Woodfield, when Miss Woodfield was across the other side of town at the same time as you were both in the cinema. So basically she went to work in the morning, went to the pictures, came back had her lunch and then went back to work. That's some woman,' said Richard.

There was a slight chuckle around the courtroom.

'Ok. Mr Walker. Look, you say that Mrs Phillips must have been cheating on her husband and got found out. In fact your exact words were: "If the truth was known the bitch was probably screwing somebody else behind her husband's back and got found out by someone." Can you explain what you meant by that?'

'I dunno, she was probably up to no good and got found out and tried to stitch me up for something that I didn't do,' said Mr Walker pointing at Sarah. Sarah hadn't noticed she was still in a world of her own. If she had noticed, she might have got into trouble by saying a few choice words.

'Look, why on earth would a woman who never knew you try and fit you up?' asked Richard.

'Because, that's what bitches like her are like. They go out pork some rich geezer get found out, blame some poor sod who happens to be minding his own business!' shouted Mr Walker, loudly and making Sarah jump. Richard was about to ask another question, but the judge spoke instead.

'Mr Walker, would you please calm down. You are not in the pub on a Friday night. If you do not wish to calm down, I have a very nice cell with your name on it. Now any more outbursts like that and you shall find that cell quicker than you think,' stated the judge, in a stern voice and looking down at Mr Walker. 'And would council please approach the bench.'

Both Richard and Mr Chevron did as the judge asked. After a bit of mumbling and whispering, they both came back to their tables and sat down.

The judge was talking to one of the ushers as Richard was just about to tell Sarah what the judge had said, when the usher spoke.

'Court is adjourned until one week from today, all rise.' Everyone stood up and the judge left.

People were talking as the guards took the two men down to the cells. The courtroom started to empty, Sarah was asking Richard why the judge had come to this decision. David meanwhile was saying goodbye to Sarah's friends. Sarah's sister and father said that they were going too. The children kissed their father and mother and told them, they loved them and then left.

Richard was telling Sarah why the judge said what he had said.

'Well, the judge wanted everyone back early next week, but I said I needed to check some things out, so he gave me a week.' Richard closed his briefcase and picked it up.

'Plus, his daughter's getting married soon,' began Richard.

'Look, don't worry, there's nothing wrong, I just want to double check on a few things.' Sarah sighed and then said ok, as she and Richard followed David and Helen out of the courtroom. They got to the car park just as her father, sister and Jamey were driving away. Sarah thanked Richard, so did David. And they both said goodbye to Helen and Richard and then left.

'Well, what do you think?' asked Helen, looking thoughtfully at Richard, who was putting the briefcase into his car.

'I don't know, I must say that she's a strong woman. Most women would have probably given up by now, but she's different,' said Richard.

'I think she's wonderful. At first when she came to my sessions, I thought, God why on earth are they bothering. They don't want to see justice done; they just want someone to do the work for them, but now after what three, four sessions, I think yeah, she might just go all the way and give them what they really deserve. I think that her husband really loves her even if sometimes she doesn't think so,' Helen said.

'How are the sessions going?' asked Richard.

'Not too bad, at first she wouldn't speak and then when she did, she didn't want to stop,' replied Helen.

'Anything useful you can tell me?'

'Yes, but I'll tell you on one condition,' Helen smiled.

'What's that?' Richard raised his eyebrows.

'Well, I'll tell you what I can about her over dinner tonight at my place.' Before Richard could answer, Helen continued.

'Seven thirty ok. Jolly good, see you then bye.' Helen walked towards her car.

Richard just stood there for a few seconds with his mouth open. He watched Helen drive away as he got into his car.

'Suppose I had plans, suppose I had a date, suppose nothing,' said Richard looking at himself in the mirror. He then started his car. 'Date my foot, you would have gone home got changed eaten a microwave dinner and watched something boring on TV.' He smiled to himself as he drove away.

Meanwhile, Sarah and David had gone for a walk in the park before they went home. David took a good deep breath then let it back out.

'God, smell that lovely fresh air.'

'Yes, lovely,' Sarah said pulling her husband towards an ice cream van that had just pulled up in the park. David with some persistence from his wife bought two ice creams and they made their way to a bench by the pond and sat down.

'God, we haven't done this in …' said Sarah.

'Blimey, years,' interrupted David.

'David, can I ask you a question?' Sarah asked as she leaned on his shoulder.

David put his arms around Sarah's shoulder. 'You can ask me anything you want darling.'

'Are we really that boring?'

'What do you mean, boring?' asked David.

'Well, you know the other day in Helen's office, when she asked us if we did anything apart from work and we both said no.'

'Yeah, but we have to work to pay the bills,' replied David

'Yeah maybe, but apart from the mortgage, we don't really have any debt as such,' suggested Sarah.

'That's true, I suppose. Don't tell me that you want to buy a five hundred foot yacht?' giggled David.

'No, don't be silly,' laughed Sarah.

You know, it's funny in the last few months Sarah and her family haven't had much to smile about. But here they are, on a rather mild afternoon talking and laughing as though everything in the world was ok – no court case, no rapists and no chance of catching HIV. For that particular moment they were happy.

They stood up and stated walking over towards the car.

'I was just thinking of something we could do together as a family,' wondered Sarah.

'There are lots of things we can do together as a family.' David unlocked the car door. Sarah shivered, she hadn't realised that it was getting cold.

'Like what?' she asked switching on the heater as David drove down the road.

'Well, there's, err… well let's see, we could, err…' stumbled David.

'See you can't think of anything can you?' Sarah smiled slightly.

'You know to be honest, I can't.' David pulled on to the drive of their house.

'We'll just have think of something,' said his wife, getting out of the car and heading for the front door.

'I think that we might have some rain soon,' David said as he looked up at the sky.

His wife was already in the house; he locked the car door and went inside.

'Well, we'll have to think of something,' said his wife, turning on the central heating.

'We will?' David took off his shoes in the hallway and checked the answering machine.

'Anybody called?' shouted Sarah.

'No,' replied David.

Sarah made a small buffet for her and her husband, sandwiches, biscuits, crisps and chocolate. David put the telly on.

'God, this bloody Gulf war, it wouldn't be so bad but they put it on every channel!' shouted Sarah.

'Yeah, true, we should consider satellite,' suggested David taking a bite of his sandwich.

'We'll have to find out more about it first,' replied his wife, pouring her husband a cup of tea. David and Sarah finished eating and drinking and settled down to watch the news.

Meanwhile, Richard was just pulling up outside Helen's house; he had brought some wine and some flowers. Helen opened the door to Richard, she smiled and took the wine and flowers from Richard and kissed him on the cheek.

'Anything, I can do?' he asked.

'No, everything's done. Oh, you can pour the wine if you like.'

Richard poured the wine into two glasses that Helen had laid out on the table, and took his jacket off and sat down. Helen came in from the kitchen and put out two plates on the table, and went back in to the kitchen. She came back out with a trolley and served the food and sat down.

'Well, what were you going to tell me?' Richard was trying to talk and eat a mouthful of food at the same time.

'Well I was going to suggest that you put David on the stand, before you put Sarah back on the stand,' suggested Helen.

'I thought of that myself, but I don't think that he'll go for it.'

'No, he probably won't, but I think that a few white lies won't hurt them or do them any harm,' suggested Helen.

'Now come on, what's the real reason behind it?' asked Richard.

'The case is going pretty well so far, but I think if you put David on the stand it will keep the ball well and truly in your court. Plus, if you play your cards right you can sway the jury on to your side. You've never lost a case yet and I don't think that you'll lose this one, but remember this is the first time that you and Mr Chevron, or stone face as some people call him, have been in court together, and he has never lost a case yet either, so he's going to play hard ball as well as you are,' Helen said as she ate some food.

'I know and I must be careful, he's been in the business a lot longer than I have, so he knows all the pitfalls, but I still get the feeling that there's something that you're not telling me.'

'Ok,' said Helen, finishing the last of her food. 'Sarah's has been having nightmares.'

'What do you mean nightmares?' asked Richard.

'I don't know, I don't know the full story, but she has violent nightmares,' began Helen. Richard could not believe that Sarah hadn't mentioned any of this to him, she usually told him everything.

'She's had three up till now. I think that it's three anyway. Apparently she wakes up screaming, shaking and sweating. I'm planning to have sessions alone with her husband, he might be able to shed some light on what's happening,' suggested Helen.

'Well, when you've found out what's happening let me know, I might be able to use this in court. Oh and get him to take her to her local GP, so we have it on record that she's been,' stated Richard.

Richard asked Helen, if she wanted a hand with the washing up. She said plainly that all she wanted to do was hump his brains out; Richard smiled and took Helen upstairs into the bedroom.

The next morning, David woke up at about seven thirty; he lay there looking at his wife who was still asleep.

My God, thought David, she looks so peaceful, I wonder what she's dreaming about. Whatever it is she seems to be enjoying herself.'

Sarah moaned and stretched and opened her eyes.

'It's weird watching people wake up first thing in the morning,' he chuckled to himself. Sarah woke up to find her husband looking at her.

'What's wrong?' she said looking as though she was still half asleep.

'Nothing, I was just wondering what you were dreaming about.'

'You wouldn't believe me if I told you,' she said sitting up.

'We'll, see,' said David.

'Ok. I was thinking about life.'

'What about life?' asked David.

'Well, how many people does it take to make a pair of shoes?' asked Sarah.

'Good question. I know it takes a lot of people to make one building,' laughed David.

'How many?' asked Sarah cuddling up to her husband.

'Well, for instance,' said David, running his fingers through his wife's hair. 'The building which they use for training young people in the town centre.'

'Yes.'

'Well, let's see that took four architects to draw and plan it out. Then you have the builders, at least thirty-five of them doing the basic building work. Then you have the engineers, at least fifteen of them, the plasterers, labourers, welders, electrician, plumbers and decorators, and the list goes on.'

'Such as shoes, people who work for next to nothing make most shoes,' said Sarah.

'Most buildings are worked out on computers.'

Yeah, but I don't think that you can beat traditional handmade things,' suggested Sarah.

'Maybe, but we must all move with the times.' David started to get out of bed.

'Why don't we stop in bed?' suggested Sarah.

Her husband said, 'Ok.'

Sarah cuddled up to her husband once again. For a while they just lay there, Sarah began rubbing her hand up and down David's thighs. She then began rubbing his cock up and down. She looked at her husband's face and knew that he was enjoying what his wife was doing. She went under the sheets and started kissing his chest, getting lower until she finally had his cock in her mouth. David was moaning in ecstasy as his wife began sucking harder and faster, David wriggled about in excitement. Sarah came up from under the sheets and started kissing her husband. David was rubbing his hand in between her legs. They were both getting excited; all of a sudden David stopped and sat up.

'What's up?' panted his wife.

'I'm sorry, I can't do it,' replied David.

'Why not?'

David sighed deeply.

'I love you, you know that don't you?' His wife nodded in approval.

'I'm just worried, that's all. Suppose you do have Aids or the Aids virus, would you really want me to take that much of a risk?' Sarah knew that her husband was right, even though she really wanted him, she knew deep down that she couldn't.

'Like the doctor said, you have to wait for the results of your blood test. Nobody likes sex more than I do, but we must be realistic. I hope and pray that you don't have it but we must assume the worst,' said David.

Sarah noticed that her husband had tears in his eyes. It was very rare Sarah saw this side of David in all the years they had been married.

David had tears rolling down his cheeks; he seemed to be crying for nearly an hour. Sarah was holding her husband and thought to herself, God, I must have been really selfish these last few months. She was thinking of all the arguments that she had caused all of them basically over nothing.

David eventually stopped crying, Sarah was still too deep in thought to notice, as David moved his wife jumped slightly.

'Sorry, I was miles away,' she said. She noticed that her husband paid no attention to what she had just said; she knew that he must have heard her; after all they were only a few feet away from each other.

Oh God, she thought, perhaps, he thinks that I wasn't listening to what he was saying, but she was she was listening more than ever before.

Her husband meanwhile had gone into the bathroom. She leapt out of bed and went into the bathroom. David was in the shower.

'I'm sorry, I'm really, really sorry. I had no idea that you felt this way and I was listening to what you said earlier,' said Sarah.

David opened the shower door.

'I'm sorry too, I just don't want them getting away with it,' he replied. Sarah got into the shower with her husband and cuddled him.

'You've still got your nightie on.'

'So,' said Sarah kissing her husband. 'I don't care what happens from now on, as long as we're together,' said Sarah as David squeezed his wife tightly.

'How did you manage to get so tough?' asked David.

'Well, let's just say that in the last couple of months, I've had to get tough and now I intend to stay that way,' replied Sarah. David and Sarah both had a shower together and then got dressed.

'What time is it?' asked David.

'Nearly twelve thirty!' shouted his wife from the bedroom. David came into the bedroom.

'Twelve thirty, are you sure?'

'Don't worry; it won't kill you or me to sleep in when we can,' said Sarah. David was watching his wife brush her hair; Sarah noticed in the mirror that he was watching her.

'What is it?' she asked, looking her husband through the mirror.

'I don't know, you just sound determined all of a sudden,' replied David.

'Oh, I am believe me, I am.' They both went downstairs.

'What do you want for breakfast?' he asked.

'I'll tell you exactly what I want,' she said, grabbing her husband and hugging from behind.

'What's that?' asked David.

'Well, I want to go shopping and spend like it's the last days of shopping,' said Sarah.

'The way that you use a credit card, it probably will be,' he said, laughing loudly.

'Cheeky,' she replied poking him in the back with her finger and making him jump.

'Well, where do you want to go shopping?'

'I want to go right into the middle of the town centre,' suggested Sarah.

'Are you sure that you are up to it?'

'I'm up to climbing Mount Everest at this moment in time,' stated Sarah.

'OK then let's go,' said David, feeling slightly apprehensive and picking up his car keys. Sarah was first to the door.

'We should get an alarm for this place. What do you think?' Sarah was out of the door and waiting by the car, before David had a chance to reply.

God, I hope she knows what she's doing, thought David, walking to the car and opening the door.

'Don't worry, I'll behave myself. I'll be a good girl.' They pulled up on to a town centre car park and stopped.

Sarah took a deep breath then said:

'Right, let's go. Oh shit, I forgot my weapon.'

'What weapon?' asked David.

'My credit card,' she said, reaching for her purse which she had previously left on the back seat.

'Don't look so nervous,' she put her hand on his knee. 'I'm not out to injure anybody that says something nasty to me, not yet anyway.' David chuckled to himself as he got out of the car.

This is going to be one long afternoon, he thought to himself.

As they strolled around town, they kept noticing that different people were looking at them and whispering to each other. Sarah made a point of making people notice them, she would purposely push people out of the way, then smile and apologise.

'What is the matter with you today?' smirked David.

'Nothing, I'm just enjoying myself,' she laughed, pushing open a shop door.

'Let's go in here,' she said, practically pulling her husband into the shop.

Sarah had decided without telling her husband that she wanted something to eat. Personally, I think that he really had no say in the matter, but still, they both found a table and sat down. David was feeling a little bit insecure, because he could feel people watching them. He looked at his wife, who didn't seem to care less who was watching them. After some persuading, a young waitress came over and took their order, they waited patiently for her to come back with their order. Eventually, she returned looking a bit more relaxed.

David and Sarah started their meal. Sarah after a while noticed that one particular woman kept looking up from her paper, every now and then and looking directly at her. After the woman had been looking at Sarah for about ten minutes, Sarah surprised her husband by excusing herself and taking herself and the rest of her food over to this woman's table and sitting down.

Everyone looked at her as she strolled across the floor with a plate in her hand. David thought, any minute now, she's going to dump the plate of food over her head. But she didn't, instead she sat down and calmly started eating. Everyone looked on curiously including David. Realising that his wife was in complete control of herself, he continued to eat his meal. He thought it funny that the whole place seemed to concentrating on what his wife was going to do.

Sarah meanwhile was asking the woman what she found fascinating about her and her husband; Sarah never gave the woman chance to reply, before she continued.

'Yeah, I know, she said, boldly. 'You watched me and my husband walk in here sit down and you think, my God you've got some balls haven't you? Strolling in as if you own the joint, and sitting down as if you're lady shit. Yeah, I know exactly what you're thinking. Huh, dumb bitch probably got what was coming to her, serves her right anyway.' Sarah was still eating as she spoke to this woman and still not giving her much chance to speak.

'Since my fake ordeal, you know people leave a shop when I enter, so called friends cross the road when they see me, people talk about you behind your back, make snide remarks to you and say nasty horrible things to your kids,' continued Sarah.

The woman was again about to speak, when Sarah carried on.

'You know the kind of things that you would kill for without question, things like your mom's a lying cow, she's a no good bitch, I hope your house burns down with you all in it.' Sarah smiled sarcastically at the woman, and then ate some more of her food.

'So what derogatory remark would you like to throw at my family and me? Oh and if you can't think of any, I've written down a few choice ones that a girl said to me once outside my shop. Let's put it this way, if I left out the swear words there would not be much left to say, and don't let the fact, that I might have Aids deter you from eating in this fine establishment again,' she said, smiling sarcastically, once again.

'I take it that you've finished whinging,' said the woman, yawning and looking as though she was falling asleep listening to Sarah ramble on.

'I don't want to interrupt you, if you have anything else to say. You can carry on if you wish, I don't mind, err… but don't take it funny if I fall asleep.' Sarah looked at the woman; she couldn't believe how bold this woman was.

'Don't let me interrupt your food,' said the woman as she sat up.

'My name is Mrs Thompson, but you call me Louise seeing as though we're such good friends. Now, it's my turn to tell you a story.' Sarah looked at this woman in amazement. I mean most women would be speechless by now, Sarah was also curious; she knew the name had a familiar ring to it but she could not place it.

'Anyway, there once was a couple who fell madly in love with each other. Love was great, sex was out of this world, but the problem was, he was black and she was white. But despite the obvious differences they loved each other all the same. Anyway one day the inevitable happened, she got pregnant, would you believe it, not only did she disgrace her family by going out with a black man she got pregnant by him. Personally,' said the woman, leaning forward slightly, 'I think that she had no moral standards.' Sarah just kept looking at this woman in disbelief.

'So the scandal ripped through the town like a hot knife through butter. Anyway, the scandal grew and grew until it reached boiling point. This woman also had her car pinched and burnt to a cinder, she had windows smashed while her and her boyfriend slept in bed, and when they went out they were burgled. Brilliant,' said this woman, getting, slightly excited. 'Anyway, the time came and their child was due to arrive into the world. His family was at the hospital giving them help and support, but her family, decided that they were too busy to come. Hectic lifestyle and all that,' she said, shaking her head and raising an eyebrow.

'Anyway, this couple had their child. A little girl seven pound two ounces, and so the happy couple eventually left the hospital with their new bundle of joy. They were both very happy. They returned home to find that someone had broken into their home, not to burgle it again but wreck it, someone had sprayed racist remarks all over the walls. I won't tell you what was said, it would only distress you. So anyway, this couple basically got on with life as best as possible until a few months later something else happened.

'One night the mother came downstairs in the middle of the night because the child was restless, she put the child down on the floor and went back upstairs to fetch her bottle, which she had forgotten. Whilst she was upstairs, she heard a loud smash and then a loud explosion, both her and her husband ran downstairs, but the room where the baby was in was already ablaze, the little tyke had no chance. Look, to cut a long story short,' said the woman, sighing deeply, she had tears slowly rolling down her cheeks.

'The child died, the parents lived but were never the same, and the bastards, who did it, never got caught, but still, life goes on as they say in the films. I think it's all bullshit, but still, what do I know.'

Sarah could tell that the woman was on about herself, even though she never said so. She looked at her watch.

'God is that the time, I must go or I'll be late for my appointment, I'll leave you the paper that I was looking at. Remember this,' she said, walking past Sarah and putting her hand on her shoulder. 'Life is like the sky, wherever you go there it is, you can never get away from it and whether it rains, snows or the wind blows heavy remember that life goes on. See ya,' she said tapping Sarah on the shoulder, as she left.

Sarah just sat there for few seconds stunned. She thought about what this woman had said and realised that what this woman said was true. Life does go on no matter what, come rain or shine, there's life larger than ever. Sarah hadn't noticed that her husband was sitting in front of her. He was reading the paper that the woman had left for Sarah; he had a big grin on his face as he read the paper.

'What are you grinning about?' asked his wife, who had eventually noticed that her husband was sitting in front of her. David never heard his wife call him; he was too engrossed in the paper he was reading. Sarah tapped the table making her husband jump, slightly.

'For God's sake woman, what are you trying to do, give me a seizure?'

'Never mind that, what are you reading that's so important?' asked Sarah.

David quickly bundled up the paper and said:

'Come on, we must go, you pay the bill.'

Sarah was trying to ask her husband what was so important that he had to rush out like that; she went to the counter to pay the bill.

'Oh the management said that your bill is on the house,' said the woman at the till. The woman looked at her.

'I think you're really brave,' said the young woman, who served them earlier, when they first came in.

'I wouldn't take any notice of the papers, if I were you; they just talk rubbish, and anyway, make sure they get what they deserve.'

Sarah was already going after her husband by then. David headed straight for the car park and was sitting in the car, when his wife arrived.

'What on earth's the matter?' asked Sarah, getting into the car and shutting the door.

David handed his wife the paper, the headline read:

Local estate agent trying to con millionaire out of fortune. Local businesswoman Sarah Phillips has accused local businessman Michael Forbes of raping her.

She claims that in February, Mr Forbes and Mr Ronald Walker raped her. Mr Forbes has at least a dozen well-respected members of the medical profession, that will swear to his whereabouts at the time of the alleged attack. Mr Forbes claims that some months before Mrs Phillips wanted to buy the house that he was living in at the time. When he said no two or three times she threatened to go to the papers, telling them what a fraud he was and that she would make up lies about him, so in the end, he unwillingly decided to sell. It was the only way to get her off my back claims Mr Forbes. Mr Forbes also claims that Mrs Phillips conned him out of a large sum of money, he declined to say how much.

The other alleged rapist Mr Ronald Walker said, that he was at the local cinema with his girlfriend and friend. He claims that Mrs Phillips was cheating on her husband and got found out by someone, and then she cries rape. Mr

Forbes and Mr Walker are currently on remand. Please we would like to know what you, the general public think.

If you have any comments or can help in any way, please call us on freephone. 0500 456456. Thomas Ford reporting for the Daily News.

'Now you know why I hurried out of the restaurant just in case you got upset, who could blame you after reading that crap? God, the things they print to sell newspapers.' David was already driving home as his wife read the article in the paper.

'Well, they don't paint a pretty picture, do they?' she sighed deeply.

'Sorry,' said her husband, pulling on to the drive and stopping the car.

'Whatever for?' asked Sarah.

'For you having to read garbage like that,' replied David. 'Oh come on, with all that's happened to us you can't tell me that you didn't expect something like this to be printed in the papers.'

'I know that I was expecting it. I mean, I am trying to get one of the richest men in our town life in prison. It was only a matter of time, before they printed something like this, and anyway, they can't hurt us any more than we've been hurt already can they?' she said, getting out of the car.

Sarah heard the phone ringing and rushed into the house to answer it.

'Hello.'

'Hi Sarah, it's me Richard.'

'Oh, hi Richard, I take it that you've read the article in the paper?'

'Yes, I did, and quite blunt it was too,' said Richard.

'Oh I don't know, it could have been worse. I picked up the paper this morning, but I never looked at it.'

'It seems as though you're taking this better than I am.' Richard sounded slightly relieved, he was expecting the same as David was, for Sarah to throw a fit and start swearing, but she didn't.

'Are you alright?'

'Yeah, of course I am. Why do you ask?' asked Sarah.

'Well, you know in light of what the paper said you should be pulling your hair out by now.' He could not believe how calm Sarah sounded. She may have sounded calm, she may even act calm, but her insides were churning over with rage. Just because she didn't show it on the surface doesn't mean it wasn't there.

'I know, normally I'd be smashing things up by now, swearing, cursing the whole nine yards, but I had a good think about it this morning and I just thought fuck the lot of them. I've done my crying, well for now anyway. I've done the feeling sorry for myself bit. There's no more slagging my family off. I would still like to kill them, if I could get away with it, but I have to face facts. I'll just have to settle for a very long prison sentence for them both,' stated Sarah.

'Well, I'm speechless,' said Richard.

'That may well be, just as long as you're not speechless in court.'

'Oh don't worry,' stated Richard.

'Are you alright?' she could hear someone being silly, on the other end of the phone.

'Yes, of course I am,' giggled Richard, 'I've got a young adolescent female, who can't control herself, I think I'll have to get the handcuffs out, if she doesn't behave herself.'

'You wouldn't dare,' said Helen, in the background.

'I bet he would!' shouted Sarah. Richard was still giggling, as he was saying goodbye to Sarah.

'Oh, by the way, Helen wants to see David on his own tomorrow if that's alright?' asked Richard.

'Yes, ok I'll tell him, bye.' They both said goodbye and put the phone down.

'They're mad, the pair of them,' she said, smiling to herself.

'Who was that?' asked David.

'Oh just Richard asking about the article in the paper, he seemed more stressed out about it than I was, but as I told him, they couldn't do any more damage to us can they?' stated Sarah.

'No, I suppose not.'

'Oh by the way, Helen wants to see you on your own tomorrow.'

I wonder what for, thought David.

They sat there cuddling on the settee and talked, David started to laugh.

'What's the matter?' asked Sarah.

'Well, when I saw you get up and walk across to that woman's table, I felt for sure that you we're going to crack the plate over her head, I couldn't believe it, when you sat down and carried on eating.'

'Neither could anyone else, I bet,' laughed Sarah.

'What did she say? I can guess what you told her.'

'I was quite polite actually.' Sarah thought about the story that the woman had told her. She thought, should I tell him or not, in the end she decided not to, she just smiled and said, 'Let's put it this way, she gave me a good kick up the backside, you know, I think I learned something from that woman today.'

David, for a few seconds pestered his wife for more information, but she just said no. He decided in the end that she was not going to tell him, so he changed the subject.

'You know what I think?' said Sarah.

'No, what?' asked her husband, talking off his shoes.

'I think we should decorate the house from top to bottom, you know, cheer the place up a bit, add a bit of colour to the place,' suggested Sarah.

'Well, I have thought about decorating, but never really that seriously,' said David.

'Really, you've never mentioned it.'

'I know, like I said I never thought about it seriously,' he repeated.

'Well, when you thought about it, what colours did you think of?' asked Sarah.

'Well, I like blue, green those types of colours.'

'Green,' laughed his wife. 'Nobody, who needs cheering up has green.'

'Excuse me, I happen to like green, I do have a green car, after all,' smiled David.

'Yes, well that says it all doesn't it,' laughed Sarah.

'Ok Mrs red car driver, what colours would you like to have?'

'Not green that's for sure.' She was still giggling furiously. Because she was laughing so much, she could not say the words properly.

'Well, I don't care, I like green, millions of people like green,' argued David.

'Yes, well, I suppose they do,' replied his wife, trying her best to calm down, she was not giggling so much as before, but she was still giggling.

David asked her, if she wanted a cup of coffee, she nodded.

'Yes, I don't know about green and she burst out laughing again. David chuckled to himself, as he walked into the kitchen. He knew that it would be a good ten minutes, before his wife calmed down, he didn't really mind, he enjoyed listening to his wife laugh.

By the time David had made the drinks, his wife had calmed down; she had put the telly on. David put the drinks down, and the phone rang.

'I'll get it,' he said, going into the hallway.

'Hello? Oh, hi, look I've told you not to call me here, yes I know you like me, but you shouldn't call me here, she might suspect something.'

Sarah was curious as to whom her husband was talking to.

'Sarah, it's for you, and he handed his wife the phone.

'And tell her to stop stalking me, as well,' stated David.

'Hello?' said Sarah, waiting in anticipation to find out who it was.

'Hi, it's only me,' said her sister, laughing. 'I'm going to kill that husband of yours, one day.'

'Not unless I get to him first,' smirked Sarah. David could hear his wife laughing.

'See!' she shouted, 'Nobody with any sense has green.' Sarah was too busy talking to hear what her husband had said back to her.

'I've just read the paper, what lying bastards, how can they print rubbish like that and get away with it?' asked Susan.

'Yeah I know, but as I told Richard earlier, I knew that this might happen.'

'Maybe you did, but it's still not very nice.'

'Now come on. I'm trying to convict one of the richest people around this town, you can't expect with all the people he knows that he wouldn't eventually do something like this,' stated Sarah.

'True, but it still pisses me off,' replied Susan.

'How's Lucy?' asked Sarah.

'Lucy, Lucy, I'm sure I know that name from somewhere. I'm pretty sure that she's my niece, but I can't be sure. Spend time with your auntie they said, Yeah right, you know sis in the past two weeks I've had her twice, maybe three times. Apart from that, Dad's had them the rest of the time.'

'Hey, has Jamie gone back yet?' asked Sarah.

'No, he goes back tomorrow, I was going to drive him, but he wants to catch the train with his mates. I think he's got a girlfriend as I overheard him talking to someone on the phone the other night.'

'Perhaps, it was one of his friends,' suggested Sarah.

'Well cricky, if that's the way he talks to his mates, we'll have to be careful, he doesn't like boys,' laughed Susan.

'I don't think he will, he likes the girls too much, it's that blond hair and deep blue eyes that does it.'

'I don't mind what he does as long as he's careful doing it,' added Susan.

'He'll be alright, he's a pretty sensible young man, I'm sure he'll be fine.'

'Anyway, how are you Sarah?'

'Oh, me, I'm alright I suppose, it's a case of having to be, I guess.' She paused slightly before she spoke. 'David was crying this morning.'

'Well, come on tell me, what funny thing did he do?' asked Susan.

'No, I mean really crying.'

'Why?'

'Oh I don't know. It just seemed like all these months, all that's gone on has finally caught up with him, and he just couldn't take any more. I couldn't believe it, he cried non-stop for over an hour,' replied Sarah.

'Well, it's about time he showed some emotions,' suggested Susan.

'He does show his emotions, he's just not one for crying that's all, I mean, not all men cry, well they say they don't, but you know they do.'

'Yeah, I know what you mean. Robert used to do it all the time, we'd watch a real tear jerker, then he'd swear blind that he's got something stuck in his eye, but you know darn well that he was just crying, I can't see the problem myself,' said Susan.

'Me neither, I guess some men feel threatened by the fact that other men might find out that they like a good cry. Anyway, a good cry never hurt anybody;

we girls do it all the time, so why can't the boys do it as well. I must say though it was a bit strange seeing a man cry that very rarely sheds a tear,' said Sarah.

'I think that's nice really. Shows he's human, anyway, it also shows that you can't bottle things up inside for too long either.'

'Any news from the doctor's yet sis?'

'No, I won't get the results for a few more weeks yet; I must say that this really and truly scares the shit out of me.'

'Hey now come on, the results are going to come back negative,' said Susan.

'I hope so, I really do hope so, anyway I'm going now, when you do see that son and daughter of mine give them a kiss and tell them we love them and miss them.'

'Ok. I will do,' said Susan. They both said goodbye and put the phone down. Sarah sighed, took a deep breath and went back in to the living room.

'How's your sister?' asked David as his wife entered the room.

'She's alright. She was just saying she hasn't seen Lucy for a while though.'

'Don't tell me, let me guess, your father's had them, I want to ask you something,' said David.

'Go on then,' said his wife, 'you know you can ask me anything.'

'Why was it your father never married again or had another woman?' Sarah had never told David much about her father's personal life; I suppose she thought that he wasn't really interested.

'Well after my mum died, he tried dating, but once they saw the car, the house, the photos lying around, they wanted his money. But they probably thought that he had another woman, he even tried a dating agency once,' she smiled. 'They got it wrong and set him up with a girl younger than me, believe me, he was not a happy man.'

David noticed a distant look in his wife's eyes.

'Look, I know what you're thinking,' he said, looking at his wife and holding her hand.

'What have you progressed to reading minds now?' smiled Sarah.

'No, not quite, but I do know my wife well enough to know when something is wrong,' suggested David.

'Well, go on then, take a guess and let's see if you're right.'

'Ok, you're thinking about those doctor's results, aren't you?'

'Sorry, you're right; I just can't stop thinking about the results.' Sarah started to cry.

'I know I should try not to think about them, but I just can't help it.'

David put his arm around his wife.

'Look, let me tell you something. One: none of this is your fault, none of it. Two: those results are going to come back negative you'll see,' said David hopefully.

'You know, I have this recurring dream, I'm running down a dark tunnel, it seems endless this tunnel, but I soldier on and I keep running. After sometime I see this light, this big bright light. As I see this light, I run faster than ever before, but the more I run the further it goes away from me and so on. Every now and then, when I think I'm finally catching up with it, I fall over or get out of breath. I know that people say that there's light at the end of the tunnel, and it's true, there is light at the end of my tunnel,' said his wife, still crying in her husband's arms.

'I just can't reach mine. I just can't reach mine.' David just sat there listening to his wife crying. He felt completely helpless.

Sarah had eventually stopped crying. She still sat there in her husband's arms for a while. David told Sarah that it was getting late and that they should go to bed, his wife agreed, so they went to bed.

The next morning, David awoke to find that his wife had had another nightmare. David cuddled her, as she was crying and panting for breath, he kept telling her that everything would be ok. His wife seemed to calm down a lot quicker this time, she kissed her husband and thanked him; she then got out of bed and headed for the bathroom.

David shouted and asked his wife if she wanted him to stay at home today instead of going to see Helen.

'Don't be silly!' shouted his wife, sounding a lot more like her normal self.

'You know what she's like; she'd probably come and fetch you,' laughed Sarah coming out of the bathroom.

'You know, I think that she probably would,' replied David finally getting out of bed. As he walked past his wife, she grabbed him and kissed him.

'I love you, do you know that?' she said.

'I should hope so; after all I'm charming, well mannered, good looking and rich.'

'Rich' said his wife, interrupting him. 'You've got no money, you're as charming as a bullfrog and you have all the good looks of a man being sick after a night out with the lads,' smiled Sarah.

'Oh thanks,' he said, rolling his eyes.

'Don't sulk, I'm only joking.'

'If I was a car, what kind of car would I be?' asked David.

'You would have to be a sports car.'

'Why's that?' he asked.

'Well because you're smooth, quick off the mark and most people like you,' said Sarah. David smiled and headed for the bathroom. 'Hey, what kind of car would I be then?' she asked as she sat in front of mirror to brush her hair.

'Well, let me see,' said her husband, standing behind her. 'You would have to be a sexy sports car, because you're nicely put together, you curve in all the right places, and like certain sports car, you only get one owner.' David kissed the top of her head and headed for the bathroom. Sarah smiled to herself, as she brushed her hair.

She felt really lucky to have a man like David to help her through these troubled times. I'm lucky, she thought, some people don't have anyone, so I guess I am lucky. Sarah left her husband in the bathroom and went downstairs and put the television on.

'God, not the bloody Gulf war again, why don't they send in the SAS to just nail him?' said Sarah out loud.

'Because,' said her husband coming into the room. 'There's a little thing called a world war, and I'm pretty sure you or anybody else wouldn't want one of those.'

'No, I guess not,' said his wife, going into the kitchen. 'Do you want any breakfast?'

'No thanks, I'll try and grab something while I'm out. What you got planned today?' he asked.

'I thought that I'd pop into the office see if everything's ok,' suggested Sarah.

'That's a good idea, it might do you good to get out on your own for a while,' said David, trying his best to listen to his wife and the TV at the same time.

'What time's my appointment for?' he asked.

'I don't know, Richard didn't say,' replied his wife, coming back into the living room with a cup of coffee.

'I suppose, she wants me to go the same time as normal then,' added David, not noticing that his wife had come back into the living room. Sarah jumped slightly.

'What are you trying to do, give me a heart attack?'

'Sorry,' replied her husband, chuckling slightly. 'I never heard you come in.'

'Don't worry, no harm done.' Sarah sat down.

'Are you going to be alright on your own?' asked David.

'Yes, I told you don't fuss, I'll be alright, like I said, I'm only popping into the office. I'll phone Dad as well, see if he's alright.'

'Ok,' said her husband as he gives her a kiss. He grabbed his wife's car keys and said goodbye.

He got into her car started the engine and started chuckling to himself, as he was looking across at his car. He was remembering what his wife had said about his green car; he pulled off the drive and drove away.

There was not much traffic on the road, so David reached Helen's office in no time at all. Helen and her secretary were talking as David came out the lift.

'Morning,' said Helen and her secretary to David.

'Morning,' replied David. Helen told him to go straight into the office, and that she would join him in a minute. David went into the office and took his jacket off and sat down. He looked around the office, he was thinking about Sarah when Helen walked in.

'You wouldn't think that you have to sign so many papers on a Friday morning, it will be at least Wednesday before I can use that hand again,' she said smiling.

'Believe me, I know the feeling,' replied David, raising his eyebrows and remembering the paper that he's had to do in the past.

'So how are you and Sarah?' enquired Helen.

'Ok, I suppose,' he replied looking down at the floor.

'Ok, let's cut out the bullshit, I know what you think about being here, I know that you feel stupid and you think to yourself, "why am I here?"'

'I used to,' said David cutting into the conversation. 'I'll be honest, I do feel a little bit apprehensive, but you must remember, I've never ever had to use a shrink in my life for any reason, so yes, I suppose I do feel a bit stupid sitting here telling you my deepest secrets. I've had my fair share of stress, but I've always learned how to cope with it, but this is something that's got me from all angles, every way I turn I hit a brick wall.'

'The quicker women come to terms with the fact that rape is never their fault, the quicker we can see justice done,' announced Helen. 'Yes ok, I know you read the papers and they don't paint a pretty picture.'

'I take it you read the paper then?' asked David.

'Yes, I did,' she sighed deeply looking at him shaking her head.

'The papers have a way in cases like this of making the victim seem like the guilty party, and when you go to court, well let's just say that you need all the will power that you can muster, and if you don't have enough, borrow some off somebody else.'

'These things are never anybody's fault. Rape is just like any other disease, you know drunk drivers, people get plastered and they kill someone in a car; the same for people who take drugs then kill a whole bunch of innocent school children; people who murder people who burgle other people houses, the list is endless. The point is, it's not your fault and it's not your wife's fault. It's not anybody's fault but the brainless idiots, who most of the time on the spur of the moment decide to do these mindless things.' David looked at Helen as she spoke.

'But, why do I feel so damn useless?' asked David.

'You will and scared, angry, hatred and pity and if you could get your hands on the two men that did this to your wife, what would you do to them?'

'I'd kill them without question,' stated David.

'So you would kill the two men right? So you would be so preoccupied with killing the two men that you would completely forget about your wife. You would then be arrested, go to court then go to prison for life, therefore leaving your wife on her own to cope,' suggested Helen getting up and heading for the kettle. She asked David if he wanted a coffee, he nodded yes.

'You are in a really fortunate position,' suggested Helen.

'How on earth do you work that out?' said David raising his voice slightly.

'Well,' said Helen, handing David his coffee and sitting back down. 'Your wife has a lot of people around her to help her. She has her sister, her dad and her children. Most of the courtroom was filled with her friends and then there's you. She has all those things behind her, but she has you her husband right at her side.'

'Some use I am,' suggested David.

'You see, there you go again putting yourself down. Ok let's put it this way.' She followed David as he got up a walked towards the window, do you love your wife?'

'That's a stupid question,' frowned David. 'Of course I do.'

This was hard for David, he wasn't one for talking about how he felt, he'd say if he was feeling ill or had a headache, or if he was hungry, things like that, but he could never really talk about his emotions, not even to his wife, even though he had started to recently.

'With all my heart,' replied David, picturing his wife in his head, as he looked out of the window.

'Right, now do you think that she's innocent or guilty?' asked Helen.

'Oh, come on that's a daft question.'

'I know it is.' She looked at David, who by this time had turned round and was leaning against the windowsill.

'I think she's innocent. No, there again, I know she's innocent without question, I know it,' said David, walking across the room and sitting back down. 'I know the wankers that did it are as guilty as sin, but it's just proving it,' he said.

'Now, you've just hit the nail on the head. It's just proving it,' said Helen.

'Let me tell you something, when something like this happens, you go through the whole thing step by step, you question everything, you say things like. If only I was with her, why didn't she call me? God, I'd like to get my hands

157

on them. But the fact of the matter is, that you were not with her, she didn't call you and you really deep down, don't want to spend the next twenty years of your life in prison, do you?'

'No, I suppose not,' he sighed.

'Nobody asks to be raped or bullied or molested or beaten up. This is the society that we live in, instead of pointing the blame we should find a solution, find a cure if you like, we should find out why people choose to do these things. Do you realise that thousands of women are raped every year, it's just that most cases are never reported and the ones that are reported, only a handful of them will ever see the inside of a courtroom, it's sad but it's true,' stated Helen.

'Can I ask you something?' said David looking oddly at Helen.

'Yes, of course you can, that's what I'm here for.'

'Well, how did you cope when you were raped?' he asked.

'Well for a start, I never had anyone on my side, not even my own mother believed me, then when my sister killed herself and all those things came to light, it was too late. The only comforting thing was that my stepfather would never come out of prison, and I don't talk to my family any more.'

'Did you ever get over it?' asked David.

'Well, yes and no. I think that I got over being raped, but I don't think that I got over the loss of my sister.' Helen got up and fetched the picture of a young girl from her desk and handed it to David.

'That's my sister, that's Judy.' Helen smiled as she talked about her sister, she had fond memories of Judy.

'She's a very pretty girl,' said David, handing back the picture.

'How old was she then?'

'Fourteen,' Helen replied.

'And how old were you?' asked David.

'I was about nine, I think,' she paused for a moment. 'Yes, I was nine.'

'So that means you're about …'

'Yes, well never mind that,' said Helen, stopping David before he said any more. David smiled to himself.

'Did you ever have nightmares?' he asked.

'Sometimes, as far as what people tell me, I just used to stare into space, I wouldn't really do anything. Then when my sister died, I just shut myself off completely from everybody. I was at school at the time she died, when everything came to light, I was then put in to foster care, and then adopted. I think now, I can say that I got over being raped. Well I say got over it, I've learned to live with it, I think in some ways it made me a stronger person.'

'Why do you say that?' asked David.

158

'Well, for one thing, I wouldn't have become a solicitor, or started running this place, I think if I hadn't been raped. I wouldn't be the person I am today, and then I wouldn't be able to help people like yourself. Anyway, enough about me tell me more about Sarah's nightmares,' suggested Helen.

'Well,' sighed David, 'She's had four so far, each time she ends up waking up screaming my name. Like the other night for instance, she went to bed before me, so when I eventually went to bed, she was lying in an awkward position, so rather than try and move her and wake her up, I put as much duvet over her as best I could and jumped into my son's bed. I woke up in the morning to hear her screaming my name. I ran into the bedroom and there she was sitting up in bed screaming my name.

'She was sweating, she was blood red, she was screaming that much, she was crying. I didn't know what the hell to do, so I just put my arms around her and gently told her to calm down. All she kept saying was don't leave and she kept saying it for a good five minutes. I sat there for over an hour, just holding her and listening to her cry.'

'Has she had any more since then?' asked Helen.

David paused for a moment.

'She had one this morning funnily enough, but this wasn't half as bad as the others.'

Helen as always was taking notes, as they spoke.

'I don't know what to do for the best,' said David.

'If you want my honest opinion, there's really not much that you can do at the minute for her, all you can really do is be strong and be patient and be your loving self. I know that it's hard, but until she comes to terms with what happened to her, I'm afraid it's a waiting game from now on. I'll give a small piece of advice,' she said, still writing things down. 'The quicker she can get this case wrapped up, the better for her and the quicker you can try and get things back to normal, you do know that you might be called as a witness,' stated Helen.

'Me, what can I tell them?' he asked sitting up sharply. 'I wasn't there, so how can I help her?'

'You are joking, right,' said Helen, putting her note pad down on the table in front of her. 'You're probably the best witness there is, in fact, you're probably in a better position than Richard and he's prosecuting for her,' suggested Helen.

'Why do you say that?'

'Well, for a start you live with her, you sleep with her, you have two children with her, God's sake. You are the one who could really make a difference in this case, because don't forget, old stone face Chevron hasn't even began to tear into your wife yet, by the time he's finished with her that article in the paper will seem quite tame. Mr Chevron has never lost a case, and believe me

159

I don't think he's going to let this one go without a fight.' David was about to speak, when Helen carried on.

'I'm not having a go at you personally, but I've been doing this long enough, I've seen women who say that they will go all the way, then back out at the last minute. Some of them even get to the last day of the trial, and then suddenly tell the judge that it was all a lie. You must understand that it's a hard road and only the best will make it to the end.'

'Well, I still don't think that I will really be much use, but if it helps my wife then I'll do it,' replied David.

'What I normally tell people who come to see me after this conversation is to go home and think it over and so on, but you and Sarah are different. I think if I said that to you, you might feel that I was taking the piss out of you and I don't want you to think that,' said Helen picking up her notepad again.

'No, I wouldn't think that, I'd just suppose that you were saying it to help us, after all, we can only say what is on our minds or what the problem is, you have to do the rest,' said David.

Helen told David that unfortunately his time was up.

'Right, I won't be seeing you for a while because of the court hearing,' stated Helen.

David told her that it was ok and if she wanted to come to the house for any reason, she could. Helen walked David to the lift and said goodbye.

David got into the car feeling quite pleased that he had got certain things off his chest. He felt relieved in a way as he decided to get something to eat. He wondered what his wife was doing.

His wife had gone to see how things were going at her office. As she walked through the door, she noticed a banner that was hanging up over the secretary's desk, the banner read: *Good luck Sarah and don't let them get away with it*, in big bold letters. Also on the secretary's desk was a notepad with names on it. Sarah picked it up, it was filled with pages and pages of names and addresses of people, who had signed it wishing her all the best with the trial. As she was reading it her secretary came out.

'That's the third book,' said her secretary. 'And each one is full, we were saving them until the trial was over.' Sarah had tears in her eyes.

'Thank you.' She had tears trickling down her cheeks as she read some of the things that some of the people had written.

Just then someone shouted from one of the offices at the back. It was Susan, Sarah's partner.

'What's happened to my coffee and the file which I asked for?' Sarah was still reading the pages in the book, she never heard Susan shouting.

The secretary noticed that Sarah hadn't heard Susan.

'I'm with an important client at the moment, you'll have to fetch them yourself,' she giggled to herself. She knew that Susan would be over the moon to see Sarah, so she kind of wanted to surprise her.

'What do you mean come and get them myself?' She banged her knee off her desk, as she got up in such a hurry to find out who this client was. She was moaning and rubbing her knee as she came out, she saw Sarah standing there, reading the writing pad full of names. Sarah had stopped crying by this time, but she still had tears in her eyes. She never knew that so many people who didn't even know her, men and women had written in it. She was as amazed that they were all on her side.

'Sarah,' said Susan, limping slightly towards Sarah. Sarah turned round.

'What happened to you?' asked Sarah, looking at Susan, who was trying to walk and rub her knee at the same time. She put her arms out and cuddled Sarah, who was also walking towards her. The secretary was still giggling.

'Remember this, revenge is sweet,' said Susan. Sarah was also giggling.

'You as well, traitors the pair of you,' said Susan.

'I've been telling you for ages now to get a new desk,' said Sarah, watching Susan rub her knee once again.

'I will one day,' she smiled.

'Yeah, when you've got no knee left,' said the secretary still giggling.

'And plus, you've laddered your tights.'

'Shit,' said Susan, looking down at the laddered tights. 'I've got no more either.'

'Don't worry,' said their secretary, 'I have to nip out anyway, I'll pick up a pair on my way back.'

Susan still had a little pain in her knee but it would pass, it always did.

'What are you doing here?' asked Susan, going back into her office, closely followed by Sarah.

'I just wanted to get out of the house for a bit.' Susan was taking off her laddered tights, as Sarah was talking.

'Will you look at that,' said Susan showing Sarah the hole in her tights. 'Are you and David, alright?'

'Yeah, fine. Well you know, as well as we can be under the circumstances,' said Sarah.

Just then, the secretary came back in and handed Susan a new pair of tights.

'Thanks.' She ripped open the box and took them out; as she was putting them on she asked the secretary if she could still have her coffee and one for Sarah too.

'David and I are ok. I keep picking fights with him though for no apparent reason, I don't mean to, but I just can't help it,' said Sarah. The secretary came in and put the two cups of coffee on Susan's desk.

'I'm sure that he understands,' said Susan putting her old tights in the bin and putting her shoes back on. Susan had a small two seater settee in her office, she picked up her cup of coffee and sat down on the settee.

'What you should do is what I do with my boyfriend, tell him that you feel like having a whinge, but you're just moaning in general, you're not moaning at him personally. Believe me, it works every time,' she said, smiling and taking a sip of her coffee. Sarah had finished wiping her make-up off her face.

'I'll try that,' said Sarah.

'What about the doctor's results? I know that you don't want to think about it, but you must face the fact that you may be HIV positive,' asked Susan.

Sarah put her head in her hands and sighed.

'I know, that's all I think about, I tell people I'm alright, but really all I want to do is just scream my lungs out. I've been having nightmares, which I just can't seem to stop having. The other morning I completely forgot that I might have Aids, and I was all set to ride the shit out of David like never before. Then just as I'd started to boil, he pulled away from me. I can't say that I blame him really,' she said, finally drinking her coffee, which by now was lukewarm.

'I know that what you're going through is a terrible thing, and yes, as sad as it seems, you may have Aids.' Susan was about to continue, when Sarah started to cry.

'I didn't ask for this, I didn't ask to be raped. I didn't really. I didn't and I don't want Aids. I want my life back the way that it was. I want to go to work, go home and play with my children, go to bed and fuck the hell out of my husband, I can't even do that now, can I?' cried Sarah. Susan had got up and had put Sarah's head, against her chest. It hurt to see her friend like this, knowing damn well that there was really nothing she could do for her.

'Stop this, in all the years I've known you, you've never let anything or anyone beat you, or get you down. Just think of this as another hurdle that you have to get over, and if I know you like I think I do, you will send those wankers to hell and get on with your life,' said Susan. Sarah eventually stopped crying. She thanked Susan and dried her eyes.

'I know when they get you back on the stand that you will not be acting, but I'd really and truly go right over the top and play on the jury's emotions. We know what your saying will be true, but they won't so really play on it. I know if it were me, they would give me an Oscar for my performance, by the time I'd finish with them, they'd die in prison. I'd make sure that they would never get out to do this to anyone again,' said Susan sitting back down. 'I know it's hard, and unless you've been through the same thing, no one could understand how you feel, and the thought of having Aids, well let's say it's more than a slap in the face, but like I said if you give up they get away scotch free.'

Sarah was still drying her eyes.

'I know you're right' Sarah said, 'but it still hurts, I just can't control my actions, I can be nice one minute and a bitch the next.'

'So can I, and I'm not in your position, it's just part of being a woman. Tell me that when you have a period every month, you don't get a little bit nasty. It's not really our fault, it's just nature's way that's all,' said Susan.

Sarah sighed, 'I could do with a helping hand at the minute. Nature may just be the thing to help.' After a while, Sarah felt and looked more like her normal self.

'So anyway, how's business?'

'Don't start with that rubbish,' said Susan.

'What rubbish is that?' asked Sarah, rolling her eyes and looking around the room.

'That coming back to work rubbish, I know that's what you're thinking.'

'Well, it would give me something to do,' suggested Sarah.

'Yes maybe it would, but you're in no physical or emotional state to come back to work, besides, nobody wants you back at work until you've won the trial,' she smiled.

'Really, you all think I'm going to win?' asked Sarah.

'Oh come on, you've seen the support that you've got, you've read some of the things that people have wrote about you. Most of them do not even know you, yet still they wish you the best of luck.' Susan looked thoughtfully at Sarah.

'You have more support behind you than you realise,' stated Susan.

Just then the secretary came in.

'Here's the file that you wanted Susan.' As she walked back towards the door, she turned round to Sarah and said, 'When we first asked people to sign the pad we didn't think they would, but we said to them, what if it was your wife or your daughter, or in our case our best friend, but anyway they signed, and now, we have all those books for you, three and a half. Look, it wasn't your fault and they should not get away with it.' She smiled and went back to her desk.

'You see, we all feel the same,' said Susan. Sarah smiled thoughtfully, she was glad that she had so many people behind her. She looked at the clock on the wall. 'It's getting late; David will start to wonder where I am.'

'No thoughts of coming back to work until after the trial,' suggested Susan.

Sarah nodded and said ok. Sarah kissed Susan on the cheek, gave her a hug and said goodbye. She also thanked Jane her secretary on the way out, who wished her good luck as she left. Sarah drove home, when she got there David was still out. As she went in, she checked the answering machine and took her coat off. She heard the message her father and children had left on it and she rang her father.

'Hi Dad, it's me.'

'Oh, hi Sarah, I've been trying to reach you all morning. I just wanted to see if my baby was alright.'

Sarah chuckled, 'I'm over thirty now Dad.'

'I don't care; you and Sandra even when you're fifty will still be my little girls.'

'You're mad, you are,' implied Sarah.

'You have to be slightly mad to cope in this day and age.'

'Dad, can I ask you a question?'

'Yeah sure, you can ask me anything you know that, you always have, go on what do you want to know?'

'Well, how did you cope when Mum died?' asked Sarah.

'I don't know really, when your mum died I thought, well what's the point in living, why carry on? I gave up on everything even you and your sister. You stayed with your aunt for months, until I could slowly try and pull myself back together,' said Bob.

'But how do you pull yourself together?' asked Sarah.

'I don't know really. In my case, I just put all my focus on my two children and then slowly but surely, I pulled myself back together. It's like you find a spot way down in the pit of your stomach where you stick all your problems. All your hate, all your emotions and then you find some way through it all. If you have a passion to do something no matter what people tell you, you will always do what you feel is right, no matter how odd or how, replied Bob.

'But suppose, I make the wrong decision?'

'Well whatever you do, it must be right for you. As long as you're happy, then you know that you've made the right choice,' suggested Bob.

'But, I might have Aids?' she said in a soft voice.

'And you may go outside tomorrow and get hit by a bus. The point is that you never know what's around the corner, you just have to take each day as it comes,' said Bob.

'I know I do, but Dad this is Aids, I could die within a few years,' said Sarah, pausing for a brief moment before she spoke.

'When your mother was diagnosed I blamed everything and everybody, I thought the daffiest of things. Things like, it must have been my fault, I must have been a really naughty child, or the best one is I'm being punished for something I did in a previous life, but I had to except the fact that it was none of those things, in a sense, I'm glad it happened,' replied Bob.

'Oh, why's that?' asked Sarah.

'Well, I really loved your mother, and if she was alive today, I'd still be the happiest man in the world, but your mother's death changed my life, it changed me emotionally, mentally and physically. I'd never felt that kind of pain before, but I decided that I was going to start enjoying my life. Don't get me wrong, if your mum were alive I'd have her to enjoy my life with, but, I thought she wouldn't want me moping around the house, she'd want me to go out and enjoy life. So I've done the house up, I bought a car that gets me from naught to sixty in less time than it takes to actually get in it and start the engine. But, I will say this, I can never really love anyone as much as I love your mother. I've had the odd relationship here and there, but it doesn't last. It's sad I know, but I can't find anybody who I want settle down with,' replied Bob.

'That's not sad, I think that's sweet.'

'Anyway, here's me rambling on when your children want to talk to you.' Sarah could hear her children in the background asking their granddad if they could talk to her.

'Ok, one at a time, Lucy you go first,' suggested Bob.

'Hi Mum,' said a little voice on the other end of the phone. 'I miss you.'

'I know sweetheart, I miss you too, but your father and I have something that we need to sort out,' said Sarah.

'But, I miss you,' said Lucy, starting to cry. It hurt Sarah to hear her daughter cry, especially when she wasn't there to hug her. She just had to try not to cry herself, which was hard. But all she could do was tell Lucy that everything would be ok. Sarah convinced her daughter to stop crying and to try and be a big girl for her mother and father. Lucy was still sniffling slightly when Sarah asked Lucy to put her brother on the phone.

'Hi Mum, are you alright?' asked Jason.

Funny thing about Jason, he always acted as if nothing bothered him, even though Sarah had caught him crying in his bedroom a lot in the past couple of months. He'd just say that he had a nightmare but his mother knew the real reason for his tears.

'Yes, I'm fine.' She knew that he was upset as well as Lucy, but he rarely cried in front of his sister. As I said, the hardest part was not being able to hug her children.

'You're going to have to be strong and look after Lucy, ok. You're a big boy now and she needs her big brother to look after her,' suggested Sarah.

'Ok. Mum,' said Jason; feeling slightly chuffed, at what his mother had said. Sarah told him that she loved him and asked him to put Lucy back on.

'Hi Mum,' said Lucy, in a soft voice again.

'You be a big girl for Mummy and Daddy, ok?' asked Sarah. Lucy said ok. Sarah also told Lucy that she loved her and that she would see her soon. Lucy handed the phone back to her granddad.

'Don't worry, life has a way of sorting itself out and try not to worry about the kids, Lucy's going back to Sandra's later. I'll ask her to have chat with Lucy, and like I said, whatever you decide, I know that you'll make the right decision,' said Bob.

Sarah told her father, how much she loved him and then he said the same. They both said goodbye. As she put the phone down, her husband opened the front door.

'Hi, what on earth have you been doing?' asked Sarah looking at her husband, who had an armful of stuff.

'Oh hi ya,' said David, just managing to give his wife a kiss. 'I've done a bit of shopping,' he replied.

'A bit, it looks like you've brought the whole shop back with you,' laughed Sarah.

'There's some more in the car.' David headed for the kitchen. Sarah went out to the car and started to unpack the boot of the car. David had come out and taken some more shopping in to the house. His wife shut the boot and took some shopping in herself. David came back out for the last of the shopping, he put the last of the shopping down as he went into the kitchen.

'You look worn out.' Sarah put her arms around her husband.

'Yeah, I am a bit,' replied David.

'How was your visit with Helen?' asked Sarah.

'Ok. I think, yeah, I think I got a huge weight off my mind,' implied David.

'Why don't you go and sit down put your feet up, I'll put the shopping away and make us a nice cup of coffee,' said his wife, kissing him on the cheek.

'Ok,' said David, as he headed for the living room and he put the telly on. He took his coat off, hung it up in the hallway and took off his shoes and sat down. He flicked from channel to channel but there was nothing on that he wanted to watch. He was wondering what satellite would have to offer, when his wife came in from out of the kitchen and handed him his coffee and she sat down next to him on the sofa.

'I have two surprises for you,' said David.

'What are they?' asked Sarah getting excited.

'Now, come on, if I told you it wouldn't be a surprise now would it?' suggested David.

'Maybe, but tell me anyway,' begged Sarah.

'I don't think so, anyway the one is being delivered tomorrow and the other is coming next Wednesday,' stated David.

Sarah knew that her husband wasn't going to tell her what the surprises were so she changed the subject.

'So do you feel better after talking to Helen?'

'Yeah, I do. I must admit she does make a lot of sense,' replied David. 'Oh yeah, Richard wants me to take the stand,' said David as he sipped some of his coffee.

'Whatever for?' asked Sarah, sitting up and looking at her husband.

'Well, he basically feels that we need some good luck on our side, basically we need to keep the ball well and truly in our court,' said David. 'What do you think?'

'Well, I think that Mr Chevron hasn't really showed us his true self yet, and if his questioning matches his cold hard looking face, I think that we'll be in for a tough time. But still, I believe Richard knows what he's doing, he's done well up to now hasn't he?' suggested Sarah.

'I suppose so,' said David.

'I mean, you never see Mr Chevron smile, but there again, you never really see him make an expression of any kind, he always has that same look,' suggested Sarah.

'I wonder what his wife thinks of him.'

'You never know, he's probably different when he's at home with his family. Remember, he's only doing a job,' stated David.

Sarah had no love for the man, after all he was trying to set free the two men that raped her, but still maybe her husband had a point.

'So how was your day?' asked David.

'My day, well let's put it this way I have come to a lot of decisions,' said Sarah finishing the last of her coffee and cuddling up to her husband.

'That sounds promising,' said David.

'You know, I thought just recently that the whole world was against me, but when I left the office today, I had a different point of view,' began Sarah.

'How come?' asked David.

'Well in the office they've put up this huge banner wishing me good luck. People who don't know me have come in and signed good wishes in a book, well writing pads actually, they've got three full pads and another that's halfway there. Until I read them, I never believed that so many people were on our side.' She smiled as she remembered some of the kind things that some of the people had written.

'It was the same as when I went shopping, people who I never knew were asking me all sorts of things. The main thing people said was, don't let them get away with it, if they walk free they may do it to somebody else. I must admit I felt like a celebrity,' said David.

'God, I bet you did, no wonder your heads swelling, would you like some ice to put on it?' smiled Sarah.

'Ha, ha, very funny, you wait until tomorrow when your surprise comes,' suggested David.

'I phoned Dad earlier,' Sarah said.

'How is he?' asked David.

'Oh you know he's always alright, I wanted to know how he coped when my Mum died.'

'Why on earth did you ask him that?' asked David.

'Well as far as I remember, he really went through the grinder when my Mum was diagnosed, he blamed himself for letting it happen,' said Sarah.

'I know what he means, I kind of blame myself for what happened to you,' stated David.

'Really,' said Sarah, sitting up and looking oddly at her husband. 'Why on earth do you blame yourself?'

'Well, you know if I had been there with you, it wouldn't have happened. If your car hadn't broken down, if you hadn't walked down that alleyway on your own, if …'

'If nothing,' interrupted Sarah quickly. 'If you were there I wouldn't have taken my car so I would not have had to walk through the ally, and if you had caught them at the time you would still be in prison waiting to be sent to prison for life, fat lot of good you'd have been to the kids and me then. None of this was your fault and none of this was my fault either, it was the fault of two brainless idiots.

'Anyway, my father said that after a while he managed to pull himself together. Eventually, he knew that he had to get on with his life, that's what my mum would have wanted by the sound of things, so that's what he did, and even though he hasn't got another woman, he seems happier than ever. The kids seemed upset though.'

'I know that's why this thing that's coming next week should take their minds off things for a while,' suggested David.

'I know you're not going to tell me what it is.' She rolled her eyes at David. 'The suspense is killing me already and I've got nearly another week to go yet,' said Sarah.

'If you're a good girl tomorrow, I'll tell you what it is, but I will give you a clue, your father's got one,' said David walking out the room.

His wife was thinking of all the things that her father had at his house. She couldn't think of what it was because they were talking for so long, she hadn't noticed that it was getting late, it was nearly ten thirty. David came back into the room. She told him the time, he couldn't believe that the time had passed so quickly.

'Well, it's a bit late to really have anything to eat now,' said David.

'I'm not really hungry anyway, I just want to go to bed and cuddle up to my husband.' She was pushing her husband trying to get him quickly up the stairs.

'Ok. Ok. I'm going, don't push me, I'm an old man and I have to be careful of my arthritis and my angina,' giggled David.

'I know,' replied his wife, in a sarcastic voice. 'And your bad back and your bad leg and your green car,' she giggled as she ran into the bathroom.

'If you don't be quiet about my car green car, I'll get you as many green things as I can think of!' shouted David.

'I don't think so,' replied his wife, coming out of the bathroom. She got undressed and slipped into her nightie.

'What's the matter?' Sarah noticed that her husband was looking at her and smiling.

'Well,' said David, walking over and putting his arms around her waist. 'I must say that you're a fine figure of a woman, I should call you Ferrari from now on.'

'Well, if I was that expensive you couldn't afford me,' she turned and kissed her husband.

'I know what you want, I want it as well, but we have to wait and see what the doctor says.' She kissed him again and then she got into bed. Her husband sighed and then got undressed and got into bed, Sarah cuddled up to him.

'If you could do anything in the world, what would it be?' she asked.

'What, absolutely anything?' asked David.

'Yes.'

'Well ok, but promise that you won't laugh,' stated David.

'Ok. I'll try not to,' smiled Sarah.

'I've always wanted to wear a pure white suit and referee a women's mud wrestling match.' Sarah couldn't help but laugh.

'Hey, you promised that you wouldn't laugh,' said David, giggling along with his wife.

'I Know I did, but come on a white suit in a ring full of mud, don't tell me, you would want to referee the whole match without getting mud on your suit?' giggled Sarah.

'No, give me some credit, of course I'd get dirty that would be part of the fun, but I would like to get as muddy and as dirty as possible then leave the suit to dry for a complete week to see which washing powder can get it clean,' giggled David, his wife was still laughing.

'Believe me, I do Lucy and Jason's washing and I know that there isn't a washing powder invented that would get their clothes completely clean,' laughed Sarah.

'A white suit,' giggled his wife.

'The other thing I'd like to do is get a racing driver to take me across those dirt roads in America which stretch for hundreds of miles. I'd like to get the fastest Italian sports car there is, fill her up with petrol and drive as fast as the car would let us and keep going until we run out of petrol,' said David who had a big smile on his face. He was picturing himself driving across America at tremendous speed.

'Hey, come back,' said his wife, nudging him.

'Sorry, I was imagining what it would be like.'

'If it's anything like when we've had sex, you wouldn't be able to walk after you'd finished,' Sarah laughed.

'I know, but boy would it be worth it, anyway, what would you do?' asked David.

'Well, I've always wanted to sit on a Caribbean island sipping something exotic whilst working on my tan. After that I'd like to make love under a waterfall,' she said cuddling up to her husband even more.

'Now I must say that does sound really nice, but I still prefer my ride in the Italian sports car,' smiled David.

'I don't know, you boys and your toys,' smiled Sarah. Her husband just smiled, they were both getting very tired so they both went to sleep.

The next morning, Sarah was already awake long before her husband was awake. When David got up, he came downstairs to find that his wife had already received the surprise, well the first of them anyway. She said, 'Good morning,' and gave him a big kiss. 'Thank you.'

'I take it by the opened box and ripped paper that you like the new stereo then?' asked David, sounding as though he was still half asleep.

'Yes I do, even though I have no idea what a CD interchanger is, or an analogue twin tape deck,' smiled Sarah.

'Is there anything that you do know about it?' asked her husband, going into the kitchen to make a cup of coffee.

'Yes, it's black and is six hundred and fifty-five watts,' said Sarah.

'Oh by the way, your secretary called this morning.'

'Misha, What did she want?' asked David.

'I don't know, she just asked me to ask you if you could pop into the office today. I told her that you wouldn't mind, seeing as though we were not in court today, it seems important anyway,' implied Sarah.

David came back into the living room with a cup of coffee and some toast.

'I wonder what the problem is; I'll give her a ring after breakfast.'

'Don't be silly, go down there it won't hurt you, you haven't seen them properly for weeks. Anyway it would give me a chance to try and figure this thing out,' she said looking puzzled as she looked at the stereo.

'Yeah, I guess you're right,' said David, eating his toast.

It wasn't long before Sarah had the stereo figured out.

'There should be a stand that goes with it as well,' said her husband, just finishing his toast and coffee.

'I know, it's still in the hallway, can you bring it in for me before you go out?' Her husband put his cup and plate in the kitchen, and then obliged his wife.

'God, this weighs a bit doesn't it?' said David, pulling the box into the living room.

'Yeah I know that's why I left it there for you to carry in,' chuckled his wife.

'Ha, ha very funny, anyway I'm glad that you like the hi-fi system, at least when there's nothing on television, we can always listen to some music, something nice and relaxing,' suggested David. 'Oh look, you get a free CD as well.'

She was glad that her husband bought her the stereo, the only music which they had was a small radio in the kitchen, or the radio in their cars.

'Anyway, I'm off, I'll see you later.' He got into his car and drove to his office.

Sarah meanwhile was still trying to get to grips with the new hi-fi when there was a knock at the door. It was their neighbour Paul, well I say neighbour, they only saw him about six weeks at a time because he worked away a lot. Wherever he worked around the country he always took his family. He would normally rent somewhere and then get his family to come down on the train or coach, he always kept his own house though. His friends and neighbours kept an eye on the place for him.

'Hi, come on in,' said Sarah, giving Paul a hug and a kiss as he entered the house.

'Well, I know it's a daft question, but how are you?' he asked.

'Oh, I'm alright,' replied Sarah.

'Ask a daft question, you get a daft answer,' he smiled.

'Well, let's put it this way I'm not a hundred percent alright, but I'm almost there,' said Sarah.

'What on earth are you doing?' asked Paul as he entered the living room and looking at the stereo on the floor.

'I'm trying to put this new stereo together. David bought it for me, but things aren't going as I planned,' smiled Sarah.

Paul had already taken his coat off.

'I'll tell you what, get me a screwdriver, make us a coffee and I'll have this working in no time and then you can fill me in on your court case,' suggested Paul, Sarah agreed.

Paul moved all the hi-fi equipment to the other side of the living room and Sarah brought him the screwdriver. She went and made the coffee, when she came back into the living room she put them on the coffee table.

'Cheers,' said Paul, unpacking the hi-fi unit.

She looked slightly puzzled as to why he was taking the hi-fi unit out of the box, he hadn't even done the stereo yet. I suppose he knows what he's doing she thought.

'I know, you're wondering what the hell I'm doing, well seeing as though you asked I'll tell you.' Sarah never said a word; she just nodded when he looked at her.

'Right, I've unpacked the unit,' said Paul.

'Well, I'd never have guessed that if you hadn't told me,' chuckled Sarah.

'Now, now be polite, anyway I'll tell you what the unit is for, because it's not a normal hi-fi unit. You see these little pins under each of the pieces of shelving.' Sarah looked at what Paul was showing her; in each corner of the shelving were little pins. 'Now, these pins are to stop you having any interference from your music like static and things like that.' Paul could tell that Sarah was only partly interested in what he was saying. 'Well, come on then tell me what's been happening in court.'

Sarah paused for a few seconds before answering Paul.

'Well for a start, it's been adjourned until next week.'

'How come?' he asked.

'Well, my barrister said he wanted to check things out. Well they put a police consultant on the stand, she told them what she found when she examined me after the well you know.' She never could get used to saying the word rape, and anyway who could blame her.

Paul had almost finished the hi-fi unit, he stopped to take a sip of his coffee.

'Anyway to cut a long story short, I might have Aids.'

Paul spilled some of the coffee he was drinking in his lap.

'Shit,' said Paul, standing up quickly.

'Hey, steady on,' said Sarah, also standing up, 'my coffee isn't that bad, you'll have to take them off and I'll put them in the wash.'

'Ok, but let me get a clean pair out of the house first.' He went round his house and was soon back with a clean pair of jeans on.

'You are joking right?' Paul still looked stunned at what Sarah had just told him.

'No,' replied Sarah, taking his other pair of jeans that he had just spilled the coffee on and putting them into the wash.

'Do you want a fresh cup of coffee?' she asked him.

'No, I've still got half a cup left.' Sarah came back in and sat down.

'Are you alright?' asked Sarah.

'Yeah, but Aids are you sure?' said Paul, looking worried.

'Well, it'll be a few more weeks until I get the results, so as people keep telling me, I shouldn't really worry until then, I'll only get myself into a state. Oh anyway back to work you.'

Paul was thinking of how calm Sarah was whilst she was talking about all this.

Sarah looked at Paul who still looked shocked.

'Before you ask, I've stopped feeling sorry for myself, I don't cry half as much as I used to and the only thing I can think of is not to let them get away with it,' said Sarah.

Paul had finished the cupboard.

'There you are one cupboard' he said. 'Where do you want it?' Sarah told him where she wanted him to put the unit; he drank the rest of his coffee and started to unpack the stereo. He had just finished putting it together when David came back. They both shook hands and said hello. David asked how Paul and his family were. Paul replied that they were alright, and that he was alright until Sarah told him that she might have Aids.

'Spilled my coffee and everything,' he said.

'Well, you know Sarah, she always likes to give a surprise every now and then,' suggested David.

'And boy was that a surprise,' said Paul.

'But, I don't think she's got anything anyway,' said David hopefully, trying his best to sound confident. Just then the stereo came on; it was extremely loud making everyone jump.

'Wow, yes, now that's what I call loud,' said Paul turning it down to a more reasonable level.

'That sounds better.' Sarah's ears were still ringing.

'I like that,' said David.

'You would,' smiled his wife. She was smiling because the ringing in her ears had finally stopped, Paul put on the CD that came with the hi-fi.

'This bloke is absolutely fantastic,' said Paul.

'This sounds like Kenny,' suggested David.

'How on earth did you know that?' asked Sarah.

'Easy my boss plays him in his office all the time, but as you know us hard working people don't have time to listen to music,' smiled David.

173

'Nonsense,' said Paul, laughing. 'There is always time for music and what do you mean hard working people like you. The last time I went into his office he was half asleep,' laughed Paul.

Nobody had noticed that Sarah was deep into the music. Paul looked at David and nodded, David looked at his wife. Her head was swaying from side to side to the sound of the CD. After a few minutes, she noticed that her husband and Paul were both looking at her.

'What?' smiled Sarah, looking slightly startled by the pair of them looking at her.

'Err… nothing,' said Paul, laughing. Sarah threw a cushion at him.

'Well, at least we know that you like the music.'

'It's alright,' replied Sarah, feeling slightly embarrassed.

'I don't know, dancing away like there's no tomorrow, what will the neighbours say?' smirked Paul.

'You are the neighbours,' laughed Sarah.

'Yeah, when we see him,' implied David.

'Look you two I've saved you the time and effort of ever cleaning up again,' suggested Paul.

'I wish you could,' said Sarah.

'How's that then?' asked David curiously.

'Whenever you don't want to dust just put something loud on, turn up the volume and the dust will move itself. I'll demonstrate shall I?' said Paul, smiling at Sarah.

'No thanks, that's loud enough for me thank you, and believe me there's not a hi-fi invented that could compare to the loudness of two children,' added Sarah.

'I agree,' stated David.

'Well, there you are anyway, one stereo finished,' said Paul.

'Hey, I thought you were doing that?' said David sitting on the arm of the chair.

'I was, but Paul came and offered me his services,' stated Sarah.

'I bet he did,' said her husband looking at her. David looked at Paul who was now sitting on the chair.

'I see she's told you then,' implied David.

'I just can't believe it. You read about these things all the time, but you never think that it will happen to one of your friends,' stated Paul.

'I know, but it's happened and the best thing that I can do is get on with things as best as possible, at least until the doctor's report comes back,' said David.

'Like I said, the results are going to come back negative, so there's no need to worry.'

174

His wife got up and headed for the kitchen. 'But what if they come back positive?' said his wife, pushing open the kitchen door.

'Is she alright?' whispered Paul.

'Well you know, I think she's doing well under the circumstances, if I could only get my hands on those two, I'd ...'

'You'd what?' said Paul, interrupting him. 'You'd end up in prison, that's what. I know what you'd like to do but trust me a stint in prison would change your mind believe me. I know I've been there and trust me I wouldn't want to go again.'

David and Sarah already knew that Paul had been in prison. He was a teenager at the time, he got into trouble for fighting all the time so in the end he got sent to prison for a year. David really didn't like the sound of prison very much.

Sarah popped her head round the door and asked Paul if he would like to stay for dinner.

'Yes, please, I did stop at a chip shop on the way down here. Blooming starving I was. Anyway I stopped at this chip shop, it hadn't been open long everything was half price so I ordered my favourite meal, chicken and chips. They looked mouth watering as the young man wrapped them up. I couldn't wait to get back to the car so that I could get stuck into them, I opened them up to find that the chips were like rubber and the chicken was red hot on the outside and stone cold in the middle,' said Paul.

'That sounds horrible,' said Sarah screwing up her face and going back into the kitchen.

'What did you do?' asked David getting up off the arm of the chair.

'Well, there was nothing I could do, I was already most of the way here. It would have been too much trouble to turn around and go back, so I just put them into my bin when I got here.'

'I bet you felt as sick as a dog?' said David getting the empty boxes up off the floor. 'I'd better keep these in case anything goes wrong, I'll put them into the garage.'

Paul got up and gave him a hand.

'What's the bottom line?' asked Paul going into the garage.

David sighed. 'You know it's funny, in this day and age you have to keep an open mind, but you still think that it won't happen to you, then when it does, well you've seen the results for yourself and the fact that she might have Aids, well that really is the bottom of the heap.'

'I've been at the bottom of the heap and I'm still here to talk about it, life is just like a prison,' suggested Paul.

'Why do you say that?' asked David.

'Well when you're born there's your sentence right away, but in a court in front of a judge, you hear the sentence that he is giving you. When you're born you have no idea it could be a year, five years. God, you could live until you're one hundred, but you never know what's around the corner. Most of the things that happen to people have no specific reason why they happen they just happen,' began Paul.

'I mean, you don't think that while you're out at the pictures some pratt's in your house rummaging through your stuff and taking whatever they feel like taking.

'Look in prison you either fight and stand up for yourself, or you let them walk all over you. It's the same as life in general, you can only let people take the piss out of you for so long then you draw the line. If you and Sarah give up now and if she has Aids, she wouldn't have achieved anything and them two shit heads walk clean out of court, then sell their story to the highest bidder, then that'll be all she wrote, but if she can stick to her guns then they get a nice healthy sentence.'

David smiled, 'Well, I've never heard it described quite like that before.'

'That's because you've never been to prison before, all I'm saying is I know it's hard, but things always find a way of working themselves out even if they sometimes need a hand,' suggested Paul.

'Yeah, well I hope that you're right, I really do hope that you're right.'

They finished putting the rest of the boxes into the garage.

'Why the hell do they need so many boxes for one stereo?' asked David.

'Beats me,' replied Paul, handing the last box to David.

They went back inside David sat down and began to read the manual for the hi-fi.

'Why they can't explain things in simple English, I'll never know,' said David, shaking his head as he flicked through the pages of the manual.

'Once you get past the jargon it's all pretty straight forward,' suggested Paul as he sat down.

'That's easy for you to say you've had one of these things for years,' smiled David.

Paul laughed, 'How can you design buildings when you can't even get to grips with a simple hi-fi?'

'Ah, but buildings are different,' suggested David.

'Not if you're talking to someone who doesn't understand what you're talking about,' insisted Paul.

'I agree,' said Sarah, coming out of the kitchen and back into the living room. 'He tells me things about his job all the time and as much as I like to listen,

I don't understand any of it, well saying that, I can't even program the video without having to ask him or one of the kids what to do next.'

'See and you have the cheek to talk about me.' He smiled at his wife. 'Anyway, I'll get the hang of it eventually.'

It was now evening time, Sarah had started to prepare dinner ages ago.

'Dinner should be about ten more minutes,' said Sarah looking at the clock on the wall. For ten minutes they just sat there talking about old times, eventually dinner was ready. Sarah called her husband and Paul into the kitchen to eat.

'What's up with you?' asked Sarah to her husband, who was grinning like a Cheshire cat.

'I was just thinking of that chicken that Paul had earlier,' he replied.

'I'll tell you what. It takes a hell of a lot to make me feel ill, but believe me that chicken nearly did it,' added Paul.

'I can imagine,' said David.

'I can just imagine the look on his face and his language,' said Sarah.

'Hey, I meant to ask,' said David, burning his mouth as he wasn't paying attention to how hot the food was.

'That's judgement on you for taking the mickey out of me about the chicken,' said Paul laughing.

'Don't look at me, you should have known that it was hot,' stated Sarah.

'Anyway' said David, fanning his mouth with his hand. 'I meant to ask, how come you're back here so soon? You don't usually come back this early.'

'Yeah I know, but I had a meeting with some people, and the information I needed was at my house. Yes I know before you say it, I did look and feel a pratt, but really I thought that the missus had packed it,' replied Paul.

'That's right, blame the woman,' suggested Sarah.

'No really, come on you've seen my packing,' smiled Paul.

'Yeah that's true, it's almost as bad as David's, almost but not quite,' laughed Sarah.

'Excuse me woman my packing is first rate,' exclaimed David.

'If you say so, there again, I take that back, you don't really pack, you throw what you think you need into a case and then you hope it shuts,' smiled Sarah.

'That's me, as my wife says I just screw everything up and hope for the best,' said Paul. Anyway I'm off about four in the morning, so I thought I'd come and say hello, don't think that I would have been forgiven if I didn't.'

Sarah looked, thoughtfully at Paul.

'Can I ask you a personal question?' asked Sarah finishing off her meal.

'Yeah, course you can,' said Paul.

'Well, if it hurts to talk about it, it doesn't matter, I will understand,' said Sarah.

'No, it's alright,' said Paul, smiling at Sarah.

'Well, I just wanted to ask what it was like in prison.'

'Now there's a blast from the past,' he sighed heavily.

'Well the only way to describe prison is by saying it's like another world. Don't get me wrong you're there to be punished, because you broke the law and rightly so, but prison is like death, it doesn't like anybody,' suggested Paul.

'What does that mean?' said David, looking at him.

'Well you see it works like this, let's say for argument's sake that you have five prisoners, ok.' Sarah and David nodded.

'Now, one prisoner is in for something silly like pinching cars, the next one's in for fighting, one's in for armed robbery, one after that's in for sex offences, then there's the big one, murder. Now as you see each person has a different level, you don't sentence a man for twenty years for pinching a car,' he chuckles. 'I know they should, but they don't and you don't give a man who's just killed somebody twelve months. Do you understand so far?' They both nod in agreement. 'So each prisoner has his own level, like there are people that are friendly, some will talk to you only if they have to, some just tell you what to do, and there's some that you don't talk to and they definitely don't talk to you.

'Let's put it another way, if you're walking down a corridor and you see a person who's what they class as a long-term prisoner, don't even think about moving out of his way, just move, because believe me, if he doesn't like you then by the time you think about moving, your throat's been cut and you're on the floor.'

'But why?' asked Sarah. 'If you don't bother him, he shouldn't bother you.'

Paul smiled. 'I'm afraid that it's not that simple, if he's never coming out of prison and you've only got a few months, they'll make your life a living hell, whether you want them to or not. The way they see it, that is their home and you're invading their territory. Anyway, I'm going I need to get some sleep, before I hit the road in the morning, but before I go, I'll just tell you this. When the judge told me that he was sending me down for eighteen months I said to myself, yeah no problem I can do it standing on my head. But when you get there you suddenly realise that you're not getting out of the place for eighteen months. Fair enough out of eighteen months I only did a year, but it was tough, I wouldn't like to do twenty years that's for sure.' Paul apologised and said that he really must go home and get some sleep. He thanked Sarah and David for the lovely meal. Sarah thanked him for sorting out the hi-fi, they said their goodbyes and he left.

'Do you think that I upset him?' asked Sarah going back into the living room.

'I don't think so, Paul can look after himself.'

'I hope I didn't upset him anyway. Would you like a drink?' asked Sarah.

'No thanks,' replied David.

'Well I'm going to have one.' She poured herself a small glass of brandy and sat down.

David had gone into the kitchen and put all of the crockery into the dishwasher. He came back in and sat down.

'What are you thinking about?'

'Nothing,' replied Sarah. David leaned his head to one side and looked at his wife.

'Ok. I give in, I was wondering what they did to rapists in prison.'

'Well if what Paul said is really true, then I wouldn't fancy their chances much,' implied David. 'Let's hope they get on the wrong side of somebody in there.'

'What did the office want today?' asked Sarah.

'Oh, they just wanted me to sign some papers,' replied David.

Sarah took a sip of her drink.

'If you could do anything right now, what would it be?'

'Well apart from make love to you, I don't really know,' smiled David. 'Err now let's see, I'd like to be at the world cup final, right in the V I P box being waited on hand and foot by the current Miss World.'

'My God, you don't want much do you?' smirked his wife.

'No not really, I'm just a simple man with simple needs, can I help it if I like the finer things in life?'

'And can you help it if your head's swelling,' smiled Sarah.

'Ok, your turn,' said David.

'Well, I'm glad that you asked that,' said his wife, taking another sip of her drink then putting it down on the coffee table. 'I'd like to see into the future.'

'What for?' asked David.

'Well I'd like to see how the trial ends up of course and I'd like to see how we are ten years from now, but most of all I'd like to see how Lucy and Jason grow up. I wonder what life they'll have,' suggested Sarah.

'Well for starters, they've got a good mother to show them the way so they do have a good head start,' said David proudly.

'They also have a pretty good father,' said his wife, butting in and making him smile.

'I think that whatever they choose to do they'll do their best and they will both be happy,' said David.

'I hope so, I wouldn't like to see them struggle their way through life. I'd like them to have a good education, decent job and a nice place to live and for them to be honest and decent,' said Sarah.

'We can only do what we can, they must learn things for themselves. They have to learn that life has its ups and downs and that life is never easy,' stated David.

'Tell me about it, life can be extremely unfair,' replied Sarah.

Sarah and David decided it was getting late so they went to bed.

The next few days went along with relative ease. Sarah and David went to see the children, at her sister's and then they went to see her father. Everyone they went to visit was ok. The children missed their mum and dad and wanted to come home, but they couldn't.

Chapter 5

It was now the day that they were back in court. David was first to wake up; he lay there just staring at his wife. He wondered what she was thinking about, he thought of all the things she could be dreaming about. David hadn't realised that he was talking as he was thinking.

'I'll tell you what I was thinking of,' said his wife making him jump slightly.

'Sorry, I never realised I was talking out loud, I didn't mean to wake you,' said David.

Sarah got her husband's hand and placed it gently in between her legs.

'That's what I was thinking about,' said his wife, also putting her hand in between his legs.

'If only you knew how much I wanted you,' said Sarah rubbing his cock up and down, she carried on talking even though her husband wanted to speak.

'But we can't not until we get the doctor's results anyway.' She got out of bed.

'Hey!' shouted her husband. 'What about me, I'm as stiff as a board now.'

'You've got two hands haven't you?' she replied going into the bathroom.

'Anyway, a bit of self-body exploration won't do you any harm.'

God, thought David. Has it really come down to that? I hope bloody not.

He got out of bed and headed for the bathroom, he asked his wife if she felt ok.

'I think so, but ask me again when I come out of court later.' She came out of the bathroom and got dressed. She had already made breakfast when her husband came downstairs; he was eating his breakfast when the phone rang.

'I'll get it.' She went into the hallway and picked up the phone.

It was Richard. They both said good morning, Sarah said something but Richard couldn't make out what it was.

'Are you ok?' he asked

'Yes, you caught me eating my breakfast,' she replied.

'Oh sorry, I do apologise.'

'Don't worry about it, what's up?' she asked.

'Nothing, I just wondered if you could pop into court a little bit early today and before you ask, there's nothing wrong I just want to go over a few things with you and David.'

'Yeah. Ok no problem.' They both said goodbye and put the phone down.

'Richard wants us to get there early so he can talk to us,' said Sarah going back into the kitchen.

'I wonder what he wants to talk to us about?' asked David drinking his coffee.

'Well he said that it wasn't serious anyway,' she said eating the rest of her toast.

'Let's hope not,' said David going into the living room.

'I think it's best if we go now,' suggested Sarah. 'Avoid the traffic.'

Her husband agreed, she drank her coffee and off they went.

They parked on the courthouse car park and held hands as they went in. Richard was talking to one of the guards. Sarah and David had to be searched each time that they entered the court alongside everyone else for that matter, strictly for security purposes. They walked over to Richard who had finished talking to the guard; they all said good morning as he led them into the courtroom, they were the only people in there.

'Don't look so worried David,' said Richard, noticing that David was slightly on edge.

'Sorry, it's just that curiosity is killing me.'

'Ok. I wanted to ask you how you felt about me wanting to put you on the stand?' asked Richard.

'Well I can't say that I'm not a little bit apprehensive, but I think I'll manage, anything that helps my wife is fine by me.'

'Now Sarah, I know you've been on the stand already but I really want to try and leave you until last this time,' suggested Richard. 'I want all the information out into the open, then when all that's out of the way I want you to have a good say, speak your mind if you will.'

Sarah nodded and said ok, she didn't mind.

'Now also I want to have David Stevens on the stand, you know, get as much out of him as possible.' As they were talking the courtroom was filling up behind them, her father and sister came in without the children so David went over and spoke to them. He wasn't able to talk long because the judge came in and the two prisoners were brought up the stairs to the dock. Mr Walker was about to say something nasty as he normally did when he noticed that the judge was looking at him, so he never bothered. Nobody had to stand up because they were all standing anyway. The judge asked if both Mr Chevron and Richard were ready to start, they both nodded.

'Would you like to call your first witness Mr Chevron?' asked the judge.

'Yes, Your Honour, I'd like to call Mr David Stevens.' Mr Stevens came walking down the aisle. Sarah remembered what a nice man he was when she had her interview with him. She was thinking how smart he looked in his suit, she never saw him in a suit before as he always wore a baggy jumper and jeans when she saw him. He took the oath and sat down in the witness box.

'Good morning,' said Mr Chevron, getting up and walking from behind his table. Mr Stevens smiled warmly and said the same.

'Could you please tell the court your name and your occupation please?'

'Yes certainly, my name is Doctor David Stevens and I'm a criminal psychologist.'

'And how long have you been a psychologist?' asked Mr Chevron.

Sarah meanwhile was asking David where the children were. He said that her father had let them stay with his friend until this afternoon when court finished.

That was a nice thing to do thought Sarah, the kids shouldn't be subjected to this even if everyone else has to.

'I've been a doctor for nearly eleven years,' replied Mr Stevens. His face seems to beam as he speaks, he seemed to be proud of his achievements and so he should be.

'So would you say that you are a professional in your field?'

'Err... yes, I suppose that I would,' replied Mr Stevens.

'Now is it true you interviewed Mr Forbes and Mr Walker three times, but you only interviewed Mrs Phillips once. Can you explain why that was?' asked Mr Chevron.

'Well my job is not to say if Mr Forbes or Mr Walker are guilty or if Mrs Phillips is lying. But she was the victim and they were the guilty party, at least that's the way I had to pursue the case. Oh, don't get me wrong, I have nothing personal against any of them, it's just the nature of my job, a bit like yours to a degree,' began Mr Stevens.

'Why do you say that?' asked Mr Chevron looking at him curiously.

'Well, you have to find out whether your client is innocent or guilty and I have to find out if they did do it and why they did it,' he replied.

'Do you think that they are guilty?' asked Mr Chevron.

'Objection,' said Richard standing up. 'It's not up to Mr Stevens to give a verdict.'

'I quite agree,' said the judge, looking down at him over his glasses. 'I maybe wrong, but I thought it was your job to prove whether a person is innocent or guilty not the witness.'

Mr Chevron apologised to the judge and then continued.

'I'd like to answer the question, if I may,' said Mr Stevens.

'Mr Stevens I must remind you that I'm not really allowed to let you answer that type of question, but seeing as though it may have some bearing on the case I'll allow it. But the jury must not allow this to impair their judgement on the case, is that understood?' insisted the judge.

A member of the jury stood up and agreed with the judge.

'You may continue.'

'Thank you Your Honour, you may answer the question, Mr Stevens,' stated Mr Chevron.

'Well, as I said I'm not here to pass judgement on anyone, but I think that Mr Walker is definitely guilty of something.' There were whispers in the court.

'Order,' said the judge. Richard was about to stand up when judge made a hand signal gesturing him to sit down, so he did.

'What do you mean?' Mr Chevron was leaning against the witness box.

'Well as I said, my job is to get as much information out of people as possible and ask all kinds of personal questions. When I first interviewed all three parties it was strange. I interviewed Mrs Phillips first, now considering what had actually happened to her she was very forthcoming, honest, polite and also scared and quite nervous, but she still told me things without really getting that upset. Ok she cried, but I expected that to happen.'

'And when you interviewed my clients?' Mr Chevron had now moved from the witness box and was walking up and down slowly.

'Well, Mr Forbes is a real smooth talker, he was well spoken and even though when I saw him he was unshaven, he still looked as though he could grace any establishment that he entered. He was also very arrogant, he basically said that he was proud of being arrogant; he said that you had to be arrogant to be a good businessman. I came to respect him in certain ways,' stated Mr Stevens.

'Oh, how come?' asked Mr Chevron, looking around the courtroom.

'Well for one, he's really good with numbers and he has a really good business sense and I suppose that most women would find him charming.'

Charming thought Sarah, looking across at Mr Forbes and Mr Walker. They weren't very charming when they fucking raped me, were they?

'So would you say that Mr Forbes was a respectable citizen?' he asked Mr Stevens.

'Err... well, yes I suppose that you would assume that, yes,' he replied.

'And what about Mr Walker?'

'Well, now he was quite the opposite of Mr Forbes. He was rude, arrogant and aggressive, I had to have two guards with him at all times,' stated Mr Stevens.

'Could Mr Walker's actions have been caused by the recent events?'

'Yes, they could.'

'No further questions Your Honour,' said Mr Chevron going back to his table.

Richard stood up to cross-examine the witness.

'Mr Stevens I have here a copy of your report on Mr Forbes, which I would like to read out.' Richard was holding up a piece of paper.

'This is the third interview that I have had with Mr Forbes. Mr Forbes is a very intelligent man, he can read most things quite fluently. He has a good business mind and is very good with numbers. He can also be very polite but is also very arrogant even though he doesn't think that he is.

'Do you have a girlfriend, I asked him.

'I have women if and when I need them. I asked him, what that meant. He said women are like food, when you're hungry you eat, so when I want a woman I take one. I asked Mr Forbes if he had any intentions of getting married. He said not for now, but I might in the future. I asked Mr Forbes if he had any children. He said the last thing on his mind were children.

'He basically said that he could not stand them, which took me by surprise, because he often gives a lot to children's charities. I also asked Mr Forbes if he liked getting his own way. He said that he never got his own way. I thought that it was too good to be true, so I tested him. I asked Mr Forbes if he wanted a cup of tea, he said politely that he would prefer coffee. I said no, have a cup of tea, coffee will only keep you awake. He still replied that he wanted a cup of coffee. I said look at the amount of coffee people get addicted to. He then swore and shouted that I should let him have a cup of coffee or else. Or else what I replied. But he declined to answer.

'I then asked Mr Forbes if he had ever raped anyone. He still declined to answer. I told him that when most people who decline to answer a question it usually means that they have something to hide. It could mean they are guilty of something. If they are not guilty of anything they would just answer the question without hesitation, he still declined to answer. I asked Mr Forbes if he ever killed anyone. He said no and got slightly edgy. I then asked if has had anyone killed, again he declined to answer. I also asked if he had ever hit a woman. He then replied that all women should be kept in line or they get out of hand and walk all over you.

'Mr Forbes was becoming extremely fidgety by this time. I asked him, if he was ok. He said that apart from my stupid questions, he was fine. I also asked Mr Forbes if he was a drug addict. He replied that he used them but was not an addict. I then asked if he injected himself or smoked them or did he just sniff then. He declined to answer. He began shouting and swearing and had to be restrained by one of the guards, handcuffed then taken back to his cell.

'Well I must say that it makes an interesting read,' said Richard putting the piece of paper back on to his table. 'Almost every question that you asked him concerning his being in prison, he declined to answer.'

'Could you have pressed him for more information?' asked Richard.

'Yes I could have but I thought it safe not to,' replied Mr Stevens.

'Safe, what do you mean by that?'

'Well, Mr Forbes wasn't what you would call outright violent, but from my talks with him, you could tell that he gets upset very easily.'

'What about his taking drugs?' asked Richard.

'Well he said that he used them occasionally, but he wasn't an addict.'

'That maybe,' said Richard walking back to his table and fetching another piece of paper from his briefcase.

'I have here a doctor's report, with a blood sample taken from the accused which gives you complete and utter proof that,' states Richard.

'I never knew about that,' insisted Mr Stevens.

'No I don't suppose that you did, but there again there's really no reason why you should've known. Could you tell us anything else about Mr Forbes?'

'Not really, all I can say is that he's a charming man, but I wouldn't like to see his bad side,' said Mr Stevens.

Richard had gone back to his table for yet another piece of paper.

'Now this report on Mr Ronald Walker makes Mr Forbes' report sound quite tame.' The judge was trying to find the sheet of paper that Richard had, as Richard carried on he found it much to his surprise.

'This is the third interview that I have had with Mr Walker. The third session is usually when I make out my report.

'Mr Walker is reasonably intelligent, he can read most things fairly well and without much trouble. Now even though I can handle most situations I felt safer having two prison guards present at all interviews with Mr Walker. I asked Mr Walker if he had a job. He said only stupid people have jobs. I can make more money on the dole than I can if I was working. I asked Mr Walker, why that was? He just replied that I have people that look after me, when I want them too.

'I asked Mr Walker if he had a girlfriend. He said that I have many women but no one serious. I asked Mr Walker if he planned on ever getting married. He said, only daft people get married in this day and age and I'm certainly not daft. The only time that I'd get married, is if the bitch has got plenty of money, but if she were skint, I'd give her one then dump her. I asked Mr Walker if he had any children. He replied that children are a pain in the arse and that he doesn't want any for now.

'Have you ever hit a woman? I asked Mr Walker

'Suppose so, he replied. I asked him why he hit them? He just replied that no fucking slag is going to ever rule me.' There were murmurs around the courtroom.

'Order,' stated the judge.

'I asked Mr Walker if he had ever raped anybody. He declined to answer the question. I also asked Mr Walker if he had ever murdered anybody. He replied that nobody fucks with me and gets away with it. Mr Walker has a very short temper.

'I started to ask him if he used drugs, he then lost his temper and broke the chair that he was sitting and went to hit me with a piece of it. He was shouting and swearing and was quickly restrained by the two guards. Mr Walker was shouting, the fucking guards planted the drugs in my cell. I'm no fucking druggie and you can tell that lying good for nothing bitch that she won't get away with fitting me up. Forbes and I will get her, we'll get her, he screamed as guards took him back to his cell.'

There were more murmurs around the courtroom.

'Order, order, Mr Thorn, do you really have to be so graphic?' asked the judge.

'Err… I've finished reading that now,' stated Richard.

'Thank heavens for that.' The judge looked slightly relieved.

'Well, you certainly have a tough job Mr Stevens,' said Richard walking back to his table and putting down the report that he had just read out.

'What a nice young man,' said Richard again walking in front of the jury box and then looking at Mr Chevron and his two clients.

'Just the type of person you could take home to meet your mother. So how would you sum up Mr Walker, Mr Stevens?' Richard had now moved from the jury box.

'Well, the only thing that I can say is that he would make a good bodyguard, but he would not do well as anything else,' replied Mr Stevens.

'What was that about the guards planting drugs in his cell?' asked Richard.

'Well as far as I can gather the guards do what they call spot searches, which means that they can search your cell at any given time. They chose random times and then a group of officers come and search your cell, in Walker's case they found a relatively small quantity of hard drugs,' replied Mr Stevens, whose eyes were following Richard as he walked around the courtroom.

'They fitted me up!' shouted Mr Walker standing up.

'Mr Walker one more outburst like that and I'll have you taken back to your cell, is that clear?' stated the judge. Mr Walker never answered he just sat down.

'I said is that clear?' repeated the judge. The judge's voice echoed around the courtroom. Mr Walker said 'yes' in an arrogant sort of way.

'Was Mr Walker fitted up?' asked Richard.

'I don't think that the warden would have anything like that in her prison,' replied Mr Stevens.

Her prison thought Sarah. How the hell can they have a woman prison warden? Doesn't she get scared of being around all those men? Probably not thought Sarah or she wouldn't do it. She was also thinking about what Richard had read out to the court. She sighed and looked across at Mr Forbes and Mr Walker.

How can they sit there as if nothing's wrong? How can you think that beating women up is a way of life? They sounded almost pleased that they beat women up, has society really gone that bad? Then she began to think about all the things that had happened to her in recent months. She thought about being attacked, beaten and raped and now the frightening thought that she might have Aids. She thought I know I told myself that I wouldn't think about it and that I wouldn't cry but I just can't help myself. I know that there are a lot of people worse off than me, but that doesn't help me at this moment. She glanced over again at the two men, they must be sick mentally. She hadn't really noticed but she was sobbing, she wasn't crying fully just sobbing.

'Ok. If the drugs were not planted, and they weren't his, whose were they?' asked Richard.

'I have no idea,' replied Mr Stevens

The judge called Richard and Mr Chevron to the stand.

'I think that we should break for an hour so we can have lunch, plus you Mr Chevron must have a strong word with your client. He needs to keep his self under control. And I think that your client needs a gentle word, Mr Thorn, if needs be, you may have her husband sitting beside her.'

Mr Thorn and Mr Chevron went back to their tables. Richard was about to explain what was going on, when the usher spoke.

'Court will break for one hour for lunch. Court will resume at one thirty sharp, thank you.' He then told Mr Stevens to step down and that he should return after lunch.

Sarah was thinking how quickly the time flew by. She was apologising to Richard.

'Why do you keep on doing that? I've told you before, if you break down and start crying then you start crying. I just wish that you would stop apologising for it. I've told you this before and I'll tell you again.' He sat down and held her hand. 'This trial revolves around you, if you get on the stand and start crying because you're upset, then the trial would have to be halted, it's a simple as that.

'Remember that you are the most important person in this courtroom. Well apart from the judge, anyway,' said Richard, rolling his eyes and smiling. Which in turn made Sarah giggle slightly. She still had tears in her eyes but she had stopped crying.

'When I'm talking to people and I turn and look at you I want to see the real Sarah Phillips, not a pretend one and if you're crying when I look at you, then all the better.'

Helen handed Sarah a hanky.

'From what I've heard so far,' said Helen. 'Those two men aren't worth breathing over, never mind crying over.' Sarah chuckled again.

'You've come this far,' said Richard, standing up and shutting his case. 'There's no reason, why you shouldn't go all the way. Anyway, I'm hungry and need food or I might start to wither away.' Richard and Helen went off together to have lunch.

Sandra had come and sat beside Sarah.

'God, you look a mess. You look like me on a Friday night.' Sarah smiled, she had no more tears in her eyes, but her make-up had run down her face.

'Look,' said her sister. 'You know that you're an emotional person. You've had all this shit happen to you, all your dirty washing out in public anyway, so what the hell.'

'I agree, what can people say or do that they haven't said or done already?'

'Listen, if you feel like crying, throwing a tantrum or you just want to do the funky chicken, we'll all be there for you,' added Susan.

Meanwhile, David and Bob had gone out to the drinks machine to get some hot drinks for everybody.

'You know every time I see those two I really want to punch them out,' said David as he put some coins into the machine.

'I know you do mate, but that would only make things worse, the best thing you can do for my daughter at the minute is to do exactly what you're doing,' replied Bob.

'But, I'm not really doing anything, am I Bob?'

'You're doing a lot more than you give yourself credit for,' he replied.

'Maybe you're right, but I still feel totally useless,' suggested David.

'Trust me you're doing just fine,' said Bob reassuringly.

They gathered the drinks and went back into the courtroom.

'I'd still like to punch them out,' said David smiling.

'I know, so would I, so would I,' said Bob. He walked over and put all the drinks on the table.

'We need the toilet,' said Sandra looking at Susan. 'Do we?' Susan looked baffled. 'Yeah, come to think of it, I could use the ladies.' They told Sarah they would be back in a moment and they took Bob with them as they went out.

'But, I don't need the toilet?' insisted Bob.

'Maybe not, but you're going anyway.'

When they got Bob outside the doors, they both explained what they were up to. They wanted David and his wife to have a quick chat alone.

'Are you alright?' asked David sitting beside his wife.

'Yeah, I think so,' she replied.

'What about you? I thought that I was the only one who cried.'

189

'I felt really stupid, I never even realised that I was doing it until your father told me and gave me a hanky.'

'I just knew that you wanted me by you, to hold you and comfort you, but I couldn't get to you. I was in two minds about asking the judge, if I could sit next to you. But I was afraid that he would have a go at me for interrupting the court or something like that, so I just sat there, I feel a bit of a fool now, crying in the middle of court,' said David.

'Well I think that it's sweet. It shows everyone that you care.' They held each other tightly for a while.

Sandra and her father came back into the courtroom.

'Where's Susan?' asked Sarah looking for her friend.

'Guess what, she really did need the toilet.' Sandra and her sister both laughed.

'What's so funny?'

'Nothing,' replied his wife; she had already guessed that her sister, father and best friend did not need the toilet.

Sarah said that she needed the toilet herself. Sandra asked if she wanted her to go with her, but Sarah told her that she would be ok on her own. As Sarah was walking towards the door, some people started coming back in and sitting down. She went to the toilet and came back with Susan; she looked a lot more like her normal self. The judge came in just as they did, they sat down in their places, Richard told David that he could sit by his wife, which pleased them both. He then carried on talking to Mr Stevens.

'When you interviewed Mrs Phillips, how did you find her?'

'It's strange really when I first meet her, I didn't really like her,' added Mr Stevens.

'Why not?' asked Richard.

'Well I can't say I didn't like her, more like I misunderstood her, I got the impression that even though she probably just had the worst experience of her entire life, I got the feeling that she was a fighter.' Mr Stevens looked across at Sarah.

'What do you mean a fighter?'

'Well she struck me as a bold enthusiastic person, she seemed that she could lift the spirits of anybody you know, you give her ten reasons why you should end their life there and then and she'll give you fifty reasons why you should carry on living, but she can also be really shy,' said Mr Stevens.

'To be honest Mr Stevens, I've never really heard of a bold shy person before.' Richard smiled at Mr Stevens.

'No, it's kind of hard to explain, I really and truly believe that she is naturally shy. But when she wants to be, I'm not saying all the time, she can really let her hair down and have a good time.'

'How many times did you interview her?' asked Richard.

'I interviewed her only once.'

'And how did she handle the interview?' he asked.

'Well for one thing, she's quite old fashioned, she has a young mind but old values'

'Can you explain what that means?' asked Richard interrupting him.

'Well most young women in this day and age like showing off certain parts of their body, some of them wear the most revealing clothes. Don't get me wrong, I'm not saying that they shouldn't wear what they like, that's really up to the individual, but Mrs Phillips believed in covering up. In fact she had a certain saying about it.'

'And what was that?' Richard asked Mr Stevens.

'Well we talked about different things, about shopping, clothes, movies, people she liked, anything like that. When she brought the subject up about shopping and clothes, I asked her what she likes to wear. She said anything that covers me up. I asked her what she meant. She replied that this is the nineties and most people know that babies don't come from storks, or they are not found under a gooseberry bush, just because people know what you have underneath your clothes doesn't mean that they have to see it.'

'Wouldn't you say that for the nineties that she's maybe just a little bit prudish?' asked Richard.

'Not at all, she said nobody sees me naked but my husband and even he's privileged. She laughed as she said that.'

'Let me ask you an odd question,' said Richard looking rather deep in thought. 'If you saw Mrs Phillips walking down the road and you were driving your car, would you blow your horn and slow down for a better look?'

'No I wouldn't,' replied Mr Stevens.

'Why not, she's nicely shaped, she's pretty,' replied Richard.

'Yes I know, but from behind you wouldn't really notice those things with the type of clothing that she wears.'

'So would you say that Mrs Phillips dresses very conservatively?' he asked.

'Yes, I would,' replied Mr Stevens.

'What about her temperament did you do a test on her too?' asked Richard.

'Yes, I did,' he replied.

'I have your report here.' Richard fetched a sheet of paper from out of his case.

'This is your report on her, I'll just quote you a few lines from it.

'I tested Mrs Phillips to see how she would respond under pressure. Now, please take into account that she was recently raped. I asked Mrs Phillips if she was telling the truth about being raped, she said yes. I then told her that she was making it all up and that she just wanted to get rich off Mr Forbes. She then shouted that I have my own business, I'm doing reasonably well and I'm not lying. She was crying by now, she sat down and said I just can't understand why they did this to me. I stopped the interview for fear of causing any more unpleasantness to Mrs Phillips.

'Now the same pressure situation that you gave to Mr Walker and Mr Forbes, ended in total disaster. Both of them were handcuffed and taken away by guards, was Mrs Phillips, handcuffed and taken away by guards?' he asked Mr Stevens.

'No,' came his reply.

'Were there any guards present at the interview that you had with her?' asked Richard still holding the piece of paper.

'Yes, there was,' he replied.

'Oh, why was that?' asked Richard looking at him.

Mr Stevens paused slightly before he spoke.

'She was too scared to be left alone with a man, that's why I requested that there be two female officers present during the time that I spent with her.'

There was a sharp intake of breath from the people in the courtroom.

'Did you at any time feel threatened by the presence of Mrs Phillips like you did with Mr Walker or Mr Forbes?' asked Richard.

'No, I felt quite the opposite.'

'Did you really?' Richard looked at Mr Stevens.

'I really felt for the first time in my career totally and utterly useless. I can usually help most people, but I couldn't do anything for her.' Mr Stevens looked again at Sarah as he spoke.

'Thank you Mr Stevens, No further questions Your Honour.'

The judge looked at Mr Chevron.

'Err… no further questions Your Honour,' added Mr Chevron.

The judge explained to Mr Stevens that his time in the witness box was over and that there was no need for him to come back to court. Mr Stevens thanked the judge and left the stand. The judge called Richard and Mr Chevron to him. As Mr Stevens walked past, David and Sarah both said thank you to him for being so kind. He tapped David on the shoulder and told him that he was lucky man for having such a strong woman. He then went out of the courtroom.

Richard and Mr Chevron came back to their seats. The usher told everyone that court was adjourned until ten o'clock tomorrow morning as the judge left.

Richard said that he would pop round and see her and David a bit later on, he and Helen said goodbye.

Sarah's father was going back to pick the children up from his friends, he said that he would phone her later on in the evening. He kissed his daughters goodbye and then left. Sarah, David, Susan and her sister all went back to Sarah's house for coffee

Sarah went into the house and sat down.

'God it's good to sit down in a comfortable chair,' she said.

'I agree,' said Susan also sitting down. 'I think that if I had sat in those courtroom chairs any longer my arse would have gone numb.'

'I'll make the coffee,' suggested Sandra, they all said ok, quite quickly.

'Well don't all fight me to get into the kitchen,' she smiled. She kind of wondered what she let herself in for, but anyway she went and made the coffee.

'I have to say that Stevens bloke was a bit of alright, wasn't he?'

Sarah looked at Susan and said, 'Don't you ever get enough?'

'Hey, there's plenty of fish in the sea, just because you've caught one doesn't mean you can't watch the rest of them swimming about.' They both laughed.

David meanwhile was fiddling with the new stereo.

'I just noticed the new hi-fi, it's about time he bought you something nice.'

'Hey,' said David looking slightly surprised. 'I buy her lots of nice things.'

'Such as?' asked Sandra coming out of the kitchen with a tray.

'Well... I can't remember offhand, but I've bought her lots of nice things.'

'Look,' said Sarah. 'We're not saying that you're tight.'

'Yeah, but it's about time that you took them tea bags off the line,' giggled Sandra.

'Ha, ha, ha, very funny,' said David listening to them all laughing.

'He's not tight, his wallet creaked like that when he bought it,' added Sarah. They were all poking fun at David and laughing at him.

'Ok, ok, I get the message, I'll go and wash the car and leave you girlies to talk rubbish,' replied David as he stood up.

Sarah asked Susan and Sandra, how many people they knew that has a green car.

Susan replied, 'A green car, nobody in this day and age drives a green car, only a right pratt would drive a green car.'

'Wait a minute,' said Sandra. 'You drive a green car don't you David?' she looked at him and was giggling as she spoke.

David was already heading for the door.

'God David, how can you drive a green car?'

'Remember not to call me when your cars break down,' suggested David as he was going outside.

David could still hear them laughing as he opened the garage door.

God, what a mess, thought David. I must sort this mess out one day. He knew that his wife and Susan and Sandra were just having a laugh at his expense.

He didn't really want to wash the car but he did anyway. He was thinking to himself, as he washed the car, I wonder what's going to happen to us after the trial. I pray to God that she doesn't have Aids. But what if she has? What then? Shit... You know that these things come in threes, maybe this is the third one. I mean, we come back off holiday to find that some arsehole has put her only sister in hospital. Sarah minding her own business gets attacked and raped and then she finds out that she might have Aids.

He forgot about having his car wrecked:

God, I bet next year's going to be brilliant and it cracks me up when people say, "Oh don't worry about it, life will sort itself out, get on with it, things will turn out ok." Come on, Aids: that must be the longest sentence in the world, there's no chance of ever getting out, it's a death penalty even if you don't want it. Yeah I know people say the more you dwell on the subject, the more that it cuts you up inside. David finished his car and started washing his wife's car.

Yeah fair enough, thought David, if you really dwell on the subject it would drive you mad, but I have to be realistic and give a life threatening disease some thought.

I'm like most people, you never really think about something until it happens to you. I used to think, if it doesn't involve you and then leave it alone. He thought about the time that he stopped a man from beating his wife up, only to have the wife turn on him and tell him off in the process for interfering.

I should have just let him kick her arse or maybe I'm just being silly.

Before David realised, time had flew by and he was so deep in thought that he had washed all the cars. His own, his wife's, her sister's and Susan's.

Ah well it saves them doing it I suppose, he thought to himself. David was putting the hosepipe away, he stopped and looked at his car. His car was green but it was a nice shade of green, the kind of green that shone like an emerald when the sunlight hit it. He knew his wife was only joking with him.

Meanwhile, while David was outside, the girls were still cracking jokes at each other.

It was good to hear Sarah laugh thought Sandra looking at her.

'What are you thinking about?' asked Sarah.

'Oh, nothing,' replied Sandra.

'I bet she was thinking about that Mr Stevens, weren't you?' suggested Susan.

'Excuse me,' said Sandra smiling. 'I admit he looked nice and he dressed well, but you were the one who said, I wonder if that bulge in the front of his trousers is real or has he put a sock down there.'

'The joke of it was I wanted to ask him when he walked past, but your sister wouldn't let me,' insisted Susan. They all laughed as she said it.

'I'm glad you two slappers came round and cheered me up,' said Sarah.

'Hey now come on, there's only one slapper in this room.'

'Yeah, Sarah,' replied Sandra butting into the conversation and laughing loudly.

'Cheeky cow,' said Sarah nudging her sister. They were still laughing when David came back in from outside.

'You lot are mad, do you know that?' he stated.

'Yeah I know,' said his wife, trying to calm down because her sides were hurting from all the laughing.

'Did you wash your green car?'

'Yes I did,' said David boldly. 'And I also washed all the other cars as well.' They all laughed and said thank you. Susan said that she would have to be going. Sandra said that she would be going as well. David and Sarah saw them out and then watched them drive away.

'Mad, the pair of them,' said Sarah still giggling slightly.

'I think that we need to talk,' suggested David going back into the living room.

'God, you sound serious.'

'I am,' he replied sitting down next to her.

'Before you say anything, I know that you're going to say that we shouldn't worry about it or that we shouldn't talk about it, but I feel that I have to talk about it to someone,' said Sarah.

'I know, I've been thinking the same thing; we should talk about this Aids problem. I've been putting it off for ages now, I know people say that you shouldn't worry about it, but I just can't think about anything else,' replied David.

'Can I ask you a question?' said Sarah, looking at him and holding his hand.

'Yeah, course you can.'

'Do you honestly think that I've got Aids?' asked Sarah.

'No, I don't,' he replied.

'You sound rather confident,' suggested Sarah.

'I don't think that people like you, get that kind of thing. Forbes got Aids because he is a drug addict, you're not a drug addict.'

'Yes but if I had VD and then had sex with you, it stands to reason that you would get it too,' suggested Sarah.

'Ok, do you think that you've got it?' asked David.

'Yes, I do,' replied Sarah in a soft voice.

'Why do you think that?'

'I just don't feel right,' added Sarah.

'Come on you were raped. That kind of thing just doesn't go away overnight, you know it takes ages just to come to terms with what those animals did to you,' suggested David.

'When I was raped it hurt not just physically, don't get me wrong that really hurt, but it's the pain afterwards that gets you. You know like when someone that you care about dies and it doesn't register right away, well that's how rape is. You walk from the road to the house and you swear blind that someone's been following you. You know that they haven't but that's what you think anyway, you get really paranoid about little stupid things, things that you would never have thought about before. I hear the floorboards creak and I think that someone's in the house. I could bathe ten times a day and I still wouldn't feel clean. It feels strange, it's a really indescribable feeling and it's like the dirt's on the inside of you. I feel angry, violated, dirty and sick, I felt pure hatred after seeing any man even you,' said Sarah.

David never said a word he sat there listening to his wife's voice. She never did really talk to him about what happened, husband or not.

'I felt that if the whole world had blown up and left me there on my own, I would have loved it. I know that it probably sounds really bitchy of me, but at the time that was how I felt. I mean I had two men beat me up and rip off my skirt. One holds me down whilst the other one takes advantage of me. Then if that wasn't enough they swapped over, they both let their sperm drip all over me when they finished and then they both give me a kick in the ribs for my trouble.

'They joked and said that I was lucky; they were lenient with me because I had been a good girl. Think about who in the hell is going to suspect a man who earns more interest in a week than most people earn in two years. I mean he can have his pick of any single woman in this area, he drives around in an expensive car for God's sake.

'What! An honest man like that I must be lying.

Now the other one Walker, he really enjoyed himself, he even kissed me when he had finished and said that he enjoyed that, it never stopped him giving me another kick in the ribs though. I wonder how many women those two have raped. And then a complete stranger tells you in court in front of your family and friends, that you might have Aids. When she said that, I just felt physically sick. I suddenly felt that all the energy had left my body, I just thought, what's the point I've been sentenced to death.

'Somebody said to me the other day. Don't worry they'll get a nice healthy sentence. And I said, what about my sentence, if I have got Aids then I'll be doing time just the same as them. I think that it's easy for them; you know they go to prison and that's it forgotten about, they have no children, no immediate family. All that pillock Forbes has is his money and all that pillock Walker has is his sad lonely self.

'I watched a talk show before, you know one of those American ones.

'Anyway this bloke had murdered this kid when he was younger. The bloke was in his late thirties and the kid was about seven or something like that. Anyway for years this bloke got away with it, when they finally caught him he was an old man with a crippling heart disease. Now instead of this talk show showing the man in his prime, they show this frail old man who could hardly breathe, he could hardly walk. Then they ask should he be sent to prison? Nearly all the audience members said no, he should not go to prison he's too old.

'Now if they had shown the man in his prime with nothing wrong with him. I bet that the same audience would have given a different answer, it just goes to show you how people think.

'Remember the nasty things that people said about the kids and us when this happened to me. I couldn't believe that so called friends and neighbours could be so heartless.

'Sorry, I've been rambling on again, haven't I?'

'I never really knew that you felt this way,' replied David.

'Yeah well, I can't help the way that I feel.' Sarah felt her stomach churning, it hurt to go over the same painful thing again and again. She sighed and took a deep breath, now normally she would have been crying for ages by now, but although she felt sad she never cried.

'Well, how did you feel?'

'That's a good question, I don't really know,' replied David.

'Now come on, seeing as though we're being honest with each other, don't bullshit me,' insisted his wife looking at him. She was hoping for something more than I don't really know.

'Ok, I felt sorry, pity, definitely anger and frustration. I felt pretty much the same as you. Ok I wasn't there and I know that this might sound silly, but I feel that I was raped as well.' His wife looked at him in disbelief.

'Yeah, yeah, yeah, I know what you're thinking, they never raped you, but that's where you're wrong. You see most men think anything that hurts their wives or their girlfriends hurt them. When those bastards did this to you I wanted blood so much that I could taste it. You have no idea how it feels to see someone that you care about in pain and there's nothing that you can do for them. When they raped you, I felt that they had raped me as well.

'As soon as I was told by the police that this had happened, I couldn't believe it. I even told the policeman that told me that he was lying, but when he described you, the car you drove, I knew that they were serious. I was shaking as I got into the police car, they seemed to take forever to get to the station and then when I got there, I couldn't see you straight away, I had to wait. I had to identify the car, your belongings and your purse; I didn't really care about the car or the stupid purse. All I kept asking was when can I see my wife. I must have asked them that a thousand times, but they just said that I had to wait, but when you finally did come out and I saw the mess that you were in, all I could do was cry, nothing else, just cry. Then when you gave your statement to the police, well I couldn't help it, I just saw red. I wanted to kill anything that moved and believe me I mean anything. All I kept asking myself was, why, why her? Yes I know that monsters like those shouldn't rape anybody, but in that room at that time I didn't give a shit about anybody else. I just cared about me and my wife, nobody else mattered. My language was probably right off the scale. When you were telling that policewoman what they had actually done to you, I felt numb all over and when I read the report that Joan Smith did, well I felt that you had been raped all over again, I couldn't believe the things that you had to go through.

'In cases like this, I honestly thought you gave a statement and that was it. I never thought for one minute that they took blood samples from you, hair fibres and even scrapped samples from under your nails. They must have taken at least twenty different things from you before they let you have a shower. And then when I finally did see you, we stood there cuddling each other and crying. I could never believe that someone could do this to another human being. I mean, you hear about this kind of thing all the time, on the news and in the papers, but when you actually see the damage for yourself. Well let's put it this way, it stopped me dead in my tracks, all I could do was cry, and when she said in court that he had Aids. Well, there are no words that can tell you how I felt and how I've felt ever since, it's hard to describe. I feel empty are the only words to describe it, really and truly empty. I know that it sounds silly, but what you say they took from you, they took from me as well. I thought that the uphill struggle was over until I realised that if you do have Aids, as I said, I don't think that you have, but if you have, what are we going to tell the children?

'I mean, you do realise that they will have to be told?'

'Yes I know. I think that more than anything that is the part that probably hurts me the most,' replied Sarah.

'I've thought about it over and over in my head, I mean, how do you tell two young children that their mother may have a killer disease?'

'Jason and Lucy are both upset as it is without telling them that I may be dying.'

'I agree the animals that did this are really getting away scotch free. Ok yeah they might never come out of prison if they get sent down, but what if they get away scotch free, what then? What if the jury decides that you're lying? I pray every day that we go to court and every day I hope we get nearer to keeping people like that off the street. I mean twenty years is some satisfaction, I just hope that they hate people who do this to women in prison,' suggested David.

'Paul told me that you could get raped in prison by some of the other prisoners. Now that would be justice,' said his wife.

'It would, most men don't like other men looking at them, never mind touching them, especially those two wankers being such womanisers. God just thinking about it seems nice,' said David.

'Well let's hope that it happens,' she sighed again. 'I must say that I'm glad that we had this talk, at least we know how each other feels now.'

'Yeah at least things are out into the open,' said David.

'Anyway what's this surprise that you've got coming for us tomorrow?' asked Sarah.

'Oh, it's only ...' began David. 'Ha, ha, nice try woman, close but no cigar, I must admit you nearly had me there,' smiled David.

'What would you like for dinner?'

'Let's go out,' suggested David.

'I've got a better idea, we'll order a pizza and get drunk, there's some brandy left,' added Sarah.

'Get drunk, when was the last time that you saw me get drunk?'

'Not since our wedding reception,' said Sarah looking at him.

'I don't really feel like getting drunk, but hey what the hell, I'm game if you are, but on one condition.'

'What's that?' asked Sarah.

'You promise that you won't start singing,' laughed David.

'Cheeky, I have a nice singing voice.'

'Yes, I agree when you're sober, but when you're drunk, you sound like a cat with its tail on fire,' laughed David again.

'Well, I can't help that,' replied Sarah getting up off the settee. 'But I'll try my best not to sing.' Sarah was one of those people who when she got drunk fell about all over the place and sang at the top of her voice. She never had a bad voice when she was sober, but when she was drunk it was a different story. But in the back of his mind David didn't really care whether his wife sang or even danced the funky chicken in the rain. He was just glad that for the moment she was in high spirits.

Sarah went and ordered a pizza on the phone, then came back in and sat down.

'What's this surprise then?' she asked.

'I told you, you'll find out tomorrow, I guarantee it,' stated David. They were sitting down talking and waiting for the pizza, when the phone rang. David answered the phone and after a few minutes he came back into the living room.

'Who was that?' asked his wife looking at him.

'Well the delivery that was supposed to come in the morning is now coming the day after,' replied David.

'Well in that case there's no harm in you telling me what the surprise is,' suggested Sarah.

'I don't think so,' smiled David looking out of the window at the pizza man walking up the driveway. David went to the door to collect it, he came back into the living room and sat down and started eating.

'Err… enjoying yourself are we?' asked Sarah looking at her husband.

'I can't help it, I'm hungry,' replied David, almost finishing off his first slice. David eventually let his wife start her pizza. David had already poured two glasses of brandy for him and Sarah.

Sarah had hardly finished her meal when she started on her brandy.

'Hey come on, slow down will you,' suggested David.

'Why, can't you keep up?' asked Sarah.

'Is that a challenge?'

'It might be,' said Sarah, knocking back her glass of brandy, she flopped back into the chair and had a glazed look on her face. Her husband laughed and then a small piece of food went down the wrong way.

He started coughing furiously, he gestured for his wife to tap him on the back.

'What, I can't understand a word that you're saying,' she joked. 'Ok, ok, I'm coming.' She then began tapping him on the back, after a few seconds the small piece of food came out. David gasped for breath.

'Good God David, you seem to have gone a funny colour.'

'Look who's talking,' said David, eventually getting his breath back and calming down.

'When you knocked back that glass of brandy I thought that your eyes were about to pop out.' David coughed again for a few more seconds. Then when he had finally calmed down, he finished the rest of his meal. David could see that his wife was getting slightly merry, even though she had only had one glass. Well I say one glass, the three-inch glass was about half full and she knocked it right the way back, brave woman. David finished his meal and also drank his drink right the way back. Now even though he didn't really drink he could still drink more than his wife. He then poured two more drinks and leaned back against the chair.

'That's gone straight to my head.'

'Don't worry it will have some sawdust to soak into while it's there.'

'Yeah, I suppose you're right,' began his wife, before realising what her husband had just said.

'Cheeky bitch,' she said after a while. 'At least I've got something up there. That's why you don't like people shouting, because when they do it echoes around in your head.' They both laughed. Surely, but steadily throughout the evening they both got drunk. Sarah was completely drunk and did not care what she was doing, whereas her husband was drunk but still had most of his faculties in order.

When David spoke he slurred his words, but you could still understand him, even though he sounded a bit funny.

But Sarah was a real joker you could hardly understand what she was talking about, well I say talk, all she did was ramble. She kept telling her husband how much she loved him, at least he thought that's what she said. She just rambled on about different things but nothing in particular. As far as his wife was concerned she made perfect sense, it was her husband who was slurring his words. They both decided that after half a bottle of brandy that David and his wife had, had enough.

As he started to try and get up, she kept pulling him back down, she did this four times until David finally got up. He was trying to put her over his shoulder. After about the third attempt, he did it. Now don't forget that they are both drunk, even though David wasn't as drunk as his wife, he was still drunk, so what would have taken them a few a minutes to get from the living room into their bedroom ended up taking them a good ten minutes.

Eventually David got his wife into the bedroom, who by now was merrily singing away to herself. He laid her down on the bed, well I say laid her down, he basically fell on the bed with her, his wife still singing and giggling at the same time. David managed just about to take off her clothes and leave his wife in her underwear and put her in bed. He then staggered back downstairs just to make sure that he switched everything off then staggered back upstairs and went to bed.

The next morning Sarah woke up about eight thirty, her husband was still asleep. She felt and looked as sick as anything, her head thumping as she made her way to the bathroom. She went to the toilet, had a shower, got dressed and went downstairs. She had made herself a strong cup of black coffee. When her husband came downstairs, he looked a lot more refreshed than his wife.

'Good morning,' said her husband, giving her a kiss on the cheek.

Every little sound echoed inside Sarah's head, it was like someone was in there with a hammer just banging for the sake of it.

'Do you have to shout?' she asked in a soft voice.

'Don't tell me, you've got a hangover?'

'Of course I've got a hangover,' she replied sitting down on the sofa.

201

'Well it was your idea that we both get drunk and anyway I feel as fresh as a daisy,' said David.

'You always do, it amazes me that you never ever get a hangover, I think there's a moral in there somewhere,' suggested Sarah.

'You'll have to go to court on your own this morning,' said her husband from the kitchen. 'I've got to wait for that delivery to come.' His wife reminded him that it was coming tomorrow not today.

'I love getting drunk, but I hate the morning after,' implied Sarah.

'Most people do,' said David, coming into the living room with his breakfast on a tray.

'God I don't know how you can eat after last night, I feel as sick as anything,' said Sarah.

'Do you know in all the years I've been drinking, I've never been hung over yet,' said David proudly.

'And in all the years that I've been drinking this is probably the worst that I've ever felt,' said Sarah. She looked slightly better after drinking her coffee. David told her that she would be ok. She just had to wait until the coffee kicked in.

She went back upstairs and she put her make up on. She came down looking a lot like her old self. David picked up his car keys and off they went.

When they got to court as usual Richard was already in there.

Richard said, 'Good morning,' then apologised.

'What are you apologising for?' Sarah asked.

'Well I said that I would pop round last night but I never got the chance.'

'Oh don't worry I was too drunk to be of any use anyway, I still feel hung over now,' said Sarah.

'Are you alright now?' he asked, looking at her.

'I don't know really, I think so. David and I had a long good talk last night,' she smiled. 'Before we got drunk and we told each other how we felt about different things, we even talked about me having Aids.'

'Now come on, you don't know that for sure yet,' insisted Richard.

'I know that you and David probably felt the need to talk about it, that's fine, but I'm not being funny with you, but I just want to win this case. I know that you think that they might still get away with it and if they get twenty years that they are getting away scotch free. But believe me they'll have a very hard time in prison,' suggested Richard.

The court had started filling up by now.

'Believe me,' said Richard. 'The one thing that they hate in prison is a sex offender.'

'I hope so,' replied Sarah.

She saw that her family and friends had come in. She went over to them and hugged them and said, 'Good morning.' Susan told Sarah that she looked hung over, she replied that she was. They also asked if she was alright, she told them that she was doing as well as she could under the circumstances. Sarah's father explained why he hadn't brought the children with him. Sarah agreed that a courtroom was really no place for children especially in this type of case.

David meanwhile had finished talking to Helen.

They all heard the two men coming up the stairs, they never even looked at Sarah, she classed that as a moral victory because usually they said something stupid, well Mr Walker did anyway. Mr Forbes never said a word he just looked her up and down sometimes. After a few moments the judge came in and everyone sat down.

The judge asked Mr Chevron if he wanted to call his first witness. He said yes and called for Mr Daniel Thomas. Soon after a smartly dressed middle-aged man came in, took the oath and sat down in the witness box.

'Good morning,' said Mr Chevron.

'Good morning,' replied Mr Thomas.

'Could you tell the court your name and your occupation?'

'Yes of course, my name is Daniel Thomas and I do not work,' replied Mr Thomas.

'Why's that?' asked Mr Chevron looking at him.

'Well I'm retired and I have more money than I could ever spend so I don't see the need for me having a job,' replied Mr Thomas.

'You must have a nice life?'

'Yes, I do enjoy myself when I want to.'

'Can you tell the court what happened on Wednesday the twentieth of February?'

'Yes, I was at my country club with some friends,' replied Mr Thomas.

'At what time was that?' asked Mr Chevron.

'I don't know really, I got there about eleven thirty in the morning and stayed there all afternoon.' Mr Thomas smiled warmly as he spoke.

'And what time did Mr Forbes get there?'

'Well he was supposed to get there roughly the same time as me, but he called me on my mobile and said that he would be late.'

'You have a mobile phone?'

'Yes I have,' he replied. A surprised look came over most of the people in the room, not everyone could afford a mobile phone.

'Did Mr Forbes give any reason for his lateness?'

'Yes he did,' said Mr Thomas.

'And what reason was that?'

'He said some damn fool had run into his Mercedes and he had to wait for the police to get there. I told him to forget it and just buy a new one,' he said arrogantly. He made Mr Forbes laugh.

'What's your opinion of Mr Forbes?' asked Mr Chevron.

'Well it's hard to say really, he's not tight with his money, but there again he doesn't waste it either,' replied Mr Thomas.

'So would you say that he's generous when he wants to be?' asked Mr Chevron walking up and down slowly.

'Well let's put it this way, he absolutely adores children. He's forever giving money to children's charities and other worthy causes. We make a joke of it at the club, we say that he spends money faster than they can make it,' smiled Mr Thomas.

'So he's really not shy in spending his hard earned money? What would you say about the idea of him being a rich and powerful man who goes around raping and beating up innocent women?' asked Mr Chevron.

'I'd say that was totally outrageous. I mean, yes sure everyone has a bad day, but if you moved in the circles that we move in, you'd know what kind of person Mr Forbes is. He can have a dozen women all at once fighting for his affections. He once bought a young lady a two thousand pound watch because he liked the way she went around helping children. Believe me, men who are as generous as that don't go around raping women.'

'Have you ever seen him take drugs?' asked Mr Chevron, who was looking quite pleased with himself. It was very rare that he showed any emotion of any kind, but he did manage to smile, which in itself was a great feat as far as most people in the court were concerned.

'Drugs, well, yes of course, he likes tea, coffee and he likes his malt whisky,' said Mr Thomas.

Sarah could see that the judge was licking his lips slightly.

He must also like his malt whisky thought Sarah and where the hell did this pratt come from? God, I've heard of stretching the truth, but that's a bit ridiculous. I mean he's making him out to be some kind of saint. Yeah, so he does give a lot to charity and maybe he can be generous, but he wasn't very generous when he was raping me, was he? Or there again, maybe in his eyes or in his own sad way he thought that he was.

'I've never seen him take any drugs. Like I said, it's tea, coffee, a glass of the good stuff but as for drugs, no,' said Mr Thomas.

Sarah whispered to Richard just as Mr Chevron had finished talking to Mr Thomas.

'Don't tear into him too early.'

'I'll try my best,' whispered Richard getting up.

'Mr Thomas, I must say that you paint a pleasant picture of your friend Mr Forbes.'

'Well like I said, he's very nice man,' replied Mr Thomas.

'Ok, let's say for the moment that he is the ideal man and every woman should have one and let's say that he is his normal giving generous self would you say Mr Thomas that I've pretty much described your friend?'

'Yes, I would.'

'Right, now what if I could paint you a seedier picture, would you believe it?'

'Not really, but I am open minded,' he replied.

'Well, ok, let's say that Mr Forbes has a history of violence against women and let's say for instance that he really doesn't care about women, and that he likes his own way a lot,' began Richard.

'Look,' said Mr Thomas, butting into the conversation. 'You may see a seedy character, but I've known him twelve years.'

'And, I've known him five minutes,' said Richard, raising his voice.

'The point that I am making is, how well do you really know a person, just because you've known him for twelve years, doesn't mean that there isn't a side to him that you don't see,' suggested Richard. 'Are you with him twenty-four hours a day?'

'No, but that's beside the …' began Mr Thomas.

'Just answer yes or no for me please, Mr Thomas,' ordered Richard.

'No, I'm not with him twenty-four hours a day.'

'So how can you sit and say all those things about him? Granted that most of them may be true, but there's no such thing as a model citizen. And if there is I'd like to meet him,' stated Richard.

'I never said that he was perfect.'

'Yes, I know you didn't, but you never said that he wasn't either,' stated Richard.

'We know for instance, that he likes to beat woman up. He said they need to be kept in place and it was his place to teach them. Do you agree with that?'

'No, I don't,' replied Mr Thomas.

'And we also know that he has a temper. What do you think of that?'

'I already know he has a short fuse, he makes no secret about that. That's part of the reason why he's so successful,' suggested Mr Thomas.

'It may be nice for business, but not when he takes his temper out on women. Now we also know that he is a heroin and cocaine addict. Now considering that he is charged with raping my client, wouldn't you say that there's a side to him that you never knew about?' asked Richard.

'I would,' said Mr Thomas, who now had different look on his face.

'So if you're not with him all the time how can you say that these things never happened?'

'I can't,' said Mr Thomas looking at Richard.

'Ok I'll put another way,' suggested Richard, who was walking back to his table. 'Now this is Mrs Sarah Phillips, married, has two children, owns her own home and has her own business, her children go to a very good school, private of course. Now granted she's not a millionaire, but would you agree that she has a stable life?'

'Yes, I suppose so,' added Mr Thomas.

'No,' said Richard, walking towards the witness box.

'She did have a normal life until the day she was raped. Then her nice stable life wasn't so stable any more. Now with all your money Mr Thomas do you think that you could ever heal that kind of pain?' Richard never gave him time to answer. 'No more questions, Your Honour.' Richard sat back down.

The judge asked Mr Chevron if he had finished with Mr Thomas. He stood up and said yes. The judge told Mr Thomas that he was free to leave the witness box and that he was no longer needed.

The judge told the usher that they would have a twenty-minute break. So he told all the people in the court that they were going to have a twenty-minute break. The judge also told the witness that he could step down. As people were leaving the court, David told his wife who was sitting down talking to Richard that he was just going to the toilet.

'I want to put you on the stand as soon as court restarts,' said Richard.

'Err... yeah, sure,' said David looking at his wife.

'Now come on, don't look like that, all you have to do is be yourself, be honest. Try not to hold too much back just be yourself, it may seem that I'm being a little hard on you when we start, but it's all for a good reason, just go with the flow as they say,' encouraged Richard.

David said, 'Ok,' and then he went to the toilet.

Sarah's father and sister had bought coffee for everybody. They chatted away idly until court was about to start back up once again.

The judge came back in and asked Richard to call his next witness.

'Yes, I would like to call Mr David Phillips to the stand.'

David took a deep breath and then headed for the witness box. He took the oath and sat down in the witness box.

'Could you tell the court your name please?'

'Yes certainly, my name is Mr David Phillips.'

'And you are the husband of Mrs Sarah Phillips, is that correct?'

'Yes, I am.'

'How long have you been married?'

'I've been married for just over ten years,' stated David.

'And how do you find married life?'

'It's nice really.'

'No real problems. No arguing, no fighting, no falling out of any kind?'

'No, well we don't really argue all that often, but when we do I always sulk,' stated David.

'So do I,' said Richard looking at him. 'So before this incident happened you had a pretty normal life?'

'Yes, we did,' stated David.

'Could you tell us what happened on the twentieth of February?' asked Richard, leaning against his table.

David paused before he spoke.

'I know how hard this must be for you Mr Phillips,' said the judge, peering over his glasses and looking down at David. 'You don't have to do this if you don't feel up to it, we quite understand.'

'No, I might as well get it over and done with Your Honour.'

'It was a pretty normal day. I got up around six o'clock and went to work, I always get up before my wife,' stated David.

'What is your job?' asked Richard.

'I'm an architect. Anyway, I went to work, finished about three thirty so I went and picked the children up from school, then we went home.'

'But doesn't your wife normally pick the children up from school?' Richard had moved from his table and was walking up and down in front of the witness box.

'Yes normally, well we have a system see. If I work over, she'll pick the kids up and if she works over, then I'll pick the kids up. Then I'll call her at the office to tell her that I've picked them up,' said David.

'Did you phone her on that particular day?' asked Richard.

'Yes I did, but her partner Susan said that she had left early to do some shopping. So I never really thought much of it at the time.'

'Then what did you do?'

'Well, I did the kids' tea and sat down waiting for my wife to come home,' replied David.

'But when she didn't return?' asked Richard looking at him. 'What did you do then?'

'Well I was just about to phone her office again when there was a knock at the door. When I opened it and saw two policemen standing there. As soon as I saw them I knew something was wrong. I mean, we very rarely have the police come to our door,' replied David.

'How did you feel?' asked Richard.

'Well as soon as I saw them, I thought the worst. Straight away I thought that she had been killed in a car accident, but when they came in they told me that she had been found unconscious in an alleyway and that she had been raped and beaten. I thought that they must have the wrong address, but when they showed me her purse, I knew that they were serious.'

'How did you feel at that precise moment, when they told you Mr Phillips?'

'Well for a while I couldn't move, I just sat there motionless,' replied David sighing.

'Then one of the policemen gave me a glass of brandy, which he told me to drink so I did.'

'Where were the children?' asked Richard.

'They were playing upstairs in their bedrooms.' He paused and took a deep breath.

'It's ok, Mr Phillips, please take your time,' insisted Richard.

David had tears in his eyes.

'I didn't have the heart to tell them what had happened to their mother. I needed someone to stay with the children while I went to the police station, so I phoned her sister and she came over straight away. I then went to the police station.'

Richard handed David a hanky. He could see the tears rolling down the side of his face. Sarah was already crying and her sister who was also crying was comforting her. In fact most of the people in the court had tears in their eyes or were just crying. Even the judge had a tear in his eye. The two prisoners just sat there giggling occasionally to each other.

'I then went to the police station,' said David.

'Then what happened when you got to the police station?' asked Richard.

'I had to wait for nearly two hours before I could see her.'

'Why was that? I know how hard this must be for you Mr Phillips, but you're doing ok so far,' stated Richard.

David paused again, before he spoke.

'She was being examined by one of their own doctors, they just seemed to take forever. They took samples of this, samples of that. I really thought that they just went, gave a statement and then went home, but when I asked the man at the desk he explained what kind of process that she would go through.'

'And what happened when you did finally see her?' asked Richard.

'Well the only way I can describe it is that she looked as though she had been in a fight. Her clothes were ripped, she had cuts on her face, she couldn't walk very well. She didn't look like my wife at all.'

'What happened then?' asked Richard looking around the courtroom. Most of the people were still crying. Richard never told anybody, but the way that the people were in the courtroom was exactly the kind of response that he wanted. Now he had most of the court in tears, he knew that he was in a winning position and that's just where he wanted to be.

'After she saw the police doctor, we spent another few hours giving a statement to them. When we got home her father was there with her sister, the children had gone to bed. As soon as they saw Sarah they just started to cry. She hugged her sister, but could not hug her father. I knew why without asking, so did he,' stated David.

'So what was that evening like?' asked Richard.

'Well unless you were there it's kind of hard to explain. Sarah and her sister went upstairs, then Sarah's sister came back down after about ten minutes. She told us that her sister was taking a shower, even though she already had one at the police station. She also had Sarah's clothes that she had been wearing which were ripped, dirty and covered in blood.

'My wife told her sister to tell me to burn them. She didn't want me to just throw them in the bin; I had to burn them in the back garden. She stood looking through one of the upstairs windows just to make sure that they were being burned,' replied David.

'So what you're saying is she could not bear the sight of those clothes,' asked Richard, looking at him.

'Well, yes, I suppose so.'

'And what did you tell the children?'

'Well we didn't tell the children straight away, their grandfather kept them over at his house for a while. He took them to school and everything.

'The night that this happened, I phoned her business partner Susan.' As he was talking, he was remembering what happened.

'Yeah, hi, can I speak to Susan Hardy please.'

'Who shall I say is calling?' said a voice on the other end of the phone.

'It's David Phillips.' Susan came on the phone.

'Hi David, what time did she get back then and how much shopping did she have?'

'Susan,' began David, trying to get a word in.

'David what's on earth's the matter?' David paused and sighed deeply.

'Sarah's been raped,' said David softly.

'No,' said Susan, raising her voice. 'Not Sarah.' Susan had started to cry.

'Susan, Susan,' said David, trying to calm her down.

'I'm coming over,' said Susan crying.

'No, look she's got her sister with her at the moment and her father's got the children.'

'What happened?' asked Susan, still crying.

'Well she was on her way home when the car broke down so she decided to walk. She took a short cut down the alleyway by the doctor's and then two men raped her.' He had huge lump in his throat and a tear in his eye. Susan was too upset to say anything.

'They beat her up pretty badly too, broken ribs, black eye, the works. I know that she had a meeting planned for tomorrow so could you sort that out for me. I'll let you tell her friends at work, I must go. Pop round tomorrow, it's not a nice atmosphere here at the minute,' said David. Susan was still crying, but said ok. Then they both put the phone down.

'Her sister stayed for a while about two weeks, I think, and as I said, her father had the children.'

'And how was your relationship with your wife?' asked Richard.

'Well, she never really spoke to me for nearly four days. I understood why at least I think I understood why,' replied David.

'And, why was that?' asked Richard.

'Well she'd just been raped and beaten by two men; the last thing she'd want to see is another man.'

'And when you did finally start talking?'

'You see that's the thing we never really spoke as such. She never came downstairs for a week, even when our doctor came he went upstairs,' stated David.

'And, when did he come?' asked Richard leaning on his table.

'He came the day after and gave her some sleeping tablets. He told her that she should eat something, even if it was only something light. But she had to eat or she would have fallen ill.' He had stopped crying by now, but he still had tears in his eyes.

'Can I ask you when did you eventually tell the children, and how on earth did you tell them?' asked Richard.

'It was at least three weeks before we sat them down and told them. It was my idea, I thought as bad as it was they had a right to know. When we told them, Jason just ran upstairs crying. I don't think that he fully understood what we told him, but I think that he understood enough to understand that his mum wasn't herself. Lucy just cuddled her mother, she never really understood at all she just said the boys who hurt her were horrible. But Jason did nothing but cry.' David was picturing the scene again, as he spoke.

'I'll go and talk to him,' I said.

'No, I think it's best if I go up and talk to him,' said Sarah, getting up off the chair.

'Why is Jason crying?' asked Lucy.

'Well, Jason's upset that your mother was hurt by someone.'

'But why did they hurt Mummy?'

'I don't know some adults are naughty like that.'

'I hope the police catch them.'

'It's hard to explain something like that to a nine-year-old girl. You tell her as best that you can because you feel they have a right to know. I mean kids tend to pick up on the slightest thing in the house anything that's not right they can see it.'

Meanwhile Sarah was upstairs talking to Jason.

'What's the matter, sweetheart?' asked his mother, putting her arms around him.

'Why did those two men have to hurt you?' said Jason crying.

'That's just the way some people are.'

'Does that mean you don't love me any more?'

'Now, don't be silly,' said his mother, who wanted to cry but she didn't. She thought that if she cried it might upset Jason even more, so she didn't even though it was hard.

'I'll always love you no matter what, remember what I always say to you:

'*I love you each and every day*
Even when the sky is grey
And when you're happy and full of joy
I'll love you still
Because, you're my little boy
And even when you're old and grey
I'll love you each and every day
And when you're sad, just think of this
I'll always be here with my special kiss.'

'I mean don't forget,' said David. 'They're only nine and ten, but still they have to know someday and I'd rather tell them than have a complete stranger tell them.'

'I gather that they never took the news very well?' asked Richard.

'As I said, Lucy never really understood but Jason understood more than he let on,' suggested David.

'So after all these months things must be back to normal?' asked Richard, looking at him.

'No, well, I think that after all we've been through, we've finally started sorting things out.'

'You have considering,' replied Richard, sounding and looking surprised, even though he was the one that recommended that they see Helen in the first place.

'Yes, we went to see Helen after the nightmares got worse,' stated David.

'Nightmares,' said Richard, looking across at Mr Chevron as he walked slowly up and down. 'I never knew that she was having nightmares. When did all this start?'

'It all started the day after she was raped. She had her first nightmare and then I just thought that she was still in shock or something like that, but as the weeks went on the arguments got worse and so did the nightmares,' stated David.

'You mean that you had fights as well?' asked Richard, stopping suddenly and then looking at him.

'Well, I wouldn't call them fights, but I did hit her once, purely out of frustration though.'

'Had you ever hit your wife before?' asked Richard, looking across at Sarah, who was leaning against her sister.

'No never. As I said, it was just the once. I know that I shouldn't have done it, and I know that I won't do anything like that again,' bleated David.

'Are you sure? I mean, some people would say that she might have deserved it,' suggested Richard.

'No, I was way out of order. No woman deserves that kind of treatment,' stated David.

'Oh come now, we know that Mr Forbes and Mr Walker both love nothing better than to give a woman a good slap or two. They should all be kept in line or else.'

'That may be their sick opinion, but not mine. Like I said, we never really used to argue, well not that much anyway. If she hadn't got raped none of this would be happening,' stated David.

'That may well be but this is most definitely for real. Now could you tell us more about your wife's nightmares?' asked Richard.

'Well like I said, her family and I kind of dismissed the first one, we just put it down to the fact that she might still be in shock in some way. Then one night, I think I was watching a movie or something on TV, so she said that she was going to bed, so off she went. When I went up she was lying awkwardly on the bed, so rather than move her and risk waking her up, I covered her up as much as possible and jumped into my son's bed.

'I awoke the next morning to hear her screaming my name. I was startled for a split second and then I jumped out of bed and ran into our bedroom. She was sitting up in bed screaming my name; this was about eight o'clock in the morning. When I finally managed to calm her down she told me what was wrong,' said David.

'And what was the problem?' Richard was now leaning against his table once again.

'She thought that I had left her, she actually thought that I had packed my bags and left, but I was only in the next bedroom. We even had a stupid argument over a packet of biscuits.'

'Why would you argue over something as trivial as a packet of biscuits?' suggested Richard.

'Well, see that's the point, I really have no idea, I mean, it's not directly her fault. I just think that she has no control over her emotions. She's not too bad now, but she wouldn't go anywhere on her own for months. She wouldn't even take the bin out on her own,' said David.

'Why not?' asked Richard.

'Well she thought that every man in the world was after her. If we went out and a man looked at her she would get upset and say that he was after her.

'As for the nightmares, well as I said we had a silly argument over a packet of biscuits and then the argument built up from there. I said some nasty things, she said some nasty things and I lashed out at her. I know that I should've just walked away, but I didn't.

'The next morning when I saw what I had done to her face, I felt so ashamed. I couldn't really touch her, I wanted to cuddle her and tell her I was sorry, but I didn't think that she would want me anywhere near her after what I had done to her the previous night. Who could blame her?' David looked over at his wife.

'And how are things between you and your wife now?' asked Richard.

'Ok, I think now that we've spoke to someone in a professional capacity. I think that we can deal with the problems a lot better than we could before. The person that we spoke to was used to seeing this kind of thing on a daily basis so she knew how to advise us best,' said David.

'Has your wife taken an Aids test?' asked Richard.

'Yes we were advised to take one by our family doctor.'

'And have you found out the results yet?'

'No, we won't get the results back for a few more weeks yet,' replied David.

'What about certain articles in the newspapers? They say that your wife is lying and she was basically having an affair that went wrong, the same article also states that your wife is only after Mr Forbes' money,' stated Richard.

'My wife and her mate built that business up from scratch and if Mr Forbes is any kind of a businessman, he'll know that not all business problems can be solved with money, there's a lot more involved than that. I agree that she may never be as rich as the queen but from where they had the business to the success that it is now, I personally think that they've done quite well. Ok she hasn't made her first million yet but believe me money is the last thing that we worry about,' replied David.

As he was about to continue Mr Walker spoke just loud enough for him to hear.

'Pratt, wife's cheating on him and he doesn't even know it.'

The judge was just about to speak, but David beat him to it.

'Maybe I am a pratt, but at least I don't go around beating women up or raping them.'

Mr Walker stood up, so did David. They continued having their slanging match even though the judge and the guards were trying to calm them both down.

'The bitch is fucking lying, I never touched her,' shouted Mr Walker. 'All this is because she was porking somebody else behind your back.'

'Look!' shouted David. 'My wife doesn't need anybody else, she's got me and as for that pillock of a friend beside you, he can take his money and shove it up his arse, because we don't bloody need it.'

In the meantime, the judge kept banging away and shouting order. There was one guard holding David back and two holding back Mr Walker.

David managed to calm down and told the guard that he was going to be fine. He also apologised for his nuisance to the guard. The judge's voice echoed across the courtroom.

'Take that man down to the cells, I think that he needs to think about his stupidity in my courtroom,' insisted the judge.

Mr Walker was swearing at the judge as he was being led away. The judge stopped the guards just as they were going down the first step.

'Mr Walker can I ask if you are really stupid enough to say that again?' asked the judge.

So as stupid as Mr Walker was, he did, which did not please the judge at all.

'Mr Walker I find you in contempt of court, further more I do not want to see your face in my court until you're needed for questioning is that clear?' The judge only had to say it once.

Mr Walker nodded and dropped his head. 'Yes.' I think that he knew that he had really upset the judge.

'Yes, what?' said the judge loudly.

'Yes, Your Honour,' came his reply.

'Right take him down,' and he was led away to the cells below.

'Will counsel please approach the bench?' So Richard and Mr Chevron did just as the judge had asked.

'If you cannot keep your clients in order, believe me I will not be a happy man, is that clear?' stated the judge.

'I agree Your Honour,' said Richard quickly. 'But my client's husband was doing ok until Mr Walker started saying things about him and his wife. I'm not excusing what Mr Phillips has done, but he wouldn't have said anything if Mr

Chevron's client had kept his mouth shut. My client is under enough stress as it is without Mr Chevron's clients doing things like this at every given moment.'

'I quite agree, your client has too much of a big mouth Mr Chevron and he needs to be taught a lesson in manners,' stated the judge.

The judge told David that under the circumstances he would not find him in contempt of court, but he would have no hesitation about doing it next time he carried on the way he did. David said ok and apologised for his behaviour. The judge told the usher that they would have a ten minute break.

The usher then told the rest of the court, everyone stood up as the judge left for his chambers.

There was a lot of talking around the courtroom about what had just taken place. Richard walked over to David who was still sitting in the witness box and running his fingers through his hair.

'Sorry,' said David, looking at Richard.

'Don't worry about it, Walker was asking for it anyway.'

'Yeah and it seemed like the judge gave it to him, as well,' said David.

'You know yourself that every time he comes into court he has always got something to say. Talk to your wife I think that she'll be pleased with you so far, I still need you back on the stand after though, ok,' stated Richard.

David nodded and then headed towards his wife, who was talking to her friends and family.

'Sorry, I guess I got a little bit wound up,' suggested David.

'I was hoping that you were going to run across and punch him out,' said his wife, giving him a cuddle. David smiled, he thought that his wife was going to have a go at him, but she seemed quite pleased that her husband was standing up to him.

'Well I did want to punch him, but I thought seeing as the guards were holding me, I'd better not, besides he's really not worth it anyway,' smiled David.

'I quite enjoyed that,' said Susan, smiling and making them all laugh.

'So did I,' said Helen. 'It's about time the judge did something about him anyway.'

'I've only got one question,' said Bob.

'What's that?' asked David.

'Why on earth did you wait so long?'

'Ha ha, very funny, I don't think that the judge would have liked it if I ran over and started fighting with the man who raped my wife,' suggested David.

'I think that you would be downstairs in the cells next to Mr Walker, anyway come on.' They all went and had a quick coffee.

David was back on the stand.

'Now earlier you were talking about your wife's business, obviously if she's so successful she has her own money?' asked Richard.

'Don't get me wrong, I do buy my wife things, presents, flowers, so on, but such as clothes, make-up, let's put it this way she likes her independence,' stated David.

'Can you say if her business has ever been strapped for cash?' asked Richard.

'Not really, all businesses hit a slump every now and then.'

'Why do you think that the business is doing so well?'

'I think that her and Susan her partner really try their best to make it work. I think they feel that every individual is different, I mean I like a nice sized house, but some don't like big houses. They cater for the individual house buyer, and not just for people who have money to spend on luxury houses,' said David.

'So what would you say to the people that say you are only after Mr Forbes' money?' said Richard looking across at Mr Forbes.

'Good luck to Mr Forbes and his money, but as for me and my wife we don't need it,' replied David also looking at Mr Forbes.

'What about the people that says that your wife is lying? Now I know that I asked you this question before the break, but as you remember we were interrupted,' asked Richard.

'We had a woman a few months ago that basically told my wife to her face that she was lying.' David was seeing the woman in his head, as he spoke.

'Excuse me, aren't you the one who claimed that Mr Forbes the millionaire attacked and raped you?' asked this woman.

'He did rape me.'

'Oh be real woman, the man has a dozen women after him, why on earth would he want to rape you?' asked the women 'Personally I think that you're just after his money, after all he could buy all the houses in your street if he wanted to.'

'Now, wait a minute,' said Sarah.

'Plus, you conned him out of all that money, no wonder your business is doing so well,' she said.

'How dare you,' began Sarah furiously.

'I just believe in speaking my mind,' said the woman interrupting Sarah. 'If you're not up to anything then you won't care what people say.'

The people in the shop were all listening to the argument, well I say argument, Sarah couldn't get a word in edgeways.

As the woman went to continue, David had heard the commotion and came running from another isle.

216

'Who the hell do you think you are talking to my wife like that?' demanded David in a loud voice.

'Don't tell me that she's got you to believe this ridiculous story of hers as well? Are you sure that she's told you the full story?'

'What the hell is that suppose to mean' shouted David.

'All I'm saying is that when the cat's away the mice will play. Perhaps she was making up for certain inadequacies at home in the bedroom.'

David smiled and shook his head he could not believe the boldness of this woman. She didn't know them but here she was slagging them off in the middle of a supermarket.

'Now you listen to me you sick twisted old bitch, how would you feel if it was your daughter who was raped, beaten and left for dead in some alleyway? Or then again what if it was yourself what then? Millionaire or not, what if it was the other way round? People like you make me sick, you make up bloody stories and most of the time you have no idea what you're on about,' said David.

As David and Sarah walked off the manager came and was asking them to leave the shop because David and Sarah were upsetting the rest of the shoppers.

'Oh by the way,' said David as he was walking off. 'We have two children, nine and ten, how would you suggest we tell them that their mother may have Aids? You make me sick all of you. I hope it happens to one of you someday and then you'll know how it feels.'

The manager and the security guards were asking them to leave the store.

'Don't touch me I'm going, I never liked shopping here anyway.' He never told Richard the full story, but I guess that Richard got the point.

'Thank you, Mr Phillips, no further questions Your Honour.'

It was now Mr Chevron's turn to ask David some questions.

'Mr Phillips, did your wife ever like my client?'

'I really can't say, I've never really asked her.'

'What is your personal opinion of Mr Forbes?' asked Mr Chevron.

'Well to be honest I really don't know that much about him only what I read in the papers.'

'And what's that?' asked Mr Chevron, looking rather oddly at David.

'It's the classic story: the man who had nothing then within a few years built up an empire. You have to respect him for that if nothing else.'

'You said earlier that you only hit your wife purely out of frustration, is that correct?'

'There was a lot of tension in the house, I just snapped,' stated David.

'Just answer yes or no please Mr Phillips.'

'Yes,' said David reluctantly.

'Then Mr Phillips, might I be as bold as to say that you are no better than my clients. Are you?'

'Yes, I am better than both your clients,' insisted David.

'How can that be? Let's put it this way. You say that you acted purely out of frustration, so would you say that my two clients also acted out of frustration?'

'No, I wouldn't,' replied David quickly.

'As far as I can gather, it was your wife who delivered the first blow,' stated Mr Chevron.

'That's a lie,' David insisted.

'Mr Phillips your wife clearly states that she was defending herself.'

'She was defending herself,' said David.

'Defending herself from what? As far as we know my clients never hit your wife until she hit them first. So you could say that they acted in self defence.'

'She was all alone in an alleyway with two complete strangers,' said David.

'So are you saying that it's alright for your wife to go around hitting people, but they aren't allowed to defend themselves?'

'My wife doesn't go around hitting people,' stated David.

'But she attacked my two clients,' suggested Mr Chevron.

'Yes, because she was in fear of her life,' said David getting slightly angry.

'But her life wasn't in danger then, was it? The only time her life became threatened is after she attacked my clients. If she had gone along on her merry way without resorting to violence, perhaps she may not be in this courtroom now. No further questions, Your Honour,' Mr Chevron sat back down.

The judge asked Richard if he wanted to question David some more. Richard replied that he had finished with Mr Phillips. David was told that he was no longer needed on the stand so he sat back down by his wife.

The judge asked Mr Chevron to call his next witness. He called Miss Donna Woodfield once again. Miss Woodfield walked to the stand a lot differently than she did the first time. It may have been because the judge had a go at her the last time she did it or it could be that she just thought better of it. She took the oath again and sat down.

'Miss Woodfield you've been at this particular job for, how long was it you said, was it three years?' asked Mr Chevron.

'Yes, that's correct,' she replied.

'So would you say that you know your job inside out?'

'Yes, I would,' she replied.

'Then it's safe to assume that it's very rare that you make any mistakes?' asked Mr Chevron. 'I mean, you can't really afford to make any mistakes.'

'Well I'm not perfect but I make a real effort not to make any mistake. I'd only be putting lives at risk if I did,' stated Miss Woodfield.

Lying bitch thought Sarah to herself. She doesn't care about what happens in people's lives.

'Then would you say that what you said in your statement is true?' asked Mr Chevron walking back to his table.

'As much as I can remember, yes,' she replied.

'Then let me remind you of what you said,' said Mr Chevron picking up a piece of paper off his table.

'In your statement you said:

I came back from my lunch break, opened the door to the surgery and went in. I put the kettle on and I then sorted out some prescriptions for the doctor to sign when he got back off his lunch break. I sat at my desk drinking my cup of coffee and reading the paper when I thought that I heard voices coming from outside the alley, but after a while there were no more noises, but as I said, I'm not sure that there were any noises. After about ten minutes I knew that I heard someone shouting, so I got up to have a look. Just as I opened the door to have a look to go outside, I heard two men jump into a car and drive off fairly quickly. The car also hit another car as they drove off. At the time I remember saying to myself that the person who was driving was a maniac.

'Anyway, I was just about to go back into the surgery when I heard faint moaning noises coming from down the alley. Curiosity got the better of me, so I walked down the alley and I heard the noise again. I looked beside the doctor's car and that's when I saw the victim. I was just about to see if she was alright, when the doctor came back from his lunch break. He saw me bending over and asked what I was doing. I told him to come over to me and he did and that's when he saw the victim. He began treating her and then I went and phoned for an ambulance and the police. I never saw the two men get into the car I just heard them drive off.'

Sarah was thinking about what she had just heard. She had never heard Miss Woodfield's statement before. In fact the only statement she had read was her own, because in the police station they were not allowed to show you anybody else's statement.

'If you had gone outside and seen the two men what would you have done?' asked Mr Chevron.

'I don't know really, it's hard to say until you are in that situation, but by the sound of things there wouldn't be much that I could have done to help anyway.'

'Oh come on Miss Woodfield give yourself a bit more credit, you did phone the ambulance and the police and plus you stayed with her until they came. You even helped the doctor attend to her when he came off his lunch break. That in itself is commendable. I mean, suppose they decided to come back, they would then have had two people to abuse would they not?' asked Mr Chevron.

'Well yes, now you put it like that I guess I was quite helpful.'

'Did you enjoy your lunch break?' asked Mr Chevron.

'Yes I did I always do,' replied Miss Woodfield smiling thoughtfully.

'Now in your statement, you said that you heard two men running away and getting into a car, is that correct?' asked Mr Chevron holding Miss Woodfield's statement in his hand.

'Yes it is,' she replied.

'So as you were just coming out of the door, there was no way that you could have seen anybody or if there was anybody running away or see any faces for that matter?'

'Well as I told the police, I was just coming out of the door,' stated Miss Woodfield.

'Do you know Mr Forbes?' Mr Chevron looked over at his client.

'Well yes, only by reputation I mean who doesn't, he's rich, good looking. Who wouldn't want to know about him?'

Anybody who's ever felt the back of his hand thought Sarah to herself.

'So you admire my client then?' asked Mr Chevron.

'Yes I suppose I do,' added Miss Woodfield.

'Thank you Miss Woodfield, no further questions Your Honour,' said Mr Chevron going back to his seat.

Sarah meanwhile was waiting for Richard to get up and tear this woman in half now that Mr Chevron had said his peace. But all he said was:

'I reserve the right to question the witness another time, Your Honour.'

'Very well you may step down Miss Woodfield, but you will be called again,' stated the judge, looking as though he was going to sleep.

'Would you like to call your next witness, Mr Thorn?'

'Yes, Your Honour. I would like to call Mr Josh Mackoshie to the stand. Mr Mackoshie came down and took the stand and the oath.

'Mr Mackoshie, how long have you been a businessman?' asked Richard getting up from behind his table.

'Twenty-two years,' he replied.

'That's a long time,' said Richard looking at him and feeling slightly surprised that for someone who looked so young could be in business for that long.

'Mr Mackoshie that's a long time to be in the same business.'

'I know,' he replied thinking back to when he first started his business.

'How did you start up your business?' asked Richard.

'This particular business is part of my family's business. We have our main business at home in Japan, that's why I'm only in this country for so many months of the year. My main work is in Japan,' he replied.

'Can I ask what sort of business that you and your family run?' asked Richard.

'Well the main part of our business is computer programming, but we also make and design computer games and we also deal in oriental jewellery,' stated Mr Mackoshie.

'So would you say that you have to pay reasonable attention to detail?'

'Yes I would,' he replied.

'So you're sure that you heard two screams on that particular day?' asked Richard.

'Yes I did,' he replied.

'When you heard the first scream didn't it bother you?'

'No not really,' stated Mr Mackoshie.

'Why not?' asked Richard.

'Well as I said before, it's a hectic part of town. The top part of the alleyway is more hectic than the bottom part of the alley, there's always someone shouting or screaming or kids being silly, so after a while you learn to ignore it. Well I wouldn't get much work done otherwise.'

'So what you're saying is that you just thought that people were just being their loud normal selves?' asked Richard.

'Yes,' he replied.

'If, err… you don't mind Mr Chevron, I'd like to ask Mr Mackoshie what might seem to the court as an odd question,' said Richard. Mr Chevron nodded as if to say he didn't really care less.

'At a guess, could you tell me roughly how long it was when you heard the second scream after the first one? I know it's a long time ago and I don't expect you to be perfect.'

'Well, I think it was about three minutes,' replied Mr Mackoshie.

'If you don't mind me saying so Mr Mackoshie, that's a bit more accurate than I'd imagined, is that a guess or are you sure?'

'I'm pretty sure,' he replied.

'Any particular reason for being so sure?' asked Richard curiously.

'When I heard the first scream I had just started printing something on my printer and what I printed normally takes about three minutes.' Richard smiled as he heard what the witness was saying.

'What's he smiling for?' whispered Sarah to her husband.

'I think that he's figured something out,' replied David. Sarah felt a warm sense of anticipation through her body.

'Now, when you got up when you heard the second scream, what did you see?'

'Well I saw as I said before the two men running from the alleyway.'

221

'When you were called up the last time, you were asked to point out the two suspects. Now because there is only one suspect here, can you still say that he was one of the men that you saw running out of the alleyway?' asked Richard.

'Yes he is,' insisted Mr Mackoshie.

'Now in your statement you said that you saw the two suspects tidying themselves up as they were in or by the car, is that correct?'

'Yes they were,' insisted Mr Mackoshie.

'Could you tell the court, which one was in the car and which one was by the car?' Mr Mackoshie pointed out who was where at the time.

'Now also in your statement, you said that they drove off fairly quickly and hit another car. Also when you were making your statement to the police you asked for something to be left out because you were unsure about what it was that you saw. So rather than make a false account of what happened you asked for this particular thing to be kept out of your statement. May I ask what that particular thing was?' asked Richard, who was now leaning against his table.

'It was really odd because as the two men were running out of the alley I thought I saw a woman in the alleyway behind them. I just caught what I thought was a glimpse of a woman but because of the sunlight I could not be sure,' added Mr Mackoshie.

'So you thought that you saw someone lurking in the shadows?'

'Yes, but as I said I wasn't sure.'

'Thank you, Mr Mackoshie, that will be all, I have no need to call this witness again Your Honour.'

'Thank you, Mr Thorn,' replied the judge. 'Have you any questions for this witness Mr Chevron?'

'Yes, Your Honour,' replied Mr Chevron standing up and walking around his table.

'Now if there were someone lurking in the shadows they would have seen my clients would they not? Theoretically speaking of course.'

'Yes I suppose so,' replied Mr Mackoshie.

'But seeing as though no one came forward to say that my clients had been seen running past them, we can only assume that there was nobody there, because everybody who witnessed anything has come forward and given a statement,' stated Mr Chevron.

'Yes I suppose that's true, like I said, it may just have been the sun playing tricks on my eyes,' added Mr Mackoshie.

'So there are no witnesses to say my clients raped Mrs Phillips is there? All we have so far is a lot of wild allegations and assumptions.'

What a bastard thought Sarah, I'm a witness, I'm the best bloody witness there is, what more do they need?

I know it happened, I've no reason to lie and make it all up and that pratt has the audacity to stand there and say that people have only made wild allegations about his clients. Sarah was just about to start cursing to herself when Richard asked if she was alright.

'Did you hear what he just said? Pratt, how can he say things like that?' whispered Sarah.

'What he said was true, if there's no one there, then nobody can say what his clients were doing there,' whispered David.

'I know what they were doing there, I was there remember,' whispered Sarah.

'Calm down,' whispered David. 'I can guess what you're thinking, we'll talk in a while ok.' Sarah agreed in a fashion. Mr Chevron told the judge that he had no further need for Mr Mackoshie.

The judge told Mr Mackoshie that he was no longer needed as a witness and that he was free to leave the courtroom. The judge told everyone in the court that court was adjourned until tomorrow morning at nine thirty. He banged his gavel and got up and headed for his chambers.

'Now look,' said Richard. 'I know what you're thinking, but Chevron's trying to say that there was nobody in the shadows right, but what if there were someone in the shadows?'

'But Mr Mackoshie said that it might have been the sunlight,' said Sarah.

'Yes he did, but he also said that he caught the glimpse of a woman. Come in early tomorrow morning and we'll talk,' said Richard shutting his case. They all said goodbye then left. Sarah and her husband kissed their children goodbye. They told everybody that they would see them tomorrow. Richard meanwhile was seeing if Mr Mackoshie was still in the building, he wanted to ask him something.

The next day seemed to come rather quickly and everybody was soon back in the courtroom.

'Mr Chevron would you like to call your next witness,' asked the judge.

'Mr Chevron,' repeated the judge. Mr Chevron was deep in conversation with his client and never heard the judge. The judge banged his gavel a few times.

'Mr Chevron,' said the judge loudly and making most of the courtroom jump. Mr Chevron looked up to find the judge staring at him.

'Are you ready to proceed?'

'Err... yes Your Honour,' replied Mr Chevron, looking surprised at the judge staring at him.

'Then would you like to call your next witness, Mr Chevron?' asked the judge again.

'Yes, Your Honour,' replied Mr Chevron looking slightly flustered.

'I'd like to call Mr Michael Forbes to the stand please.' There was a sharp intake of breath throughout the courtroom and people began to whisper. Mr Forbes walked over to the stand and took the oath. Sarah just kept giving him a dirty evil look, the kind of look that would melt concrete.

She was pondering on whether she should think about all the nasty horrible things she could do to him and Mr Walker, but as she pondered she glanced at her husband. He put his hand in her hand and gave her a warm comforting smile. The kind only a loved one could give, he gave her hand a gentle squeeze. She then thought to herself, I'm going to have to listen to his bullshit sooner or later, besides the bastard can't do any more than he and his mate haven't already done.

'Can you state your full name please?' asked Mr Chevron.

'Michael Anthony Forbes,' he replied.

'And your age?'

'I'm thirty-five.'

'And what is your occupation?' asked Mr Chevron walking up and down in front of the witness box.

'I'm a businessman.'

'Are you married?'

'No,' replied Mr Forbes.

'Do you have any children?'

'I have no time for children,' he added.

'Oh, why's that?' asked Mr Chevron.

'My lifestyles to hectic, I would not be able to spend enough time with them, so it would be selfish of me to even think about having children at this stage in my life.'

'I have here a copy of your statement which I would like to read to you if I may,' stated Mr Chevron walking back to his table and picking up a sheet of paper.

'I came down the alleyway after doing some shopping in the town. I saw a young woman in some distress. I offered to help her to her feet, but she declined my offer.'

Sarah had put her head on her husband's shoulder. David noticed that she was sobbing. Not a lot but just enough for someone who was close enough to notice to see her.

He gave her a hanky and then put his arms around her and whispered that not to worry that he was there for her.

David and Sarah just sat there listening to Mr Forbes, knowing that all they could do was listen and wait.

'I tried again to assist her, but all she kept shouting was leave me alone you bastard, just get away from me and leave me alone,' continued Mr Chevron. 'Even though she was shouting, I still tried to help her, but she kept shouting and screaming at me. She then began to scream very loudly that's when I decided it was better if I left and forget about the whole thing, so I went about my own business. Got into my car drove off fairly quickly as I didn't want anybody thinking that I had harmed such a beautiful woman,' read Mr Chevron.

Each time he spoke, it was like being slapped repeatedly to Sarah and David, probably her friends and family too were hurt and sickened by all these lies Mr Forbes was telling.

'I had no accomplice as you would call it, I was on my own. I have never seen this woman before in my life. I don't know who she is for all I know she could be a mad woman. I have never raped anybody in my life. She must be doing this to see if she can get money off me, she's probably jealous of my fortune, most people are jealous of my wealth and me. This woman had a stroke of bad luck and was raped. Now, because I tried to help her she wants to blame me. If the truth was known she probably had an argument with one of her lovers and wanted to end it but he or she thought better of it.

'I've never heard of Mr Walker, perhaps he's the one that raped her, all I did was try to help,' read Mr Chevron.

Sarah could not take any more. She jumped up and started screaming abuse at him. David was holding his wife back, he was trying to get her to calm down and stop shouting but Sarah was having none of it. The judge was asking for order in the courtroom. Richard told David to take his wife outside. David carried his wife kicking and screaming outside the courtroom. The judge told Mr Forbes to step down and he then called Richard and Mr Chevron to the bench.

'Is your client alright?' asked the judge, to Richard.

'Yes, well she will be anyway. I'll have a word with her.'

'I think that we should have a break,' said Mr Chevron. Sarah must have touched Mr Chevron in some small way, because most of the time it was Richard who asked for the case to be adjourned or anything like that normally.

'I agree.'

'This case has to be finished sooner rather than later, or this kind of thing will keep happening,' said the judge.

'My client doesn't do this on purpose, this must be really hard for her and her family,' stated Richard.

'Nobody's blaming your client we are just saying that it's inconvenient when these things happen,' said the judge. Richard knew that for the time being he was out voted. The judge told the usher that they would adjourn until the fifth of August. The usher then told the court.

Richard was putting his papers back into his briefcase, as he sat down he sighed deeply.

'Look,' said Sarah's father putting his hand on Richard's shoulder. 'We all believe in you. Ok, I know that my daughter's actions put you in a difficult position, but you know that it's not her fault and it's not your fault either.'

'I know but you must understand my job is to convince the jury that my client, your daughter was raped. Now Chevron plays hardball as well as me, so he's going to try to prove that his clients didn't rape your daughter,' said Richard.

'I can believe how difficult your position is, but I've watching and listening and I know that certain things do not add up. I mean Mr Mackoshie for instance, as far as I see it, he seems a pretty bright intelligent man and I personally think that he did see a woman there as he thought he did. Keep with it morally speaking you've already won this case. So if you give up now, you will let thousands of sick individuals think that it's alright to do this and get away with it, you want to show them that they cannot get away with it no matter how much money you have,' said Bob.

'Come on,' said Richard. 'I'll buy you a pint.'

Everyone had gone from the courtroom except Sandra, who was waiting outside.

'Where is everybody?' asked Bob.

'Well,' said Sandra. 'Helen said that she would call you later, and David and Sarah have gone home.'

'How was Sarah?' asked her father.

'She calmed down a little bit when she got outside. Personally I think that she just needed to let off a bit of steam, anyway where you going?' Sandra asked.

Richard told her that they were just going for a quick drink in the pub. Bob asked Sandra if she would like to join them, she said yes just for a quick one and off they headed to the pub across the road.

Back home David asked Sarah if she was ok. She said that she just wanted to go and lie down for a while, she went upstairs and fell asleep within a few minutes. As David sat down to relax the phone rang, he sighed and let it ring for a while. He decided that he had better answer it or it might disturb his wife. He picked up the phone, it was Helen.

'I'm not going to keep you long,' said Helen. 'How is Sarah?'

'Oh she's fine, well you know what I mean, she's as well as you'd expect under the circumstances.'

'And how are you?' asked Helen.

'Oh me, I'm fine I'm ok,' said David.

'Liar, you and I need to talk. Richard phoned me and said that he wants to see you and Sarah in my office at ten thirty tomorrow morning and if you've made plans cancel them because this is important.'

'What's it all about?' asked David.

'Don't ask me I'm just the messenger.'

'Ok we'll be there,' said David. They both said goodbye and put the phone down.

David sighed again and sat back down.

'I wonder what he wants.'

You know thought David to himself. It's amazing how people can just sit up there and lie. I mean you take the oath, swear by almighty God that the evidence given will be truth, the whole truth and nothing but the truth and so on. But I mean you expect people to lie a bit or even lie a lot, but distort the truth completely is a bit much. How can Forbes have the audacity to sit in the dock and say that he tried to help her, but she declined his offer?

Am I the only one that thinks that Forbes and Walker are both pratts? David was lying on the settee, his mind must have been wondering because he never heard his wife come into the room and speak to him.

She kissed her husband on the top of his head making him jump slightly.

'Sorry, darling I was miles away,' said David stretching and sitting up.

Sarah seemed a bit more relaxed than she did earlier.

'Come on then,' said his wife sitting down beside him. 'What were you thinking about?'

'Well,' said David, putting his arm around his wife. 'I was thinking of getting absolutely plastered. I want to go to the pub on the corner and get absolutely wasted.'

'You know that sounds like a great idea, I'll just go and get changed,' said Sarah.

'Come on, we'll go as we are,' said David.

Sarah was quite surprised at her husband's spontaneous gesture. She got her coat, as did David and off they went. Sarah and David were a little bit apprehensive as they entered the pub. Everyone who was in there went silent. David and Sarah thought to hell with them and headed for the bar.

The bar man greeted them warmly.

'Yes sir, madam. What would you like to drink?'

The pub was still quiet. David and Sarah felt as though the whole pub was watching them and they were right. David glanced around the pub to see everyone staring at him and his wife. David spoke out loud. 'My wife and I came here for one reason, and that was to get totally and utterly plastered. None of you can say anything that we haven't had said to us already. So you all have five minutes to say whatever nasty horrible things you want to say to us and then you can leave us alone, and let us get completely pissed.' David looked around the room. 'Come on, who's first to slag us off?'

Sarah meanwhile was enjoying watching her husband. She just thought that he was great. I mean, here they were in a pub full of people that they hardly knew, they may have seen some of them about, but they don't really know them as such. As David was looking around he saw a man get up and head towards him. Sarah looked at the man heading towards her husband.

He was bit bigger than the average man, a lot taller too. Sarah knew that David would have his work cut out if he was to fight this man who was at least six foot tall and six foot wide. They were quite surprised when the rather large gentleman offered to buy David and Sarah a drink. David and Sarah looked shocked, they expected the man to come over and start punching David. David and Sarah were still in shock as the man gestured a small woman to come over to him.

'Don't worry about Mick,' said the woman. 'He may look bad, but believe me the only thing bad about him is his bad breath, believe me, once you've been married to him for eighteen years you get used to it.'

Sarah burst into small giggle. The woman took Sarah by the arm.

'Come on sweetheart, come and sit with us girls. If you stay with the men, you'll end up talking crap and liking football.'

'Come on,' laughed the woman, leading Sarah to a table and gesturing her to sit down. There were about five ladies at the table. Meanwhile people wanting to buy him a drink surrounded David.

'Now,' said the barman. 'Did I hear someone say that they wanted to get pissed?'

'Err… yes, yes you did,' stuttered David.

The man served them with a load of drinks. He told the two women helping him behind the bar that he was going to sit with the guys for a while.

'Typical landlord,' said one of the girls. 'We do all the work and he has all the fun.'

'I heard that,' said the landlord as he walked over to where the other guys were sitting and talking to David. David glanced at his wife, who was laughing hysterically with some other woman. He was glad that she was enjoying herself, he felt that they both needed to relax.

'So come on then mate,' said Mick. 'Who's Forbes paid to bullshit for him now?'

'Mick, come on the man came here to get pissed not to talk about the court case,' said the barman cutting into the conversation.

'Sorry, I wasn't thinking alright,' Mick apologised to David.

228

'Don't worry about it, I don't mind if you want to talk about it. I only know Forbes by his reputation,' said David.

'Is that what you call it?' said one of the men sitting next to David. As David went to speak, the man carried on.

'Let's cut the crap, Forbes has screwed too many people in this town out of money, or pissed them off in some way. Most of us here had our own small business each of us doing ok in our own way. Then that pratt comes along with his money and his big development ideas and bang, you're out of business.'

'Yes, I know how you feel,' said Mick. 'I lost my business because of him too.'

'Are you sure Forbes is a pratt and not a wanker?' asked David putting his glass down after taking a drink from it.

'That's a good question.'

'Forbes has screwed people over and put people like yourselves out of business, how come he's never been charged with anything?'

'You really don't know much about him, do you?' said Mick.

The man who was sitting next to David spoke again.

'Look mate, when you've got a bank account as big as Forbes and you've got millions in there and I mean millions, you can buy almost anything that you want.'

'And anybody,' added Mick.

'Look,' said another man, 'People look at Forbes and they see money, they don't see a man, they see pound signs, they see expensive cars, a thousand pound suit, a ten grand watch and all they see is money nothing else matters.'

'Yeah, but people say that he's a damn good businessman,' said David.

'Ok,' said Mick. 'He may be a good businessman, but come on you've heard him in court, I know I have, he talks to people like he just stepped on them and wiped them off his shoes.'

'I agree,' said the barman, 'but I know for a fact that at least half his money came from dodgy dealings, you might say that he has an expensive habit.'

'You know he takes drugs,' said David, beginning to slur his words slightly. 'They said so in court, he sniffs it, injects it, smokes it and sells it.'

'If you want anything to do with drugs anything at all, see him,' said Mick. 'And if you owe him any money, he'll send his bodyguard round to kick the shit out of you or worse.'

'Don't tell me, Walker,' said David, who was beginning to find it hard to put his words together.

'Yes, the very same,' said the man next to David.

'Look,' said the barman. 'Mr Forbes is a very convincing character, he's rich, smooth and as evil as that Saddam Hussein. You and your wife may be the first people to ever cross him and Walker and actually get away with it.'

'That is unless you and wife give up the case?' said Mick.

'Oh no,' said David, who now could not put a sentence together properly. 'I'll make sure he pays for what he's done to my wife.'

It was getting late; David and Sarah by this time were well and truly drunk.

'Well,' said Mick. 'The man and his wife came here to get drunk and I must say that I think that they have done a superb job.'

They all laughed as they watched David slump further into the chair. Mick's wife had come over and suggested that Mick and some of the lads take them home. They were used to this drinking lark but David and Sarah weren't. But I guess they enjoyed themselves nevertheless. 'And don't forget those things from behind the bar for them.'

Mick and the lads he was drinking with got up and took them home. One of the men took David's keys out of his pocket. There weren't many keys on the key ring, so it wasn't long before they had the front door open. They struggled to get Sarah and David up the stairs, but they managed it eventually. They put Sarah in the main bedroom, took off her coat and shoes and put her in bed. They did the same to David, even though David was trying to sing and slurring his words, as he was doing so and trying to thank all the guys at the same time.

He was too drunk to know what he was thanking them for, but he thanked them all the same. Eventually they managed to get him into Jason's room. They put the things from behind the bar downstairs and then wrote a short note and then they left.

In the morning Sarah was the first one up and out of bed. Apart from having a mouth that felt a dry as a desert considering the amount that she drank, she was reasonably ok.

She was having a shower, when she heard David come into the bathroom.

Now, he sounds terrible thought Sarah smiling to herself. She pulled back the shower curtain a little and saw her husband looking in the mirror.

'You look a pretty site,' said Sarah.

'God I haven't felt this good in ages,' replied David, looking as though he was going to be sick.

'I suppose you'll be off on your ten mile run? All uphill today is it?' Sarah broke into a small chuckle as she finished her shower.

'Not today,' said David, leaning his aching head against the mirror over the washbasin. Sarah had finished her shower and was standing behind her husband, drying herself off.

'So you look a horrible mess,' said David, looking into the mirror again.

'I know I've got a headache like you would not believe. I'm feeling as sick as anything and my body aches from top to bottom.'

'Still you look great.'

'Well I really don't feel great,' replied his wife tapping him gently on his backside.

David turned round and held her close to him.

'No, I mean you really look great,' said David looking deep into her hazel eyes. 'And I'm sorry, I'm really, really sorry.'

'Sorry for what?' Sarah could see her husband could not find the words to say what he meant.

'It's alright,' said Sarah putting her head on his shoulder. 'I miss sex as much as you do and there's nothing that I would like more than to have the man I love throw me on that big bed in there and ride me silly. But you know what the doctor said.' David sighed deeply.

'Suppose the doctor gets the all clear, just suppose I am completely Aids free, we'll both be on top of the world. For me it would be just like winning the pools. But suppose I do have Aids, David?' Sarah looked at him with a tear in her eye. 'I'm being really and truly selfish as I am.'

'No you're not,' whispered her husband.

'Yes, I am. The people I love and care for the most, I treat them like shit most of the time and if I do have Aids.' Sarah sighed deeply, as she looked into her husband's eyes.

'If your wife, the woman you love and married and had children with is going to die. And then, I don't want my children to be orphans. I want their father to love and care for them as much as he does now, because I'm not going to let what happened to me happen to them, not to them.'

Sarah carried on talking, as David was about to speak.

'But anyway I'm not dead yet and I'm not planning to go for the next two hundred years, so you won't get rid of me that easily.' She walked out of the bathroom and into the bedroom. David just stood there and watched his wife's curvy figure as she walked away. He smiled to himself as his wife began singing. He had a quick shower and went downstairs.

'Hey, you know,' said David going into the kitchen and joining his wife. 'We should find somewhere nice to take the children, I don't want them thinking that we've deserted them.'

'Yeah, you're right,' replied his wife handing her husband a cup of black coffee. He walked in the living room.

'We should do some shopping today or tomorrow.'

'Somehow I don't think that we'll need to do any shopping for a while.'

'Why on earth not?' said Sarah, walking into the living room.

'Where did all this come from?' asked Sarah, looking at all the boxes in the living room. David had already picked up the note that was left by the barman the night before. Sarah meanwhile had put her coffee down and was looking at some of the things in the boxes, as David was beginning to read the note.

Dear David and Sarah,'

'If you are in any kind of shape after the amount that you drank between you last night, you will by now have seen all the boxes and things in your living room. It started a few months ago, when a woman came into the pub and asked if she could leave a few things behind the bar for a Sarah and David Phillips. She had a writing pad with her as well as some cuddly toys and a small box. The woman said that Sarah would know who she was.

Anyway to cut a long story short, things just seem to catch on from there and before we knew it people were leaving things left right and centre. Money, tins of food all kinds of stuff for the kids. That's why I made the pub a sort of drop off point. People didn't have to leave things, but they did. All I asked was, if they bought a drink in the pub that they would sign the book of sympathy, which we had on the bar. Up to now we have filled five notepads, we also have a sign outside on the pub wall. I must go Mick's moaning at me for another pint. So anyway the best of luck with the case and enjoy the stuff. P.S. David is a terrible singer and if you ever need anything, anything at all just pop into the pub. All the best from Rob and gang at the pub.

David and Sarah were speechless. David said that he had no idea that so many people were on their side. He picked up one of the notepads and read some of them.

Good luck to Mr and Mrs Phillips. All the best, from Pam and Terry.

Win the case George.

All the best Sarah and David.

Good luck to Sarah and her family.

The writing went on page after page with good wishes and condolences on each line.

'Hey, look come on we'll have to sort these things out when we come back from Helen's.'

Sarah asked her husband if he could pop round to her office.

'What for?' asked David.

'Well seeing as though we are both going to Helen's we'll need someone to watch the house and wait for my surprise to come today,' said Sarah.

'Shit, I forgot all about that,' said David.

As they were getting into the car Sarah told David that the people at her office had done the same thing with getting people to write words of condolences on the pads every time they came in.

'Yeah, I remember you telling me something like that, didn't you bring them home with you?' asked David.

'You know I don't think I did, I'll ask Susan when we get to the office. So the people at the pub must have brought us home and put us to bed.'

As they turned to come out of the street, David noticed the sign on the pub wall. It read, *Good luck Sarah and David all the best.* The sign was that big you couldn't really miss it.

'You know the amount of times we've driven past this pub and never noticed that sign.'

'We never went in really until last night, did we?'

'I know, we normally go to work, pick the kids up, watch TV and then go to bed.'

'I mean, we are in bed by ten o'clock most nights.' David checked his mirror then stopped the car suddenly in the middle of the road.

'God, are we really that boring?' said David turning and looking at his wife.

'God, I hope not,' said Sarah, putting her hand on her chin. A car horn sounded behind their car. It was a driver of another car gesturing them to hurry up and drive on, so David did so. They pulled up outside Sarah's office. Sarah got out and went in. After a few minutes Sarah came back out and got back into the car.

'That's that sorted, Kate said that she would watch the house for us,' said Sarah.

'That's good of her.' David pulled up outside Helen's office building.

'Remember the first time we came here and you were apprehensive about going in to see Helen.' David locked the car door.

'I must admit that the thought of coming here the first time, did not appeal to me.'

'Me neither I suppose,' replied David holding his wife hand and crossing the road.

'But now, I feel like I've known Helen for years.'

'I know what you mean.'

They knew that they did not have to see the man at the desk any more because they knew exactly where to go. They reached the floor of Helen's office and got out of the lift, Sarah wondered why the secretary was not there.

'Perhaps she's talking to Helen in the office,' said David looking around.

As David was looking around Sarah was opening the door. She caught Helen and Richard getting changed.

'Oops, sorry,' said Sarah, shutting the door just as quick and blushing slightly.

'What's the matter?' asked her husband, looking at her. Sarah giggled and said. 'I must be the first person in the world in a rape case to have seen my barrister's backside and quite nice it looked too from the glimpse that I got.'

David smiled as he bent down to have a look through the keyhole of Helen's office.

'What are you doing?' asked Sarah, looking at him strangely. As David got down on one knee and was just about to look through the keyhole the door opened. Helen was quite surprised to see David down on one knee in front of the door.

'You won't see anything the keyholes too small and besides we've got dressed now.'

Sarah burst into laughter. Then Richard came to the door.

'What on earth are you doing down there David?' asked Richard, looking oddly at David.

'Whatever he's trying to do, I'm sure there's a law against it.'

Sarah and Helen just laughed as David got up all red faced. Richard just looked at them oddly.

'I'm sure that I've missed something.' Helen and Sarah were still giggling as they all went into the office.

'Coffee anyone?' Helen said yes, but David and Sarah said that they had just had one before they came out of the house.

'Before we start, I'd just like to apologise for the way I acted yesterday,' stated Sarah, looking at Richard. 'I know I should learn to control myself but I can't seem to help it, I just got so wound up.'

'Come on Sarah,' replied Richard, handing Helen her coffee. 'Nobody blames you for the way you acted yesterday. Ok, I'll be honest and tell you that all it does is slow things down a little, but as I've said before, your outbursts are not nice to see or hear. I mean for instance yesterday, if you took away the swear words you would not be able to talk. I know it can't be easy to sit there and listen to the man who raped you telling complete lies about you, but be realistic Sarah. What did you think that he was going to do, go up on the stand and say? I'm the world's biggest druggie, and I raped this woman, of course he's going to go up there and lie through his teeth. Don't forget, he's convinced his barrister that he was not there. Walker has convinced his barrister that he was not there and as he's defending them, he has no choice but to believe them. His job is to make you sound as dirty and cheap, and as much of a lying cow as much as he can.'

'Yeah fair enough, but I can't help it if it winds me up.'

'Yes, well that may well be but you're going to have to try and not let these men get to you. Anyway that's not what I wanted to talk to you about. I had a nice long talk with Mr Mackoshie yesterday and I found out some very interesting things.'

'Like what?' asked David curiously, remembering how Richard rushed off yesterday.

'Well for one thing, we were led to believe that Forbes and Walker don't know each other, but we all know they do. And we know that both Forbes and Walker are both drug users, but according to Mr Mackoshie, Forbes and Walker are in that particular part of the alleyway all the time. Why?' asked Richard, looking at Sarah and David.

'The doctor's surgery as far as I know, that's the only thing that's really on that corner.'

'Yes, but why are they there so often?' Sarah had no idea what Richard was leading to, and just told him that she had no idea.

'What do doctor's surgeries have in them to cure a patient's illness?' asked Helen.

'Drugs,' said David, looking slightly bewildered.

'You're not suggesting that they get drugs from the doctor. He couldn't risk his job to do that,' asked Sarah.

'No he couldn't,' insisted her husband. 'But a secretary could.'

'Couldn't she exactly, we know the doctor is not that type of man. I think that there's more to Miss Woodfield and Mr Walker than meets the eye.'

'What. You don't think that there's more to their relationship do you?' asked Sarah. 'She may be a scheming lying bitch.'

'Absolutely right, but we now know that she's Walker's girlfriend. She also told the court, that when you were raped she phoned the police and ambulance straight away. Now, we know from the emergency services logged calls that she waited for some time before she called them. Why was that?'

'Good question.'

'I'll tell you my theory' suggested Richard, getting up and walking about. 'I think that when they raped you Miss Woodfield knew exactly what happened. I don't think that she actually saw what happened, but I think that she caught enough to put two and two together. And because her boyfriend, Mr Walker, probably said that she'd get the same treatment if she told anyone, so she kept her mouth shut.'

'Well, don't expect me to feel sorry for the bitch because you can forget that.'

'Look,' said David. 'Let's say that what you say is true. It all makes sense apart from one thing.'

'What's that?'

'How did they know Sarah was going to be at that particular place at that particular time?'

'You're not listening are you?' said Helen. 'If Sarah's car had not broken down she would not have been anywhere near that alleyway, because she would have been able to drive straight home with the shopping, therefore she would have had no need to walk through that alleyway, and therefore would not have been raped.'

'Look,' said Richard, looking at Sarah. 'I'm going to tell you something and I don't want you biting my head off, ok. But what happened to you was an accident, they didn't have to rape you but they did. They could have walked away, they could just as easily left you alone but they never. Those men meant to do long term damage to you and that's exactly what they did. But think about it, if your car hadn't broken down you would not have had any need to go through that alleyway.

'Ok. When was the last time that your car broke down and you had to walk home through that alleyway?'

Sarah shrugged her shoulders and shook her head, as if to say she had no idea.

'You see, and I bet if the truth was known, that was probably the first time that you used that particular alleyway in ages.' Sarah just looked at him, as if to say well that might be true, I can't really remember.

'So you're saying Sarah just happened to be in the wrong place at the wrong time,' suggested David.

'That's exactly it. Sarah, I know it's probably the worst thing that you want to hear at this moment in time, is that it was all an accident, but it seems you being raped as bad as it is, it seems like that's all it was. Like David said, you were just in the wrong place at the wrong time. But anyway, I still have a case to win and as for you being on the stand again, I'm leaving you until dead last.'

'Why's that?' asked Sarah, in a soft voice still trying to take in what Richard had said.

'Well I want anybody and everybody who has to take the stand to go up there before you. When it's your turn to go up, I don't want any more witnesses having to be called up. No more statements to be read, no more police telling the court about how they arrested Mr Forbes and Mr Walker or any consultants telling the court what state you were in. I want nobody but you and when I mean you, I don't mean the swearing, aggressive, abusive Sarah. I don't want the angry Sarah,' stated Richard.

'But I am angry. I'm very angry that this accident had to happen to me. Out of all the people out there, this had to happen to me.'

'You still don't understand do you?' suggested Helen. 'This case is not just about Sarah Phillips and her family any more. This case is a benchmark for all women who suffer any kind of sexual abuse. It may be physical, mental it doesn't matter. This case will be on record and say this one guy was a millionaire, the other guy was on the dole, but still they did not get away with it. And that's the message that we need to send out.'

'As I've told you before I've handled a lot of rape cases, even cases where you know as in this case, the men are as guilty as sin and they walk away scotch free. And the worst part about it is that the people who do this time after time, do it, knowing damn well when they get caught that they will just get away with it, just to do it all over again. Believe me, it's just one vicious circle, one that we hope that you can set the standard for other women to follow and say no more.'

'If I could kill those two bastards and get away with it, I would. I would believe me, but I know that it would only make things worse than they are already. That's why I promised myself, my husband, my children and my family and friends that I would not let them get away with it. And on my children's lives, I will not let them get away with it even if I die trying,' stated Sarah.

'I have to go, I'll see you in court tomorrow morning,' said Richard standing up and putting on his coat. 'Oh one more thing before I go, what do you think about getting some sort of compensation out of this? It's worth thinking about.'

'I'll come down with you,' said David, also standing up and getting his coat. 'I just want to pop out for a while and get something to eat. After last night I could eat a horse, be back in a bit.'

'What did you do last night?' asked Richard, opening the office door.

'Come on, I'll tell you on the way down.' Richard said goodbye to Helen, and said that he would call her later.

'Coffee,' said Helen, yawning widely.

'You should go to sleep at night.' Helen chuckled to herself, as she made the coffee.

'So how is Sarah?' Helen handed Sarah her coffee and sat down.

'Fed up, pissed off and happy all at the same time.'

'We'll start with you being fed up.'

'Oh, I don't know.' She put her head in her hands. 'It hurts to know that you might just have been in the wrong place at the wrong time. That you were an accident.'

'What happened to you was an accident. Not the rape itself that was on purpose. They didn't have to rape you, they could have just as easily left you alone and gone about their business and none of this would be necessary.'

'I suppose so, but it still hurts, it hurts a lot. It hurts more than most people know.'

'And what about you being pissed off?' asked Helen.

'Well, I'm pissed off with myself for making things as bad as they are.' Sarah took a sip of her coffee.

'How did you make things so bad?' asked Helen, looking at her.

'Well ok I never started the situation, but I can't say that I've done that much to help speed things a long now have I?'

'Maybe, but none of this is your fault, none of it. At least you can say that you have a good barrister. You've identified the suspects, they're on trial, what more can you do apart from wait to see the outcome of the trial. I mean, most rape cases never get this far, not many rape victims get this far. Most of them just never tell anyone, because they feel that no one will believe them or that something else might go wrong, if they go to court.

'Most victims are scared to tell anyone, let alone identify them in person at the police station and start beating the crap out of one of them and have to be dragged off by a police officer. That's definitely the mark of someone wanting to see this thing through until the end, no matter how hard it is,' said Helen.

Sarah laughed.

'You know as I kicked Forbes right between the legs and punched him it felt great. At the time it felt great, but now I think that it was really a silly thing to do. It made me feel good for a few minutes and then it was gone. But I said then in the police station that I would not let them get away with it and I won't,' stated Sarah.

'Good for you, well come on then, let's hear the good news,' replied Helen.

'Well,' said Sarah, kicking off her shoes. 'It all started about three weeks or so ago, I think it was about three weeks. Oh I can't remember I tend to lose track of time a lot these days for some reason. Anyway, I hadn't been into the office for ages so I thought I'd pop in and say hi to everyone. I was talking to one of the secretaries and she told me that they had got people to sign best wishes on a notepad and before she knew it they had filled the writing pad.

'After a while people just came to sign these pads. Now most of the time, I was thinking before I really started going out on my own again that nobody cares, nobody gives a shit about some dumb old estate agent who got raped. And as I got myself to the point where I thought fuck the lot of them, I noticed that people were beginning to show signs of caring. But I saw these pads that people had written things on, well you can imagine the state I was in, I was crying, my make-up was running. You know all these people didn't know a thing about me, apart from the fact that I was raped by two men. One happens to be one of the most respected millionaires in the whole town and here's this little businesswoman accusing him of rape and as I'm thinking about what people might read in the paper. I thought that nobody cared and I was wrong, but lots of people cared, I was just too stupid to notice.

'Last night for instance, David and I went to the pub by us and as we walked in the whole pub went quite. I stood there looking at everybody, who in turn were looking at David and me. Ha,' giggled Sarah slightly. 'All of a sudden David said Ok now my wife and I came to get pissed anybody who has anything nasty to say has five minutes to get it out of the way and say what they want. I thought that David was going to get his head kicked in, but I never told him that. All of a sudden this guy walks over built like a brick shit house he was.' Sarah drank her coffee, which by now was stone cold.

'I thought that's it, I'm going to spend the night in casualty and all of a sudden this guy asks to buy us both a drink? Well, I was dumbstruck. I mean, my husband can look after himself but this guy Mick would have killed him. God he was a big guy, but funny enough though he turned out to be one hell of a nice guy. David and I, apart from getting completely pissed, found out some very strange things about Forbes and Walker.

'I thought Forbes was rich, drives a convertible everyone must like him but not so. From what those women told me about him, he seems one hell of a nasty man and not many women like him, most of them can't stand him. In fact the ones I spoke to last night in the pub said the only thing good about him is his money and as far as they said, not all his money was earned legitimately.

'I know that as far as rumours go, he's been taking and selling drugs for years, so what Richard said earlier could well be true.' Sarah paused for a brief moment.

'You know, it might be true. It all makes a bit of sense now that you mention it,' said Helen.

Suddenly there was a knock at the door; it was David coming back in after having something to eat.

'You look like you enjoyed yourself,' suggested Helen, looking thoughtfully at him.

'Yes I did.'

'I was telling Helen about last night,' said Sarah.

'You mean, Mick?' His wife nodded her head.

'God the way he walked over to us, I thought that my time was up. When he handed me a pint later on in the evening, his one hand covered the whole glass so he would have slapped me all over the place if we had fought.'

'Did you tell Helen about the stuff they left us last night?' asked David.

'Yeah, they took us home and then they left all this stuff for us. I can't believe how much stuff there actually is,' said Sarah, thinking about all the boxes and bags in her living room.

'It's worth taking a look at it.'

'You know that's not a bad idea. Would you come and have a look?' Sarah asked Helen.

'I think I might actually, I haven't got anything on today anyway, well apart from seeing you two that is. It sounds like quite a sight.'

'Well we might as well go now that's if nobody minds.' Everyone agreed that they might as well go now, so they did. On the way down, Sarah asked Helen why her secretary was not at work.

'Well, I felt that she's been working really hard for me these last few weeks and I just thought she could use a few days off.'

'Ah, isn't that sweet.'

'I know I'm a darling aren't I?' replied Helen, rolling her eyes and smiling to herself.

It wasn't long before they got to the house. Sarah had begun telling Helen all about the sign on the outside of the pub, when she noticed a satellite dish on the wall outside the house. She ran excitedly around the car and kissed and hugged him.

'Well now you know what your dad has.' His wife was over the moon.

They went into the house, Sarah picked up her keys and a note that was on the floor.

'I'll have to read it later.' She was still excited about the satellite dish. 'As I was saying we just hadn't noticed the sign on the pub before.'

'God, you weren't joking when you said that there was a lot of stuff was you?' said Helen, not quite knowing what to focus on because there was so much.

'Sit down if you can find somewhere to sit.' David moved a few boxes off a chair so Helen could sit down. Sarah hung her and Helen's coat up.

'Right let's sort some of these things out, then you can show Helen some of those pads,' suggested David.

'Come on I'll give you a hand,' she sat forward on her chair.

'Where do you start?' said Sarah, picking something up then putting it back down.

'The best thing to do is any food comes to me and I'll put them in the kitchen. Any clothing, toys, things like that go over by you or Helen.'

David went over to the stereo and after some fiddling about managed to put a CD on. He turned the volume down a little and started moving boxes. He groaned slightly as he tried to move a large box.

'I bet Mick carried that,' suggested Sarah.

'What's in it?' she asked. David opened the box and saw that it was full of tins.

'You'll never pick that up in a thousand years,' said Helen. 'Not without pulling something anyway,' she giggled with Sarah.

David struggled, but managed to get the large box into the kitchen.

God thought David I don't envy the person that had to carry that box. It didn't take him long to put the things out of the box into the cupboards. David noticed as he was putting the tins into them that the cupboards were basically empty.

Damn Sarah, thought David to himself you weren't joking, when you said that we needed to do some shopping were you? He quickly put the things in to the cupboard and went to get another box.

'Here these would look great on you,' said his wife, showing him a pair of long johns as he entered the living room.

'You can laugh, but in certain parts of the army they have to wear things like that to keep them warm in very cold places, but there again I'm not in the army.' He had a look as if to say, there's no way in the world that I would wear them. He carried a somewhat smaller box considering the size of the last one into the kitchen. He chuckled to himself as he carried on putting some more groceries away in the cupboards.

Imagine what I'd look like in those long johns, he thought to himself. When he went back in the living room, it was beginning to look more its old self.

'God, I'd like to know how long they were collecting things at the pub.'

'I know I can't get over how many people actually cared about what was going on in my life, but there again I suppose that was the selfish part of me.' Sarah sighed deeply.

'Why do you do that?' asked Helen, looking at Sarah.

'Do what?'

'Do what? Beat yourself up all the time, you act like you're supposed to apologise for being raped, you should know by now that being raped was not your fault.'

'I know, but I just feel so damn guilty all the time. I feel all I want to do is say to the world, fuck you as loud and as long as I can and then just curl up in a hole somewhere where nobody can see me. I feel as though any man who looks at me in any way whatsoever is after me,' stated Sarah.

David was still in the kitchen; he had already finished unpacking the box that he had brought in. He was just staying in there so that his wife could have her talk to Helen in private. Sarah was holding a teddy that someone had sent to one of the children.

'I have a husband who I love and adore and would give my life for him. That's how much I love him and most of the time the poor bloke doesn't know what to do for the best. Most of the time all he tries to do is help and I just have a go at him. Start crying even when he tries to comfort me sometimes I just push him away. I want to hump his brains out but I can't yet and even if I don't have Aids, I still don't want him to touch me. How much can one man take? I have two children that I love and I've probably seen them twice maybe three times in the past few weeks. I want to see them, talk to them, but I don't want them near me. My dad and my sister, well let's just say, I treat them like I treat everybody else in my life: like shit.'

'When I was raped.' Helen looked sad, as she recalled what happened to her all those years ago. 'When I was raped, I was a young girl and believe me I hated people with a passion, but most of all I hated myself more than anybody else. But as I grew up, I learned to turn what happened to me around. I came to realise as you will in time that my anger, my hatred could help other people.

'At first, I would help nobody but women, but when I first helped out a male friend of mine, as I listened to him I realised that most of the people that do this kind of thing: rape, domestic violence, physical and mental abuse, were just sad lonely children trapped inside men's bodies, that's all. And as I spoke to more and more men, I just felt that to understand the man, you first have to understand the child inside them that's crying for help. I found out through lots of research, that people who commit these kind of crimes are just crying out for help in some way. All they want is someone to understand them.

'You didn't ask for this, no woman in the world asks to be raped. No families say, come over here and ruin our lives. Tragedy strikes at every turn, remember that you have death on one shoulder and life on the other and anything else goes straight down the middle.' Sarah felt as though she wanted to cry, she had tears in her eyes, but she never cried. At the end of the day, how do you cope?

As David realised that it had all gone quiet in the living room, he went back in.

'That's it, typical,' said David, smiling broadly, hoping that it might perk up his wife a little bit. 'The women stand there gossiping and the men do all the hard work.'

'Well you can do some more hard work, and make a nice cup of coffee for us all.'

'By the way do you know how many jars of coffee we have so far?'

'Go on, surprise us.'

'We have seven jars of coffee and five boxes of tea bags, just out of those two boxes I carried into the kitchen.' Helen and Sarah both looked surprised, because there were still quite a few boxes left in the living room. David went and made the coffee, and then came back into the living room.

'Can I ask you a question?' said David to Helen.

'Yeah course you can. You can ask me anything you want.'

'From what you know of Sarah and me, do you think that we are boring people?' David cleared a space and sat on the floor. Helen paused for a brief moment.

'Err… yes you are.' Helen was not one to mince her words.

'In fact, I think that you two are probably at this time, the most boring people I know. You're both very nice, but as lively as watching paint dry.'

Sarah burst into laughter, and consequently spat out some of the coffee that she had just taken a sip of. She was still laughing as David handed her a tissue.

'Are you alright?'

'Yeah, fine,' said Sarah, coughing and still trying to laugh at the same time. Which in turn made Helen and David laugh even more than they were already.

'Oh God,' said Sarah, putting her hand to her chest and doing one large cough and clearing her throat. 'Well, I've been called some things over the past few months but that is certainly one to remember.'

'Yeah, but come to think about it, Helen's probably right.' David was calming down on his laughter.

'You are ok. You went out last night for the first time in how long?'

'I couldn't tell you,' replied David thinking back to when they last went out.

'I think that the last time we went out,' said Sarah, 'was when we went out for a meal and as I recall that went wrong.'

'I bet you get up, go to work, pick the kids up from school, come home, eat a pizza, watch the ten o'clock news, then go to bed. Probably make love two or three times a week and do absolutely nothing at weekends, well am I right?' suggested Helen.

'About eighty percent right, apart from the fact that David and me love to cook if and when we can, but you're basically right about the rest.'

'See I told you boring as paint drying.'

'We went to Disneyland for a few weeks.'

'Fair enough, but before you went, when was the last time that you all went on holiday together?' asked Helen.

'About seven years.'

'See, haven't you ever thought about things like family days?'

'What's that?' asked Sarah.

'Well, it's a thing where you take turns in doing things with different members of your family. For instance one weekend David could take his son fishing. You and your daughter could go shopping, no boys allowed of course. Another time you all go somewhere nice together. Think about some of the places that are out there to visit. Even just taking the children for food can be for them a fun time. There are so many options available to you, it's really all just up to you. It's worth thinking about.'

Fishing, thought David, I bet Jason would love that, just me and him.'

A family day thought Sarah to herself. As David and Sarah were deep in thought thinking about what Helen had just suggested the doorbell rang, it was Sarah's father.

'Hello,' said Bob, giving Sarah a kiss on the cheek.

'Hey you two,' said Bob entering the living room. 'I've picked up two strange children off the street, look. Just then Jason and Lucy came running in behind him. Sarah and David were over the moon to see them. Lucy gave her mum a big hug and a kiss. Jason did the same to his father.

'Oh God I've missed you,' said Sarah, squeezing her daughter.

'I miss you Mummy,' said Lucy, looking at her mother. Even though Lucy was quite cheerful Sarah could see a little bit of sadness in her eyes.

'Hey don't I get a cuddle too?' Jason moved as Lucy gave her dad a kiss and a hug, Jason did the same for his mother.

'Wow,' said Jason, just noticing the toys on the floor. 'Are all these toys mine?'

'I don't think that you would be happy playing with Lucy's dolls.' All Lucy heard was the word dolls and she quickly leapt off her father's lap to see what her mother was on about.

'Thanks Dad, Mom,' said Jason and Lucy, excitedly looking at some of the toys on the floor.

'Hey thank you, but we didn't buy them.' Sarah picked up another cuddly toy and looked at it for a brief moment.

'Some very nice people gave them to us.' Sarah was thinking of how kind and thoughtful these people were to give them all these things. David asked the children to take all of the toys that belonged to them upstairs and into their bedrooms and off they went. Both Jason and Lucy took their time carrying all the toys upstairs bit by bit, both having a bit of a play with them in their bedrooms before coming back down for some more to take upstairs.

Meanwhile Helen and Bob were putting some more things away in the cupboard.

'I can't believe that all these people gave all these things to you lot,' said Bob. Helen had gone back into the living room to help Sarah.

'I know,' said David. 'Just as you think the worst of people, they turn round and do things like this.'

'Well, how did all this come about?'

'Well we both went down to the pub last night.'

244

'What you mean, you and my daughter actually ventured out of the house on your own initiative?' Bob looked at him and raising an eyebrow.

'Yeah, yeah,' said David, smiling at him and shaking his head. 'Anyway, we went out intent on getting completely pissed and we did. Anyway we woke up this morning to find a note and all this stuff. Apparently people just came in the pub and asked if they could leave them for us because they did not know where we lived so basically the pub became a sort of drop off point for people wanting to wish us well and all that.'

'Tell him about the fight that you nearly had with that guy Mick,' said Sarah, walking into the kitchen with another box, closely followed by Helen also carrying a box.

'Oh God Bob, you want to see the size of this guy.'

'Not Mick Thompson?'

'I never got his last name. I just know he was a big guy.' David described Mick to Bob.

'Yeah Mick Thompson, he was in the army, ex-paratrooper,' said Bob.

'I've no idea what he was, I just know that I'm glad that I never picked a fight with him,' smiled David.

'So am I, because if you did you would now be lying in hospital hooked up to a load of machines, believe me they don't call him big Mick for nothing. He's put many a bloke in hospital before now. He and I go fishing together sometimes.'

'Actually,' said Sarah. 'He turned out to be a really nice man.'

'Likes his beer as well, I know the pub on the corner is his local.' Bob was smiling to himself.

'Anyway, where's Sandra?'

'Ah, I can answer that' said Helen. 'Your father and Richard decided to go for a drink yesterday after coming out of court and well to cut a long story short she went with them and got completely drunk and had to be carried home, pretty much the same as you two did last night.'

'She said she might phone you later if she feels well enough that is. She never could drink that much,' said her father. Helen said that it was getting late and that she had few things to take care of at the office.

Bob said that he had to be going himself.

'The children are going away with a few friends of mine for about a week, so you won't hear from them for a while.' Bob offered Helen a lift back to her office.

Sarah called the children down from upstairs; she and David cuddled them tightly. They then told them that they loved them and that they should behave

245

themselves for their granddad's friends. Jason and Lucy both gave their mom and dad a kiss and waved goodbye from the car.

There were only a few more boxes to be put away now and it only took them about ten minutes to put them away.

'I'll put the boxes in the bin in the morning,' said David, sitting next to his wife who had turned off the hi-fi and was flicking through the channels on the TV.

'Not a damn thing on, all they keep on about is that bloody Gulf war.'

'Hey, we have satellite TV now.'

'I'd put it on if only I knew how to work the blooming thing.'

'All you have to do is press number six on the remote control for the TV and then you can use the control for the satellite.' Sarah was looking quite pleased as she flicked from channel to channel.

'Hey you know this is quite good,' she said, finally leaving it on a channel she liked the look of.

Family day thought David.

'Are you alright?' asked his wife, realising that he had gone quiet all of a sudden.

'Yeah, I was just thinking about what Helen was saying earlier, about us being boring.'

'Well she has got a point, don't you think?'

'Well yeah she has and she hasn't. I mean, think about it in the beginning we had to work all those silly hours. You and Susan had to make the business work and I had to prove each time that I was good at my job to get that promotion. Then the kids came and I tell you I never really realised how expensive having children actually was.'

'When I was at school, my sex education teacher used to say, you young girls think that having kids is easy, you wait until you eventually have your own, then you'll see how expensive they are. We always took the piss out of her at the time, but now that I think about it she had a point. I just wish that I had paid a bit more attention to her now. I might have learned something,' said Sarah, thinking back to her school days.

'Anyway it's ten thirty and we have a long day in court tomorrow, we should go to bed.' His wife agreed. They turned everything off and then they went off to bed.

They got up at about eight o'clock the next morning, had a shower and went downstairs. Sarah told her husband that she never fancied any breakfast. David made himself a cup of coffee and three rounds of toast.

As David entered the living room with his breakfast the front door knocked. Sarah said that she would get it; it was Sandra.

'Morning, feeling better today are we?' Sarah asked giving her a kiss on the cheek.

'Yes I am and as hungry as horse,' she replied, looking at David eating his breakfast.

'Don't even think of pinching my breakfast.'

'Oh come on, it's only eight thirty, which gives you plenty of time to make some more toast and coffee.' David gave in and said ok. Sandra kissed him when he stood up to go into the kitchen, she then sat down.

'First my breakfast, now my chair, what do you want from me next?'

'Oh I don't know, how about five million quid and a house in the Bahamas.'

'Sorry you can only have four million, we need the other million and the house in the Bahamas.'

She sat next to her sister on the settee.

'So how are you? Sorry you must get fed up with people asking if you're alright all the time,' said Sandra.

'I used to, I used to hate it, but now I know that they only say it because they care. But anyway I'm alright, as well as I can be anyway.' They were talking as David came back into the living room Sandra looked at him and started laughing.

'I see she told you then,' said David, sitting down.

'I know that curiosity gets the better of most people, but that was a bit much, I mean literally getting down on your hands and knees outside the door of your therapist's office is a bit much.' She was still giggling and so was Sarah.

'You should have seen his face when Helen came and opened the door, it was a picture.'

'Anyway, we'd better get going or you're going to be late.'

'But, I haven't finished my breakfast yet,' said David, still eating his toast. He watched as his wife and her sister get ready to go.

'Come on,' said Sarah opening the front door. David sighed he took a quick sip of his coffee and took his toast with him. His wife had already started the car and was waiting for her husband.

'Come on, Mr Keyhole,' said Sandra, winding down the window. David shut the front door and got in the car.

The court was only about twenty minutes away from the house and it wasn't long before they reached it. Richard, Helen and their father were already in there, so was Susan her business partner and a few of her work mates. Sarah gave them all a quick hug, and told them that she would speak to them later. She then hugged and kissed her father. Most people were already standing up when the judge came in.

'All rise,' said the usher. As the judge sat down the guards brought up the two prisoners.

'They look in a bad mood and how come they've brought Mr Walker back up?' said David, looking across at Mr Walker.

'Well Mr Chevron said that he had talked to his client and that he would behave himself in court, so the judge let him back in. But by the time I've finished with them today, Mr Walker will end up being his normal nasty self and they'll be in a worse mood by the end of today,' stated Richard.

Both Richard and Mr Chevron were asked to approach the bench.

'Is your client alright today?' asked the judge.

'Err… yes she is, Your Honour, but I would very much appreciate it if Mr Walker didn't keep making stupid remarks at her and her husband all the time.'

He was still wondering why the judge asked him such an odd question.

'And I hope that you will keep yours under control Mr Chevron,' stated the judge.

'Err… yes, Your Honour, I have had a strong word with him about his attitude.'

'Very well then you may begin Mr Thorn.' Richard thanked the judge and went back to his seat.

'I'd like to call Miss Donna Woodfield to the stand Your Honour.' Miss Woodfield came to the stand and was reminded that she was still under oath.

'Miss Woodfield the last time we spoke you claimed that you knew Mr Forbes by reputation only, is that correct?'

'Err… yes it is as far as I can remember.'

'As far as you can remember, what does that mean exactly?'

'Nothing, I just meant that I've heard of him.'

'What do you think of Mr Forbes?' asks Richard.

'Well he's generous, good-looking, rich and he seems a really nice person.'

Yeah right, thought Sarah.

'And we already know that you and Mr Walker are an item. But what I want to know is if you've never met Mr Forbes, why did you let him pay for all your abortions?'

She was about to speak when Richard continued.

'Now considering that you do not know each other, why do you suppose that he paid for all your abortions?'

'I don't know,' said Miss Woodfield, looking at both Mr Walker and Mr Forbes. 'He just did, that's the kind of man he is.'

'How long were you at the surgery before you heard the first scream?'

'I think that it was about twenty minutes or so.'

'So you came back, made yourself a cup of coffee and sat down, is that correct?'

'Yes, it is.' She glanced at Mr Forbes and Mr Walker once again.

'So how long was it, between the time you heard the first scream and then the second scream?'

'Well it was about ten minutes or so I think.'

'Are you sure?' Richard was remembering what Mr Mackoshie had told the court.

'Did you hear anything else?'

'No.'

'Why did you wait so long before you phoned the emergency services?'

'I don't know, I guess that I was just scared. I mean it's not every day you see something like that is it?'

Richard was leaning against his table. 'Oh come now, you're a doctor's secretary surely you've seen some terrible things in your time working in the surgery.'

'Well yes, I suppose I have, but all the same it still scared me.'

'So you're not one of the friends that Mr Walker was at the pictures with on the day of the raping of Mrs Phillips?'

'No, I was at work.'

'Oh yes of course my mistake. Do you take drugs at all?'

'No I don't.'

'Then would you care to explain how certain hard drugs go missing from the surgery from time to time?' asked Richard in a rather stern voice.

'I never knew that there were drugs going missing until just recently,' she replied.

'So you had no idea that this was going on? Even though you and the doctor are the only two people who have a key to the drugs cupboard,' asked Richard.

'Yes but as I said, the doctor only asked me about it just recently.'

'Did you know that Mr Walker and Mr Forbes both use drugs, but only Mr Forbes uses hard drugs?'

'I've heard rumours.'

'I'm sorry to disappoint you Miss Woodfield but they are not rumours, they happen to be true Miss Woodfield.'

'No, I never knew that.'

'Do you know Mr Josh Mackoshie?'

'No, sorry I don't.'

'Are you sure, his office faces the alleyway to the surgery.'

'As I said, I don't know him.' Miss Woodfield was looking slightly upset.

'According to Mr Mackoshie, the time between the first scream and the second scream was three minutes. He was most insistent about his accuracy.'

'Perhaps he was wrong.'

'Perhaps you were wrong.'

'Well I'm not,' she replied sharply.

'I have another one of my theories Miss Woodfield, would you like to hear it?'

Miss Woodfield just shrugged her shoulders.

'I believe you when you say that you never saw what happened to my client, but I do believe that you know what happened. Now, I think that you came back to the surgery early, feel free to stop me when you think I am exaggerating the truth, Miss Woodfield.

'You came back early because you knew that Mr Forbes and Mr Walker were coming. They were coming to see you, but I think that something went wrong. Either they got held up, caught in traffic, who knows, but I believe that they came to see you because you supply them with small quantities of drugs.' Richard looked at Miss Woodfield.

'Objection, Your Honour,' said Mr Chevron abruptly. 'He has no solid evidence about these wild accusations.'

'I agree, but let us see if Mr Thorn is actually leading to something.'

'I am Your Honour.'

'I hope you are Mr Thorn.' The judge peered down at Richard over his glasses.

'Do you think that Mr Walker and Mr Forbes are perhaps very close acquaintances?'

'No, I wouldn't think so.'

'Why not?' asked Richard.

'Well, Mr Forbes is a rich man, he'd have a better class of friends wouldn't he?' came the reply.

'Oh come now, just because he's a rich man, doesn't mean that he can't have a friend like Mr Walker.'

'I still don't think so.'

'I'll continue with my theory if you don't mind. As I was saying feel free to stop me when you think that I'm telling something that is not true. Now as well as supplying them with a small quantity of drugs from the surgery you also help them out in other ways. We know from our previous witness that Mr Forbes and Mr Walker are down that part of town on a regular basis. I mean the nearest shop is right at the other end of the alleyway, so why are they always in that part of the alley? The only thing there are some loading facilities for lorries and the surgery. We know that you took a considerably long time phoning the emergency services, but as you said you were scared. You then helped the doctor when he came. Now when the doctor came his bag was already there beside you waiting for him, according to what you told the police you said that it would save time.'

'Are you alright, Miss Woodfield?' asked Richard, noticing that she was looking slightly edgy.

'Err… yes I'm fine,' she replied.

'Now why would you take your time calling the emergency services, unless you wanted to give someone a bit of time to get away, which otherwise they might not have had?'

'I had nothing to do with that women being raped ok, I just found her there in that state, and yes I may have panicked a little bit.'

'We know Mrs Phillips was raped between twelve o'clock and one o'clock. Now we know that it was three minutes between the first time Mrs Phillips screamed and the second time that she screamed. Yet you say that it was fifteen minutes.

'We know that Mr Forbes and Mr Walker are there by the surgery almost every day. Why you seem slightly nervous Miss Woodfield are you sure that you are alright?' Miss Woodfield just looked at Mr Forbes and Mr Walker.

'Err… yes,' she replied, nervously.

'Is there something which you want to tell the court?'

'You tell him anything and I'll have you!' shouted Mr Walker, from across the courtroom.

'Mr Walker would you like to spend the remainder of the trial in the cells?'

'No,' replied Mr Walker, sarcastically.

'Well, then kindly shut up. Please continue Mr Thorn.'

'Thank you Your Honour.'

'It seems Miss Woodfield that every time that I ask you a question, you look at the accused. Why is that? In fact don't tell me, I'll tell you. Now I really do believe you when you say that you had nothing to do with my client being raped, but I still think that you know what happened. I think that you came back early from your lunch break to meet Mr Forbes and Mr Walker to give them some more drugs, but something went wrong, not on your part though. I think that you did as you always did, wait for them to come and knock on the door or something like that, but they never did, so you probably just assumed that they were not coming. Then after some time you heard a scream, but I believe that you paid no attention to it. After all people shout in that part of town all the time as we know. But I think that when you heard the second scream you went to see what was going on outside. I think that at first you looked out of the window, saw nothing and then you went outside.'

Miss Woodfield began sobbing.

'They said they'd kill me if I told anyone. I had to do as they said.'

Mr Walker jumped up.

'Shut the fuck up you stupid cow. They don't know anything, they can't do anything if you keep your mouth shut!' he shouted.

'Officer, restrain that man and take him back to the cells.'

'You stupid cow, you bloody stupid cow, I'll get you for this.' Mr Walker was kicking and screaming as he went down the stairs being held by two big guards.

The judge called for order in the court. It all went silent.

'I warned you about your client Mr Chevron, now seeing as though you cannot control Mr Walker, I only want to see him when he's called to give evidence, and then I want two guards with him at all times. And I want him to be handcuffed, when he's in court is that understood?' said the judge loudly.

'Yes,' said Mr Chevron, who sat down as quick as he stood up. Mr Forbes just looked like he was on another planet. It seemed like his body was there but his mind was somewhere else altogether. Either that or he was suffering the after effects of not being able to have an unlimited amount of drugs to take. Sarah meanwhile loved every minute of it. She was thinking that finally people might start to believe her, she knew that a lot of people cared but then again a lot of people didn't, especially the local newspapers. Now the truth was actually starting to come out she hoped that more of the general public would be on her side.

'Would you please continue, Mr Thorn.'

'Yes Your Honour.' He took a tissue out of his pocket and handed it to Miss Woodfield.

'Who would kill you?'

'I suppose it was my fault really. I thought well you know, ok, he may be a bit of a rough reputation but he's still nice. He was nice to me anyway.'

'Are you talking about Mr Walker?' asked Richard, looking at her.

'Yes I am,' she was sobbing as she spoke.

Bitch, serves you right thought Sarah. If you knew his reputation why did you agree to go out with him?

'Surely you knew what life would be like with him?' Richard was now leaning against his table.

'I know but like I said he was nice to me at the beginning. He still is sometimes.'

'So what about the drugs?' asked Richard.

'It was just to stop him beating me at first, but then he'd beat me whether I got him the drugs or not.'

Sad cow thought Sarah, when you were lying your ass off, you thought that you would be ok, but now look at you. You knew that you would be caught out sooner or later, but you carried on lying. Now that you're sitting there crying, you want the world to feel sorry for you, well not this bitch I hope that you rot in hell.

'And how did the doctor find out that the drugs were missing?'

'He found out when he did his quarterly checks on the drugs cabinet. I denied it of course but he's not stupid he knew who was taking them.'

'But Mr Walker as bad as he is does not use hard drugs, so who were the hard drugs for?'

'They were for Mr Forbes,' she said, looking nervously at him.

'What did happen on the day my client got raped?'

'Well when they never showed up as they normally did, I thought that they were not coming, I was glad in a way that they never showed up. When I heard the first scream, I never really paid it any attention because there are always people being silly around there anyway. When I heard the second scream and the voices, I went out to have a look to see if there was anything going on. As I opened the door to go outside I saw Mr Forbes and Ronald coming from behind the side of the surgery. I asked Mr Forbes what was going on. He just laughed at me and walked off, so I asked Ronald. All I got off him was tell anybody about this and you're dead. He then slapped me and grabbed me by my hair. He got right into my face and said you do not ask Mr Forbes anything do you hear me, you do as you're told and that's it.'

Miss Woodfield was remembering what happened on the day.

'I could hear them laughing as they drove away. It never occurred to me at first to go and have a look at what they were doing, I was just too scared that's why I never called the police straight away. You can't mess with these people you don't know what they're like.'

'So what made you go out and have a look?'

'I don't know really, I guess I thought that they had killed somebody again.'

'Are you telling the court that they have done this kind of thing before?'

'Yes,' came the reply.

'Objection Your Honour,' said Mr Chevron. 'There is no proof that my client has done anything in the past apart from a few speeding tickets. It is not for Miss Woodfield to make accusations that she cannot prove.'

'I agree please stick to the matter in hand Miss Woodfield. This is a rape case not open forum, we can only deal with what we have in front of us not anything else.'

Miss Woodfield nervously agreed to what the judge had said.

'So when you found my client, what did you do then?'

'Well when I saw her, I was sick literally, I mean how could anyone do that kind of thing to someone?' She looked at Sarah who was giving her the coldest of looks.

'I've heard stories of things like that. I've even seen terrible things in the surgery, but nothing like that. I kneeled down to check if she was still alive; she jumped and started screaming at me to leave her alone. That's when I went in and phoned the police.

'I got the doctor's bag out of his office because I knew he would soon be back from his lunch. When I went outside I saw him walking down the alleyway and I called him over and showed him the woman on the floor. He said that she was slipping in and out of consciousness. I told him that I had phoned the police and it wasn't long before they showed up.'

'Wasn't there something about a security tape?' Miss Woodfield never spoke she just looked at the floor. Richard asked the same question again and still got no reply. He then looked at the judge.

'Will you please answer the question Miss Woodfield,' stated the judge, leaning slightly towards the witness box and looking down at her. As the judge was about to speak again Miss Woodfield spoke.

'I got rid of it,' she said and began to cry.

'You did what?'

'I got rid of it. Look you don't understand. You don't know what these people are capable of they would kill me.' She looked at Richard, who was walking up and down in front of her.

'You mean to say Miss Woodfield that you deliberately withheld vital evidence from a crime scene. Do you realise what you have done?'

'Did you look at the tape before you destroyed it?'

'No, when I phoned the police I took it out of the machine and put it in my bag. Then when I got home I destroyed it.' She obviously couldn't tell anyone that she had watched the tape. She just cried as she watched the two men, beat rape and kick Sarah. She even heard them laugh as they walked away and basically congratulated each other on a job well done.

'So, as well as lying to the police and your boss, you lied to this court. You do know that you may be charged with destroying vital evidence from a crime scene? Withholding vital evidence and taking evidence from a crime scene and also aiding and abetting two criminals. That's at least a four year term in prison, maybe longer.'

'You don't understand,' she began.

'No, you do not understand,' said Richard, loudly. 'You deliberately lied while in court. You took the oath and promised to tell the truth, but you lied. You destroyed probably the most vital and conclusive piece of evidence in this case.'

'I'm sorry, I wasn't thinking straight I was scared,' cried Miss Woodfield.

'So was my client, she was raped, beaten and left for dead. Her life can never be the same. Her family will never be the same, but I suppose that you feeling sorry makes everything alright.' Richard walked over to the witness box.

'Look at Mrs Phillips. I want you to take a good long look at her because that could so easily have been you. It could easily have been you.'

'No further questions Your Honour. I've finished with Miss Woodfield for good.'

'Do you want to …' began the judge. The judge was going to ask Mr Chevron if he wanted to question the witness, but Mr Chevron knew that there was no point in asking her anything. He knew that he was beginning to lose the case. The judge told Miss Woodfield that she would no longer be needed in court, and that she was free to leave the witness box. As she walked away she noticed that Mr Forbes was staring long and hard at her. Sarah laughed at Miss Woodfield as she walked past.

'You do know now that you will not be safe?' said Sarah laughing. Miss Woodfield just looked sad as she ran out of the courtroom. It was now almost dinner time. The judge called for a recess until after lunch. He then banged his gavel, stood up and headed for his chambers.

Everyone in the court was talking about what they had just heard. Sarah smiled at Mr Forbes as the guards brought him past her to take him downstairs to the cells. She breathed a huge sigh of relief.

'Are you alright?' asked Richard, shutting his briefcase.

'Yeah I think so.'

'Have you thought any more about what I said about compensation?'

'Well I suppose I could always put the few quid in a trust for the children,' she said, looking at him.

Richard leaned over to her and whispered.

'You'd better make it a big trust fund, because I'm not talking about just a few quid. I'm talking about your grandchildren's children never having to work at all ever.' Sarah just sat there with her mouth slightly open. She watched Richard as he walked out of the courtroom door with Helen.

'Are you alright?' asked her husband. He hadn't heard what was going on he was too busy talking to family and friends.

'Sarah,' he said, making her jump slightly.

'What sorry, what were you saying?'

'I was asking if you were alright, but I'm not sure that's a good idea now that I think about it, but still I think I'll risk it.' Sarah's family and friends asked them if they were coming for lunch. Sarah and David said that they would join them in a few moments.

'Well Richard was talking about compensation.'

'I didn't think that you wanted to bothe,' said David.

'I know we never really discussed it did we? I only thought about it when he was talking to that bitch Woodfield. You know, I thought why not if my health is going to go from bad to worse I won't be able to work and as nice as your wages are it wouldn't last forever. I want my children to have a real future not have to scrimp and save the way we had to.'

'But how much is he talking about?' asked David, looking at her.

'Well put it this way. Richard reckons our grandchildren's children will not need to work ever. I think that he's talking millions. I need something to eat, I'm starving,' said Sarah.

'We'll have to talk about it more when we can,' suggested David opening the courtroom door for his wife to go out. They met everyone in the café at the far end of the courthouse.

'We thought that you weren't coming,' said Susan, standing up.

'What are you going to have to eat?' she asked Sarah and David. They both said what they wanted and sat down at the table.

'You alright Sis?' asked Sandra, putting her arm around her.

'Yeah, well you know,' replied Sarah, shrugging her shoulders. Susan asked David to give a hand bringing over what they had ordered.

'Can I ask you a favour?' David waited for Susan to say what she wanted of him, before he took the food over to the table.

'I don't want to be sad, but can you disappear for a few hours tonight? I wouldn't ask but I feel Sarah could use a bit of female company. You don't have to, I mean I will understand.'

'We'll talk after court's finished,' said David, as he noticed Sarah looking at him and waiting for her food.

'Come on you, hurry up she'll wither away if she doesn't eat something soon.'

'What with her waistline,' replied David, giving his wife her food.

'Oh, you cheeky sod,' said his wife, smiling at him. It was plain that everybody was thinking about something. Perhaps they were thinking about Miss Woodfield and the things she said in the court. They may have been thinking that but nobody spoke about it. They all just made fun and laughed at different things. It wasn't long before they were back in court. It wasn't long before the judge came back into the courtroom. As before because almost everybody was standing up and there were still people coming into the courtroom, the usher never told the people in the courtroom to stand up. The judge laid his papers down on the bench and sat down. The judge watched as the guards brought Mr Forbes up from the cells. Sarah watched him as they walked him across the room.

'He doesn't look very well.'

'I know, but that's Mr Chevron's problem, not mine. Don't forget if he's in prison they can only give him so many drugs prescribed by the doctor, so if he's used to taking a lot of drugs, his body will have to try and cope as best as it can.' The judge asked if both Mr Chevron and Richard were both ready to begin again. They both stood up and said yes.

'Then would you like to call your next witness, Mr Chevron?'

'Yes, I would like to call Mr Daniel Thomas to the stand.'

The usher called for Mr Thomas to take the stand. Once again a very smartly dressed Mr Thomas came down to the stand and took the oath and then sat down.

'Mr Thomas could you tell the court what you and my client were doing on the day of the alleged incident?'

There was nothing alleged about it thought Sarah. Believe me I should know I was there.

'Well, we normally play a short round of golf in the morning and then we normally have lunch.'

'Did you play golf on that particular day?'

'No, we didn't.'

'Why not?' asked Richard.

'He had some charity function to go to.'

'Charity work?' asked Mr Chevron, looking at him. 'So Mr Forbes is a charitable person?'

'Well yeah, well I thought that everybody knew about his charity work.' Mr Forbes just smiled as he listened to Mr Thomas.

'How much charity work does he do?'

'Well, I couldn't give you a precise number, but he's done four charity events in the past six weeks.'

'And how much has he raised in that time?'

'I think it was about twenty thousand pounds, or close to that sum anyway.'

'That's an awful lot of money,' stated Mr Chevron.

'Well that's the kind of giving, charitable person that he is,' replied Mr Thomas.

'I see,' said Mr Chevron, looking thoughtfully at his client. Who seemed to be a lot perkier than when he first came in.

'What about the drug allegations?'

'Everybody does a bit of drugs every now and then. It doesn't hurt anyone.' The judge looked down at Mr Thomas over his glasses.

'Drugs kill people Mr Thomas and they are illegal, and any drugs, no matter how small the amount carries a stiff penalty in my courtroom. Please remember that when you enjoy yourself.'

'Err… sorry Your Honour,' replied Mr Thomas.

Mr Forbes was grinning widely.

Meanwhile Sarah was thinking to herself, how can anyone take drugs? Imagine all that poison running through your body. It's bad enough getting drunk and feeling like shit the next day, but imagine taking drugs and getting drunk, it would take at least a week to get over it, if you got over it at all. She looked across at Mr Forbes.

Well if that's what drugs do for you, I'm happy doing without them. It's bad enough having a needle from the doctor without having to stick it in yourself on purpose everyday. I can understand people who are diabetics and have no choice, but people like Forbes who take drugs and say that they are fun. I for one can't understand the logic behind it, but maybe that's just me I don't know.

'Would you class Mr Forbes as a drug addict?'

'No way,' said Mr Thomas, interrupting Mr Chevron. 'Look having money is not a crime, not as far as I know anyway. But because you have money people always want to try and see how much they can get from you. Of course if they don't get any they make up all kinds of things about you. Mr Forbes is one hell of a nice man and too generous for his own good, his generosity may be his downfall.'

'So did you attend this charity event?'

'Well, I couldn't stay for long I had a few things to do.'

'How long did my client stay?'

'Well, he was there when I got there. He was there for most of the morning.'

'And then what happened after that?'

'He went home and I went to catch my plane to go on holiday.'

'Are you sure that he went home?'

'Well I can't see him lying about saying that he's going home, there's no point.'

'Does Mr Forbes have a steady girlfriend?'

'He doesn't have a serious relationship as far as I know, unless he's been keeping secrets from me,' said Mr Thomas, making Mr Forbes smile again.

'So basically Mr Thomas you have nothing bad to say about my client?'

'No, I haven't.'

'Thank you Mr Thomas, no further questions.' Mr Chevron sat back down and looked at Richard and smiled slightly.

'Mr Thomas, you say that Mr Forbes your good friend does not tell lies, but let's say that hypothetically he does. What would you say then?' asked Richard.

'Well, I don't know. I suppose that I'd have to question his morals.'

'Well, we know that Mr Forbes has lied about his involvement in drugs. We know that he is an addict, a proper drug addict. He sniffs, uses needles and everything.'

'Well, I must say that this is the first time that I have heard about it.'

'Well, believe me it's true. This is not a lie, but my point is if he has lied to you about that, what else would he lie to you about? I mean he could lie about anything couldn't he?' suggests Richard.

'Well, I suppose so now that you come to mention it.'

That's made him think thought Sarah, perhaps after Richard has finished with you. You may begin to say what a bastard your so called friend is.

'He told you that he was going home, but still speaking hypothetically seeing as through you were off to catch a plane to go on holiday, you only have his word that he went home. I mean not being funny but you can't prove that he was where he said he was going to be, can you?'

'Err... well no I can't prove that he was actually where he said he was,' replied Mr Thomas.

'So he told you that he was going home, but what if he never actually went home? What if he went on one of his weekly visits to a doctor's surgery to collect drugs from the secretary who works there, and who supplied them with small quantities of drugs?'

'Well, I couldn't really say I mean I wasn't with him,' said Mr Thomas, who was now looking at his best friend in a different light. He never had the same smug tone which he had earlier. Maybe he has put two and two together and realised that he may not really know his friend as well as he thought he might.

'I mean how well do any of us really know anybody? In fact how well do we know ourselves? What if Mr Forbes is the opposite of what people see him as? Ok people see the kind giving generous Mr Forbes, but what if there's a nasty side to him that nobody really sees? What if he has a violent streak in him?'

'Well, he's well known for his ruthless business streak. He'll do anything to get the job done,' suggests Mr Thomas.

'Anything to get the job done,' said Richard, walking up and down in front of his table and glancing occasionally at the witness box. Would you explain that?'

'It's just a business term, it just means that he doesn't give up easily that's all.'

'That may be, but what if that term applies to any business, inside the office or outside the office, what then?'

'Well ...' began Mr Thomas.

Richard continued, 'I mean just because he gives to charity and is an all round generous man, doesn't mean that he can't take drugs or commit any other offence.'

'I accept your point, but you asked me my opinion of him. I think drugs maybe but nothing else.'

'He may be a stand up man in the circles that you move in but from what we have found out about him he's nothing but a lying drug taking threatening violent man with more money than sense. After al, Mr Thomas, he is in court and he is on remand for allegedly raping Mrs Sarah Phillips. Do you think that Mr Forbes raped my client?'

'No, I do not.'

'But if you do not know Mr Forbes as well as you thought you did. Then how do you know what he's done from what he hasn't done. But if you say he wouldn't do it, then you may be right. So if that's the case my client must by lying.' Richard was now leaning against his table and looking at the witness.

'No, I never said that. I just don't think that my friend is capable of those things, not when he can have any woman if he wants one. I bet he has a dozen women after him even as we speak. He has never had trouble getting one in the past. So why should he have trouble now?'

'Mr Thomas we know many things about Mr Forbes, most of them are very strange and most of it has shocked this courtroom.' Richard was now walking up to the witness box. 'Let's suppose that you are right and my client is lying through her teeth and you can say, yes I told you I knew my friend. I knew that he was innocent, but what if he's guilty? What if the multi millionaire really did rape Mrs Phillips? What if the person you know and the person that raped Mrs. Phillips are one and the same. What then?'

'Like I said, I don't think so.'

'Ok do you remember some while ago Mr Forbes sold a house to my client. Do you think that he was conned out of money by her company?'

'From what I heard about the sale of his house, yes I do.'

'But surely she's a ruthless businesswoman, who will do anything to win. Nothing stands in her way she'll do whatever it takes to get the job done. That's business.' Richard was walking up and down once again.

'Yes, fair enough,' began Mr Thomas.

Richard continued, 'If she agreed a price with Mr Forbes and then a made a profit after the house was sold on. Isn't that just good business?'

'I suppose so.' Mr Thomas looked as though he was bored with Richard.

'I just don't believe that a man of Mr Forbes' stature would stoop to such things.'

'You see now that's just the problem Mr Thomas. He's a rich well-respected member of the community. Who's going to believe a silly little insignificant estate agent who's just out to get him and his money? Well Mr Thomas we are not out in the community now, we are in a court of law and money, wealth, power, whatever you call it means nothing. It's evidence that counts and believe me Mr Thomas, we have a lot of evidence so stick around and we'll see how well you know your friend. No more questions Your Honour.' Richard went back to his chair.

The judge asked Mr Chevron if he wanted to question Mr Thomas any further. He said no. He then asked both Richard and Mr Chevron if they needed to question Mr Thomas again at any time. They both said that they had finished with him for good. The judge leaned over slightly and told Mr Thomas that he was no longer needed in court and that he was free to leave. He then asked Richard and Mr Chevron to approach the bench, they did. He told them that he was adjourning the court session until tomorrow morning. They both said ok and then they both went back to their seats.

Richard seemed slightly distant as he walked back to his chair. The judge told the usher, who then told the people in the court that the session was over for today and that they would need to be here at the same time tomorrow morning. Everyone stood up as the usher shouted 'All rise' as the judge left the courtroom.

'Are you ok?'

'Well, yes and no' said Richard. 'I was hoping that Mr Thomas wouldn't be so stubborn. I was hoping that he would have given something damaging about Mr Forbes.'

'Well perhaps he did and never realised that he did.'

'He claims that he knows his friend like the back of his hand. What's he going to do when he really finds out the truth about him? I bet he wouldn't be friends with him then, nor will anybody else for that matter.'

'Yeah, maybe you're right, but I still feel like I've achieved nothing today.'

'Look,' said Sarah, standing up. 'You, my family and a few close friends are the only ones that believed in me when the whole town was against me. You said that you believed enough in me to represent me. I could never repay you whether we win or not. I could never thank you enough.'

'Hey, now come on, I may be disappointed, but I still genuinely believe that we are going to win.'

Susan had grabbed David and was talking to him.

'I think that Sarah could do with a girl's night.'

'That's a nice thought. What can I do to help?'

'Well, we need you to disappear for a few hours, I'll understand if you don't want to.'

'I think that it's a great idea, and I would like sometime on my own to be honest. I really need to think.'

'Sorry to interrupt,' said Bob. 'But I couldn't help over hearing you. Why don't you stop at my place for the night David? Leave all the girls together and if you want you can still be on your own at my place.'

'If that's what you really want, yeah alright. That's a great idea, I might as well come straight to yours now with you. I don't really need to go back home anyway.'

'I'll just tell Sarah I'm staying at yours Bob.'

'Tell me what?' said his wife, walking up behind him.

'Well the girls have kicked me out the house.' Susan and Bob had gone to wait outside with Sarah's sister.

'The girls want a girlie night and I need sometime on my own, so I'm staying with your dad for tonight.'

'But I need you with me,' said his wife, cuddling him.

'I know but you'll have the girls.'

'But not you,' replied Sarah.

David looked deep into her eyes.

'I haven't asked you for anything since this happened, but I'm asking now. No before you ask I'm not leaving you. I haven't found somebody else. I just need sometime on my own that's all.'

'Promise,' said Sarah, with a tear in her eye. 'I don't want to lose you not now.'

David smiled. 'The only person you're losing me to is your father for the night and I don't think that he has any romantic intentions. Please Sarah I need this.' David held her close to him.

'Ok.' David could sense that she didn't want him to go, but he felt that he needed to do some thinking.

I suppose he just needs a bit of space thought Sarah, as they walked out of the courtroom. It can't be easy for him. David gave her a kiss goodbye and said that he would see her tomorrow. He then got into Bob's car and drove off.

Sarah felt a little bit sad, but was also looking forward to a girlie night.

'Well what times the stripper coming?' said Sarah to Susan.

'No such luxuries I'm afraid it's just old-fashioned cooking and some talking rubbish with Susan and me.'

'Probably get drunk we don't know yet,' said Susan. They all got into their cars and drove off. Sarah was glad to get home; she took off her coat as she went through the front door. She hung it up in the hallway and went into the living room, where she sat down kicked off her shoes and had a nice long stretch.

'I know,' said her sister. 'Those chairs in the courtroom are not the most comfortable in the world are they Sis?'

'Tell me about it my bum's as numb as that stupid bitch Woodfield's brain.' Susan gave both Sarah and her sister a strong drink, and then she poured one for herself.

'God, she had some nerve. Anyone could see that she was lying her ass off.'

'Well it's a damn good job that you've got a good barrister,' said Susan, sitting down.

'Yeah, I know. Do you know when I first went to look for a barrister none of them wanted to know? They all said that it would be bad for business to take my case on, so they respectfully declined. I don't know what I would have done if Richard would have said no.'

'Yes but he didn't say no did he?'

'I was glad that he tore that bitch apart,' said Sarah, interrupting her sister. 'Fancy knowing all that about those two wankers and still defending them in court.'

'Did the police know about the tape?' asked Susan, sipping some of her drink.

'God knows. If they did they never told me about it.'

'I bet they knew.'

'Even if they knew it would be a waste of time telling you about it. Think about it, because they don't want to get your hopes up. When you heard that the tape was in there, and that stupid cow got rid of it. What was the first thing that entered your head?'

'God, I just wanted to tear her head off. I just wanted to grab her head and keep banging it off the witness box until she died or I got tired, one of the two.'

'See if the police had told you about the tape, you would have battered her. Then where would you be?' Up shit creek without a paddle,' said her sister.

'But believe me if you push for it you can have her prosecuted, she may get a nice few years in prison. I hope that you prosecute the bitch anyway.'

'Yeah I know, but in some small way I feel sorry for her. You know if they did threaten to kill her she didn't have much choice did she?'

'Get lost, she had plenty of options. She could have told the bloody truth for one. You may feel sorry for her, but I don't. Come on, she left you there to die. She waited ages before she called the police. Destroying the main vital evidence and pinching drugs from the surgery for those two arseholes,' said Susan.

'Come on, she has a point Sis. If it was the other way around I bet that she would have no hesitation about sending you to prison, so you do the same,' implied Sandra.

'Don't give me that look. Ok, I'll admit it, I felt a little bit sorry for her too, but that was before I heard about the tape. Look, she already knew what happened to you before she ever got to court. She knew just being in court that they might kill her, but she came anyway. She lied to protect them, even though they seem the type that would probably kill her anyway, just for the hell of it.'

'That's the point, you look at Walker and you see that's he's capable of anything from murder to pinching bicycles. But as much as I want to kill him, I still get the awful feeling that he never wanted to rape me.' Sarah had tears rolling slowly down her cheeks.

'You know, I think that he would have been happy just beating me up and talking my money.'

Sandra had moved and sat beside her sister.

'It's been a long day you don't have to talk about this if you don't want to, me and Susan will understand.' Sarah never seemed to hear her sister she just cried softly and continued talking.

'All he basically said was, we've got the money let's go, but I think that Forbes was the main instigator. I even remember him saying that he didn't want seconds, or words to that effect meaning that he was going first. Sarah was trembling as she spoke. But I still feel that Walker was not really interested in raping me. Personally speaking, I think that he gets upset in court because they had a sweet thing going on with drugs and so forth. But now he's in prison and can't do anything apart from sit there and think about what he's done. I blame myself.' Sarah was still trembling.

'How can you say that? This was never your fault.'

'I feel it was you know my car breaking down. If I hadn't walked through that alleyway, I know people keep saying that it's not my fault, but I just feel that it is.'

'I know how you feel, when that guy beat me up and I was in hospital, I blamed everybody and anybody, but what turned me around was a little girl. A little nine-year-old who said, "Don't worry Auntie Sandra, it wasn't your fault". It was then with that look on her face, and the words she said that I realised that it wasn't my fault; she turned me around. The only one I blame now is the person that did it. And as far as I know he's never going to do this to anyone else, but that's history and I realise now that life goes on, and I'm stronger and better than I have been in my life.'

'Really?' said her sister, sitting up and looking at her.

'Absolutely, now I don't take any crap off any man or woman. One little girl made me realise how short and precious life can be and now I live everyday as if I'm going to die tomorrow and I tell you it's great,' said Sandra.

'Yeah, but you and Susan have always been like that. Me, I've never been like that.'

'I've been telling you for years, the only person that can change the way your life is, is you. Nobody is going to come and change it for you.'

'Yes, but it doesn't stop the pain,' said Sarah.

'You have to learn that life has its ups and downs, but you just have to take the rough with the smooth sometimes.'

'Let's send out for pizza and then we can slowly get drunk and you can whinge and cry until your heart's content, or you get so drunk that you pass out,' smiled Sandra.

Sarah got a hanky and dried her eyes. Meanwhile her sister phoned and ordered the pizza.

'What you've been through won't be solved in five minutes, and you'll more than likely be blaming yourself for a long time to come yet. One thing I've learned about life, time just keeps ticking away, the clock never stands still and waits.'

'If I never get my life back to how it was, then how can I make a better life for my family and myself,' said Sarah.

'Don't worry about things too much.'

'But Susan, I may have …' began Sarah.

'Later,' said Susan, interrupting her. 'If you feel that you need to talk about that that's fine, but as least wait until were drunk, because I don't want to think about that as yet. And until the results of your tests come back, you shouldn't think about it too much either.'

They all sat down and were waiting for the pizza to arrive. After about forty minutes the pizza came. Sandra paid the young man and said goodbye. They all shared the pizza.

'It doesn't matter what people tell you, only you can figure out the best way of dealing with it. If you feel that you want to scream every day for a month that's your choice. Whatever you do you must feel that you need to do it, otherwise you wouldn't do it.'

'Yeah, I suppose so, but I love and hate people at the same time. I love my husband, but when he touches me sometimes I feel like throwing up. It's not so bad now but that's how I feel sometimes. I love my children but at the moment I'm glad that they're not here. Besides I don't want them to see me like this.'

'Maybe, but they'll find out the truth eventually. It's better that it comes from you or David rather than a complete stranger.'

'I've told them as best as I can. It's hard to explain something to someone when you don't understand it yourself.'

'I can believe how hard it is. When I was attacked, I found it hard to tell my son and he's seventeen years old. I just mumbled a load of rubbish basically. It's a good job really that he was clever enough to put two and two together.'

'Personally,' said Susan. 'I think that the one you should worry about is David. I'm not saying that the children don't matter, but they have years to grow up and can try and understand this for themselves.'

'But oh, I don't know. I watch David sometimes in court and I think any minute now that guy's going to snap, but he doesn't. Ok fair enough he's had a bit of a slanging match with Walker, but that was about it. Now come on don't you two look at me like that you know I'm telling the truth. Well think about all that built up anger it has to be released at some point.'

'That's true, and what if it's just some innocent person who was in the wrong place at the wrong time.' Sarah was thinking about what Richard had said about her rape being an accident.

'But what can I do?' She had hardly touched her pizza.

'Take it easy on him. We can sympathise with you and the way you feel. But if you lose your husband who loves you, I think that you would go downhill from then on. Because that bloke doesn't understand what you're going through inside, you have a go at him for no apparent reason. You wake up screaming in the middle of the night.'

'A person can only take so much stress before they snap.'

'I think that the best thing that you can do is as soon as this case is over let him go back to work. Let him take his aggression out in his work.'

'Perhaps you're both right, but I don't mean to be nasty to him, but most of the time I can't help it. Most of the time, I don't remember having a go at him and when I do remember I can't even remember why I did in the first place. Then all I want to do is cry, I could cry day and night and never stop. I have a shower twice a day sometimes three times a day and I still feel dirty and the dirt never seems to come off.'

'You've been through a lot, in time you'll learn to live with it. You won't like it, but you'll learn to live with it.'

'Did Richard say anything to you about any compensation?' asked Sandra, looking at her.

'Yeah, well we haven't spoken properly about it yet, but he has mentioned it.'

'What compensation?' asked Susan, also looking at her. 'And how much are we talking?'

'Well, he's thinking in the millions. I must admit I'm not completely comfortable with idea.'

'You're not,' said Susan, raising her eyebrows in amazement.

'Look Sis, thousands of women are attacked every year and the ones who do get to court never get a penny, never mind millions. The most I got was a smile and a good wish card. Well I had lot of good wishes from different people actually, but I never got a penny. You can get millions and you're not sure if you want it or not?'

'If you can get something positive from all this mess then you go for it girl.'

'If you don't want to do it for yourself then do it for your children, because you should do your best to make sure that this never happens to them. And if anything happens to you or David you know that they will have no money worries at all.'

'I know, oh I don't know. I know what you mean, but you must understand I'm not in the least bit comfortable with this situation as it is. You know I hate the people and they haven't done anything to me. I'm beginning to get to grips with things a little better. I don't lash out at people as much as I used to. I still feel ashamed of myself and I still think that this whole mess was my fault but deep down inside I know that it was nothing to do with me. I can understand what everyone is telling me, but it doesn't make things any easier for me.'

'I know that you may not want to answer this, you might even throw something at me, but still I'll have to take my chances. What for you is the worst part of all this mess?' Sandra looked at Sarah, wondering what she was going to say or do.

Sarah just sighed deeply.

'It's hard to explain. I feel that something has been taken away from me something that can never be replaced.' She put her head on her sister's shoulder once more and began to sob.

'It's like I don't know, before I felt like a whole person. I felt like I could fight the world and win, get away without so much as scratch on me. I felt like I could run for a thousand miles without stopping. I felt good for a bit of a laugh, Sarah Phillips that was me. Now I feel like, I'm on the outside looking in not the other way round. The rape as I've said before, it's not even the sex, Ok yeah fair enough, of course if it was my choice I'd rather become a lesbian than have sex with anyone but David. But most people can't understand, they say, oh my God the sex, being raped. Those men had sex with you but I disregard the sex. If I was brutally honest with myself the sex was not my main concern. Those bastards took something from me that cannot be explained.' Sarah sat up and shouted as she spoke. She was still crying but all of a sudden in a soft sweet tender voice, she said:

'It's also something that can never be replaced.' She rested her head once again on her sister's shoulder.

'For the last few months, I've been really selfish. I've been one hell of a stubborn nasty bitch. I've never been one for violence of any kind, but now believe it or not I could quite easily injure those two wankers and still sleep easy at night.

'Remember when we asked Dad about how he felt when Mum died and he said that he felt like someone had just ripped out his heart and threw it away and that he lost his best friend. Dad must have really loved her, if you ask him about finding someone else, he's not the least bit interested. You know I feel a bit like Dad, like my heart has been ripped out, there's a big empty space where it used to be. My whole body seems to echo every time I talk.

'In the last few months, I've had some really nasty things said about me and my family and my children. Well, let's just say that they won't be going to school for a while not after what they suffered.'

It hurt Sandra and Susan to listen to all this but they really had no choice. Ok yeah, Susan could just say sod it I'm off, but she was Sarah's true friend. They've known each other since they were small children and were basically like sisters. What kind of friend would she be if she deserted her now? Fair enough, she may feel like crying herself but would that make Sarah feel better or worse?

'I just felt that nobody cared,' said Sarah. Sarah sat up and stared in to her empty glass. Susan took it off her and poured another drink. 'Thanks.' Sarah took a sip of her drink.

'I felt like the whole world was against me, family, friends, everybody. But then one day I decide to pop into the office just to see how things were going. And I see these writing pads. You know the friends who I thought hated me and were against me were actually helping and supporting me behind the scenes. I never thought that people who didn't even know me would come in off the street and put nice things about my husband, my children, my whole family and me.

'David and I decided to go out to the pub just down the road one night. We found out that Forbes and Walker have been pissing people off for a long time. They carried us home. I tell you.' Sarah was smiling, she still had tears in her eyes, and most of her make-up had run, but she seemed a lot more cheerful than before. 'David and I were in no fit state to walk home. We got up in the morning to find this note.'

Sarah got up and took the note that Rob the barman had left them. She handed it to Susan, and then after she had read it she handed it to her sister. She sat back down.

'All these people who I thought never cared really did give a shit about me. And in their small way were helping me, supporting my family and me. Here's me thinking that nobody cared. Now my children can't move in their rooms for toys that people had left at the pub for them. Toys, clothes, moneyboxes, boxes of food and drinks, believe me you name it they left. It's a good job really that I have got a big kitchen and lots of cupboard space.'

'See, more people care than you might imagine,' said Susan, looking at her.

'I know, so if I fail or give up now, I won't just fail my family or myself. I'd be failing all those hundreds of good people. All of them who took a little time out just to wish me and my family the best of luck, I couldn't let them down that is worse than letting myself down.' As they carried on talking Sarah began to think about David and how he was getting on.

'At the end of the day there's nothing at all you can do, nothing. The only thing you can do is be there for your wife, that's it,' said Bob.

'It's easier said than done,' said David.

'Ok,' said Bob, handing David another drink. 'We know that you can look after yourself in a fight, but this is a fight that you can only win one way, and that's going to court suffering the crap in there, putting those two monsters behind bars where they belong.'

I know,' said David, getting up and looking out of the window. 'But I just feel so damn useless.'

'So what would you do if you could?'

'I'd kill them, both of them plain and simple,' replied David, turning around and looking at Bob.

'So you'd kill them, end up in prison, what then? Yeah ok, for a while life would be sweet for you. You'd be on cloud nine, but what happens when you come down from that cloud and then you realise that for the next twenty years this prison is your home. What then?' asked Bob.

David sighed, as he sat back down.

'I heard a story once,' said Bob. 'It's only a short one. Anyway this guy was in prison; don't ask me what for because I have no idea. Anyway for sometime this one prison guard kept on taking the piss out of him. Well, I'm off to the pub now that I've finished my shift, and you're stuck behind bars for being a stupid man. So anyway one day he says to this guard, while you're in here somebody could be screwing your missus and the guard said that's probably true. So while you're looking after me, somebody could be screwing your wife or raping your daughter. Remember that you're doing time the same as me. The only difference is, you can go home at night and I can't. Look no matter how many rapists, murders and child molesters you kill or get rid of there are always more of them somewhere else. We have to send a message to these people that this has to stop and stop now. We must tell them if this is what you want to do then you will get a stiff penalty not just a simple slap on the wrist. You know like by the time you get out of prison if you get out at all, your two-year-old daughter will be married with children of her own.'

'I understand what you mean, but that doesn't take the pain away. That doesn't help me now. I have a young beautiful wife who will never ever be the same again, because two morons have decided that they wanted to have a bit of fun. Do you have any idea how it feels to know that another man touched your wife and had sex with her. Sorry, forced her to have sex after they beat her up. I can't touch her now, because she might have Aids and may die. I'm sorry for being so direct Bob, but it's true,' said David.

'I'd rather face that sooner than later.'

'No, you wouldn't because when that time does come, you'll wish that you had done a lot more than you have done.' He was thinking about his wife who had died when Sarah and Sandra were young children.

'You're a smart man David, if I was in your shoes I would probably be reacting exactly the same as you are right now, perhaps worse. And yes, we should face the fact that one day my daughter, your wife will no longer be with us, but she isn't dead yet. You get the results pretty soon and then we'll know, but for now just take each day as it comes. That's the best you can do, that's all any of us can do, is to be there for Sarah. You'd better try and get some sleep, we have another long day ahead of us tomorrow, and we'll need all the energy we can. They both went to bed. David thanked Bob and then headed for the spare room. He got into bed and thought about what Bob was saying, and before he knew it he was soon fast asleep.

In the morning, David was the first to come downstairs. He made himself a cup of coffee and sat down. I must start drinking more tea, thought David to himself, thinking about all the teabags he had in the cupboard at home.

I suppose Bob's got a point, thought David. I don't suppose that killing them would make the situation any better for Sarah. I suppose that it would make things worse than they are already. As he was thinking to himself Bob came downstairs.

'Morning,' said Bob, sounding as though his body was still in bed, and what was standing there was only an illusion. 'I'm getting too old for these late nights.' Bob was yawning and scratching his head.

'Do you want a coffee?'

'Yeah, thanks,' he said, stretching and then sitting down.

'About last night.' David handed Bob his coffee.

'Last night was last night, forget about it. Let's just concentrate on today ok.'

'Ok,' replied David, smiling and sitting back down.

After his cup of coffee, Bob looked a lot more refreshed. He looked more like his usual self.

'Right, shall we get going?' David got up and put his coat on, and sighed deeply.

'Yeah, come on let's get this over and done with,' and off they went. They pulled up onto the court car park as Sarah, Sandra and Susan were just getting out of the car. David looked at his wife.

She looks very nice this morning, more than usual thought David, beaming all over his face. He looked at Bob, who had already seen the way David was looking at Sarah.

'What?' said David, looking at him.

'Nothing,' replied Bob, laughing as he got out of the car.

Sarah walked towards them. 'Morning, what's so funny?'

'Nothing sweetheart.' Bob was still chuckling to himself and giving his daughter a kiss on the cheek and then a huge cuddle.

'I'm sure I've missed something.' Sarah looked at her husband.

'You look very nice this morning,' said David, putting his arms out for her.

'I missed you in bed last night.'

'I missed you too.' He gave her a kiss.

'Here, I thought that you might like a fresh change of clothes,' said his wife, handing him a bag.

'Oh yeah, thanks,' said David, holding her hand as they headed towards the court.

'I'll just go and get changed.'

'Can I come and watch?'

'Oh God, if only you could. If only you could.' As Sarah walked away she was still smiling to herself. She was met in the courtroom by lots of people wishing her good luck, and asking her if she was alright.

'And you said that people don't care,' said Susan, as Sarah walked past her. Sarah just smiled warmly and shook her head.

'Morning,' said Sarah, to Helen and Richard.

'Morning,' came the reply from both of them.

'I've brought some of those pads that you wanted to see,' said Sarah, handing Helen a bag.

'Oh thanks, I'll have a look at those later,' and she went to say hello to David, who had just entered the courtroom.

'How are you?'

'I'm getting better,' he replied.

'I know you get the results of your tests pretty soon,' Richard sighed.

'I'll worry about that when it comes, let me deal with today,' replied Sarah.

Richard sighed again, 'Ok, ok.' Richard looked slightly down in the dumps.

'Look, if the results are positive, then there's nothing you or anybody else can do for me, so please just let me take each day as it comes. Anyway I'm still here and I'd like to ask a favour if possible,' said Sarah.

'Anything you want, just ask.'

'Well it may seem a strange thing to ask, but would it be possible to have Walker stay up here no matter what happens?' Richard looked at Sarah.

'I know it sounds strange, but I feel that if he hears everything there is to hear, we might get a better response from him when he's back on the stand.'

'I see your point. If he's downstairs in the cells he can't get upset, can he?' said Richard. That's a good idea actually, because I'm having the police on the stand today. I'll ask the judge when he comes in.' As Richard spoke the guards were bringing up Mr Forbes, who looked a lot worse than he did yesterday.

'He looks ill,' said David, walking over. He had just finished talking to Helen.

'Are you sure he's alright?'

Richard just looked puzzled.

'Oh don't worry I'm not concerned about his welfare. I just don't want him dying in the middle of the trial. That would only mean that he'd be getting away with it too easy, and that's not going to happen.'

Richard was slightly surprised by Sarah's sudden change in attitude. As he was about to speak, the judge came in.

'All rise!' shouted the usher. 'The right honourable William Thorp, QC. Preceding.' Richard asked the judge if he could approach the bench. The judge said yes, Mr Chevron followed Richard to the bench. The judge asked Richard what he wanted and Richard told him. The judge said ok just as long as he was handcuffed and had at least two guards with him at all times.

After the judge spoke to the bailiff, two guards brought up Mr Walker from the cells. He looked a lot better than Mr Forbes did. The judge just looked at him as the guards walked him to his seat. They both stood behind him and he was handcuffed.

'Would you like to call your next witness Mr Thorn?' asked the judge, looking down at him over his glasses.

'Yes, Your Honour,' said Richard, standing up. 'I would like to call Mr Jassed Agpatel to the stand please.'

'Can I ask you what your name is for the benefit of the court?' Mr Agpatel said his name.

'And may I ask what you do for a living? I know that you've been on the stand before, but I just want to refresh the court's memory of who you are and what you do for a living,' stated Richard.

'I'm a doctor.'

'And how long have you been a doctor?'

'I've been a doctor for nearly fifteen years,' replied Mr Agpatel.

'So you're a man with lots of experience, a professional in his field.'

'Yes I am,' he replied.

'Could you tell us what happened on the day that you found the victim?' asked Richard.

'As I said I went for my lunch as usual and then I came back down the alley and saw my secretary standing by my car. It was then she told me about the victim. As my bag was already outside I treated the victim until the ambulance arrived. I then gave a statement to the police.'

'In your statement to the police you claim that you heard a car speeding down the road as you sat in the restaurant. Did you see the car at all?'

'No, I did not. I wasn't sitting by the window,' implied Mr Agpatel.

'So you had no idea what the car looked like or who was driving the car?'

'No, I did not.'

'So all you heard was a speeding car. Why did that surprise you?'

'Well the restaurant I use is in a small quiet street and the street is very narrow, so anybody who was doing more than ten miles an hour would have to be good not to hit anything.'

'All you heard was a speeding car, nothing else?'

'No nothing else.'

'When you first saw the victim, what was your initial reaction?'

'Well I was shocked and disgusted.'

'But you're a doctor surely you've seen some horrendous things in your time,' suggested Richard.

'Yes I have, but this was one of the worst that I've ever seen, simply because of the nature of the crime,' replied Mr Agpatel

'Why was this particular crime so bad?'

'I'm sorry, whichever way I say this it's going to sound awful.'

'This whole crime is awful and I don't think that you can damage Mrs Phillips or her family any more than the people who did this to her already have, so please,' said Richard, smiling, trying to put Mr Agpatel at ease.

'Well, I've seen a lot of nasty things in my time, but this was strange to say the least. I really don't want to sound too sexist. But if you take a typical Friday night you go walking around the town any time after ten o'clock and you see these young girls wearing the skimpiest things that you could possibly imagine. I mean, basically they invite this kind of thing to happen. Now, I'm not saying that women deserve to be raped or they shouldn't wear whatever they like, but in this day and age, these young girls should dress a bit more conservatively.'

'Was Mrs Phillips dressed in this way?' asked Richard.

'You see that's the strange part. It's not a nice thing to say, but if she was, then you could say that the person who did this saw a woman wearing next to nothing and grabbed his chance, but Mrs Phillips, the only part of her body you saw was her neck, face and her hands. Oh and from the knees down she was showing nothing at all.'

'Should she have been showing anything?' suggested Richard.

'No, that's the point, if you compare her to some of the young woman you see walking about, even the school girls are wearing less now a days. Let's put it another way. When I was interviewed by the police, I said to them that this should not have happened to her.'

'I see your point. So basically what you're saying is, if Mrs Phillips was somehow acting in a provocative manner or even dressed in a provocative way, then there may be some kind of reason for this to happen,' stated Richard.

'Basically yes, but I stress, I'm not saying that any woman deserves to be raped or that they cannot dress the way they please.'

'We understand Mr Agpatel,' replied Richard.

'You've spent some time with Mrs Phillipss, you treated her at the scene of the crime and you visited her at her home. What's your impression of her?'

'Well, she's pleasant, well mannered. I don't know she's just a genuinely nice person. I suppose she has her bad days the same as the rest of us. From the short time that I have spent with her, I just found her to be a nice person.'

'Your secretary Miss Donna Woodfield, did you not know that she was stealing drugs from the surgery and giving them to Mr Forbes and Mr Walker?'

'Well, I did have suspicions, but I couldn't prove them.'

'What suspicions were they?' asked Richard.

'Well it was always the same two people hanging around the surgery. Always the same substances taken, always on a regular basis. But without any proof I could do nothing. I did inform the police though, they said that they would check things out for me.'

'Are the two men that you saw on a regular basis here in the courtroom today?' asked Richard, looking at Mr Agpatel.

'Yes, they are,' he replied.

'Would you please point them out for the benefit of the court?' Mr Agpatel pointed to the two accused men sitting by Mr Chevron. There were murmurs and whispers around the courtroom as he pointed at them.

'Order,' stated the judge, banging his gavel two or three times. Then the court went quiet as before.

'Has Miss Woodfield ever acted strangely at any time in the past few months?'

'Yes, a few times,' suggested Mr Agpatel.

'In what way?' asked Richard.

'Well, little things really, turning up late for work, having personal phone calls in the surgery. Arguing over the phone with people and coming to work with bruises on her face. Oh of course I tried to get her to tell me what the problem was, but she wouldn't say. There's only so many times you can ask someone what the problem is, if they don't want to tell you, there's not a lot that you can do.'

'How did she say she got the bruises?'

'Oh you know the usual, she'd say that she walked into a door or cupboard or something like that. In the end she just covered it up with make-up, but you could still tell what was underneath.'

'Did you know about the videotape?' asked Richard.

'Not until the police told me about it. I just thought that I never put a fresh tape into the machine. Even though, I thought that I had put one in at the time, but because of the situation at the time that didn't seem that important.'

'But that's the thing that was probably the most solid piece of evidence apart from Mrs Phillips. As well as Mrs Phillips' own personal physician, you have also done an Aids test on Mrs Phillips. Have you had the results back yet?'

'No not yet. They are due back any time this week, so she should find out within the next couple of days.'

'Mr Agpatel, you've been very helpful. Thank you very much indeed.'

'No further questions Your Honour.' Richard sat down in his chair.

'Do you have any questions for the witness Mr Chevron?'

'Err... yes Your Honour I do,' said Mr Chevron, standing up.

'When you were sitting in the restaurant you only heard the speeding car, you didn't see it?

'Yes, that's correct.'

'So you couldn't say that my two clients were driving the car?'

'No as I said, I never saw who was driving the car.'

'And just because you saw Mr Forbes and Mr Walker outside the surgery a few times doesn't really prove that they are guilty of anything, does it?' stated Mr Chevron, looking at him awkwardly.

'No, it doesn't.'

'Why couldn't you prove that Miss Woodfield was taking the drugs from the surgery?'

'Well, I needed strong proof that they were being stolen,' replied Mr Agpatel.

'But surely you have paper work for the drugs that you keep?'

'Yes I do, but Miss Woodfield used to fill out supply forms, so I guess all she had to do was add a few extra items each time, and nobody would be any the wiser.'

'Thank you Mr Agpatel. No further questions Your Honour.'

Mr Chevron and Richard both told the judge that they had finished with Mr Agpatel for good. The judge then told Mr Agpatel that he was free to leave and that he was no longer needed in court. Mr Agpatel thanked the judge and left.

'Would you like to call your next witness Mr Thorn?'

'Yes, I'd like to call Mr Tony Begia to the stand please.' Once again, Mr Begia came down and took the oath and sat down.

'You're Mrs Phillips' and her family's doctor are you not?'

'Yes I am. Well I must admit that I do not have a lot to do with them now that Mr Agpatel is taking over my practice.'

'And you said before that you delivered Mrs Phillips into the world?'

'Yes I did,' smiled Mr Begia proudly.

'So you've been a doctor for over thirty years. How long have you been the Phillips' family doctor?'

'Well, I delivered Mrs Phillips and her sister into the world.'

'I never knew that you delivered her sister too. So you've known the Phillips family all of their lives, basically?'

'Yes, that's correct.'

'Did you deliver her children as well?'

'No, I didn't.'

'Have you treated Mrs Phillips for any serious illnesses at any time in her life?'

'No, I haven't.'

'Have you treated her for anything at all in the past?'

'Well, as a child she had mumps, chicken pox, measles that sort of thing.'

'What about when she got older?'

'No not really. Well she's had the odd cold or flu apart from her prescription for the pill she very rarely comes to me for anything.'

'So as far as you know, she's just a normal woman or should I say was a normal woman until she was raped?' asked Richard, looking across at Mr Forbes and Mr Walker and then at the jury, who seemed a little saddened at the thought of Mrs Phillips not having her life, as it was before.

'Can you tell us anything which we may need to know about Mrs Phillips at all?'

'Well, no, not really. I've known the family for years and I find them to be very nice people. If they have got faults, which I should think that they have faults the same as anybody else, but I've never seen them.'

'You also said that you done your own tests on Mrs Phillips. Have any of your results come through yet?'

'No, not yet but it should be any day now.'

'Thank you, Mr Begia, that will be all. No further questions Your Honour.' Richard sat back down.

'Watch this,' said Richard, quickly to Sarah. 'I bet Chevron won't question Mr Begia.'

Sarah looked at Mr Chevron. Who had stood up and was telling the judge, that he had no questions for Mr Begia. The judge asked Richard, if he wanted to question Mr Begia at any other time. Richard stood up and told the judge that he had finished with Mr Begia for good. Richard sat back down. The judge told Mr Begia that he was no longer needed in court and that he was free to go. Mr Begia wished Sarah and David good luck as he walked past. They both said thank you. Sarah felt slightly chuffed with herself. Both of the doctors thought that she was a reasonably nice person.

'See, I told you that Chevron wouldn't question him.'

'But why not?' asked Sarah.

'Well think about it. What could he really ask him that I didn't?'

'I suppose you're right.' The judge told everybody that they would recess for lunch, and that they would be required back in court at one thirty. He then left the courtroom. Everyone left the courtroom and went and had lunch.

At lunch Sandra and Susan noticed how cheerful Sarah looked. It may have been the fact that sometimes all she needs is a damn good cry, or the fact that everything in the courtroom was finally going her way. They both smiled to themselves as they watched her. They talked for a while about some of the events that had happened in the courtroom, before they broke up for lunch. It seemed that the time had passed really quickly and it was time to go back into the courtroom.

Sarah and David held hands as they walked back towards the courtroom.

'Are you alright?' asked her husband, stopping and looking at her just as they reached the door.

'Yeah, well, you know, I'm not brilliant but I'm getting there slowly but surely,' replied Sarah, giving her husband a warm smile. Sarah's father walked past them. Once again, he started chuckling to himself.

'Now, I know that I've missed something,' said Sarah, walking into the courtroom behind her father. He was still smiling to himself, as he sat down.

'Don't look at me, I think that your dad's going senile,' smiled David.

'Are you ok?'

'I'm getting there,' said Sarah sitting down.

'Well' said Richard, also sitting down. 'I'm hoping that Chevron will call the police up next. A good statement from the policemen who arrested Forbes and Walker.'

'And suppose that he doesn't?'

'No, I dunno, I think that he will. He'll probably try and say that his two clients were unfairly treated or something silly like that.'

The judge came and they all did the usual standing as he entered, and then sitting back down.

'Would you like to call your next witness please, Mr Chevron?'

'Yes Your Honour, I'd like to call Mr Morgan to the stand.' Mr Morgan was called to come and take the stand. Sarah really liked Mr Morgan. He was one of the few policemen who was really honest and up front with her. Mr Morgan took the stand and the oath and sat down.

'Could you state your name for the benefit of the court please?'

'Yes, certainly, my name is Darren Morgan.'

'And what is your occupation?'

'I'm a police officer,' replied Mr Morgan.

'And what rank are you?'

'I'm a Detective Chief Inspector,' replied Mr Morgan, looking quite please as he spoke.

'You were the arresting officer for my client, Mr Ronald Walker?' Mr Walker was just giving Mr Morgan a cold stare. As you might expect, he didn't like the police very much, in fact he didn't like them at all. He was daydreaming as he watched Mr Morgan; he started thinking about when Mr Morgan arrested him.

Mr Walker was at home in his flat, when suddenly he was woken by a lot of loud noise. It wasn't long before he realised what the noise was and where it was coming from. It was the police breaking down his front door and not for the first time either. He also had a woman with him, but it wasn't Miss Woodfield.

'What's going on?' she mumbled. She was still high from the nights drinking and drug smoking.

'Nothing, just shut up and go back to sleep.'

The police were almost through the flat door. The young woman was scared and stumbling and she tried to cuddle him.

'Look, I said get off me bitch.' As he pushed her she fell out of bed onto the floor. She groaned as she hit the hard surface as she hit the floor. The police had broken the door down and were in his flat.

'Detective Chief Inspector Morgan, it must be something special for you to come in person,' exclaimed Mr Walker.

'Morning Mr Walker nice to see you again.' As Mr Morgan was talking, the young lady who was on the floor made a slight noise. A young policewoman walked round the bed and saw her.

'Who's she Walker?'

'Just someone I met, why?' asked Mr Walker, looking at the woman on the floor, and smiling to himself, as he thought about the night's bingeing they had both done followed by sex.

Mr Morgan told the policewoman to take the young woman into another room.

'See if you can get her to wake up as well. Although what he's probably given her, she'll be lucky if she ever wakes up again.' The policewoman put a blanket off the bed around the body of the naked woman. She looked really bad. She was hardly walking as the policewoman and another officer struggled to get her into the living room.

Mr Morgan looked at Mr Walker and sighed deeply.

'Ok what has she been taking?' he asked.

'Hey don't look at me. I just gave her a drink or two maybe three or four, can't really remember now.' They could hear the officer in the living room radio for an ambulance.

'Let's hope for your sake Walker that nothing happens to that young woman.'

'Look, enough shit,' said Walker, getting slightly annoyed.

'Now now, let's keep this civil.' Mr Morgan threw Mr Walker some clothes that were lying on a chair in the corner of the room.

'Get dressed now please,' said Mr Morgan in a firm voice.

'Why, what are you arresting me for? I haven't done anything,' said Mr Walker, getting up slowly out of bed. There were four more police officers in the bedroom with Mr Morgan. They knew from previous visits that he was a very violent man and they didn't trust him one bit. When they came to arrest him some while ago, he put a female officer in hospital, so they were not going to take any chances with him.

'Walker you know damn well why I'm here, so don't act silly with me. I'm tired, hungry and I need a cup of coffee badly, so just be a nice boy and get dressed.'

'I'm not going anywhere until you tell me what this is all about.'

'Ok seeing as though this is being done by the book. I'm arresting you in connection with the raping of Mrs Sarah Phillips, you do not have to say anything, but anything that you do say will be taken down and used in court as evidence against you. If you cannot afford a lawyer, one will be appointed by the state for you. Do you understand the charge as I have stated it to you? And do you understand your rights?'

Mr Walker quickly lost his temper and hit Mr Morgan. He then tried to make a run for the door, but he never got very far before he was restrained by all the other officers. They held him down and put handcuffs on him.

'Nice try Mr Walker but that's not going to work, as I said, this is being done strictly by the book.' Mr Morgan was in pain. As the other officers were picking him up off the floor, the ambulance men turned up. An officer directed them to the living room whilst another officer was putting a pair of shoes on Mr Walker's feet.

'Be careful that he doesn't kick you in the face,' said Mr Morgan holding his cheek, which by this time had started to swell up. As two of the officers were taking Mr Walker down to the police car, a few more policemen had turned up.

'My God, I see Walker's his normal happy self,' said another detective, looking at the bruise on Mr Morgan's face.

'Yeah, I know. Look the ambulance men are in there with a young woman. Walker's given her something, but we're not sure what it is. Look, do me a favour search the flat and see if anything turns up,' said Mr Morgan walking towards the lift. 'Oh and send someone to hospital with the ambulance, if the woman wakes up I want anything she's willing to give us about Walker and what happened.'

The other officer said ok and went into the flat. Mr Morgan headed for his car and went back to the station.

'When you got into the flat, what was my client doing?' asked Mr Chevron.

'When we got in the flat he was just sitting there in bed like he was waiting for us,' stated Mr Morgan.

'Did you knock on the door before you decided to break it down?'

'Yes, we did.'

'What was Mr Walker's response when you entered the flat?'

'When we entered the bedroom, he just greeted me like an old friend. His actual words were.' Mr Morgan took out a small note pad out of his pocket and began to read from it. It read: "Detective Chief Inspector Morgan, it must be something special for them to send you to arrest me".'

'How would you say Mr Walker's attitude was?'

'Well, he was very aggressive.'

'Do you think that breaking down his flat door at three in the morning had anything to do with his attitude?'

'No, not really, Mr Walker just doesn't like policemen.'

'Did you identify yourselves as police officers?'

'Yes we did, several times.'

'When you were at the police station, there was some fuss over a solicitor to represent Mr Walker. What was all the fuss about?'

'The brief that Mr Walker requested was not available, so we offered him a temporary replacement, but at first he declined. That was the first time we tried to question him. Then when we went to question him the second time, he asked for the duty solicitor.'

'When you questioned Mr Walker what was he like?'

'Well, to be honest he was not very co-operative.'

'Did he give you an alibi for the day that Mrs Phillips was raped?'

'Yes, he did.'

'And what was his alibi?'

'He claimed he was at the local cinema with his girlfriend and a few friends. But we checked out all the people who were working on that day but nobody remembers seeing him there. But they did say that a large group of people did come into the cinema on that particular afternoon.'

'So just because they never saw him, does not mean that he wasn't there?'

'Well, yes I suppose that could be true, but he was seen across the other side of town on that same afternoon. Roughly at the same time that he said he was at the cinema.'

'Didn't any of his friends verify his story? I mean what about the girl he was with?'

He wasn't with anybody thought Sarah to herself. The bastard was raping me at the time. She felt a big lump come into her throat as she thought about it. She wanted to cry, but tried her best not to even though it wasn't easy, but she tried all the same.

'When we asked them, they all said he was there. The girl even told me what they were getting up to in the back row of the cinema, but really he couldn't be in two places at once. But for some reason when we asked them if they would testify in court they said no, all of them.'

'You and Mr Walker seem to have a bit of history. You have arrested him well over a dozen times and he's assaulted you on more than one occasion. I get the feeling that you and Mr Walker do not like each other.'

'That's perfectly true. I dislike anybody who breaks the law.'

'Have you ever arrested Mr Walker on any drug related offences?'

'Yes, we have.'

'So my client has a bit of a criminal record?' suggested Mr Chevron.

'Yes he has,' stated Mr Morgan.

'Would you say that because of Mr Walker's attitude it makes him a target for people to accuse him of all sorts of different things? Anything that happens, blame Mr Walker. Is that right?' asked Mr Chevron, being slightly sarcastic.

'No, it's not like that. Mr Walker is known for doing some very dodgy things. He moves in certain criminal circles, but most of the things he does we can't catch him at them.'

Why on earth is Mr Chevron bullying him? It must be hard enough catching people like Mr Walker thought Sarah. Never mind trying to get him convicted. And here's that pillock basically having a go at him. A police officer a member of the law, which Chevron is suppose to be a part of and he makes Walker out to be some kind of misunderstood person. Who somehow gets blamed for things that he doesn't do and then he makes the policeman out to be a criminal. Maybe I'm thick, but for some reason I just don't understand the law these days. Mr Chevron had just finished telling the judge that he had no more questions for Mr Morgan. Mr Morgan seemed quite relieved that Mr Chevron had for now finished with him.

Richard stood up.

'Mr Morgan, even though you identified yourselves as police officers why did you feel it necessary to break down Mr Walker's front door?'

'We were told by our superiors not to take any chances with Mr Walker given his past history.' Mr Morgan felt slightly more at ease with Richard than he did with Mr Chevron.

'And what a past it is.' Richard picked up a small folder off his table. 'Indeed Mr Walker has quite a history.'

'By the age of sixteen he had been in juvenile prison three times for stealing cars. By the age of nineteen, he had done a further two years for assaulting a police officer. After that, he spent six months in prison for driving while disqualified. Four months for defrauding the DHSS out of over eleven hundred pounds. Twelve months for robbery with violence. Six months for attempted burglary, and currently under investigation for other crimes. Well, I'd say his file makes for quite interesting reading,' said Richard, closing the file and looking at the jury. He then puts it back on the table.

'Now you see why we couldn't take any chances with him,' stated Mr Morgan.

'But wouldn't it have been simpler to ask him to open his door?'

'No way, the last time we tried that, when we walked in he ended up putting a female PC in hospital. His excuse was, he thought that she was going to attack him, so he defended himself.'

'And was he trying to defend himself?' asked Richard.

'Defend himself from what? All she was trying to do was put handcuffs on the bloke.'

'What were you arresting him for?'

'Murder,' replied Mr Morgan, making everyone in the court take a sharp intake of breath. They started whispering amongst themselves.

'Order, order,' demanded the judge in a deep voice, banging his gavel at the same time. After a few minutes everyone had calmed back down. Richard looked at the judge, wondering what he was going to say but to his amazement the judge said nothing. He just looked at Richard.

'Did you have any proof of this?'

'I'm afraid not.'

'I don't want to dwell on this subject and my learned colleague may stop me at any time if he feels uncomfortable with this question.' Richard looked at Mr Chevron, who gestured him to continue.

'Very well, who and why was he under suspicion for murder?'

'Well, the gentleman in question was called a Mr Jeffries. He was a major witness in a drugs case that we were investigating involving Mr Walker and Mr Forbes. But he died in a horrific way suddenly, but we are still currently investigating the case.'

Bastard thought David, I knew it, I knew I had heard those two names before. He looked at Forbes and Walker. David knew Mr Jeffries through certain circles. He had met him a few times; they had even had lunch once together with Jonathon Miles, David and Sarah's friend. The investigation wasn't public knowledge, but because of certain friends David found out a lot of things that maybe he shouldn't have. This murder was one of them.

'Have you ever arrested Mr Walker for any drug offences?'

'Yes at least a dozen times, but we could never prove anything, so reluctantly we had to let him go.'

'So did you ever try to reason things out with Mr Walker?'

'You can't approach Mr Walker with reason, because he just won't listen.'

'Have you ever tried?'

'Yes, lots of times, but he wasn't interested in anything like that. Look, we arrested him for something, I can't really remember what but when we took him back to the station he spat in my Superintendent's face and called him every name he could think of. Believe me, there's no reasoning with people like Mr Walker.'

'So basically, there was no way he was going to open his front door to you, was there?'

'No, he would not.'

Look at them thought Sarah, sitting there as if butter wouldn't melt in their mouths, when they are probably one of the country's biggest criminals. How in the hell do they get away with it for so long? I remember getting a speeding fine once, and they nearly took me to court over that just because I missed one payment. You know if the truth was known, I bet they've probably done more crooked shit than people really know about. And murder, I mean bloody hell. How can they say they don't have enough evidence on them? How much evidence do they need for God's sake? But there again, if it's anything like this case, you can guess how much trouble they're going to have with it.

'Why did Mr Walker hit you when you told him that he was under arrest?'

'Like I said, that's the way he thinks. He thinks with his fists.'

'But you haven't pressed charges against him. Why is that?'

'I didn't feel that there would be any point. If he's found guilty in this case, then he'll have gotten what he deserves, so adding a few extra months won't really make that much difference to his sentence.'

'I see your point, Mr Morgan. When you were in the flat there was a young woman with him. What happened to her?'

'We already know that Miss Woodfield is his girlfriend, but this was someone else, wasn't it Mr Morgan.'

'Yes, when we got into the flat the young woman was lying unconscious on the bedroom floor. We knew that he had probably given her drugs, but he wouldn't tell us what kind, so one of my police constables radioed for an ambulance for her.'

'And was the young girl alright?'

'Everyone in the court waited with baited breath as Mr Morgan paused before he spoke.

'Yes, she was.' There was a huge sigh of relief all around the court even the judge and Mr Chevron seemed relieved.

'Well after having her stomach pumped out and being in hospital for a day or two, she was reasonably ok. A bit wiser perhaps, but ok nonetheless.'

'Did you ever find out, what he had given her?'

'Yes, it was cocaine and acid mixed together, a very lethal combination.'

'And has he been charged with any offences relating to this?'

'No, he has not,' replied Mr Morgan, looking around at people gasping in disbelief.

Don't tell me thought Sarah, not enough evidence to charge him with anything.

'Why not?' asked Richard, looking and sounding as surprised as everyone else.

'Well basically without his confession, we could not really charge him with anything. All he said was that she took them of her own free will and she wouldn't press charges against him, so we had no choice but to let him go.'

'When you were at the station as my learned colleague mentioned earlier, there was some disagreement about which solicitor he was going to have but what I want know is, what was so important about this other solicitor that he wanted?'

'I don't really want to ramble, but there is a bit of a story behind this. Each time in the last three years or so that Mr Walker has been arrested he has had a top solicitor. Now what people at the station wanted to know was how he could afford such an expensive solicitor.'

'And what was the reason for him having this solicitor?'

'I asked one of the duty solicitors, whom he worked for. He told me that a Mr Michael Forbes employed the man.' There was a sharp intake of breath around the courtroom.

'And how many times has this solicitor seen Mr Walker at the station?'

'Basically each time that he was arrested in the last three years.'

The judge asked Richard and Mr Chevron to approach the bench.

'Look it's getting late, I'm giving you one more hour Mr Thorn and then I'm going to call it a day.'

'That's ok another ten minutes and I've finished with him anyway.' The judge seemed pleased perhaps at the thought of finishing earlier than he expected. Richard and Mr Chevron went back to their tables.

'Do you dislike Mr Walker?'

'Not really dislike. I guess I just feel that he thinks getting into trouble and being arrested must be fun and for that I feel sorry for him.'

'Thank you, Mr Morgan. No further questions Your Honour.'

The judge then asked Mr Chevron if he wanted to question Mr Morgan. Mr Chevron also told the judge that he had finished with Mr Morgan. The judge then told Mr Morgan that he was no longer needed in court and that he could leave. Mr Morgan thanked the judge and then he left the court.

Mr Morgan let out a huge sigh of relief as he shut the courtroom door behind him. One of his work colleagues was waiting outside the court for him.

'That bad, was it?'

'I'll tell you what, that was bloody hard work. Here we are trying to put these criminals behind bars, and in the process were made to feel like criminals ourselves.'

'Look,' said his friend. 'Nobody said that this job was easy. When you join the force, they only tell you the basics. They can't tell you what would happen in a real situation, because not all situations are the same. Anyway come on, I'll buy you a pint,' and off they went.

It wasn't long before people started coming out of the courtroom. There was a lot of talking about some of the things that was said in the courtroom that day. David was talking to Richard. Sarah's father had said his goodbyes then left.

'Shit, I wanted to find out what Dad was laughing about?'

'You mean you still don't know why Dad was laughing at David?' Sarah looked at Sandra and Susan.

'You really don't know, do you?'

'Look,' said Helen, from behind. 'Think back to nature, think man and woman in a sweet embrace.' Sarah just looked bewildered.

'Oh for heaven's sake woman,' said her sister. 'Man, woman, short skirts, horny, randy and frustration.'

'Oh, you mean sex,' said Sarah, finally realising what they were all talking about.

'My God, I think she's finally got it.'

'Seriously talk to him about it. Men have problems just the same as us girls. It's just that we admit our faults. But all they do is bottle theirs up, and then they explode when they least expect it.'

Sandra and Susan said that they would call Sarah when she got home. They said their goodbyes and then they left. Sarah looked at David, who was just finishing talking to Richard. He smiled warmly as he looked at his wife. Richard was singing to himself as he picked up his briefcase.

'No need to ask if you're in a good mood,' said Sarah, walking towards the courtroom door.

'Well, aren't you? Today was a very good day for us. I think that finally were getting the court on our side and in a case like this with this amount of pressure, that's a good sign.'

Richard held the door open for everyone.

'I agree, but I have also learned in a case like this that you can take one step forward and two steps back. I don't want to put a downer on things, but I think I'll wait until I hear the end result in this case before I celebrate.'

'Hey come on, don't be so optimistic.'

'I never used to be, but don't get me wrong, today was a very good day.'

'Don't be late in the morning the days can only get better.'

'Let's hope so,' said David. They all said their goodbyes and drove home.